Me an' Gus

Me an' Gus

James D. Crownover

FIVE STAR
A part of Gale, a Cengage Company

Five Star Publishing, a part of Gale, a Cengage Company
All scripture quotations, unless otherwise noted, are taken from the King James Bible.

LIBRARY OF CONGRESS CATALOGING-IN-PUBLICATION DATA

Names: Crownover, James D, author.
Title: Me an' gus / James D. Crownover.
Other titles: Me and gus
Description: First Edition. | [Waterville, Maine] : Five Star, a part of Gale, a Cengage Company, 2023. | Identifiers: LCCN 2022022696 | ISBN 9781432899042 (hardcover)
Subjects: LCGFT: Novels.
Classification: LCC PS3603.R765 M4 2023 | DDC 813/.6—dc23
LC record available at https://lccn.loc.gov/2022022696

First Edition. First Printing: February 2023
Find us on Facebook—https://www.facebook.com/FiveStarCengage
Visit our website—http://www.gale.cengage.com/fivestar
Contact Five Star Publishing at FiveStar@cengage.com

Printed in Mexico
Print Number: 1 Print Year: 2023

For Joel

Preramble

I ain't goin' t' do it, ain't gonna be a blackland farmer. By th' time you're thirteen, you've done it all. By th' time you're nineteen, you've got two kids, you're stooped an' turnin' gray, doin' th' same old thing year after year, prayin' for rain, fightin' weeds an' Injuns an' wonderin' if th' locusts is comin' agin. And you die of old age, wore out at forty.

Lose one crop an' starvation's at your door, so you go to th' bloodsuckin' banker an' he loans against your land and gives you enough t' get to spring—at ten percent. Gradually, th' weather, an' th' banker chips away 'til th' weather has th' crops, th' banker has th' land an' offers you sharecroppin' rights where th' risk is all on you an' he gits th' gain. Got a nice cabin he'll rent you at a good rate. I ain't goin' t' do it.

Workin' cattle? Now that has its advantages, fresh air, open range where th' grass is right-side-up, an' a good horse between your knees. It's hard work, but there's variety to it; you never know which way that hoss is gonna jump on a frosty mornin'. Longhorns got minds of their own an' th' variety o' thought and action is endless. Shore, you don't get a lot of sleep, an' it rains and blows some, but ya got three squares most days, sometimes a roof over your head, an' th' Old Man pays *you* thirty a month, free an' clear. A little mavericking' on th' side gits you a start in th' business an' before long, you're a rancher lookin' for a range of your own, out where Injuns an' wolves is your nearest neighbors—an' greatest threat.

Well, you an' th' army kin take care o' th' Injuns, an' those longhorn cows'll take care of th' wolves. Yes sir, seems like th' cattle business is th' thing for me. I'm gonna give it a try, but *I ain't gonna be a blackland farmer.*

My name's Sutter Lowery, the eldest son of the four children of Ira and Mary Lowery. When the fourth child, Baby Kay, was near weaning, Pa moved us from that blackland farm near Tyler to a place on the West Fork of Keechi Creek south of Jacksboro. We were the next-to-last settlers on the creek, the Bells a mile south of us bein' the last. We'd of starved if it weren't for hunting, for Pa spent as much time fighting Injuns as he did farming.

August Bell was a year younger than me and we became best friends. The day the Comanches swooped in an' killed Pa and Gus's Dad, we became th' primary workhorses of our families. It wasn't long before Ma married Manley Ryman and that sorry Ben Young took over the Bell place. It made me an' Gus feel crowded out.

Chapter 1
Justice on the Prairie

June 1871

You don't sleep in a bed when it's a hunnert an' ten at sunset. We was all sleeping on the dogwalk, laid out from the door to the back edge of the porch where I was sleepin' to keep little ones from rollin' off. The moon had set and the dipper was three fourths the way around th' polestar when the dogs began barkin' an' growling at a wagon rattling up th' trail. Ma an' me herded all th' kids into the house from th' breezeway, an' Manley checked his load in that old muzzleloader of his. I grabbed a pitchfork an' circled around to be b'hind that wagon when it drove across the yard. When it passed, I caught th' silhouette of a lone driver. *Must be Gus, not big enough for that sorry Ben Young,* I thought, and trotted along b'hind.

The wagon pulled up near our stoop an' Gus called out, "It's me, Gus Bell, Mr. Ryman. Ma's hurt."

"Set still, boy. Mary, bring a light." Th' old man was bein' cautious, an' I didn't blame him. Ma came with a candle under a pot.

"It's me, Gus," I said and jumped up on a back wheel and peeked over th' sideboard. All I could make out was th' form of someone layin' wrapped in a quilt. Manley took the candle and lowered it into the box an' what we saw liked t' scared me t' death. It was a woman by her hair, but there was no recognizing her by her bloody face. Her eyes was swole shut, her nose lay to one side, an' her lips were just a raw mass. I was pretty sure she had a tooth or two missin'.

"Oh, my Lord," Ma said and dropped to the ground and retched. She didn't say a word, just hurried to the house.

Manley said soft-like, "Take that tailgate down, Sut, an' we'll carry her in on it." Nancy Bell was not conscious and Manley rolled her to her side while me an' Gus set that tailgate under her. We slid the gate to th' back of th' wagon an' Mrs. Bell never said a mumblin' word. I thought she might be dead. The door only come to her knees an' her feet swung free. Me an' Gus carried from either side of her legs an' Manley carried at her head and we shuffled to th' house. One of th' kids held a candle so we could get up th' steps. As he passed, Manley blew out th' candle. "Skedaddle in th' house, child." It was dangerous t' be seen outside after dark in those days. If an Injun didn't see you, a bushwhacker would like as not take a shot at you from the dark. We lived southeast of Jacksboro, and most houses there that wasn't burned was empty.

Ma had cleared th' table an' we laid Mrs. Bell out as easy as possible. Ma was pale as death but her jaw was set an' her lips clamped shut. She already had a pan of warm water from th' stove an' began cleaning Nancy Bell's face. The lady groaned a little and raised her hand then let it fall. It was th' only way I could tell she was alive. There was a purple and blue bruise around a knot in her forearm where she had tried to ward off her attacker. "Broke," Manley whispered to no one in particular.

Ma glanced at me, "Sutter, get those kids t' bed, all except Liz."

I shooed the kids to their bedroom, but they refused to get in the bed an' I had t' gather pallets from the breezeway an' lay 'em out on th' floor. It only took a moment for them to be quiet, though I doubt they closed their eyes, afraid of dreaming of disfigured faces. Me and Gus swung our legs off th' back porch.

"Sut, I kilt Ben," Gus whispered.

"You did that a month ago."

"No, this time I done it fer real, he's dead an' buried." Gus was whimperin' an' I thought sure someone would hear him. I rolled off th' porch, and hustled Gus to th' crick.

"What's this you're tellin' me?"

"He come home mean drunk an' had Ma down sittin' astraddle her an' beatin' her somethin' awful. I got my axe an' hit him in th' back of his head with the back side, but I guess I swung too hard. Ma was out cold an' I pulled Ben off'n her an' laid him out then got Ma in th' wagon. Her eyes was already swole shut an' she had loose teeth b'hind her split lips. I spent some time doctorin' her and when I went t' see why ol' Ben didn't wake up, he was cold and gettin' stiff. I took him to that bottomless sinkhole, doused him with lime, an' rolled him in. No one will find him there."

"You couldn'a carried him that far."

"Coulda drug him b'hind his horse. Tole Ma he run away thinkin' she's dead."

There are two kinds o' folks on th' frontier, 'specially th' Texas frontier. They's good folks wishin' t' get a start by hard work an' they's frontier trash, rawhiders, we call them, those people run out of polite society back east or hidin' from th' law. They's always tensions b'tween th' two.

When th' Comanches killed Pa an' B.R. Bell, Gus's Pa, on th' same day, this Ben Young moved in an' took th' Bell place over, lock, stock, an' woman. Manley Ryman, a widower with three squalin' kids from down below Jacksboro, courted Ma a few times an' they decided to get married. Ours was th' only house that would hold seven kids, me bein th' oldest at twelve years. It was a marriage of convenience.

Manley introduced me to the hickory stick method of raisin' kids. He showed no signs of recognizing I had about outgrown that kid stage and I was pretty sure th' next time he raised his hand to me would be th' last. I was kind of disappointed that time never came, for that night, me an' Gus hit out for tall cane. I left Ma a note in our hiding place lettin' her think we was after Ben.

Anything north and west of Jacksboro was Injun country. Cattlemen were always seekin' open range and pushin' into Injun country to stay away from settlements, crops, and fences. North was the safest direction for a runaway and a murderer to go.

We rode Ben's horses, Gus with Ben's saddle and me with Gus's old kack. Me an' horse had th' same opinion of that piece of junk.

"Where we goin' Gus?"

"I heard they was an outfit over on th' Trinity readyin' a herd for the rails. Maybe they'll need a couple o' hands."

"Suits me. Th' farther away, th' better." I'd be bigger and stronger after a trail ride and could whip Manley that much easier. All we had to do to find the West Fork of th' Trinity was ride north 'til we hit the river. We turned upstream an' didn't find any sign of cattle until we got to th' mouth of Cameron Creek. The creek had already dried up and the cows was trackin' to th' river to drink, then back up the creek to grass.

"Eat 'til they're thirsty, then go drink 'til they're hungry," Gus said.

The outfit had their headquarters in a jacal a ways up the creek by a spring. Gus almost had a runaway when he saw two Injuns in vaquero garb squattin' in th' shade. I knowed they was Jake Meeker's vaqueros, the Utes Uno and Dos, and grabbed Gus's rein before he could get turned. "They's good Injuns, Gus," I hissed.

I held on to his rein until he jerked it away and growled, "I ain't goin' nowhere." Gus is about as independent as he is stubborn.

Mr. Meeker was hammering horseshoes in the blacksmith shed an' we rode over. "Howdy, boys." He eyed my bare toes in the stirrup and grinned. "Need a little shoein? Light down and look at your saddles." He examined his handywork and moved back to the forge. I grabbed the bellows handle and pumped.

"Ease up a little there, son, you'll have this shoe meltin' into a puddle."

It was a hasty
But successful funeral.

—A.H. Lewis

Chapter 2
Jake Meeker

Zenas and Jake Meeker took the last Bent train to Westport, Missouri, after Mr. William Bent died May 19, 1869. It was at Westport that the brothers' paths parted, Zenas returning to New Mexico Territory, and Jake determining to visit their family on the Middle Fork of the Little Red River in Arkansas. Though they kept in touch, it would be several years before they met again. Zenas wandered over around Las Vegas, got in th' oxen business, and did well tradin' good oxen for wore-out ones with th' pilgrim trains. Later, he drifted into the Tularosa Basin an' cowboyed there and on ranches in th' Sacramentos.

Jake soon found he couldn't be content in a quiet life of th' Ozarks. That an' some misunderstanding with a widow woman about his intentions toward her daughter convinced him to come back out west. His interest was in horse breeding and he built up a nice herd of fine horses. In th' business of trading horses, he found himself with a small herd of cattle and decided to buy more cattle and move them out beyond the settlements where the range was still open, free, and unoccupied. Of necessity, the hands he hired as he grew were pretty salty characters, as handy and quick with a gun as they were with a rope or branding iron. He had already taken a herd up the trail to Kansas shipping points by the time we left our homes in the summer of 1871. Gus had heard he was having trouble getting men, so we went to offer our services.

"We heard you were lookin' for trail hands, Mr. Meeker,"

Gus said, not being one to over-chew words.

Jake held up the shoe for examination and eyed Gus over th' top. "I am, do you know of any hands lookin' for work?"

"We are," I said.

There may have been a little smile tuggin at th' corners of his eyes when he looked at me an' asked, "You been up th' trail with two thousand head of steers b'fore, Lowery?"

"Nawsir, but I know how t' trail cattle crossways of Texas."

"Drivin' milk cows from Tyler t' Jacksboro ain't qualifying experience for a trail herd o' longhorns." He looked us both up an' down. "How old are you?"

"We're fifteen," I lied.

If you're fifteen, I'm a hundred, I could almost read Jake's mind. "We're both little for our age, but we're work brittle," I said.

"We can be horse wranglers an' that would free up two o' your men to be hands," Gus offered.

The first of June was late to be starting on a drive if you was down around San Antone, but we was near five hundred miles closer, and only one or two herds had gotten this far north. Jake's would be one of the early herds t' get to th' tracks if all went well with him—and he started right away. "I'm in a bind since two of my regular men haven't showed up, so I'm gonna take you up on th' deal. Wranglin' pays twenty-five a month and found. Get your outfit together an' let's see what you got and what you're short on. We'll start tomorrow."

Gus looked down an' scratched dirt with his toe, "We ain't got—"

I poked him hard "—it all here, Mr. Meeker, but it won't take long for us t' get it."

He smiled and hit the shoe a couple of licks, "Cookie's got dinner almost ready, go on over and eat a bite before you get too busy."

(*At the risk of belaboring the point, the editor would point out that dinner occurs at noon amongst southern gentry.*)

We tied our horses in the shade and hotfooted it to the cookhouse. "He knowed we ain't got any more'n we rode in with," Gus whispered.

"It may be we can scare up a little more stuff," I said.

"How? Rob that store there on th' corner?"

"Yore ma home?" I asked.

"No."

"Ben have a bedroll with him?"

"Yeah, an' I stashed his guns under th' house." Gus was catchin' on.

"They'll blame Ben for anything we take, an' it ain't likely yore ma'll be spendin' time there until she gets well."

"I guess yore right—an' it ain't like I don't own some part of those things," Gus said. Cookie had just started fryin' steaks, an' there wasn't much else ready. He took two steaks off th' fire, rolled them in thick slices of bread, an' kicked us out of his kitchen. They were awful pink in th' middles. We ate them anyway as we rode.

Gus started gatherin' things he had hidden at his house while I gathered quilts and clothes and kitchen stuff we would need. It didn't take long and we were riding two tired horses back to the Trinity. Near midnight, we picketed the horses an' unrolled Ben's bedroll and crawled in.

"Whew, this stinks, didn't he ever wash anything?"

"Be lucky if there ain't already things livin' in here . . ." I said. We broke some kind of record uncrawlin' that rig and rolling up in some of Nancy Bell's quilts. Daylight found us riding into th' Rafter JM ranch yard with our outfit. Jake gave it a quick look and asked if that was all the bullets we had. Before we could answer, he tossed us a box of shells. "Bring up th' cavyyard and I'll give you fresh horses. You can take yours with us or leave them here." He rode off and we gathered the horses.

"Herd's comin' down th' creek, Sut, better get these horses out'n th' way," Gus called, and we moved horses across th' creek and up on a hillside. Cookie drove his kitchen out of the yard and headed for the Trinity ford. We followed with the cavy-yard and just like that, we were on th' Chisholm Trail to Abilene, Kansas, with two thousand ornery steers, a dozen yearling heifers, sixty-two horses, one boss, six vaqueros, two green horse wranglers, an' one grumpy cook.

Cookie drove like th' devil was after him an' we soon tired of tryin' t' keep up with him. Th' cattle were a couple of miles behind us and we slowed the cavy down to a walk. Presently, Jake had us hold th' horses until the men caught up with us and turned in lathered and tired horses for fresh ones. It was all done with only a word or two spoken here and there and they were off for the herd at a gallop.

"How many's that?" Gus asked.

"How many what?"

"How many men have changed horses, dummy?"

I hadn't counted and had to think a moment, then count lathered horses. "Five, one more t' go." B'sides me an' Gus, th' Utes, Cookie, and Jake, there were Curly Treadaway, who was bald as a cue ball, Thomas Stepp, Pock, and Otha Huie. Curly an' Tom came from around Jacksboro. Rumor was that Tom had Union leanings. I just know he hated th' Rebel yell an' we used it to get his attention; Otha (we called him O) was from somewhere around Kingston, Arkansas; and we never knew where that Pock came from or if he had any other name. We was pretty sure he done time in someone's prison, but he was a good hand.

Pretty soon O, who was th' drag, came up, horse and man all th' same color as the dirt. He rode off on a different colored horse while dusty horse rolled and shook like a dog shedding water. Not knowin' how things worked on a drive, we was wonderin' if this was th' normal pace.

"If it is, we'll git t' Abilene in about twenty days, but we'll all be dead, cow, horse, an' man," Gus said.

"Bet Jake's pushin' 'em hard so's they'll be too tired to be homesick an' go back home," I said. "That's th' only way this scramble makes sense."

Cookie fed us in relays an' th' last man t' eat had hardly finished before the wagon was up an' gone again. Not havin' a head start, the remuda spent th' afternoon followin' th' cattle, off to one side out of their dust. The next day was much the same, but after that we settled into the customary routine of th' trail everyone is familiar with. It was boring enough to drive a man daft. The only breaks in the monotony were river crossings, thunderstorms, and stampedes, events we sometimes prayed for and always dreaded.

Two nights before we crossed the Red River, a couple of men rode in while we ate and called for the boss. I noticed the hands sitting around shifted their plates from their gun hands. Pock and O lay them aside. Jake stayed seated, his plate in his lap. "Light down, men, an' have a bite with us."

Uno and Dos disappeared into the gloom; I supposed they were shying from those strangers.

"Well, thankee, boss, believe we will." They tied their horses to the chuck wagon wheels, something only Jake was allowed t' do. Gus was finished eating and after putting his tools in th' wreck pan, moved to the horses. "I'll move your horses to the brush over there," he said.

The stranger that done all th' talkin' said, "No you won't, son, they're fine right there." Jake nodded and Gus left the horses alone. Curly an' Tom put their utensils up and continued on around the wagon opposite the horses.

The stranger and his partner sat across the way from the rest of us and ate their supper. The speechless one even went back for a second helping of beans. As soon as they had finished, the spokesman stood and said to Jake, "I suppose you know why we're here; I represent a group of ranchers who don't want their cattle sold off right now, and tomorrow morning you need to hold the herd on the grounds while we cut them. Any brands I represent will be cut out of the herd."

Jake stood up and while the two visitors watched closely, dumped his gear in the wreck pan, then turned and faced the men. "You got a list of th' brands you're lookin' for?"

"Yes, sir, I shore do." He reached into his shirt and drew out a folded paper and handed it to Jake who took a few moments to scan the list. "That's a pretty good list of ranches, guess it covers every brand within fifty miles of Jacksboro—including the Rafter JM, my brand, and I *didn't* ask *anyone* to cut for my brand." He refolded the paper and put it in his pocket.

The man began, "I'll need that paper—"

"You won't have any need for it after tonight," Jake interrupted. "You must not remember me, but we met just about here a year ago. I refused your cuttin' services and that night you stampeded my herd. One of my men—Johnny Jump, we called him—was killed trying t' turn th' herd and we buried what was left of him over there under that big cottonwood tree. I visited him this afternoon an' it seemed t' me his blood was cryin' out from th' ground.

"Now, I sat at my mama's knee an' listened as she read from th' Good Book. One thing I remember is that part that says 'An eye for an eye, and a tooth for a tooth.' It seems that sayin' fits this situation—"

That's as far as he got, for our two guests drew their guns—well, they started to, but were starin' down Jake's barrel before they cleared leather. Both men went pale as a vigilante's sheet and the men tied them up.

"Now, I have it in mind to appease my friend's cry the only way I know how. We'll settle this tomorrow morning."

"My men have orders to stampede your herd if we don't return to camp by midnight, so you could be too busy to settle things with us—if you're still breathin'—in th' morning." The fellow had regained his composure and stared at us in defiance.

"Reckon time will tell, won't it?" Jake didn't seem a bit worried. Later, as if they sprang up from the grass, two painted Indians in breechclouts and moccasins stood beside Jake, their lances decorated with fresh scalps. I counted five of them. Jake watched our guests closely and noted their expressions.

"Good, we got them all. Doesn't look like any yellow slickers'll be wavin' at our herd tonight," Jake said.

One of the Indians grunted and nodded. They left as suddenly as they came and I felt a chill on the back of my neck.

"D-a-a-m-m," Gus whispered.

Jake showed his confidence in the Indians by not increasing the night watchmen around the herd. It was a peaceful night. Me an' Gus had stayed with the cavyyard just to be safe. Feller could do without a few head of beef, but we needed horses. We drove the horses to camp for the exchange of night horses for morning horses. Seemed like everyone was especially quiet, not a lot of joshin' going on until Curly's horse lowered his head an' tried to break in two. It broke th' gloom and they rode out laughin' and joshin'.

Cookie had dished up two plates for us so he could get a jump on cleaning up an' getting on to th' noonin'. "The boys left you a decent saddle over there, Sut. You can get rid o' that piece of junk you been riding."

I'll put it on Johnny's grave. My glance at the tree turned into a shuddering stare, for there were two figures hanging from a limb over the grave.

"Well, I'll be . . ." words failed as Gus stared.

Cookie looked at us and said, "It's a long way to a court, an' bein's it would be a Yankee court, th' likelihood of convicting those two is right at zero or lower. They'd most likely get a slap on th' back and be in business stealing cattle an' getting men killed in no time. That out there is a permanent solution to the problem. Other would-be cutters might see them hanging there and decide th' job is too risky t' try, thereby savin' himself and other people a lot of trouble.

"A feller might talk about finding strange fruit on a cottonwood tree, but only a fool brags about putting them there or th' men he has killed. His life is sure to be short and full of strife. When good men catch a horse thief or cattle thief 'out on the prairie,' they does what they has to and be done with it. A man don't brag about it, he don't talk about it—ever. That is good advice you ought to put to memory and bring it up every once in a while for review. Now, get them dishes in th' wreck pan an' wash 'em up. Time's a-wastin'."

It's worth mentioning that in all the years I worked with and associated with the men of that crew, there was never a mention of the incident, or other incidents that happened from time to time afterward. Truth be known, me an' Gus had a secret we never mentioned between us again.

"That Cookie gives good advice, don't he?" Gus just nodded.

After we had our chores done, I rode down and laid that old saddle at Johnny's head between the two scalp-decorated poles stuck in the ground, one either side of the head of his grave. The big man looked like his neck was broke. A sign pinned to his coat read, "He Cut His Last Herd."

The little fellow was all contorted and purple, his tongue out. He must have danced a bit before he strangled.

★ ★ ★ ★ ★

They were born to be hanged.

—Old Saying

CHAPTER 3
COMANCHEROS

Curly Treadaway cut a chew off his twist and stuck it in his cheek. He chewed and spat a stream before he spoke, "Once you cross th' Red River goin' north, th' Lord looks the other way, you're in th' devil's hands."

For two days we had watched the Red River water level climb our gauging stick and now it was slowly receding—too slowly for us.

"This ain't a good crossin' at its best," Curly said. "We should try it when it is a little high, might keep us outa that quicksand."

"Might wash us down t' climb out'n th' river on th' banks o' Louisiana, too," the feller we called Pock said.

"Don't care, so long as Cookie makes it over with th' chuck," Curly replied.

"How's she going?" Jake asked as he walked up.

Curly spat and said, "She's going down—receding, some might say—might be down to our first mark by suppertime."

"I'd like t' cross it when it's a little higher than last year and avoid some of that quicksand if we could," Jake said.

Pock was standing a little behind Jake and rolled his eyes 'til th' pupils near disappeared. "Good idea, boss."

We started the herd across midafternoon and had th' whole outfit in Indian Territory by sunset. Th' north side of that river looked just like th' south side, red dirt and all. What told us we were in a different land was th' demeanor of the men. Every man caught up his night horse and had him tied close to his bed. His rifle was always in his hand or within reach under his covers. No man kept it in th' boot unless he was in th' saddle. Where he could, Cookie parked out of sight and now he traveled closer to th' herd. Our big meal was breakfast, with dinner bein' holdovers from that. Supper was late because he didn't start cookin' until th' herd was settled for the night.

"Reason for all this caution is that we are a long ways from the main cattle trail and help if we needed it. Jake's dependin' on all th' Injuns bein' along th' trail seein' what mischief they can stir up there while we sneaks by b'hind 'em," Pock explained.

O spat and said, "He's bettin' his whole herd on it since if we get caught out here, th' Injuns would have the herd and horses and a few of our scalps t' boot."

"Won't be this way th' whole trip, just while we're in Comanche, Arapaho, Kioway, an' Cheyenne country," Pock assured us.

"That's good t' know. So we don't get to sleep until we're clear o' these killin' grounds?" Gus asked.

"Don't worry about that, you can catch up this winter," Tom Stepp said. He wasn't smiling.

The Ute vaqueros were especially alert; one or th' other of them would take off and scout ahead in their Injun garb. The fifth day we camped about four miles south of where Buckhorn Creek joins Little Beaver, and Dos rode in after dark, dished up his supper, and ate. When he finished, he looked at Jake and said, "Comancheros."

Jake swore, "Where are they, Dos?"

Dos took a stick and drew in the dirt. He drew three streams coming together in one place and tapped the western stream, "Whisky Creek." He put a dot southeast of the creeks to indicate our camp.

"How far, Dos?" Pock asked.

Dos held up three fingers horizontally, meaning three hours, and from the way his horse was lathered, it was about fifteen miles at a goodly pace.

The thought struck me that if the comancheros had sent someone to find the Indians, they would cross our trail and, knowing we were a lone herd, would tell the Injuns, who would find the temptation to attack too strong to resist. Without our scouts, we would be unaware of the danger we were in.

Pock looked at Jake expecting some decision.

"Dammit, we can't afford t' waste time chasin' after comancheros." He thought for a moment then said, "Dos, you take Sut and go over there and see what kind of mischief you can do those rascals. You have two days. We will lay over at Rocky Ford on the Little Washita. Take a spare mount for each of you and don't get yourselves killed."

Dos nodded, "We go."

Well, that caught me flat-footed and I had to scramble to get my gear ready. Gus caught my spare for me, a lineback buckskin named Stripe. He was a good traveler. I had already saddled Dusky, my night horse. He was black with a blaze face. Dos had a quarter mile head start when I finally rode out of camp. *You can stay up there,* I thought, *I ain't runnin' t' catch up,* but I did hurry a little so as not to be lost when it was full dark. We crossed upper Cottonwood Creek about midnight and when we got to Beaver Creek, picketed the horses, rolled up in our blankets, and slept.

After we ate breakfast, Dos said, "You should be Indian." I fished through my possibles and found my moccasins and a piece of cloth that could serve as a breechcloth, but when I took off my shirt, Dos began to laugh, "White as a catfish's belly."

All my exposed skin was as tanned as he was, but under my clothes I was a sickly pale white. I couldn't help grinning at the thought of me dressed in a breechclout. "Forget that, Dos."

He nodded, "You be vaquero, Catfish." And that's what he called me from then on.

The Mexicans had camped at the mouth of a deep cut made by the creek to form a natural corral for their animals. It wasn't very big, but held water and enough grass for the short time they anticipated being there. "Dos, do you think they sent someone to find the Indians?"

"Yes."

"They'll find th' cow's trail, we got t' warn them."

Dos grinned, "Jake knows."

It only took me a moment t' think about that. Of course, they would know—and a long time before a newcomer would. I pointed to myself, "Pumpkin Roller."

"Yep." And he didn't even grin.

Right then, I decided to apply one of my pa's sayings, "Flies don't enter a closed mouth."

We rode to the edge of the canyon and watched the camp. In all my years with the Mexican people, I never knew one who would voluntarily rise from his bed before midmorning. They are night people, late to bed and late to rise. These comancheros fit th' pattern. The sun had been up an hour before there was any stirring in the camp. There were six carretas, those screaming two-wheeled carts with wooden wheels and axles, circled around a central firepit. Underneath each carreta was a bed laid out where the traders slept. It looked as if there were two men for each cart.

"What are we going t' do, Dos?"

"We run and burn," he said with a grin, then he explained, "We will run the cattle through the camp and when the amigos chase them, we will burn the carts."

I nodded, "Nothin' much t' do before dark, then."

He shook his head no, "We do this at siesta time."

"In th' daylight?"

"Sí."

He was really serious, and as I thought about it, I could see that it had a chance of working. "All right, what do we do?"

He pulled back from the brink and we mounted and rode to the head of the canyon. The bluff there was tall enough the cattle couldn't climb it, but not so high our horses could not jump down into the gulley. Once there, we waited until siesta time and slowly gathered the animals into a herd and bunched them toward the carts. With a sudden move, Dos whipped out a panther skin and waved it at the bunched animals. I unfurled my slicker and the race was on. The herd was at full speed when it ran through the camp. Comancheros could do nothing but cower under the carts. A wheel broke on one and it canted as the men under it ran to another cart. One man was struck by the shoulder of a passing ox and propelled under the cart faster than intended. The rush of the small herd was quickly over and men crawled out from their refuges pondering what had just happened.

"After them!" someone shouted, and there began an exodus, gathering steam as the men realized the fix they were in without their animals.

When they were safely away, we rode into the circle and added fuel to the firepit. Then with firebrands we began burning carts. I found a cache of new Winchester repeating rifles in the last of the carts with enough ammunition to stock an army and rued the fact I could only take two guns and one carton of shells. I broke open a keg of powder and salted down the guns and shells and looked to see Dos setting fire to his last cart. After he grabbed two more rifles, I lit the cart and threw the keg into the firepit and we ran for the horses. They needed no urging to run and when the keg blew, it added more speed to our departure. I still don't know how I mounted that nervous horse with two rifles and a box of shells in my arms, but I did.

Dos gave the long yell and we cut to intercept our herd. The ammunition began popping off as the fires reached them, keeping the comancheros from rescuing much from the fires. An occasional boom when a keg of powder went off was followed by a billowing of black smoke above the fires. We could hear them from several miles away.

Dos led us across that mostly featureless country straight to Rocky Ford. It took me several years of ridin' these plains to be able to develop that talent. It's more of an instinct than a skill, and I still don't know how it works.

Gus liked his new rifle and we stored the old ones in the wagon over Cookie's protests. Jake grinned at us and said, "Crossin' a cook is as risky as braidin' a mule's tail." We learned th' proof of that sayin' later.

There was no way a trail herd could outdistance angry Injuns, so we stayed bunched and rode with our eyes on our back trail and our rifles across our laps. Turned out we were looking in the wrong direction an' it almost did us in.

The era of the comancheros opened with the Comanche-New Mexican Peace treaty negotiated in 1786. It was never broken.

—C.L. Kenner

Chapter 4
Two Kinds of Indian Trouble

"Trade sides with me, Sut, I'm gettin' a crick in my neck from lookin' over my right shoulder all th' time. I need t' look left t' balance it out some." We were wolfin' down a quick dinner b'fore th' afternoon drive. Jake had started using us with the herd some, and me and Gus was ridin' th' swing on each side of the herd, keeping up the corners so they didn't spread too much or bunch too much and overheat.

"Shore, Gus, it'll ease my left neck some, too." I never thought ridin' th' east side of th' cavyyard would have me squintin' into th' sun morning *and* afternoon, but I bet Gus did. You can bet that's th' last time I traded sides with that scamp.

The threat of a visit from mad Injuns kept us alert and wary of every little dip in th' ground. Jake did a good job keeping us on th' divides away from draws and arroyos that might hide trouble. We only drove to water after making a good scout of the place. It was the Injun's favorite place to start something.

About every other day a thunderhead would rear up over us an' give us a good soakin'. Sometimes it was water, sometimes ice. Hail made all God's creatures hunker down an' we tried to draw up under our sombreros. It was during one of those downpours that the Injuns struck.

Tom was ridin' right swing, his hat down on his ears an' his blanket wrapped up to meet his hat. I was on th' right side of th' drag wringin' out my sombrero when I spied a figure riding out of a draw and walking his horse toward Tom. I could have shot him—and stampeded a herd already prodded three steps from a run. The next best thing t' bring him out'n his shell might be th' rebel yell, so I gave it my best.

Tom busted out of his cocoon, swinging his horse toward me and in the process seeing th' now charging Injun outa th' corner of his eye, turned right on around to charge him. His cow horse, being bigger than the Injun pony, took th' charge on his shoulder without losing his footing, while that pony fell to his knees pitchin' his rider forward and spoiling the thrust of his lance. It passed through Tom's blanket and missed his ribs.

My yell had warned others, including the herd, which stepped up its pace, still not running. There were two other battles goin' on across th' herd at th' same time: O was hanging onto a warrior's lance for dear life and Curly was down with a warrior about t' plunge his lance into him. I brought my rifle up but didn't have to fire because a loop fell over the Injun an' he was jerked out of his saddle and skidded off behind Pock's horse.

Uno and Gus drove the cavyyard right into the cattle herd and we circled the combined animals, guns ready. Pock returned to his place next to me, looping his rope across his saddle horn. "That Injun's gonna have a raw ass for a while," he called. "Hope he brought his squaw with him t' pull cactus spines outa his backsides."

"You didn't kill him?" I asked.

"Nope, thought his little ride might put him outa order an' he'd behave." Pock chuckled. "He's gonna ride standin' up for a while."

We were in a bad fix, out in the open with a herd, and no way to protect them. Come dark, we would be lucky to have our scalps and th' horses between our knees—all else would be gone. We had been driving above the breaks of the Little Washita River where it flowed northeast to the big Washita. Jake signaled and turned east and we followed with the herd. He took us to the very edge of the caprock where the cliff falls sheer down to the river breaks. There were two places where the caprock twisted and made big necks of land with sheer bluffs on three sides—culs-de-sac, the French called them—and just a little neck at the mouth. We drove the herd into one of them and set up our camp to guard the mouth. There was enough grass to hold the herd one night, but no water. Only lizards could climb those cliffs.

"Well, this buys us another night with our hair," Gus said.

Uno and Dos painted up and disappeared into the gloaming. We wouldn't see them until morning. "They don't ever sleep," O said. "I don't know how they do it."

"Herdin' cows is work to them. Huntin' Kioway is play," Pock said.

"Good hunting, fellers," Tom said after them.

We strung rope across the neck of the cul-de-sac and hung cans with gravels in them along the length of the rope. "Another sleepless night," Gus groaned.

"Jake said twenty-five a month and found, Gus. Sleepin' wasn't mentioned," I said.

Five vaqueros spaced themselves along the rope and prepared to spend the night guarding the herd. Far, far to the northwest, the towering top of a thunderhead caught the last rays of the sun as it sank into the Pacific. Periodic flashes lit up the whole interior of the cloud making it look like a huge popcorn kernel. The absence of longhorn-disturbing thunder was welcome. Cloud-building energy left with the sun and an anvil formed the top portion of the cloud, reaching out hundreds of miles and reflecting the fires in its belly below. Gradually, the cloud died, leaving the wispy anvil to drift across the sky. It too was gone by sunrise.

Cookie hooked up and drove off northwest to find a place by water to cook breakfast. Curly and Tom sat their horses by the mouth of the cul-de-sac to pinch the cattle down to a narrow path to avoid any being pushed over the cliffs. We greeted the cattle as they came out and strung them along after the wagon.

Presently, the scent of water encouraged thirsty cattle to pick up their pace and they were soon full and contented enough to lie down and ruminate thoughtfully—and yes, a cow can think. All hungry vaqueros could think of was food and sleep. There was plenty of the former and thoughts of the imminent visitation of angry Indians postponed the latter.

It was as if our two Utes could read their minds, for every time the Indians tried some trick to steal the herd, Uno and Dos knew their plans and prepared us for them. They wanted the whole outfit including Cookie's six mules. The comancheros put a premium on mules, for they were in high demand with the homesteaders set on plowing their bit of land into a farm, and praying for rains that never came.

For several days we had been paralleling the Chisholm Trail tracking east of us and the dust of the herds convinced us there was no place to enter the line of march. "We'll either have to stay where we are or go back to San Antone and get in the back of the line," Jake said. That, plentiful grass and unsullied water, was incentive enough for us to stay on the track we had begun.

"Those fellers are in a hurry. We'll be going slower and reach th' tracks with slick-fat steers that'll garner top price," Jake explained.

"Only drawback t' this trail is th' danger of Injuns," Pock said.

"S'long as we got Uno an' Dos watchin' out for us, we should be in pretty good shape," Tom answered. The two Utes had ceased herding and were constantly scouting around the herd.

"It leaves us a little shorthanded, but the herd has settled down in th' routine an' we don't need as many hands on the herd," Jake said.

"I'd rather do a little more work and have them out there lookin' after us," I said.

The next Kiowa try for the herd came from the east. From down below a bluff, they had found a gap and were able to lead their horses up the scree to hide in the bushes there. Their plan was to stampede the herd west and eliminate us as we rode to control the runaway. Uno found them and told Jake.

Instead of moving the herd away from them, we crowded the cattle until they were forced to push through the brush at the very edge of the cliffs. This made the Indians retreat down the slope of the cut a ways to avoid being swept up by the herd. The sudden appearance of a half dozen vaqueros with rifles caught them without cover and they scrambled down that steep loose slope, sliding and tumbling all the way to the echoes of our rifle shots. As if that were not enough, a posse of Choctaw Lighthorse policemen gathered their remnants at the bottom and herded them east to trial at Boggy Depot. That was the last attempt to steal our herd by the "Wild" Indians—on that trip.

Now the so-called civilized tribes took over with a different kind of harassment. Before we could start the herd the next morning, a delegation of Choctaw hailed our camp. Cookie quickly filled the coffeepot with water as Jake invited them in. "Have a cup of coffee, men, we are just about to get this outfit on the road," Jake Meeker said. The natives dismounted and dug their cups out of their bags. The coffee was just tepid, but they didn't seem to notice.

"I woulda throwed that swill right back in Cookie's face," Gus whispered.

"And collected an ass full of bird shot or might be it would be buckshot," I replied.

"This whole outfit runs on beans an' salt pork an' Cookie controls it all," O said.

"No doubt about who runs th' outfit, is there?" Tom asked.

The Indians drank their coffee and never showed a bit of distaste. I suppose it was because their "coffee" was made from something b'sides coffee beans. When they had finished, the head man stood and addressed Jake: "You have been in the Choctaw Nation for two days and now we must ask you to pay the tax."

"What is the tax?" Jake asked.

"Two cents the head for cattle, five cents for horses and mules."

"Two cents! Last year it was a cent," Jake exclaimed.

"It is still a cent down on the trail, but you are breaking a new trail and it will cost more."

"Look at that trail down there; when the drives are over it'll be a mile wide, no grass left, an' cut to pieces by a million hooves. Water fouled, too," he added. "Now, go back and look at our trail. Th' grass got cropped, but it is growin' back an' we hardly left a track. We have done less damage and this time next year you won't see where we've been except for th' cow piles. You should charge me less."

"But it is a new trail," the man insisted.

"I will not pay two cents a head," Jake declared.

"Won't pay one cent a head, either," Pock said under his breath.

They noticed the cattle stirring, so accustomed to the routine of travel that they were preparing to leave the bed ground on their own. Without guidance, they were likely to take up any direction. Curly motioned to me an' Gus an' we rode out to guide the herd down the path of righteousness. The rest of the crew stayed with Jake except for Cookie who poured everyone another round of hot coffee, then poured the remainder on the fire, to the consternation of our visitors. Soon, the kitchen was rattling over the prairie for the nooning.

Me and Gus had to be swing and drag while Curly guided

the lead steer. "We'll wear out these horses tryin' t' do it all," Gus called.

"Let th' drag go. Those scamps b'hind us can pick 'em up if they ever get this way," I called back, and that's just what we did. It didn't take those cows long to miss pressure t' keep up from behind an' there were more and more "drags" falling behind. We took turns applyin' coiled rope encouragement to lazy rumps.

Near high noon, Tom and O drove up th' cavyyard an' we were able to change horses. Now we could stay at the swing positions while Tom caught up some of th' drag and O kept th' horses. "They're about done palaverin' an' should be catchin' up soon," Tom called as he rode back to the drag. Only a few steers looked his way and nodded their understanding. The rest didn't care. We let them spread a little and stop for the nooning. When Cookie threw his hat in the air, Curly an' me and Gus left Tom with th' herd and rode to the wagon.

"My steak's pink in th' middle," Gus whispered and Cookie glared at him. He was too far away to hear, but he knew any talkin' during a meal most likely was about th' food.

"Sh-h-h, eat it an' don't say a word," I whispered behind my cup.

Jake and the rest of the crew rode up while we were eating and Jake said, "Sut, you and Gus go back to the drag and cut out the two slowest steers and take them back to those Injuns. They'll be waitin' near where we ate breakfast. Then you hotfoot it back to th' herd and take up th' drag."

"That's all they wanted?" I asked.

"That's all they're gettin'. They never were part of the Choctaw Nation's tax collectors, just pretendin' to be. You watch them, they're tricky."

It didn't take long to cut out the two drags we hated th' most and move them—at their pace—back toward the Injuns.

As we approached, I spied a disturbance in the brush. Gus rode over close to me and said, "They got a steer tied in th' brush over there."

"That's what I thought, an' there they sit down there innocent as a Sunday school class, waitin' on their two-steer dinner. We'll push these dogies down to them and get that steer on our way back."

We moved the steers on down to where the Choctaws waited and sent them the last hundred yards by themselves. Then we turned and ran out of there, something tingling between my shoulder blades.

When we crashed into the brush, we found that the steer had company and the company had a long rifle. My pistol shot was close enough to make him flinch and his shot went wild. He ran a few steps into the brush and I watched him while Gus freed th' steer.

"Hurry up, Gus, he's reloadin'," I yelled.

"Reloadin'?" He couldn't get near th' steer and was struggling with the knotted rope.

"Cut it and git goin'!" I yelled again.

"Reloadin'?" He cut the rope and chased the steer through the brush into the open. I made my own path through that brush, and just as I got clear, the rifle boomed again and clipped a limb above my head. Gus was already a hundred yards ahead, following a one-steer stampede dragging a long rope. I caught up.

"All he had was a muzzleloader?" Gus was still unbelieving.

"And be glad he did, or one or both of us would be displaying our hides on some Injun's wall."

"Na-a-ah, you would have gotten him if you wanted to . . . a muzzleloader?" He laughed.

★ ★ ★ ★ ★

Crossing a cook is as risky as braiding a mule's tail.

—Old Saying

Chapter 5
A Right Pleasing Feast

"Those fellers didn't pick up a single drag as they come up," Gus griped.

"Too busy lookin' for dinner," I said. There must have been more than a dozen head scattered all over the back trail and we ran ourselves ragged tryin' t' get them out of the brush and back to the herd. When someone finally seen th' trouble we was havin', O came back and helped us. Our horses were so tired we had to change again.

A strange thing was happening on the right side of the herd. When it got to a certain spot, the cattle would all stop and face the brush and stare, frozen. It looked like they were one step from a runaway, and Curly, who had the front swing, had to make them turn back to the herd. From that point on, th' whole herd curved far away from that area, watching it with th' whites of their eyes showin' and trotting on once past the danger zone. Even the drags didn't like that spot.

"I'm gonna find out what they were pointin'," Gus called.

"You're gonna go in there and find out how much a mountain lion likes horseflesh," I called back. "Don't do it, Gus." Of course, he done it. I couldn't sit there and let that drag go and watch out for Gus, he was a big boy an' would have t' take care of hisself. That bobtail steer headed for th' high lonesome the hundredth time, but I convinced him t' return to his friends after a short run. Shoulda sent him with th' Injuns.

I was past the area that spooked th' cows when Gus busted

th' brush comin' out on the run. At his horse's heels, nipped a sow javelina, her hooves throwing up little spurts of dust as she sprinted across the prairie after man and horse. Seeing the futility of her chase, she stopped and with head high snorted after the horse. She turned and trotted back toward the brush where a dozen piglets stood, only their heads showing.

She was only a few feet from the safety of the brush when an arrow pierced her side and she fell squealing and biting at the arrow. Dos ran up and slit her throat and she lay still. The piglets disappeared into the brush, probably already dealing with the prospects of no more of mother's milk.

It only took Dos a few moments to cut out the sow's musk gland and skin the animal. Holding the carcass out away from his horse, he galloped to the chuck wagon where he and Cookie quickly set up the iron spit and had the wild pig turning on it.

Gus had dismounted and was inspecting his horse's off hind leg and I rode over to see if he needed help. There was a lot of blood from a long cut between his fetlock and hock where the javelina's razor sharp tusk had slashed him.

"Got anything t' stop that blood, Gus?"

"Not with me," he said and began unbuttoning his shirt. Folding it in half up the back, he wrapped it tightly around the leg, wrapping sleeves in opposite directions and tying them together tightly. It seemed to stop the flow and Gus rode him slowly to the wagon.

"Gonna have to stitch him up, Gus," I said. "Leave him at the wagon an' I'll get you another horse." I trotted out to the cavyyard where O, who had seen us working on the horse, had caught up Gus's afternoon horse and had him waiting for me. "Had a round with a javelina, did he?"

"Dang cows had more sense than he did, goin' into th' brush like that," I said.

O chuckled. "Kid'll do a man's job, but once in a while

stoopid sneaks up on him. Be careful, Sut, that stuff is mighty catchin'."

"It broke out on Gus for shore," I replied. "Jake's gonna be mad."

"Can't blame him for that," O said. "What one man gits into affects th' rest of th' outfit one way or another. He's lost a horse from his string and th' rest of th' string will have to take up th' slack. *They'll* tire quicker an' th' rest of us will have to pick up that part of the load Gus can't carry. You see how 'little things' can work against th' whole bunch?"

I hoped I wouldn't catch a dose of "stoopid." It would not be hard for a kid with no experience to mess something up, and I hoped to avoid it if possible.

The combination of catching a wild hog and the horse's injury persuaded Jake to hold th' herd over the rest of the day. We spread them out and let them graze the afternoon away while we turned the spit and sewed up the horse's leg. He would be sore for a while.

Jake didn't say much, and I think it hurt Gus more than if he had blown up at him. It's for sure we both thought twice afore we done anything out of the ordinary after that. That wild pig was th' best pork I had ever eaten. I didn't think at the time it could ever be beaten and if it ever was, it was darned seldom.

We were back on the cavyyard detail forty miles north of th' javelina incident and had not slept since the third watch the night before. Gus rode over and said, "Sut, someone's stalkin' us over in that brush b'hind me. He's been there followin' us along for th' last two–three hours."

"I been noticin' you actin' skittish over there. Wonder is you haven't spooked th' horses."

"We need t' fetch him outa there afore he creates a situation we can't handle," Gus said.

"What's that vow you made when th' javelina operated on your horse? That leg hasn't healed yet and you're proposin' t' break your word?"

"I'm proposin' that *you* flush that feller out so we can see what he's up to," Gus answered.

"I ain't doin' it, Gus. Think up somethin' new that they ain't told us not t' do an' go do it yourse'f—or I might do it if it looks like it might be fun."

"Sutter Lowery, you go straight to hell."

"You're th' on'y one I know could show me th' way."

"I'm gittin' 'im outa there your help or not," Gus yelled, then turned and trotted south out of sight in a draw. In less than half an hour, he emerged from the brush with a figure matching his description.

He had on a deerskin breechcloth and there were crude moccasins on his feet. The only thing well kempt about him was his hair, which fell halfway to his waist.

"This here's Chickasha, Sut—leastways, that's what he keeps sayin' an' beatin' his chest," Gus called. "Don't know anything else he says in that Injun gibberish."

When they came closer, I could tell that the Injun was close to our age, somewhat shorter, but heavyset with a deep chest and strongly muscled. "What you gonna do with him, Gus?"

"Guess I'll feed him and turn him loose somewhere far away from th' herd," he replied.

"Why not turn him loose and avoid Cookie's Irish?"

"Cookie be damned if he can't feed a hungry man."

"Boy. What was he doing in th' brush?"

"Guess he's livin' there. Had a lot of cowhides layin' 'round, none with th' same scripture on his rump."

"Don't tell th' boys, they'll be elevatin' his feet under some cottonwood limb."

"Better not," Gus said.

The first dinner shift was returning to the herd and we trotted on over to the rope corral and saddled fresh horses. As we approached the kitchen, Cookie looked up and called, "Well hello, Chickasha, how you been?"

"I've been fine, Orville, how about you?"

Gus grabbed the boy's arm and spun him around, "You speak American?"

This Chickasha puffed himself up and replied, "Carlisle Indian School—"

Gus hit him hard on the shoulder, "You been messin' with m—" Had he said more, it would have been to th' blue sky he was trying t' focus his eyes on. I guess this Chickasha was used to one-blow fights, for he had turned to speak to Cookie again when Gus's fist landed in his kidney. For an Injun, this Chickasha was quite a fighter. He must have learned to fight at that school he went to, and it was a very even match. Gus's shirt was ripped from top to bottom, and the fight only ended when he jerked Chickasha's cloth down to his knees and shoved his bare ass on a prickly pear. I'll say Chickasha was a gamer. He first tried to pull his breechcloth up, but had to stop when it hit the cactus spines, and when he tried to shove it off his feet, Cookie stepped in and said, "No more, Chick, I call this a draw. Here's th' tweezers, Gus, de-spine him."

Gus stared in disbelief, "I'm not gonna . . ."

"*You're* not gonna eat 'til them spines is outa his ass," Cookie interrupted. "Now git with it . . . and you, Sut, wipe that grin off your face an' help out here."

"I didn't . . ."

"You'll git fed when they eat," Cookie said over his shoulder. I believed him.

It took a while to figure the best way to get at the spines, and we ended up breakin' him over the wagon tongue like a breech-loading shotgun. I started at his shoulder blades and worked my way down, trapping the spines between my thumb and my knife blade and pulling, while Gus started at his hind legs and worked up. The spines were so thick, he didn't get far. A lot of those needle pricks drew little drops of blood and when we were finished, his rear looked like it had th' measles. Pulling his breech up disclosed a few spines we had missed.

Chickasha was a Choctaw Injun who spent his summers out by the cattle trail, picking up strays and some not so strayed cattle and horses. He made a good living returning these animals to their owners who rewarded him for the service. Those that didn't reward him never got a second return and the lost animal got a good home—or made a good meal. Chickasha became famous for his whole beef roasts and a Mexican taught him how to barbeque beef. In the fall after the last herd passed and the frost got the ticks, he applied his cooking skills to feral hogs with good results.

After we ate, Cookie sent us to dig out one of those heifers and drive her to Chickasha's. The third heifer we caught passed our sleek and fat test and we drove her back to the camp. There was a large firepit with a spit over it and a kid was there to do the overnight tending and turning. We heard the shot that signaled a feast before we got back to the horses.

Chickasha fussed because Cookie rushed the process somewhat. Jake had said we couldn't afford another layover right then and the carcass had to be done by midmorning so that Cookie could get to the nooning grounds on time.

The smell of the meat cooking made for restless sleep, but no one was complaining. Cookie beat us to the grounds by only a half hour, but there was little cooking that had to be done, and he was ready in time.

Gus learned quick that there was no "doing" with Chikasha; he took care of himself. The reason he was this far from the main trail and for his cautious approach to our outfit was to be sure a certain bunch of hands was not in our crowd. These men were bootleggers hiding from Judge Parker's deputies and often hired on to outfits passing through to hide and travel unobserved to Kansas towns to stock up on liquor. Chickasha was feuding with them over something he wouldn't talk about.

Cookie usually reserved the evening for the big meal of the day, reasoning a heavy meal at noon would not set good on th' back of a horse, so we weren't used to eating so much at noon as that barbequed beef.

"Oh-h-h, I ain't never eatin' that much agin at noon. This horse has tamped my beef down so tight I may need dynamite t' break it loose," Gus groaned.

"Ugh, white eyes eat like hungry Injun, no sleep it off," Chickasha mocked. "Do not worry, Gus, Cookie has an old Injun remedy, but you cannot take it sitting on a horse." His proper speech had a remittance man lilt to it.

"Better git enough for th' whole outfit," I called as I pursued a wayward steer, standing in my stirrups. The back of a horse was sure not the place for a full stomach.

When we went to eat that evening, Cookie gave each of us a large spoonful of castor oil before we ate a small supper.

"Old Injun remedy," Chickasha said. "Castor oil to oil your casters." It worked well, for there was more than the usual moving around in the night, and everyone awoke in a better mood.

"We git more company out here than a Fort Worth crib on Saturday night," Gus muttered out of the side of his mouth when he saw the three strange horses tied to the wagon wheels of a dilapidated wagon. "Always showin' up at feedin' time."

Chickasha was still with us, Jake having hired him for th' rest of th' drive. He looked closely at the horses and turned back to the herd.

"Must not be any of his friends," I said.

"Prob'ly owes 'em money," Gus growled.

The three strangers were eating and gave little notice to our arrival. They were a shabby lot with an odor that kept us shy of their downwind side. Pock rode in to eat with us, his friendly greeting only receiving a grunt and nod or two from the visitors.

"Who's yer friends, Cookie?" he asked in a normal voice. He took offense at being snubbed and showed no concern that he could be heard by the three.

"No friends of mine, Pock," Cookie replied. "Came in to eat and talk to th' boss."

"Seems they're good at offendin' one an' all," I whispered to Gus.

"Yeah, reg'ler ambassidors of goodwill," he replied.

The three continued eating, seeming to ignore the conversations and people around them. A little weasel-faced fellow rose and made to get seconds and Cookie waved him away, "No seconds until all have eaten," he said.

Weasel Face hesitated, then made to proceed toward the bean pot. Pock stepped in front of him. "Must be deef or hard o' hearin', Cookie." Then placing his face close to the little man's face, he said in a loud voice, "No seconds 'til th' whole crew's eaten, fellow."

"New rule, ain't it?" Gus whispered as we watched Weasel Face put his hand on the bowie knife at his waist.

"Go ahead, feller," Pock muttered through clenched teeth, "draw it."

Possibly the other two men had seen our guns resting in our laps, but in any case, they seemed to ignore the little scene by the bean pot.

We could see Pock's face an' he never blinked the whole time they stood there. After what seemed five minutes, Weasel Face shrugged and turned back to his companions.

"If Pock had blinked, that bitch wolf's offspring would have cut his gizzard out," I whispered.

"He's a sneak killer, if I ever saw one," Gus said, "an' I ain't blinkin' 'til he's gone far enough away from here, he can't git back afore daylight."

We had finished our meal and should have left for the herd, but we stayed, watchin' our guests. Pock finished his meal and with a meaningful glance at us, mounted up and rode back to the herd. The three watched him go, then watched as Jake rode in from another direction. He gave us a questioning look and nodded slightly when I cut my eyes to the visitors.

"Hello, men, did Cookie get you fixed up?"

The midsized man looked up and smiled, "Just fine, boss, good grub."

"Here comes th' charm," I whispered.

The man rose and followed Jake to the grub line. "We have come to offer our services," he said, "to the state line, and we only ask for our meals for pay."

Jake nodded and studied the proposal a moment, then shook his head, "Sorry, but I have all the help I need. Besides, I'm short some on horses right now an' don't have anything you can ride. You're welcome to this feed, but I don't need any more help. One of those herds over on th' main trail might have use of you."

"We like it over here out of th' bustle and dust of the main trail. We'll stay with you and try to make ourselves useful," the man replied.

"Someone's lookin' for them," Gus whispered.

"They're prob'ly used to that," I replied.

"Must be someone determined and likely to have them stretchin' hemp."

"Lead poisonin's cheaper, we need our r—" Gus's sharp elbow cut my wind off and I looked up to see that the other two bums had risen and joined their partner. They crowded Jake against the wagon. I fired two shots into the air and let out a yell, "Whoopee!"

The two larger men whirled toward us, but the little weasel's knife flashed and Cookie standing by the fire shot him.

Me and Gus were on our feet and across th' thirty feet that separated us holding our guns in th' faces of the two men standing before they could react.

"Git outa my way," Cookie shouted at us, "I'm gonna finish th' job."

A horse skidded to a stop just before hitting the fire and Tom Stepp bailed off, and pushed Cookie's gun skyward as he pulled the trigger.

"Let me go you . . ."

"Hold on there, Orv, we got things under control," Pock called as he walked around the back of the wagon, his rifle levered.

Stepp held Cookie's gun barrel high until the man took a deep breath and relaxed. "You ain't gonna shoot me if I let go, are you?" he asked.

"I just might," Cookie flared, "but it'll be after I shoot those two pups for interfering in our fight an' gittin' in th' way."

Gus looked at me, eyes wide. "He's talkin' 'bout us! What'd *we* do?"

"Looks to me like you got into his line of fire b'fore he was through shootin'." Tom grinned. Other riders were converging on us, having heard my danger signal.

"I'm glad they did," Jake spoke for the first time. We looked, and he was holdin' his arm, blood oozing out b'tween his fingers. Doctor Cookie rummaged in the boot and brought out the doctoring box. "Let's stop that bleedin', Jake."

"Gus, you aiming for th' sky or that fellow's goozle?" Curly Treadaway asked.

I looked at Gus for the first time and he shore presented a comical sight, him bein' barely five feet tall and holding his gun on that six-foot-four-inch-tall feller.

"Look 'em over close, fellers, an' seize their weapons," Pock said, "I got th' drop on 'em."

Curly stepped over behind the giant, "You search from th' ground up high as you can reach, Gus, an' I'll git th' rest."

"Company's comin'," Otha Huie said.

We could see a man carefully riding around the herd. He wore dark clothes and a peaked sombrero. His horse was all black except for a white blaze face. As he came closer, I could see he was a black man and he had a peso star on his chest.

"Well, it's ol' Baz Reeves," Cookie said, and called, "Unload that horse, Baz, and fill yer plate."

"B'lieve I will, Orville, seein's how you're th' cook. Wouldn't want to eat this outfit's cookin' if you wasn't here."

He stepped down and stretched his legs. He was fully as tall as our prisoner and wore two guns on his waist. The stock of his Winchester peeking out of its boot was polished.

"You boys have saved me a lot of trouble chasin' these three. Judge Parker has sent me with an invitation to visit him. He's gonna be disappointed Creepy there ain't gonna make it."

"Creepy" lay crumpled and still at our feet. "Better lay him out straight, or his grave is gonna have to be short and awful wide," Bass said.

"You two straighten out your friend there," Jake ordered. "None of my men are gonna touch him."

"Aw-w-w after he cools a little, th' critters'll all leave an' hunt a live body," O said.

Curly grinned. "Well, you just stand here close to th' corpse a while."

I laid my prisoner's knife and guns on the wagon seat and grabbed Creepy's knife before the two could get near. I hesitated a moment, tempted to ram that knife into the killer's chest, and Jake said, "Let me have that knife, Sut, I think I earned it." It was a nice knife with a ten-inch blade, broad and very sharp. The coffin handle was made of some black wood and I noted the large brass guard had several nicks in it. Someone must have had several fights, but I doubt it was Creepy's way of using it.

"How many ribs that thing has parted?" wondered Pock.

"With that Creepy, it was mostly the back ribs or the throat," Bass said. "Say, Cookie, them beans smell good. Is that a ham bone I see floatin' 'round that pot?"

"Shore is, Baz, you can thank that short feller there for that. Only cost him thirteen stitches in his horse's leg. This steak will be done to a turn soon an' I'll plop it in a plate for you. Fill yer cup."

While we were waiting and visiting with Bass, his tumbleweed wagon drove up with two bored mules in the lead, the driver and cook on the seat, and two morose prisoners shackled in the cage.

Bass let us shackle his prisoners and put them into the wagon. The crew returned to their chores. Cookie sewed up a three-inch cut in Jake's arm and bandaged it good. O snuck around and gave us Jake's horse for the cavyyard to keep him in camp and quiet. Bass was still there when we drove the horses in for the switch to night horses. There was a fresh grave over by th' trees.

"Would you believe Jake wouldn't let these buzzards go with me until they had buried their friend and I preached th' funeral?" Bass asked.

The two looked tired and, if possible, dirtier than ever. They sat shackled to their own wagon wheel and kept their occasional conversation to themselves.

Jake lay on his bedroll, propped up by his saddle. He looked pale and said his arm ached. Cookie boiled some willow bark and made him drink the tea. It seemed to help. We ate supper in silence, then gathered around his bed and talked and smoked our pipes.

"Any rustling goin' on around here, Baz?" Curly asked.

Bass put that in his pipe and smoked it a couple of puffs. "Not that I recollect, Curly, unless you count them hog rustlers I caught last month."

"Before you tell that tale, tell us about those two Texans you caught," Jake asked.

Bass chuckled, "Played my letter trick on 'em. We got warrants for these two Texans wanted for murder down in Texas. I taken the warrants and was going to the last place they had been staying when I met them on the road. 'Morning, gentlemen,' says I.

" 'I don't speak to blacks,' one of them said. 'Say, ain't you Bass Reeves?'

"Me being the honest deputy I am, I answered, 'No.'

" 'I think you are,' the big man said, and throwed down on me with his gun.

"The little man said, 'Let's take him with us until we meet someone who knows him.'

"So they turned me around and marched me down th' road, but we did not meet anyone and after some time, the two got tired of th' game and stopped.

" 'We ain't got no more time t' mess with you, feller, so we're gonna have to kill you. Git down off that horse.'

"The other feller asked me, 'You got any last words you want to say?'

"Well, I starts shakin' an' says, 'I got a letter from my wife an' I'd shore be grateful if one of you two would read it to me.' I got the letter out of my saddlebag. Them two got down too an' I laid the letter on the pommel of my saddle.

"The big feller said, 'What difference does it make?' He took his eyes off o' me and looked at the letter.

"I grabbed him by the throat with one hand and jerked his gun away with the other, 'Son of a bitch, now you are under arrest,' I said. Would you believe it? That little feller was so scared he dropped his gun. I took them to Muskogee."

We got a good chuckle out of that, as Bass reloaded his pipe. When it was well lit, he said, "Now, as I was saying, we got word that a bunch of hogs had been stolen and Marshal gave me the warrants to bring in the thieves. One of them had been named and I went to his house, had supper with him. I noticed some hog hairs around the fireplace. After supper, we were smoking our pipes on the stoop and by-'n'-by, I said, 'Now, I know you have stolen those hogs an' you couldn't have done it by yourself. If you tell me who the others are, I'll put in a word for you with the judge.'

"We discussed that a few minutes and he named three other men who had helped and showed me where they had butchered the hogs. I only found one of the other men by nightfall and determined to take these two to jail and come back in the morning for the other two. We were going along in my buggy when someone shot at me from the brush. I told the men in the buggy to sit still and when the ambusher shot again, I fell over.

"That brought two men out of the brush and I gutshot the man with the rifle. The other man started to run and I convinced him to stop. Ended up, I brought all four of the hog thieves to jail at once."

All was quiet for a minute as we digested those tales, then Pock said, "At least we won't have t' worry about those hog thieves upgrading to cattle thieves." He knocked out the embers of his pipe on his heel and with his knife cleaned out the dottle before stowing it all away. "Time for me to git some shut-eye. I'll sleep good knowin' Creepy's safe an' no Texas murderers is lurkin' about."

We heard Bass pull out with that rattletrap tumbleweed wagon and his prisoners well before daylight. It seemed only a minute or two later Cookie called breakfast. "Always too soon, ain't he?" Gus asked as he rolled out of the covers.

Chickasha was relieved his enemies had been captured and no longer looked over his shoulder every minute or two. Jake put him out in front of the herd as the whooper. His job was to run off the buffalo and wild horses that might interfere with the progress of the herd.

"What did you do to those men to make them chase you?" I asked.

"They brought down a bunch of quart jars of that rotgut they peddle and hid them in the Boggy Depot Cemetery, knowing those Injuns would not go in there and steal. 'Good as a bank safe,' I heard that Creepy say, but he hadn't counted on a Carlisle-educated Injun who wasn't scared of the cemetery spirits. I snuck in there and emptied those jars and took them over to Aunt Birdsong to can her jams and t'maters in. Got two dozen the first trip, but those fellers almost caught me my second trip. They been chasing me ever since. Now they're gone, I can go back and get the rest of the jars. Shore made a bunch of those spirits happy, pouring that whiskey on their graves."

"It's a wonder you didn't join them," Cookie said, plopping a steak in his plate.

"Might be those happy spirits was protecting him," I said.

"It had a lot to do with that jar my Uncle Tall Oak found that I had 'forgotten' to dump," he said with a grin.

★ ★ ★ ★ ★

Bass Reeves won a reputation as the
"Most feared U.S. marshal in the
Indian country."

—Baird and Goble textbook

CHAPTER 6
COOKIE TELLS A TALE

It was the custom for one of us to tell a story or sing a song before turning in at night, and this night Cookie came over after the chores were done and shared a smoke with us. "Orville, you haven't told a tale this whole trip," Jake said. "How about tellin' these two kids about your coon hunt with Uncle Jess?"

Cookie puffed on his pipe a couple of times, frowned, and relit with a stick from the fire. Two or three puffs satisfied him that the pipe was lit, and he looked at us and grinned.

"Dis here tale started 'way back whin we was wukin' for da massa on da plan-ta-shon in *South* Carolina. South Carolina da state whur da revolution turn in favor ob da colonies whin dem w'ite mans turned deir squirrel guns on dem Red Coats frum ahind trees an' rocks an' such."

"He's talkin' another language, Sut, can you cipher it?" Gus whispered.

"Sh-h-h, I'm concentratin'."

(I know how tiresome this dialect can become to you, faithful reader, so I have taken the liberty to translate some of Cookie's "plantation" talk into modified English for the remainder of this story. Ed.)

"Ennyhow, that's not a part o' *this* story." Cookie continued, "We wus short o' meat after massa sold off all our hogs an' th' men decided it were necessary t' have a coon hunt. Now due to th' absence o' hogs, th' coons and possums been hunted down all 'round th' place an' it were necessary t' go a long ways t' find coon country.

"We set th' nex' night for th' hunt, th' moon bein' in th' right phase, an' gibbin' massa time t' notify th' Pattyrollers we was coon huntin'. That warn't necessary, for no Pattyrollers went into th' woods, night *or* day. Lots o' them what went in never comed out. We hardly ever ate 'gater meat, knowin' whut they fed upon.

"Uncle Jess heered 'bout our plans an' comes to us an' says, 'This be my las' hunt if you says I kin go.'

"Now, Uncle Jess be our bes' coon hunter, but he gettin' old an' a little feeble, 'specially for a long walk, so that why we didn' ax him t' go with us. We talks it over an' 'llows he might not live long e-nough to go on th' nex' hunt, seein' he past th' 'lotted three score an' ten. So we says 'yes' to him, but he hafta keep up with us on his own. That satisfy him, an' nex' night he sittin' on a stump at th' edge o' th' woods waitin'.

"Even though we say we not wait on him, we goes slow an' takes more restin' times than usual. He struggle along an' refuses enny helpin' hands, sumpin' we appreciate in him. 'Way deep in th' woods, them dogs treed an' we hurried on.

"They had treed in a great big sweet gum tree, thirty feet to th' first limb an' not a knot b'tween, an' from th' sounds, there was more than one coon up that tree.

"Well, we had set to with our axe by th' time Uncle Jess got catched up to us. He sat on a log back away frum th' flyin' chips an' watched an' listened. Whin th' axe was changin' hands, Uncle Jess say, 'I doesn't t'ink that there tree is a coon tree, boys. Look an' sound more lak a bear tree, t' me.'

"Now that hurt th' feelins o' th' hound men an' they takes offense that their *coon* hound would tree a *bear.* No, sir, that tree be full o' coons, an' Uncle Jess be dammed.

"Now th' chips really flew an' folks was grabbin' dogs an' haulin' them out o' th' way 'fore that tree fall on 'em. It hit th' groun', an' only bounce once b'fore them dogs was into it. Theys some onlikely growlin' lak a coon never make an' with a bunch o' yippin', th' dogs come tail-tucked outa that tree wi' a big black bear swipin' at their hind ends. That whole pack takes th' back trail home followed by their masters at their best pace, but much slower.

"That first two mile seem lak five mile t' our lungs an' th' whole crowd set new speed records fo' themselves. Sounds o' those dogs had long faded.

"First breath someone catch, he say, 'Poor Uncle Jess,' an th' rest o' us starts wi' th' cognation that he was left b'hind in th' 'mergency runaway.

"O-o-oh th' grief o' those mans over th' loss o' th' beloved Uncle Jess. 'How we gonna tell th' widow Julia?' they asked.

" 'He a hero,' one say, 'giving hisself up so th' rest o' us could ex-cape.'

" 'Yes, ma'am, he a hero, an' we gonna go back soon's it's light and gather his bones, we are,' we rehearsed. With heavy hearts we entered th' row of shanties. Seeing a light on in Uncle Jess's house, the hunters gathered close to th' door an' someone knocked softly. In a moment, th' door cre-e-ak open an' there stood Uncle Jess! There was a stir in da back o' th' crowd as several made a hasty e-vac-u-ation. One nearest th' door was held by th' press o' that crowd long enough to perceive that Uncle Jess weren't no spirit.

" 'Uncle Jess! How did you get home?'

" 'Oh,' he say, 'I comed 'long wif th' dogs.' "

"Huh?" said Gus as I laughed and the rest, who had heard the story a time or two before, chuckled. "That really happened, Cookie?"

"It did sure as I'm sittin' here an' this pipe is cold," Cookie returned.

"What was that language you was talkin'?"

"That was the way we talked on th' plantation, Gus. The old folks used t' talk th' old country language when they didn't want us youngsters t' know what they was sayin'."

"What were the Pattyrollers?" I asked.

"They was white trash the landowners hired to catch us out at night or without permission, Sut."

"It shore was a different world, Cookie, an' I'm glad you ain't in it no more," I said.

"Me, too. There were some good things there, but this is better. Now, I've stayed past my bedtime and it's off to bed I go."

With that, we all retired and Gus got to giggling about th' story; I had t' kick him to shut him up.

The only real casualty
In tellin' the story
Was the truth.

—Old Vaquero Saying

Chapter 7
The Ninemile Canyons

We had crossed the Canadian before it sank into the quicksands. Even so, the bottom was boggy and we had to pull several steers out. Jake steered us around the headwaters of Sixmile Creek. The North or Dry Canadian was running, but easy to cross. The only water between there and Dead Indian Creek was in tanks and old buffalo wallows, and they were all full, so we didn't suffer for water. We crossed the Cimarron twice because it had split into two channels against the two banks of the riverbed.

From there, we drove up the west side of Turkey Creek; the main trail ran up the east side of the creek. When Turkey veered northwest, we crossed and followed it a ways to get more distance from the main Chisholm Trail. Where it made the big loop west and back south, we stopped to noon and let the stock get a good drink. The boys said it was a long ways across the plains to the next stream, and it was the Salt Fork of the Arkansas. We would be depending on tanks and wallows for our water.

"Gettin' a little far from th' main trail, ain't we?" I liked it when we were in sight of the trail and other herds moving along it.

"Nah, Sut, we're not that far from it, five or six miles is all," Gus said through his sombrero pulled over his face. "Now quit your yammerin' an' let a feller nap a little."

Tom was sitting against the wagon wheel next to Gus. "We

veered west to miss what they call the Ninemile Canyons, Sut. It's an area full of canyons and Injuns and stolen stock. Anything lost in them is gone forever, and that includes men looking for their animals."

"What tribe is in there?" I asked.

"Whichever gits there first in th' spring, Comanche, Kioway, Cheyenne, Cherokee, or any of the other so-called civilized tribes."

"Cherokee?" A hat-muffled voice asked.

"They come early and the 'wild Indians' run them off when they get there," Tom replied.

"Not a lota difference atween th' two is there?" I said.

"I got a feelin' we ain't gonna get a lot of sleep th' next couple of days," said Tom.

"Nothin's new there," the sombrero said.

It was later than usual when Jake stirred around and told us, "We're gonna start now, and drive all night. I hope we can get by Ninemile Canyons without being seen. Maybe those Indians will be too interested in what passes on the trail to look for us west of them. Sut, you and Gus keep the remuda even with the herd on the west side. Any trouble out there, give the long yell. Ride with your rifle on your laps. Bring the horses close at sunset for the change to night horse, and again at midnight by th' dipper. The password is 'kettle,' shoot anyone that approaches and doesn't say it. If the stock stampedes, let them run and keep them running north." He moved on to talk to Pock and Cookie.

"Sounds serious, don't he?" Gus observed.

"We lost nearly two hundred head comin' up on the trail last year," Curly said. "I think Jake came this way just to get past the place."

"There was a lot of talk about getting together an army and cleaning out th' canyons, but it would have to be done every year, and our 'army' was needed to drive herds to market," Tom said.

Gus nudged me, "Won't be any supper tonight, drop by an' rustle us some grub while I saddle our horses."

Cookie was waiting on me and handed me a sack of biscuits and salt pork. "Share that with Gus, now."

"Yes, sir." And we were off.

There was a cold wind right out of the north and it was a lot of work keeping the animals facing it. When it swung around coming from east of due north, we let the herds turn west of north and the going was easier. The wind kept the dust we kicked up close to the ground and harder to see from a distance.

"Those canyons are not real deep, just a bunch of drainages lined thick with trees and brush scattered over a big area of the plains," Curly said. "They are an ideal place to hide stolen stock and easy to defend."

It was a lot of work convincing the cattle that we were not stopping for the night, and it was a good thing we had strayed somewhat west of our intended track, away from Ninemile. The horses were not as hard to handle, but it was going to be a strain on them, for they were worked more often and didn't get the rest they needed. Being grass fed, they couldn't be pushed as hard as corn-fed stock.

It was a long hard night and the grub sack had been emptied long before sunrise. Half the morning was over before Jake allowed the cattle to slow somewhat, but they kept them bunched and moving so they wouldn't lie down.

Cookie had driven ahead and we could see the little dot of white wagon sheet far ahead where he had selected a spot close to several tanks of water.

"Sut, I ain't gonna make it to that chuck wagon. Just tie my body over my saddle an' don't bury me out here alone on this prairie. Put me where there's people t' come by occasionally an' say 'howdy.' "

"You ain't gonna die. Hop down an' munch some o' this grass. If cows get fat on it, you might get by."

O rode up to change horses and I called out, "What's th' password, O?"

"Th' password's forty-four."

"Forty-four?"

"Yeah, th' caliber of this rifle, now get me that grulla of mine." Some people just don't have a sense of humor. The grulla didn't have much more in him than the horse he turned back, but none of the rest of the whole cavyyard were any better off.

"These horses gotta rest soon," Gus said. He was actually chewing on a grass stem.

"Probably not before th' Salt Fork."

Cookie had parked on the upper drainages of Wild Horse Creek where some of the branches had pools of water. The herd stopped and spread to the several pools and tanks, then grazed a little before lying down and ruminating—that's what Tom called chewing the cud.

I watched the horses while Gus went in and ruminated on a thick steak and frijoles. He came back with a pocket full of biscuits and waved me in. I drug up th' top of a dead tree for Cookie's fire, then ate. When I finished, Cookie took my plate and handed me the axe. "Now, chop that wood up and throw it in th' possum belly. I got plenty of wood for now."

There I was chopping that wood when a couple of men rode in from the east and Jake met them at the wagon. "Howdy there, Clay, how are you?"

"That's Clay McSparren, Shanghai Pierce's trail boss," Cookie whispered. "Fill these cups with coffee and take it to them."

Clay McSparren was a slim feller, not too tall, but walked erect, back straight as an arrow, legs bowed in the cowman fashion; someone used to spending most of his waking hours—and probably some sleeping hours—in the saddle. His black hair was long and ragged, like all trail men at this stage of the trip; his month-old beard was speckled with gray. It was hard to tell his age under that sombrero and beard. When he had his pipe lit, I offered him the coffee and he nodded his thanks.

The young vaquero with him was about my age or a little older. He stayed in the saddle and waved away my offer of the cup. Something Mr. Clay said caught my attention and I sipped the coffee and listened.

". . . thirty head of Shanghai's prime cows he was planning on showin' for braggin' rights. If I don't try to get them back, I will be lookin' for a new job."

Jake nodded, "They got two hundred head off us last year, but they haven't bothered me this year—yet."

"You're never out of danger from these Indians, even if you get to Kansas," Clay said.

"How do you propose to get your stock back?"

"Damned if I know, Jake. Do you have any ideas?"

"We could go in with an army, but some of us would sure get killed, and all th' cattle in that place aren't worth one man dyin'."

It looked like Mr. Clay wasn't so convinced of that, but he said, "How else can we get our stock back?"

There was a long silence while the two trail bosses mulled the question over in their pipes. "If we can't go in there and get them, we need to get them to come out to us," Jake said.

"That 'how' question still hasn't been answered," Mr. Clay said.

"Burn 'em out!" I hardly realized I said it out loud until it was out there.

Jake frowned, "You can't do that without burning off the rest of the prairie, and that would be a calamity for the herds comin' up the trail. My Utes have been in there and tell me there are separate Kioway, Comanche, and Arapaho camps, and that they have some pretty good horses in their herds."

Mr. Clay drew on his pipe. "It's possible they could stir up a little trouble so that one of those camps would be invited to leave." He paused long enough to relight his pipe. "If one of those camps could be suspected of stealing from the others . . ."

"What if one of the tribes 'stole' horses from the other two?" Jake asked.

"Cause a fuss, for sure," Clay mused. "Might work. If your Utes could take horses from two of the herds and put them in th' third . . ."

Those two Indians broke out in grins when Jake put the question to them. Shore they could do that and more if need be. That night, Uno and Dos took Chickasha and rode back to the canyons. Chickasha was to hold their horses while the two stole horses from the Kiowa and Comanche camps and mixed them into the Arapaho herd. They were gone all night and Chickasha came back dead tired, but excited about what was happening.

"They got ten of the best horses from the Comanche herd, and three of the Kioway chief's best horses and mixed them into the Arapaho herd without a problem," he said. "Now all we have to do is wait until they get caught with the goods. Uno and Dos stayed to watch. I don't think they ever sleep."

"They'll prob'ly git more sleep than you do today. Jake wants you t' go with me an' Gus to drive the cavyyard out a ways and graze them all day. Curly's scoutin' a good place for us where there ain't no Injun-hidin' gulleys."

"I'll catch up my night horse. He'll keep an eye on th' herd and let me sleep."

"What you gonna ride tonight if you ride your night horse all day?" I asked.

"When th' devil does he think I'll git some sleep?"

"Last I heard, it was some time 'bout November th' first," I answered. I couldn't spare too much sympathy on the boy. Bein' out all night playin' horse thief was his idea of fun.

We weren't so far away that we couldn't see one of the Utes riding in and talking with Jake. Soon, Dos rode out and traded his horse for another of his unshod horses. He caught one of Uno's horses and rode straight for Ninemile Canyons. All he said to us was, "Big fight, Arapaho leaving."

Jake told us the rest of the plan when we drove the cavyyard in for the night. "We are going to let the Arapahos go and the Utes are going to steal some more horses from the other two tribes. The Kioways an' C'manches'll think the Arapahos did it and send people to get them. *Then* we spring our trap and gather them all up."

"I'm goin' t' bed," Gus whispered, and he did.

I ate supper, stole a pocket full of biscuits for Gus, and followed him to our bedroll.

When I heard the hoofbeats of the night guard returning for us, I nudged Gus and pulled on my boots. Gus munched cold biscuits and turned right at the herd when I turned left. Chickasha was absent. We had the next-to-last watch, so we caught a couple more hours of sleep while Cookie made breakfast.

Jake had a hard time keeping enough hands to handle the herd while the rest rode to catch Injuns and stock on the open prairie. It ended up that he stayed with Gus, O, and Cookie to watch things and let the rest of us go with strict orders to report to Clay McSparren and do what he says to do. Cookie was mad because he had to ride herd, but he didn't have to cook for the outfit. He wouldn't even cook the steaks for O, Gus, and Jake.

There must have been fifty men mounting up when we rode into the Pierce camp and Pock found Clay. The two Utes and Chickasha had just given the information that a large group of

Indians had ridden west out of the canyons, hot on the trail of the retreating Arapahos. The plan was to ride in between them and the canyons, send half of the army into the canyons to drive out what stock they could while the other half corralled the retreating Arapahos and their pursuers. We would be outnumbered, depending on surprise to carry the battle.

Clay looked me over and ordered me to stay on the prairie with Curly and Pock while the others went east into the canyons with a man who had been an officer in the Confederacy. He seemed very competent to lead the fight.

Clay formed us in a line, spaced about ten yards apart, and we rode out at a trot. I was next to him in the middle of the line. Their dust showed the Injuns to be about three miles ahead of us and the Arapahos were at least that far ahead of their pursuers. The Comanche-Kiowa would catch the Arapahos about the time we would catch them, and if they could figure out the trick before we caught up with them, we would have to fight the combined force instead of one bunch at a time. Clay called us in close and shouted as we ran, "Bunch up in one line and we will run through the Indians and stampede the herd."

The Comanche-Kiowa couldn't tell through the dust who we were and must have thought us to be more Indian reinforcements. They paid us no mind until we burst out of their dust and shot our way through them and across the three hundred yards or more right into the Arapaho warriors lined up to protect their herd and the women and children beyond them.

The mixed herd needed no more prompting to turn and stampede to the northwest with us following on the run. We didn't know what the Indians behind us were doing. The natural tendency of a stampeding herd is to turn to the right and we took advantage of that to guide them to the northeast and the trail. We let them run until they were tired, then kept them moving, spread out so they could cool.

A few Comanches had followed us, but we discouraged any interference from them. The Arapahos were more concerned about their women and children. The herd had run through the north edge of the tribe and there were several injuries and a few were killed. Some of us felt sympathy for them.

Pock spit and eyed the retreating Indians. "Damned scoundrels won't come out here in th' open an' fight us. Rather ambush us or sneak up on us in the dark when they can't be seen. Just ignore 'em, boys an' let's get these dogies out of harm's way—harm bein' those damned scoundrels."

"Would you look at that herd," Curly said as we rode to catch up.

"Must be over five hundred prime steers and at least a hundred horses, mostly cow horses, too," Pock observed.

"And that's from only one tribe," I said.

"You can bet there's more than that with the Comanches, Sut. They always have the king's portion," Curly said.

"Wonder how those boys are getting along." I was concerned because of what Jake said about them getting shot up.

"The Lord said, 'Sufficient unto the day is the evil thereof,' " Curly quoted. "Another word just like it is, 'Don't borrow someone else's troubles,' Sut. We'll know about them soon enough. Clay's callin' us up."

Clay picked ten of us to stay with the herd and push them on up the trail away from the Indians. The rest of the men he sent back toward the canyons to help out there. I didn't wait to be told, just took up my customary place with the drag. Twelve long, hot, dusty, dry, foodless hours later we crossed the Salt Fork and drove three more miles to the fresh waters of Pond Creek where three chuck wagons were parked and three fires were cooking up grub. The watered steers didn't bother to graze, just laid down and rested. It made it easy to separate the horses and drive them to one side. There was a big dust a few miles behind us. Speculation was that it was from the canyon crowd.

I called to Curly, "I counted twelve different brands in th' horse herd."

"Can't be that many outfits ahead of us, must be some left over from last year," he replied.

"The six brands we saw in the beef herd probably represent the outfits ahead of us on the trail," Pock said.

Clay sent a couple men back to see who was under the dust cloud and to give them instructions if it was another herd of stolen stock. I washed up in the creek and got supper from the nearest wagon. The cook filled my tin with rice and poured hot beef gravy with big chunks of beef on top. "Eat this with a spoon," he instructed, "and come back for more if you want. Biscuits are in the oven."

I got some of them with my second plate of that rice and gravy.

"We got the third watch, Sut," Pock said when I stumbled to my saddle. I don't remember answering him, but I was rested enough to hear the second watch ride in and unwrapped myself from the saddle blanket. I didn't even have to pull on my boots, and a horse from the herd was tied there waiting on my saddle.

One of the great tragedies of history
Is that the Indian and the white man
Had to meet.

—Struthers Burt

Chapter 8
A Sioux War Bonnet

The raid on the canyons had been successful in that the raiders had run a large herd of steers and horses out of them, but it was at the cost of four men wounded, one seriously. We heard later that he died. Word was passed from herd to herd ahead for outfits that had lost cattle to send a rep to gather their stock. With no branding to do, the separation went fast, and me and Gus found ourselves the custodians of the Circle Dot cut. There were thirty-two head and when the cutting was complete, a couple of men presented Jake with a letter authorizing him to release the animals to them.

The letter was written by someone who didn't write very often and Tom said most of his spelling was by sound. I guess that means he couldn't spell.

Jake noted the brands on the horses were not Circle Dot. He studied the letter a long time, then looked up and said, "All right, men, the herd's yours. Gus, you and Sut stay with th' herd an' help the men get them back to their main herd, then mosey back this way. We'll meet you somewhere west of the main trail."

"Yes, sir." Gus noted the absence of any food and scrounged a couple of steaks wrapped in sourdough bread.

Cookie threw him a greasy sack and he stuffed the steaks in it. "Now git, Chow Wrangler, I got work t' do."

The man called Nick took point and the other man, Ray, took the left swing; me and Gus flipped for right swing and he lost and went to the drag.

The point man signaled turn right and we turned, expecting that their herd was on the main trail somewhere. There was an outfit camped just west of the trail and Ray rode over to see who they were. He came back and said, "Our outfit is two herds ahead and we should get there before dark. You two have been a lot of help and we thank you. We can get them there by ourselves, now." They turned and began driving the stock up the trail.

Gus shook the greasy sack at me and said, "Dinnertime."

You can be sure I was ready. "Suppose that outfit would give us a couple cups of coffee?"

"Shore they would, let's go ask."

Of course, the boss and cook were very generous, even offering us a whole meal, but they seemed a little cool, for some reason. We settled for a cup of coffee and plate of beans t' go with our steaks. When we were finished, I washed our plates in the wreck pan and put them in the cook's stack. He poured us both another cup of coffee. "You got time for another cup before you catch up with your herd." He nodded to the disappearing cattle with Nick and Ray.

"We're not going with them. They said they could handle those steers from here and we are going back to our outfit over west of here," I said.

"You fellers know who those two are?" a red-bearded cowboy demanded.

I glanced at Gus and said, "They are two men from the Circle Dot trail herd picking up their steers cut out of the herd we captured from the Injuns."

"They had a letter from the trail boss authorizing them to take the cattle," Gus added.

We heard a plate slam in the wreck pan, "Damned slickers," the cook said.

The trail boss stood and said, "Those two are the biggest thieves on the trail. We thought you two were in with them and a couple of the boys are out looking for a tree tall enough to hang you on without your feet dragging the ground."

"Jake Meeker of the Rafter JM is our boss and he sent us to help them move the steers back to their herd," I said.

Two riders trotted in to the camp and without dismounting, a short, weathered vaquero said, "They turned east as soon as they were out of sight. Looks like they have a good start on a ranch with that herd and the Rockin' R bunch."

Gus poked my ribs, "They stole another bunch!"

The other rider was shaking out the loop of his latigo. "These th' two we gonna stretch?"

"Naw, they're victims of th' Cottrel scam," the red-headed cowboy said.

The rider looked disappointed and kept his loop ready as if he expected us to run any moment. Gus eyed the man, his hand on his gun. "Be careful with that rope, feller, it might get you hurt."

I stepped in front of Gus, "He's just mad 'cause we got robbed. Thank you for the coffee an' grub. We have to go now." We mounted up and headed toward the stolen cattle.

"Hold on there," the trail boss called. "What are you goin' t' do?"

"Get those cows back and make life miserable for two thieves," I replied.

"Just you two against th' Cottrel boys?" the would-be hangman asked.

"If we have to. They lied to our boss and stole cows in our care. It's our responsibility to make it right."

The hangman grinned and looked at the trail boss. "Boss, I request permission to assist these two whelps in retrieving stolen stock from the Cottrel gang."

"Me, too," a half dozen voices joined in.

"Hold on, now, I can't let th' whole crew go. We still have to protect our own herd, and these Injuns ain't gonna let this go that easy." After a pause, he said, "I'll let Red and Al," nodding toward the mounted man, "go if the rest of you agree t' take up th' slack—*for two days only*—after that, I'll look for two replacements."

There would have followed a long discussion on the merits of other men eager to go, but the trail boss cut off debate and called for a vote, and the two chosen were given grudging approval to pursue the thieves. All four of us changed to fresh horses and rode into the gloaming with many words of advice and threats ringing in our ears.

"They weren't pushin' 'em hard when we saw them," Al said. "I imagine they will find a place near water and bed them down for the night. They had a dugout over on Deer Creek and that's where they will hide the critters 'til fall when the trail herds are gone."

"They might hold them over until next year and be the first to ship," Red said. "We could go find their dugout an' let them bring th' cows to us."

"That'ud take more than two days an' I ain't crazy about lookin' for a job out here."

"We could go partway until we're sure to be beyond them an' let them come to us," I said.

" 'Specially since we don't know where they are," Gus added.

It seemed like a good plan. "Instead of bungling around in th' dark with a chance we might stumble into them and get ourselves shot up, we could get ahead of them, watch where they are going, and set up an ambush for them," Al said.

"Sounds good t' me," Gus said, and we turned east and rode until the dipper was under th' polestar.

I picketed my horse and lay down on the saddle blanket.

"Don't know how t' sleep without wakin' up for th' third watch."

"Just listen for the second watch t' ride in," Gus said.

It did seem strange to sleep the remainder of the night without any interruptions, and I did wake and listen for the second watch's return. When they didn't, I slept again.

A bag of jerky and water served us for breakfast. "I'm gonna have me the biggest steak Cookie can fry and drink my coffee straight from th' pot when we get back," I said.

"Buttermilk flapjacks an' maple syrup," Red said. "an' a half gallon of th' coldest milk you ever drank."

"Sunrise in a few minutes and we'll be seein' their dust," Al said. "Throw your dishes in th' wreck pan an' I'll wash 'em after we get th' herd back."

Al looked at me as we saddled and said, "Watch that critter, Sut, he likes t'buck, but he'll wait 'til he thinks you aren't paying attention."

"Thanks, I'll watch." *I'll watch out and strangle my saddle horn, I will.* It was ten minutes later, when I was scratching my head with my saddle horn hand, that the scoundrel tucked his head between his legs and tried to stand on it. I lay back almost on the horse's back, kicked free of the stirrups, and raked my spurs down his shoulders. He was so surprised he stopped and stood still, looking back at me. "Any time, old boy, any time."

Horses can't shrug, so he shook his head and ambled on. We stopped on a little ridge, maybe three feet above that flat plain, and watched. The dust was already there, we knew. It would just have to get light enough for us to see.

"There it is," Gus said, pointing southwestward.

"Too small," I said, "but we better keep an eye on it. Might be trouble." The big dust of the cattle was about three miles north of the little cloud and pointed just a little north of where we sat.

"Injuns stalkin' th' herd," Al said of the smaller dust.

"If there are only two men with those steers, they are gonna lose them and prob'ly some of their own hair," Red observed.

"We could possibly tip th' scales for them," I said.

"The enemy of my enemy is my friend," Al said.

"Sorry, boys," Red said aside to us. "He has spells like that ever' once in a while."

"Runs fever with it, does he?" Gus asked as we gigged the horses into a run for the herd. Seeing the two groups of riders converging on them was inducement enough for the two thieves to abandon their booty and scoot for the relative safety of the trail herds. We easily won the race to the cattle and set ourselves up between the herd and the oncoming Indians. We were caught on the plain without any cover for the steers or us.

". . . sixteen, seventeen . . . I count twenty of them," Gus said.

"Only five apiece? That ain't quite fair to them," Al said. "Let's flip to see which one of us has t' sit out, t' even th' odds for those Injuns." He jerked off his saddle and pulled his rifle out of its boot, and I noticed for the first time that it was a Sharps .50 breech-loading buffalo gun. Lying down and using his forked stick for a prop, he sighted the oncoming Indians.

"Sa-a-ay, ain't that a Sioux in that war bonnet?" Red asked.

"Not likely, since they don't git along with the Comanches," Al replied. "Prob'ly it's a C'manch who killed a Sioux warrior and got hisself a bonnet." He adjusted his sights for five hundred yards and aimed. We could hear the Indians whooping. *Kabam* went the .50 and we jumped. A couple of seconds later, the bonneted Indian fell from his horse.

"Got him," Red said.

Al's second shot missed his target, but an Indian behind him toppled forward off his horse. The warriors milled in confusion and one rode toward the fallen chief. "That's my bonnet, Injun, leave it alone," Al said and shot the would-be rescuer. That settled the matter for the remaining Indians and as one, they turned and ran, three riderless horses with them.

Al clicked his sights up to a thousand yards and fired three more rounds at the retreating crowd. A horse fell at his third shot and he quit, "Sorry, hoss, I meant t' hit your rider. You shouldn't be runnin' with that crowd—gits you in trouble ever' time." He saddled and we rode over to the fallen Indians. Al retrieved the bonnet and tried it on. The two long tails touched the ground either side of his horse and the horse didn't like it. "Here, here, hoss, them feathers ain't gonna hurt you." He gathered the tails up in his lap, hung his sombrero on his horn, and wore the feathers.

"Those Injuns is still running," I said. "Time for us to gather those steers and head for the trail."

"I'll help you," Red said, "Chief Jackass can watch th' Indians for us."

The steers knew what we wanted when we started gathering them and they lined out for the march. "Look at them goin' north like they knew which way t' go," Gus said.

"Turn 'em west, Sut," Red called from the left swing. "Let's get them to the trail." Gus slipped over behind me and helped turn the cattle. We reached the comparative safety of the main trail before noon.

We had lost ground with the herds moving up the trail; Red and Al's T bar T herd was two herds ahead and we had to drive the Circle Dot two herds above that after we traded back for our horses. Every outfit we passed sent men out to help us and the Circle Dot boys were sure glad t' see their cattle. They fed us near to founderin' an' early next morning we headed for the Rafter JM herd.

★ ★ ★ ★ ★

In most Indian languages the words
Stranger and enemy were the same.

—Jubal Sackett

Chapter 9
The Dog Town Dance

"That sun can stay b'hind that cloud 'til it sets," Gus said as he rested a moment and drank deep from his canteen. He let the last drops in the canteen splash on his upturned face. There wasn't a dry stitch between us, down to our socks. Even our sombrero brims were soggy.

"Better fill that canteen right away, you'll need it again in about ten minutes," I said. "This plain is as flat and hot as Cookie's skillet an' we're a big fat hunk o' meat fryin' on it. Sure would be nice t' get a cooling rain."

"S'long's it doesn't spook th' herd," Gus answered. The cattle were really suffering in this heat. For the last two days, we had been driving them early and late and letting them rest through th' heat of the day. Even so, with no shade, the stopovers were not much comfort.

"I been drinkin' water by th' gallons an' still ain't peed but once in two days," I said. "Even gave up coffee for water." Our saddles were wet top and bottom and we had to change horses twice as often. They were as tired and dirty as we were. Now we were thankful for the cooling shade of that great cloud that rose over the western hills and just kept climbing and climbing. We could hear a few rumbles of thunder.

About four o'clock Pock rode up and changed to his night horse and said, "Keep away from the white horses, and keep an eye on that cloud; I never saw one climb that high. We are in for a time with this herd." He rode to the wagon and dumped all the metal he had on, including his belt buckle and spurs, into the wagon.

"Why keep away from the white horses, Sut?" Gus asked as we switched to our night horses.

"White horses draw lightning, Gus." He should of knowed that. It was already dark as night under that cloud and the cattle bedded down on their own. The air was still—deathly still—and little balls of fire appeared on the tips of my horse's ears and danced around the cattle horns. Several of the riders dismounted and walked beside their horses when they were beside and behind the herd. When they got toward the front of the herd, they mounted and lay low on their horse's neck. "We're likely to be wrangling horses all night," I called as I rode to the west side of the cavyyard.

My night horse, called Aciago, for his moods not his color, told me trouble was coming as plainly as if he could talk. I stared through a heavy mist rising from the ground to watch his ears for more warnings. He suddenly stopped and lowered his head to the ground and groaned. I lay on his neck, afraid to dismount.

There was a snapping, crackling sound coming across the sky and a blinding flash as lightning struck a tree east of the herd and exploded into a fountain of fire flying high in all directions. The crash of thunder was simultaneous with the lightning and before its echo died, the herd was on its feet and running. Rain as cold as ice descended so thick it was hard to breathe. Just seconds ago, I was sweating and now we shivered, man and horse.

"One jump to their feet and the next jump to hell," Curly had said of a stampede, and I now believed him.

The horses didn't run! They milled a little and stood legs spread and heads to the ground, probably the better to breathe. A figure appeared through the rain and Cookie called, "Gus,

Sut, go after the herd, I'll watch the horses."

We were a few yards west of the cattle and I joined Gus running after the herd. "Where are they?" he called.

"Let your horse find them," I called back.

I thought I could hear hooves above the roar of the storm, but I couldn't be sure. I was almost among them before I saw a portion of the herd, and it was a long time before I could get them to milling and stopped. Even in that cold rain, I could feel the heat coming from the bunched cattle. They steamed like a cup of coffee on a frosty morning. "Spread 'em out, Gus, before they settle down," I called, not knowing where he was. There was no answer. I spread them as best I could and the cattle gradually settled as the lightning and rain subsided.

Gus was nowhere in sight or sound and I began to worry that he may have fallen in the run. I backtracked, looking for him or his horse, afraid that I might find him and afraid that I might not. "Where are you, Gus?" I called several times. The only answer was the swish and drip of the softening rain.

Satisfied that he wasn't alive behind us, we turned toward our little herd. It had stopped raining. I wrung out my sombrero while Aciago drove and had my shirt pulled over my head when we both heard the rattler warning. Hoss jumped right out from under me, and I landed face first in red mud still wondering where that cussed snake was. It's just as scary when he *stops* rattling as when he rattles since you don't know *where* he is. Not knowing the snake's location, Aciago tip-hoofed away and resumed his journey back to the herd in spite of my calls to wait up.

I slowly sat up without protest from the snake, removed the wet and muddy shirt from my head, and wrapped it thickly around my forearm and hand. Then bracing on it, I arose from the mud. My hat was somewhere on the ground and I gave it to the snake.

It was the blackest night I remember and there was nothing I could use to get my bearings. My best bet was to follow that horse and hopefully catch up with him. He would have been going northwest to the cattle, so I took my bearings with great care, and assuring myself I was right, struck out—southwest.

Fate plays many tricks on us and she must have been in a whimsical mood after that storm, for I walked into the New York City of prairie dog towns. They have three main occupants; prairie dogs, of course; then there are those little owls who rent rooms from them; and the rattlesnake who just moves in without invitation and sometimes eats the landlord's progeny and renter. I hadn't gone ten steps when I stumbled on a mound of dirt and nearly fell. There was an immediate protest from, I supposed, that snake and I detoured to avoid him only to hang my toe in a burrow.

I began to suspicion what was happening and after another ten yards and a warning rattle, I was pretty sure I had literally stumbled into a prairie dog town. There was nothing to do but to continue on my journey and get out of town as fast as I could. So I continued—right into the heart of that city. All night long I danced through town in those tight high-heeled boots, turning one ankle then the other. Knowing a rattler won't strike a moving object, I danced all night, detouring from buzzworm to buzzworm, stumbling over uneven ground, and occasionally ducking an owl mistaking me for a good perch.

Lady Fate finally revealed her joke when the clouds lifted and faded to show the dancer a setting half moon and the first glimmers of sunrise. It certainly didn't feel right when I turned north in opposition to my instinct. The coming of light signaled a changing of the guard, the welcome whistles of the dogs replaced the whirr of rattles, and I soon left their city limits.

Daylight and leaving the dance soon brought to mind another problem: Range cattle, regardless of the breed, get pretty used to a man on horseback and if he doesn't bother them, they leave him alone. However, a man afoot causes much curiosity and must be investigated by the whole crowd.

It doesn't take them long to determine that this strange creature is a threat to public safety and the vote for elimination is unanimous. Another dance begins, its ending not good for the pedestrian.

Me and Gus once found a dead cow in the big pasture and were surprised to find it had been shot. A couple of hundred yards away lay another cow shot, and we followed a line of carcasses across the pasture until in the distance we saw a crowd of bodies. In the middle of the circle of dead cows were the remains of a man. By what was left of his clothes, we knew he was a stranger to the west and by the seventeen dead cows, we knew he wasn't aware of their danger until it was too late. He had put up a good fight. We found his broken rifle several feet from the body. There was one live round in the chamber, indicating what he intended to do with it, but he never got the chance.

We learned that he was from back east visiting a neighbor and had gone out hunting alone and violated his host's admonition that he not cross any fences as he hunted. His widow could not believe cows could behave that way, but we guessed that there must have been more than fifty head in the battle.

Now, I faced that same possibility with only my six-shooter and a belt of shells. I was in real danger unless someone came to my rescue, and that was not too likely to happen soon. Where was Gus? Where was Aciago? Where was a tree or a hole in the ground?

I could have found the trail by the dust, but there was no dust after the rain and I had no idea where anything was, including myself. The stampede had been north or northwest and we had chased a splinter group that must have veered west or even south of west. How far we had run, I couldn't guess. My best chance to find or be found would be to walk north to northeast and hope I hit the trail without being discovered by cattle. Man, how I hated those boots.

About midmorning, a slow-moving herd to the northeast of me came into view. It was at least twice as big as the bunch I had rounded up, and there was only one rider with them. When they were within a mile of me, I fired my gun and waved. The vaquero saw me and turned and led a riderless horse from the far side of the herd. Those poor horses were almost on their last legs and I moved forward to meet them. It was Gus, and the riderless horse was Aciago.

"I thought you were dead when I found your horse with those steers. He had rounded them up by himself, but didn't know what else t' do with them . . . where you been, Sut? I had give you up."

"They was a dance at Dog Town an' I went," I said. "Didn't break up 'til sunrise."

"Must not have had much of a dress code," he replied, looking at my muddy clothes. "An' you left your hat there."

The white skin above my hat line had gotten hot and I had tied my bandanna around my head to shade it. "Checked it with the hat check snake and left by another door."

Aciago nodded and nipped my shoulder. I hated to ride him, but it was necessary. "He insisted on herdin' from th' left side and did a good job of it," Gus said with a grin. "Didn't seem to miss you at all."

"You got any idea where you are going?"

"Nope, just lookin' for that pillar of cloud by day. Must have settled with th' rain."

"We didn't run more than three or four miles, did we?"

"I ran farther than that, I think. The mob must have split and you stayed with the one in back while I stayed with the one still running," he said. "That's how we got separated."

Those steers were as tired as we were and they didn't give any trouble, just needed a little encouragement to keep goin'. We stumbled into camp near sunset, watered the stock and ourselves, and looked for grub. Jake thought we had about our entire herd and called for a count in th' morning, followed by a march if we were close to a full count. I caught my second night horse, Dusky, stripped off and put on clean clothes, and crawled into bed. Gus was already snoring. We rode our third watch and fell back in bed until Cookie called breakfast.

Jake and Curly counted out two thousand and nineteen head in th' count an' Jake allowed that was close enough to two thousand to move on. We only made about ten miles that day, ever'thing in th' outfit was tired an' sore. All the stock needed good grazing to catch up with what they had lost in th' run, so ten miles was a productive drive.

Toward noon, another cloud popped up south of us and we watched it climb into the sky, happy that it posed no threat to us. "Ever' bit as high as ours," Pock said as he saddled his night horse. It was interesting watching it grow. Sunset on the cloud was really pretty—if you didn't think about the hell goin' on under it.

The rattlesnake is harmless when
He is making love or looking for food or water,
But he is seldom harmless.

—Mexican Vaquero

Chapter 10
Crossing Salt Fork

The rain had helped where we camped, but five miles up the trail we started kicking up dust and it was a hot dry pull to the Salt Fork of the Arkansas River. Jake bent th' herd east a little and led th' herd to a spring branch about ten miles south of the river. The steers were grateful and drank their fill. While the horses drank, I drained my canteen and headed for the spring for a refill with that cold water. Being on the south side of the water and the south wind blowing, I didn't smell the sulfur in it until I washed my face.

Curly had been watchin' me and laughed. "Go ahead and drink that water, it'll kill any critters on you and clean your bowels out at th' same time. It's good for you ever' once and a while."

"Guess I'll have to wait until I get to th' wagon barrel," I said. "Why did Jake bring us to this stink-water, anyway?"

"Sulfur will make th' ticks drop off and th' herd will put on weight better without them bloodsuckers," Curly said. "We'll make a wider circle around th' bed ground tonight, an' by th' night after, won't be a live tick in th' crowd. Just don't cross that bed ground in th' morning or you'll founder in hungry ticks."

"That is th' stinkinest herd of cows I ever smelt," Gus said as we ate. Cookie had parked an extra distance from the herd, making sure he was upwind.

"It's enough t' gag a maggot," I answered.

"You just wait 'til those scoury cows stand up in th' mornin'," Curly said. "Folks pickin' up prairie coal around that sulfur spring look funny stickin' it to their noses an' sniffing it, but worse than that is burning it in th' dugout. Makes biscuits taste funny, too."

"Does it make the horses scoury, too?" I asked.

"Let's just say their biscuits would not stand up in a pan," Tom said.

"And if you want to see a mad cook, just water my mules at that spring an' see what you'll be eatin' for supper," Cookie warned.

Pock laughed. "Mules is th' worst animal there is for th' vapors. Cookie's liable t' suffocate b'hind 'em."

Just for fun, the boys made me an' Gus ride drag th' next day, but we had a stiff tailwind an' they suffered th' most. After noonin' we took the horses again.

"The three most dangerous and dreaded river crossings are the Salt Fork, Cimarron, and South Canadian. All three of them are boggy, shifty, and treacherous," Jake told us. "I want you to hold the horses and take them over after the herd. We may need them on this side if it's boggy."

We were a couple of miles above th' trail crossing. "Jake must have planned this out pretty careful," Gus said. "This crossing looks pretty good."

"Not a very wide river, is it?" I observed.

Jake had chosen to cross just above a little riffle over a rock shelf and the herd had no trouble crossing.

"Why's he goin' up th' riverbank, Sut?" Gus asked. The herd had crossed and turned left sharply to follow the riverbank.

"I don't know, Gus. Reckon he was jobbin' us about th' crossin' bein' hard?"

Gus rode ahead a little and watched the herd turn north again. "Wasn't jobbin', Sut, we're only halfway across."

By then, I had rounded the point and could see the main channel twice as wide as that little relief channel. We were on an island. The main channel was flowing stronger than the other one.

"He led those cows around in the open so they wouldn't scatter in th' brush," Gus said.

That shelf of rock ran under the island and across the main channel also, only it seemed higher and that made the water swifter. It was still a good place to cross and we had little trouble getting across, except for the wagon.

The men tied on to the four corners of the wagon to keep it from tilting, and Cookie drove into the water above the track of the herd to give the two downstream men room above the riffle. The mules took the water with a little bullwhip talk and proceeded across, feeling for footage and avoiding boulders. Unfortunately, the wagon was not as good at dodging the big rocks and near midstream slipped off into a hole and busted the offside front wheel. Cookie's face, already red from the strain, turned even darker, but he didn't say anything. The mules stood still in water near to their bellies.

Pock and O were on the downstream side and Pock climbed onto the wagon and stripped down to the skin. While he untied the spare front wheel from the wagon, O stripped and hauled out the axle jack.

"Sut, don't just sit there, get down here and help us with this jack," O called, and I stripped and waded into that cold water. Belly deep on those mules was waist deep on me and the current kept trying t' push me over.

"Feel around and get a flat space to set this jack in," O ordered, and I couldn't do that and keep my head above water. Hanging onto the axle kept me from washing away and I rolled a big rock out of the way somehow and set the jack down in its place. O was cranking away before I cleared the water from my eyes.

"Hold there, O, I can get this wheel off," Pock called above the rush of water. He applied the wrench to the hub nut and pulled the washer and broken wheel off.

We had to raise the axle to get the new wheel on and when it topped out, Pock said, "Dive down and dig us out a trench for the wheel, Sut." It took three trials and two mashed fingers, but I got it deep enough at last and Pock slipped the wheel onto the axle.

Pock slapped the washer over the axle end and fumbled around for a few seconds. "Cookie, hand me the nut and wrench."

"I have the wrench, but you never give me the nut."

"I gave you the nut with the wrench; look around and hurry, this wheel won't stay on long without it."

"Pock, *I ain't got th' nut,*" Cookie vowed.

"You had it, where is it?" Pock hollered.

"I didn't have it you . . ." and we will expunge the rest of Cookie's words in deference to those of tender ears. It is sufficient to say that there was a long discourse on Pock and his ancestors back almost to Adam.

"O-o-oh, here it is," Pock called over the bellows of the cook. "I had it here all along. Sorry, Cookie." He had to duck under the wagon to avoid a blacksnake lash. O got the nut tightened down and when we had the jack stowed, he picked me up and threw me over the little falls and dove after me. The water was deep and cold, but it felt good to wash off a little.

Cookie was so mad he grabbed up the pile of clothes, including mine and O's and threw them into the river. We had to scramble to recover them and Pock lost a sock.

The two vaqueros switched places so Pock could be behind the wagon out of reach of that whip and we rode the rest of the way out of the river naked.

We had killed a heifer the night before and Cookie fried us steaks as we came in to eat. "Oh no, you don't pick my steak," Pock said as he arrived for his supper. "I'll choose . . . that one," he said pointing to his choice out of the half dozen slabs of meat lying on the table.

Cookie growled and laid it in th' skillet. He hardly gave it time to get warm on one side before he flipped it over. A minute later, he forked it into Pock's waiting plate. Now, you know a cowman likes his meat well done. Any sign of pink is strictly forbidden and would be positively rejected by them.

Pock swore that with a little help, this meat could have recovered. "Cookie—" Pock began.

"That's all th' cookin' you're gittin' here. If you don't like th' way I cook, you can do your own from now on."

"A-w-w—"

"Take it or leave it, Pock," Cookie said. Pock was teetering on th' edge of becoming cook for the rest of the trip, and that would be no good for the rest of us.

"Take it, Pock," a half dozen voices urged, and Pock took the meat to the fire and finished cooking it himself. When he was satisfied it was done to his taste, he sat down and began to eat it right off his cooking stick. Carefully peeling his lips back so they didn't get burned, he bit a corner, but couldn't bite it off. He tried another corner with the same result. Laying it in his plate, he managed to cut a piece of meat and plop it into his mouth. He chewed and chewed, but the tough meat resisted his mastications, and he had to swallow it whole.

The rest of us watched with great amusement, though not a word was spoken, and many a sombrero was pulled low over eyes to hide smiling faces.

It took a long time, but Pock ate the whole steak, washing most of it down with coffee. When he finished, Jake said, "Pock, before you switch to your night horse, let's ride around the herd and see that everything is in good shape."

We watched them go in silence until Tom chuckled, figuring they were out of hearing him, and we all laughed. Cookie had this smug look, like he was saying, "Trifle with me, will you?"

"How did you get him to choose the tough steak, Cookie?" Curly asked.

"They were *all* tough, Curly. We'll be havin' stew tomorrow after these are cut up and cooked all night."

"If you can't bite through it, make stew," three of us quoted the saying almost together, and we had a good laugh.

"Bet Pock ain't gonna let it lie," Gus whispered to me.

The next day, Cookie introduced me an' Gus to hickory stakes and spokeshaves, and we spent the next ten days carving out new spokes for the broken wheel. In their "spare" time, the others repaired the broken wheel and stored it for any future needs. Jake had us make two more spokes for spares.

Never argue with a skunk,
A woman, or the cook.
—Old Vaquero saying

CHAPTER 11
EAKIN'S CROSSING

"Ain't nothing healthier'n them longhorns," Otha Huie said, watching two steers butting heads over a heifer. "Like they could do something about it," he snorted. "They's several reasons t' take she-cows along on a drive, Sut. One, you don't put a bunch of steers on th' trail an' eat them as you go. Two, a cow bawls as she runs an' th' steers listen to her. They won't run as far as a steer and that induces th' steers to slow down and stop also."

"Cookie says Rafter JM meat don't taste good an' he's always after us t' find a steer with different markings," Gus said. Me and Gus was back to bein' cavymen, and Jake had us taking th' horses a little farther west of our track to give them and the herd more grazing. O showed us how far to stay out, then left for the herd. Sometimes it got a little spooky out there so far from the rest.

We came to one of those unnamed dry washes that cut through the plain, and the horses had to go a ways to find a place to cross. It was a narrow cut in the high bank and only one horse could enter at a time. There were two trails cut out of the opposite bank and the horses preferred the left trail. An occasional horse impatient to wait in line would start up the second trail, shy, and then butt himself back into line. Gus went across early and after the last horse had crossed, I descended the south bank and, out of curiosity, started up the unused trail. A few steps into the cut, Stripe stopped, snorted, and turned around. He had smelled something he didn't like and I had glimpsed a horse hoof showing around a bend in the cut. "Ok, scaredy-cat, stay here and I'll go see what bothers you."

The cut was steep and sandy and traction was not good. Around the bend, I found just what I had expected, a dead horse. Some of his hide still clung to the bones, especially under the saddle he still wore and against the bank. Eight or ten yards up the cut lay the horse's head where the coyotes had carried it. The body lay hard against the vertical bank and there was cloth pinned between the horse and the bank. I reached over to pull the collar of a coat free of the horse and glimpsed an object that had fallen into the crevice between horse and bank. There, staring back at me with empty sockets, was a human skull. I screamed and jumped back, my heart racing and a thousand black spots swimming across my vision.

"Whatsa matter, Sut, dead horse kick you?" Gus was peeking over the bank ten feet above and grinning. "Thought you scared some girl into screaming."

Let's hear you scream. "Come down here and see what I found."

In a moment, I heard him enter the top of the cut, and here he came, sliding on his butt in the sand. He maneuvered around the horse skull and slid to a stop at my feet, "What?" he said with his usual impatience.

"There's a coat of some kind pinned between the saddle and the bank; see if you can pull it out."

"That can't be too hard, sissy." He reached over the carcass and grasped the coat collar and, with the other hand braced against the bank, pulled. "What's holding it back . . . *ah-h-h-h,*" he screamed and stumbled backwards across the cut. The far wall kept him from falling.

"What was that?" he yelled, eyes wide and bugging.

"What?" I asked in all innocence.

"Someone stared at me."

"Was it scary?"

"Shut up. What is going on?"

"I'm not sure, Gus, but I think there is a human body back there under that horse."

I leaned over with both hands braced on the bank and studied the coat. "There are bones buttoned inside the coat, and an arm bone going into a sleeve, and the ribs are crushed all against the backbone. The skull has fallen or been knocked off the skeleton and lodged between horsehide and bank, faceup." It grinned at me, mocking. "Bet you screamed like that when this horse fell on you."

"Don't talk to him, Sut. He might say something back," Gus whispered

"I don't think so, Gus." Bein' younger, he wasn't as mature as I was. I didn't hold that against him, he was learning.

"We better get back to those horses before they scatter from hither to yon. One of us should go tell Jake about this. I imagine we'll have a funeral tonight." Nothing could have held Gus out there by himself knowin' that dead man was down in that cut, so he went to the herd to spread the word. He caught up with Curly riding swing and told him what we had found. He didn't talk to Jake until we brought the horses in for night duty.

"How far back is it to the man?" Jake asked, his eye on the twilight.

"It's about three miles from here," I said.

"Be pure dark before we got there and we'd be as likely t' walk over one of those banks as not. We'll look at it in th' morning."

That was good enough for us, and me and Gus had supper and went to bed. He was restless and must have dreamed all night. It seemed every time I closed my eyes, I saw that skull grinning at me until I got mad and told myself, *It was just a skull, stupid, go to sleep*—and I did, only to wake at the start of my watch with those empty eye sockets staring at me.

The crew changed to their morning horses and we had breakfast. Jake put Uno in Curly's place and sent Curly with us to see what to do about the dead man. I got the shovel out of the wagon and we took the cavy out to pasture.

"I ain't goin' back to that place," Gus declared, and we left him with the horses and rode to find the cut. It was easier to climb up from the bottom, so we went down and scrambled up to the bodies.

Curly studied the carcass and the remains of the horse. "Where's his head, Sut?"

"It's down in between the horse and the bank."

He put both hands on the bank and leaned as far over the horse as he could and looked the man over from head to shoulders. There was a leather strap over the shoulder of the coat and Curly pulled on it until it broke. Then he followed the strap down between the man's bones and the horse and pulled out a possibles bag. "Now, we might get to know your name, feller." We hunkered in the shade of the bank and Curly opened the satchel. There were several papers in envelopes, some sealed and addressed to people back in the states. Two or three letters were from the states addressed to Hiram Eakin. "That must be ole Hiram, Sut," Curly nodded toward the bones. "Wonder what brought him here."

He had me read two of the letters and we discerned they were from his wife, Martha, who lived with her parents in Illinois. They had three children.

We found an unsealed envelope addressed to Martha and opened the letter. Actually it was several letters he had written over time and the newest was dated December 14, 1867.

"That means he's been here about four years," I said.

" 'Bout right, I 'magine. Wonder what kilt them." He crawled over to the carcass, lifted the petrified hide over the horse's ribs, and peeked into the cavity. After a moment, he whistled low and said, "Lookee here, Sut."

I crawled across the sand and peeked into the dark cavity of the horse's rib cage. It took a moment for my eyes to adjust to the dark and when I did, I saw a long shaft passing through the left bottom ribs and almost to the other side. There was a rusty arrow on the tip. Curly was poking around on the ground where the arrow shaft was buried. The horsehide was brittle and flaked away from around the arrow to show that it had gone through the saddle skirt. There was a scrap of wool cloth poking through the hole with the shaft. Curly gave a low whistle, "I know what happened, Sut."

"Let me see if I can tell you," I asked.

"Go ahead."

"Somewhere back along his trail, he got shot by an arrow. It must have been by someone standing to his side or hidden in ambush. The arrow went through his leg, through the saddle skirt, and into the horse, and they ran, man and horse pinned together by that arrow. They must have escaped the killer and who knows how far they came after getting hit. When they started up this cut, the man must have known the horse wasn't going to make it and swung his good right leg over to dismount, only the horse fell the wrong way and lay on top of him, driving the arrow deeper into the horse."

"And here they died, man and horse together," Curly said quietly. He sat back and we both were lost in our own thoughts about the man and his horse and how their lives and deaths had been tied together—literally—by that arrow and how much a man and his horse depend on each other for survival in this country.

"Wonder if they got to talk a little before they died," I asked more to myself than to Curly.

"A man alone should talk to his horse a lot. They don't keep secrets from each other, probably more than you could say about a man and his wife," Curly said, and grinned. When we were at Dodge City, Pete Harding's cream horse, Cookie, died and he buried him on Boot Hill—with his shoes on.

"Well, Sut, we have done as much as we can here; let's have a buryin' and get on with our lives." He took the shovel and dug out the bank above the two corpses, letting the dirt fall on them. I brought the horse's head back to him, and Curly propped Hiram's skull on his shoulders. Then we climbed out on top of the bank and caved it off on them. When we were finished, they were buried under four or five feet of soil. It would be many years before weather would uncover them again.

"Well done, Sut. Now they can really rest in peace." He put the possibles bag in his satchel and we rode for the herd.

We called the place Eakin's Crossing and used it until the cattle pens got moved to Dodge City. Cookie kept the bag with its letters and Jake said we would mail them first post office we came to. The next year, I brought a cross and stuck it up over the grave. I only heard of one other time a man was buried with his horse, and it was an occasion much like Hiram's.

The cowboy sees that horses are people
And that people are horses
And that both are queer.

—Struthers Burt

Chapter 12
Pock's Tale

"Next town or granger we hit, I'm makin' you a gift of a hundret pounds o' spuds, Cookie," O said. "Not that I don't like your cookin'," he hastened to say, "but I'm shore gittin' tired of rice, any way you cook it."

"Don't think I'm not tired o' cookin' and eatin' it," Cookie retorted.

"I like rice myself," I said. I could have added that rice doesn't have to be peeled, and me and Gus knew who would get that chore with potatos.

"Did you ever eat wild rice cooked in prairie hen sauce?" Tom asked. "Th' Tonkaways make it and it's the best you ever tasted."

"You eatin' with them dirty Tonks?" O asked.

"When there ain't nothin' else t' eat from here to El Paso, I do," Tom responded.

Jake sat up on one elbow and said, "Listen, don't never get outnumbered by them Tonks, an' if you travel with them, always be last in line. If they run out of food, run like the devil."

"Why's that, Jake?"

" 'Cause they eat people."

"Not so much," Pock said.

"What does that mean?" Gus asked.

"They only eat a little, maybe a leg roast or a liver. They ain't big people eaters, not like them Attacopas was." Pock lay back and puffed his pipe.

"Who are Attacopas?" I asked.

"Was," Pock said. "So bad the Tonkaways and Mexicans killed 'em all off."

"I never heard of them," Gus said, which was not unusual for him. He never heard of a lot of things. Didn't believe in Republicans until he saw one after the war.

"Seems I hear a story comin' on," Jake said, grinning at Pock.

Pock took a couple of puffs at his pipe, looked in the bowl, and reached for a burning stick from the fire. "Well, I know a little about them, but my Great-Grandpa Nix on my mother's side knew a lot about them." He puffed until he had a good light.

"He came down here with th' Old Man Austin when the Spaniards gave him all that land for a colony. All the while, them Spaniards was laughing up their sleeves, knowin' Colonials and Attacopas couldn't live together peaceably. One would kill off the other and it didn't matter to them which went and which stayed.

"While Old Man Austin went back to the states to recruit settlers, Great-Grandpa Nix stayed on and explored the land grant. He did good until he got down near the coast in those swamps and meres and got lost—"

Gus elbowed me, "What's a mire?"

"Just think swamps and marshes," I growled.

Pock eyed us. "He wandered for days in those salty waters without food or dry feet and when he was about to lay down and die, out of the bushes stepped these Injuns. They were friendly fellers and took him to their village where he caused quite a stir, bein' the first white man some of them had ever seen. The whole village took him to the chief and had a big powwow and after much talk and gesturing, th' chief stood and made a long speech, at the end of which the people all cheered and dispersed on what seemed a lot of errands. Great-Grandpa kept askin' for food, but the people looked sad and shook their heads. There was no food in the village.

"Along about midafternoon the women came back into camp with baskets full of wild rice straws. They winnowed out the grains of rice and when the hunters returned with a dozen prairie chickens, they were quickly cleaned and thrown into a big copper kettle the Indians had taken from the Jesuits when they were run out of the country. Soon, there was a kettle full of chicken and rice boiling happily away while the people stood around and rejoiced at the bounty. Great-Grandpa could hardly contain himself. Finally, the rice was ready and the chief dipped a bowl out of the kettle and gave it to Great-Grandpa to eat.

"He pitched in right serious-like and it wasn't until he was half through the third bowl and his stomach come unstuck to his backbone that he realized that no one else was eating. That was mighty suspicious and he wondered if he was being poisoned. He made the chief eat with him, which he gladly did, and Grandpa began to taper off by the end of his fifth bowl. One of the women offered him more but he signaled with his hand under his chin that he was full 'up to here.'

"With that, the people cheered and the little red ones rushed the kettle, dipping out rice with their hands. Still, the adults didn't eat." Pock relit his pipe and puffed contentedly, contemplating those long-ago days.

"Did th' Injuns ever eat?" I knew better than to ask, it just slipped out.

"Yeah, they did, but it was late that night after Great-Grandpa Nix was well roasted and they ate him whole. They always claimed that was the best rice they had ever eaten."

"I knowed it was a tall tale," Cookie said.

"Weren't no tale, Cookie," Pock said. "Really happened. Fortunately, he had left a wife and house full of kids back in Arkansas to carry on the name."

"They must have been pretty bad for the Tonkawas to want rid of them," Jake said.

"Yeah, I think they ate one too many Tonks," Pock said. He tapped out his pipe, reamed out the dottle, and unspooled his bed.

"You believin' that?" Gus whispered.

"Pock says it's so, I ain't arguing with him, are you? Go to sleep."

It's a good thing that life is not
As serious as it seems to him.

—Oren Arnold

Chapter 13
Texas Fever and Mustang Chasers

Kansas settlers have been complaining about Texas cattle spoiling their crops ever since th' first herd of longhorns passed through Kansas.

"Like them cows know not to cut through unfenced cornfields an' snatch a bite or two," Gus said.

"If they're gonna plant a farm, at least they could do is fence it in," I said.

"You don't expect a man living in a soddy house or dugout t' have th' money to buy posts an' wire, then have th' ambition t' put it all up, do you?" Jake asked.

"Smart granger wants th' herd t' bed down on his place so wife and kids can pick up enough cow patties t' burn all winter," Pock added.

"Yeah, and shoot th' neighbor who tries to poach his crop," Jake said. "Imagine two sodbusters fighting over a cow patty."

"Fence it in an' you can't charge a drover twice the value of th' damage," said Pock. "It's a business. Spring comes an' th' old man says, 'Cattle drives coming, got t' plant th' crops so's they'll be up when they git here.' "

"Now, they're saying our cows is carrying a disease that kills their livestock," Tom Stepp said. "If they have a disease, why ain't *they* getting' sick?"

"Seems our longhorns have worked up a resistance to th' sickness, but those northern cattle haven't," Jake said. "It ain't a pretty sight, I'll tell you, and it will wipe out a whole herd. The strange thing is that if the Texas herd winters up here, they don't carry th' disease anymore. Th' smart thing t' do is avoid places where grangers are an' they'll not bother you. That's one reason we are west of th' main trail. Another being they will be so busy fightin' those trail herds, they might miss us."

That very day, we veered northwest and hit the state line several miles west of a little place called Caldwell that had built up on the trail. Sure enough, we heard later that a bunch of grangers were there waiting to stop the Texas herds. Smart trail bosses avoided any conflict. Those that didn't suffered for it, for the grangers were determined. A thinking man understood.

We overnighted on th' north bank of Bluff Creek, "A sure sign we were in Kansas," Jake said. He doubled the night guard until we crossed the Chickaskia River where our enemies changed from white to red.

Chickasha came in at noon soon after we crossed the Chickaskia and filled his plate and cup and ate without saying a word. Coming in at noon was unusual for him because we only saw him at night. He got up with Cookie and ate breakfast first, then rode out to whoop the few buffalo left away from our path. With his utensils safely stored in the wreck pan he turned to Jake and said, "Injuns around."

"Who are they?"

"Sioux."

"Sioux? They're a long ways from home, ain't they?"

"They came to steal Pawnee horses and fight a little, not too far for that, but they'll find us, and our horses are easier pickin's."

It was our custom to keep the cavyyard close through the noon hour so every man had a chance to change horses. While they were that close, me and Gus would ride in an' eat. Chickasha's news made me nervous. Gus got up with me and we threw out our unfinished meals and hurried out to the cavy, Cookie cussing us for wasting food. We pulled our rifles across our knees as we rode. The horses hardly looked up from their grazing, which was a good sign, for any whiff of Injun made those horses awful nervous.

"Of course, no Injun would come in upwind of th' herd," Gus would say.

To which I would answer, "Only if they wanted t' stir up the cavy an' get them ready to run."

"You're always makin' exceptions to what I say," he would say and ride away mad.

We had hardly gotten settled in our patrolling when Chickasha rode out and joined us. We shore didn't need Jake t' tell us to keep th' horses close to the herd.

A few minutes later, Uno and Dos rode out stripped and painted for war and changed to their war ponies. The Sioux were the Utes' favorite enemy; a Sioux scalp counted equal to two scalps of any other tribe.

Chickasha watched them leave with a long face. He would have given anything he had to go with them, but he was never invited. Instead, he would stay here nursmaidin' two wet-behind-the-ears white kids and a bunch of cow horses—ignoring the fact that he was the same age as we were.

We watched the horses closely, and they showed no nervousness, just grazed the hock-deep grasses and looked contented. Not so calm were the cavymen, who spent as much time watching behind as forward. We took the horses in a little early for the evening switch and Jake sent Curly and Tom out to watch the cavy while we ate.

"Just takes two men t' watch what it takes three boys t' do?" Gus grumbled as he shoved his rifle into its boot on his night horse.

"Makes you want t' do more, don't it?" I asked.

"I'll 'do more' them." He kicked a rock and found that most

of it was buried and didn't move, but jammed his toes into the end of his pointed boot, which caused him to stumble. "Dang it!"

Jake laughed. "That rock's like an iceberg, Gus, nine tenths of it is underground."

Cookie grinned and slapped a big steak on his plate, "Here, Gus, see if this takes yer mind off your sore toe."

We sat down to eat and Gus whispered, "What's an iceberg, Sut?"

"I don't have any idea, except nine tenths of it is underground."

After we had eaten, Jake said, "See that everyone has changed horses, then drive the cavy up close to the cattle and take the bell off the mare. If there is a disturbance of any kind, you could ring the bell in the hope that it calms the horses."

While Gus and Chickasha came near to blows over who was in charge of the bell, I found the mare, removed the bell, muzzled the clapper, and stowed it in my saddlebag. The two yahoos spent the next two hours looking for that mare and cussing her for not ringing her bell. They suspected I had the bell, but wouldn't ask and I didn't say. At least it would keep them alert and their minds on the horses.

"I won't beef up the watches until we are sure of the danger, but be especially alert on your watch," Jake had said to the crew. "Don't let any Indians sneak up on you and don't hesitate to warn us if they show up, even if it means scaring the herd into a run. Keep one eye open when you sleep."

"Tell you what, Gus, since you are gonna have *both* eyes open all night, I'm gonna close both my eyes and sleep. That way, one of us will be alert tomorrow," I said in passing.

"You close both eyes an' you're gonna havta worry about *me* scalpin' you."

"Shush, you're too loud."

"What did you say, Sut?"

"Wasn't me, it was that brindle steer. You are disturbin' his sleep."

Near noon the next day, we saw a dust rising in the west and watched as it approached. Under the dust we could eventually see riders in a row two by two. "Could it be Indians?" Gus asked.

"Don't think they would ride organized like that for long," I replied. "One of us better ride in and tell th' others."

"Not necessary. Here comes Jake."

"What do you make of it, boys?" he asked as he rode up.

"Too organized to be Injuns," I said. "Hope them grangers ain't that organized."

Jake took down his glasses and said, "Looks like th' army. Gus, go tell Cookie t' warm up for a feed and I'll stay here."

"Yes, sir," and Gus trotted off. I waited until he was gone to grin.

It took the soldiers a long time to get to us, I guess because the air was so clear we could see farther, and they were very slow.

"Horses are played out," Jake said as we watched the whole bunch dismount and walk the last mile to us. Two of the men had no horse. "Men are, too."

I realized with a start that the soldiers were all black except for one man in th' lead.

"You're lookin' at one o' th' best cavalry units in the whole army," Jake said. "See the flag? That's part of the Ninth Cavalry, Sut. You're gonna like 'em."

We rode out to meet them, and dismounted and walked the last quarter mile. "Hello there, Lieutenant Ashley, looks like you've been on a patrol," Jake called.

"We certainly have, Mr. Meeker, what are you doing out here so far from the trail?"

"Avoiding squatter farms, and Texas fever vigilantes. Come on in to the wagon and rest yourselves; Cookie's put on th' big pot, killed the fatted calf, and added water to the coffee."

The soldiers trudged on, their horses barely lifting their feet to take a step, heads hanging low. They would have been in poor condition if they had been rested and fed up; and from the light loads on the packhorses, they hadn't had grain recently. Grass-fed horses are much better off out here than corn-fed horses.

Jake walked with the lieutenant and I sorta fell back behind.

"Nice lookin' horse, young man. My name is Corporal Casey," the man said.

"I'm Sutter Lowery, the cavyman for Mr. Meeker."

"Bet they calls you Sut, don't they?" His grin was friendly and I liked him in spite of his color.

"When they're not callin' me Catfish," I said.

"We got a feller back to th' fort called Catfish, may be you're cousins," the man beside Casey said with a grin.

"They named me Catfish 'cause under my shirt I'm white as a catfish's belly. Is that how your friend got his name?" I replied.

The troops laughed, "Got you right back, Bandy, what you gonna say to that?"

The man was laughing also and said, "My name's Bandy, and this here is Bull, Silent Sam, Oke, Sad Sack, a-a-nd Fears Nothin'."

Their grins showed white teeth through dust-grayed faces, and I felt at ease with them. Their uniforms were in tatters, their boots held together with leather thongs, and I was sure they would be mostly barefooted before they got back to their fort. But they were a cheerful bunch, not at all dissatisfied with their lot.

I stayed with Gus and the cavy while the troops trudged on to the wagon. Later on, they told me they were a detachment from D Troop of the Ninth Cavalry. When we rode in for the noonin', the troops had washed up in Slate Creek, the horses were watered, and the men were currying them. "Two hours above the hocks an' two hours below," Bandy crowed. They were singing a song I had never heard while they worked. The horses really enjoyed the attention.

Jake loaned Lieutenant Ashley two horses and two pack mules to send Corporal Casey and Fears Nothin' after corn for the horses. "Was you t' give our horses corn t' eat, they'd might near starve first," Curly said.

"They'll take to it sooner if you leave it on the cob," Tom added.

Currying stopped abruptly when Cookie called dinner for the troops. He had killed a heifer and the meat was fresh, the son-of-a-gun stew even smelled good. Each man had a large steak and the choice of beef stew, frijoles, and son-of-a-gun. As soon as a man finished one stew, he dipped into the other flavor stew.

"How long since you ate?" I asked Bandy.

The black man cast his eyes to the heavens and thought a moment, rolled his bite of steak to his cheek, and said, "Bes' I can recolleck, it were night b'fore las' whin we ate that las' bean. Oke's horse give out this mornin' but didn' die so we couldn' have steak."

"Oke would not let us kill him, an' b'sides he wouldn't hev et any of him," the man called Silent Sam said. His boot tops were the only things left of his boots and his feet were wrapped in blanket cloth.

"He has th' miss-fortune to have th' same boot size as Oke, an' when Oke's boots failed him, they traded so's Oke could walk out Sam's boots, too."

"What did you do to get so wore out like this?" Gus asked.

"Well, it's lak this—" Bandy began.

"—Hush up yo' mouf, Bandy, I'll tell th' boy th' trouf o' th' matter," Bull spoke up for the first time. He paused for a moment, collecting his thoughts, then said, "We lef' Hays—"

"—That's *Fort* Hays, Gus," Bandy explained, ignoring the baleful stare of Private Bull Boone, who began again, "We lef' Hays ten days ago to scout out wes' an' south for some Injuns rumored to be out an' about doin' mischief. All was quiet until this granger come runnin' into our midst all lathered an' hatless three days ago wi' th' news that a hull army o' Injuns was seen waterin' at th' crick near his place. We follered him to where the trail was then follered the tracks o' about fifty horses for two days."

"Them Injuns didn' seem in too great of a hurry," Sad Sack put in.

"Then on th' third mornin' we spied their dust an' knowed we was close," Bull continued. "So we spread out in a wide skirmish line to hold th'a dust down an' urged our ganted horses to hurry. We knowed they was heading for water in Bluff Creek, an' sho' nuf when we topped th' breaks, there was that flock o' horses drinkin' in th' creek—an' not a Injun amongst 'em."

"It were jist a herd o' wild horses out for a little stroll," Sad Sack said.

"We used up our horses an' beans an' corn chasin' a bunch o' wild mustangs," Bandy said.

"Might near used me up, too," Sad Sack said.

"Sad, youse mos'ly used up afore we lef' th' fort," Bandy said.

"I was fresh as a Easter mornin' lily," Sad protested.

"An' nex' time you sleeps in th' saddle, I'm not gonna hold your rein so's your horse don' stray off wi' you," Bull said. "You jus' might find yoself all alone on th' great prairie."

"My horse don' stray," Sad vowed.

"We'll find out," Bull said.

Lieutenant Ashley and Jake had been sitting opposite the fire talking and sometimes listening to the banter as the troops told their story. "Be careful, men," Ashley said. "Sometimes the tales they tell leave out a bunch of the truth. No taps tonight, men, we will wait here until Casey and Fears get back."

When we left them the next morning, they were digging a pit to roast the rest of that beef carcass to go with that big bait of dried rice Cookie left for them.

They still had a week of traveling to get back to Fort Hays. "Come see us some time, Gus," Bandy called as we rode away.

"Bring Catfish with you. He would want to meet his brother," Bull called.

Why do you murder my people for those who made you less than cattle?"

—Victorio, Apache Chief

Chapter 14
Prescience and Other Troubles

I used to think my mother was the best at predicting the weather of anyone I knew. By the time I was ten, I depended on her word, for she was never wrong. "Foresight," she called it. One day she said, "Sutter, stay to high ground after noon, the creek will be in the willows." It had been dry for a couple of weeks and Pa had me hoeing corn in th' bottoms, but I kept my eye on that creek.

I was on the third middle from the bank when I heard the water take on a different sound, and I saw a little foot-high wave of brown dirty water washing over the top of the clear water in the creek. Right there, I dropped that hoe and headed for the hillside. The rest of the afternoon, I watched the water rise until it was bank full and *over* the willows. Pa whipped me for losing the hoe, but I found it down the creek in a brush pile. Pa didn't take the whipping back.

I realized when Pa got killed that Mother was blessed with second sight and could see things other than the weather. The alarm went out that Comanches were raiding and Pa made preparations to go with the militia. Ma was very upset, but all she said was, "Ira, don't go."

Pa had to know that Ma had some sort of foresight, but he was duty bound to go on. When he left, Ma dried her eyes and got Pa's Sunday suit out of the trunk and pressed it. One of the kids asked her why, and she just said, "He'll need it when he comes back."

They brought Pa back in a wagon, laid out beside B.R. Bell, Gus's dad. Folks came in from as far away as Jacksboro to prepare the bodies and help any way they could.

After that, I paid close attention to Ma and listened to the things she said. She must have noticed, for she said one day, "It's a gift and a curse, Sutter." That was all she ever said about it. I began to discern when she had a premonition until one day I realized I was having foresights the same as her. It liked to scared me to death.

Ever since we left Slate Creek, I would have this dream of standing on the top of a bluff and looking down into the creek bottoms and seeing two people standing there looking up at me. I couldn't tell who they were, only that it was a boy and a girl and they were in some kind of trouble. Once I saw a burning wagon not far from them. The longer we were away from the creek, the more persistent the dream was until I avoided sleep.

Gus knew about the dream and finally said, "You got t' do somethin' about it, Sut, or die."

That night after our tour of the herd, I caught up Dusky and Stripe, pointed them west, and departed the drive. Ten miles and midmorning later, I came to the limestone bluffs above Slate Creek. Instead of standing on the bluff as I had in the dream, I crawled the last twenty yards and peeked over the rim. The creek ran against the far side bluff and there was a wagon-track trail running along this side. About a quarter mile up the creek to the right, were several burned wagons, still smoldering. I thought I could see several bodies laying around, but nothing seemed to be alive there.

The horses were restless and nervous when I got back to them. At first, I thought they were thirsty, then I caught the unmistakable odor of Indians and understood. There was no need to hide anymore and I rode up the bluffs past the five burned-out wagons, watching the bottoms closely—and there in a clear spot in the brush stood those two children, just as I had dreamed.

The slight movement of a branch against the wind told me they were not alone, they were decoys. As casually as I could, I moved the horses away from the bluff out of danger and returned on my hands and knees to the brink of the bluff. The children were still standing there and from the direction they looked every once in a while, someone was in the brush to their right coaching them. I now had two of the Indians located, but there had to be a dozen or more of them scattered around waiting for me to do something.

There was nothing I could do by myself to save those children. I would have to go get help. I turned to my horses, and there sat Uno grinning at me, painted for war.

"Hello, Sut."

"Hello, Uno." I got scared later when I had time to think about how he walked up on me without my notice, and whacked my horse on his shoulder. "Thanks for the warning."

"Sioux make good trap." For him, the issue was the trap, not the rescue of the bait. In fact, the Utes could not understand our concern for the children. This was the wrong bait for catching Indians. These Sioux were fishing for whites.

"I have to save them, Uno, how do I do that?"

"Not know. Dos wants horses."

"Yeah, and so does Uno," I said. He just grinned and rode down the creek.

There was some movement down in the bottoms and the boy and girl were moving toward where I had last shown myself. They stood on the low bank of the old stream where it had flowed against the bluff below us.

"Mister? Can you come git us?" the boy called.

"I'm hungry." The little girl began to cry. They were both

barefooted, dirty, and ragged.

Now, I was hesitant to show myself and greatly suspected the Indians were moving to trap me and keep me alive only for some lucky buck to count coup on a living enemy.

I remember taking a deep breath and saying to myself, "Well, if you don't do *something,* you're gonna be down there with them kids, or dead." So I rifled three or four shots into the brush nearest the children and ducked. There was a big stirring of the brush and firing came at me from a dozen different places. I had a busy time returning fire, probably with no more effect than to keep the Sioux from chasing the children who were running up the road. The next time I looked for them, they had disappeared, and I concentrated on the gun smoke nearest the kids' last position. I couldn't keep up this firing much longer, for want of more shells.

There was a swirl of dust and hoofbeats beyond the creek and I saw Uno and Dos running off the Sioux horses. "More about the horses than . . ."

"Mister, we got away from them."

I turned and there stood the two kids more dusty and dirty than before. "How did you do that?" I asked and didn't wait for an answer, but scooped up the little girl and ran for my horses. I put the kids on Stripe, regretting that I had saddled him earlier. Now I had to ride a tired night horse again. He was gonna be mad. "Do you see that butte way up there?" I asked, pointing a little north of east. The boy nodded. "Ride straight for it and find a trail herd of cattle. Go to the wagon." The boy nodded. I'm sure bare heels on ribs was a welcome sensation for the horse and he was soon in a long lope.

There were no Sioux coming over the bluff, preferring to chase after their horses than a couple of captives and a man with a gun. I hopped on Dusky bareback. "Don't fuss about it, hoss, this is gonna hurt me as much as it hurts you." I followed the kids, keeping my eye on the back trail. No one appeared after us. The dust of the stolen horses was disappearing to the south with what looked like a dozen men following afoot. Uno and Dos were going to have a time keeping those horses away from the Sioux.

The kid was pretty savvy and found the wagon easily enough. It was noon and the boys were eating. I turned Dusky into the cavyyard and found Stripe standing alone and neglected as the attention was all on the two kids.

Jake looked at me, but saved any conversation for later.

The little girl was sitting in Pock's lap, eating from his plate, and the boy sat with a plate of his own.

"Where did you find the orphans, Sut?" Tom asked.

"Over on Slate Creek. Sioux had burned their train and were using the kids as bait for a gringo trap."

"An' you sprung th' trap by yourself?" Cookie asked.

"No, Uno and Dos helped by running off their horses. Last I saw, the Sioux were chasing them and the herd south."

"They'll play Whaley keeping them horses," Pock said.

"May be that they don't want to keep all of them," Jake said.

I rustled up a plate and tools and Cookie grinned and plopped a big steak on my plate. He whapped me on the butt with his long-handled turner. The steak was well done, just like I wanted it. Instead of coffee, I got a cup of branch water from the barrel—several cups, in fact.

Tom watched the little girl, who must not have been more than three years old, drinking water and said, "Too bad we don't have a fresh cow t' give these kids a little milk."

It must have been more than Jake could take, because he said, "Fellers, we've done just about everything but move cattle the last couple weeks. It's time we concentrate on herdin' cattle an' gettin' them to market fat and happy. I'm glad Sut rescued the kids, but it's time to concentrate on the job."

Gus just looked at me and rolled his eyes.

I shore hoped that was the gist of the conversation he had for me, and I guess it was, for later all he said to me was, "I had heard your ma had the gift, didn't know you did, too." I decided then and there to keep my premonitions to myself as much as possible.

Cookie packed up and left the nooning early with the girl sitting beside him, and the boy standing behind the seat. When we went in for supper, they both were clean and in fresh-washed clothes. It shouldn't be necessary to say that those men spoiled the kids. The boy was named Frank Pierce and the girl was Jessie Smart, but we just called her Angel.

The next few days we did concentrate on the herd and gradually turned them into the main trail for the crossing of the Arkansas at the only ford for some distance either way along the boggy river. We had heard the rumor that there was trouble at the ford. Some enterprising fellers had set up a ferry and being a monopoly, they charged what they wanted. They were a tough bunch that enjoyed fighting and bullying people. Two days before we got the herd there, Jake took Pock and rode to the ford.

In an era when leadership was based on brawn and not brains, the leader of the Wichita Ferry Company was a man called Burly Barnes. His gang called him Captain, though he rode the ferry only to confront irate would-be customers and collect fees. He met all trail herds. "For there was always trouble with those Texas drovers. Rates are based on the flow of the river," he explained. "Average flow is ten cents a head, man and beast. High or low flow, price goes to fifteen cents per head."

"Rate's ten cents right now," a wizened little man with no front teeth and squinty eyes grinned.

"Been a lot of clouds over the mountains the last week and

we expect the price to go to fifteen cents any time now," Burly said.

"Too rich for my blood," Jake said. He had considered shipping the cavyyard across on the ferry. "We'll take the ford."

They turned to go and Burly said, "Cost for the ford is five cents per head, regardless of the water level."

Jake turned back to him, "You're charging for the ford also?"

"We own the ford."

"You can't own a ford, it's there for everybody."

"Five cents a head, cows, horses, and men." Burly's hand rested on his pistol.

Jake stared at the man until Burly blinked. "Five cents a head," the little man said and laughed.

Pock shoved the man in the face and he yelped. The captain turned and stared at Pock. "I can take him, Jake."

"Don't doubt that at all, Pock, but while you're eatin' his lunch, he's gonna have a sandwich or two and I can't afford for you to be handicapped right now. You may have your chance later."

Pock shrugged and turned away. He could be patient.

That night Jake told us about the problem at the crossing. He told us to be particularly vigilant and watch for anyone skulking around the herd—as if we were not already.

I went to bed with the seed of an idea in my head and by the time we rode night herd, it had taken root and sprouted. When I met Gus on one of our circuits, I told him what I was thinking. "Fellers living this far up in a dry land must have a hard time finding whiskey. What if we could get them all too drunk to fight when we crossed the river?" Several bovine heads popped up when the singing stopped, and I couldn't say anything more for singing to those blasted cows.

When we met on the other side, Gus sang a question. "Where are we gonna get whiskey?"

"Lots o' secret bottles hidden in bedrolls," I sang back.

Half a circle later, he asked, "We gonna steal all of them?"

"Don't see any donations comin' our way," I sang to the tune of "Shall We Gather at the River."

"Why do you go lookin' for trouble when it just comes to us natural?" he sang at the next meeting.

"We'll get them when Cookie takes his afternoon nap tomorrow," I whispered a half-circle later. Gus just grunted.

Nothing is as easy as you think it will be, and getting those bottles was no exception. We ran late and Cookie caught us in the act. "What kind of mischief are you two up to now?" he demanded, and we had to tell him. He thought a moment and said, "Sounds possible. Here, take one of my medicinal bottles—and put a little of this laudanum in each bottle."

We divided and poured and got eight half-bottles of whiskey and laudanum and hid them in a hole in the sand under our bedroll. "After our tour tonight, we'll ride to the ferry," I said.

Gus groaned. "I'm gonna sleep from Christmas plumb through January."

We wrapped the bottles in our spare clothes so they wouldn't clink and after waking up our reliefs and stowing our bedroll, me an' Gus rode north.

When we found the ford, the boat was on the other side, so we spent our time looking over the layout and examining the cable where it was anchored to a big cottonwood. It didn't look too hard to undo, but an axe applied in th' right place would be faster. "We can't leave the whiskey here now; they would be sober by nightfall and we would not get any good out of it," I said.

"So-o-o, what are we gonna do?" Gus asked.

"We're gonna get back to that remuda as fast as we can an' act like ever'thing is normal. Somehow, we will have to get the whiskey to them tomorrow afternoon so they will get good and drunk and sleep it off tomorrow night so we can do our mischief." We might have been a little later than usual getting the cavyyard to camp, but no one said anything or noticed two sweating night horses—right then.

Curly was changing horses at the nooning and he asked Gus, "What you two up to now?"

"Nothin'," Gus said.

"That bulge in your sidesaddle and the absence of every whiskey bottle in the camp says different."

"I-I-I can't talk about it," Gus stammered.

Curly stepped toward Gus and looked him in the eyes from about four inches away. "I know better, Gus, an' you better tell me what my whiskey is doin' in your pack, *right now.*"

Gus stepped back and confessed, "We gonna get those ferry men drunk an' cross the river afore they wake up."

"Well, b'fore you do, I'm gonna have one last drink." Curly opened Gus's sidesaddle and fumbled around inside for a bottle. I saw Gus was in some kind of difficulty with Curly and rode up in time to hear his last remark.

"It's got laudanum in it, you'd sleep a week," I warned.

"Laudanum? Where did you get *that*?"

"Cookie."

"That rascal. So you are gonna get them drunk and while they sleep, we'll move the cattle across and they can't do a thing about it?" Curly rubbed his whiskered chin, "That just might work, but I doubt you can pull it off by yourselves—"

"Me an'Gus can git it done."

"Be a lot easier if you had help. How about O and me takin' the whiskey to the ferry boys late tomorrow afternoon while you two rest up and you can do whatever mischief you're up to after dark. We'll be ready to cross th' next morning."

"I-I guess that would be alright, but if you drink any of that stuff, Cookie said you'll sleep longer than Rip Van Winkle," Gus warned.

"I 'magine he's right," Curly said with a grin.

We transferred the saddlebags to O and Curly and rode to supper. "Why did you tell Curly what we were up to?" I asked Gus.

"He figgered most of it out an' was goin' t' get a bottle out, 'til you told him about the laudanum."

"I shore hope they don't mess it up for us," I said.

"I shore am glad t' get that extra sleep," Gus replied.

After the herd was bedded down and before sunset, Curly and O rode out of camp on some excuse and rode north. Me an' Gus went to bed early. We hadn't heard them ride back, but they both were in their beds when we went out to ride herd. As soon as we were relieved, we headed for the river. It was on the rise, and the ferry was on the other side.

"Looks like one of us is goin' for a swim," Gus said. He knew it would be me because he was not good at it. There was a light in the ferry's cabin and that was a worry, but we were committed to our work. I stripped, put on my belt and knife, and took off my horse's saddle. Aciago and I waded into the river. The water was cold, thick with mud and lumpy. Things kept bumping into us and we both were pretty jumpy. Aciago had to swim just a little bit and it felt good when he struck ground again. We like to froze when we waded out on the bank. When I hopped off, Aciago shivered, "Cut that out, hoss, you got fur an' I got nothin'," I whispered.

I crept up to the boat and climbed aboard for a look. The lantern was bright and swung lazily from its hook in the cabin roof. Seven men lay about in all kinds of positions, all sound asleep. All the bottles in sight were empty. The lantern needed to be off and I tiptoed into the room, took it down from its hook, and was about to put it out when one of the men groaned and looked up. "Sh-h-h," I said, "I gotta go pee." I tiptoed on through the cabin to the river side of the boat, put out the lantern, and since I thought of it, peed into the river.

The rising river had put the boat afloat and there was a lot of tension on the ties. If it rose much more, the crew was gonna get wet and the boat sunk. It bobbed up some when I cut the ropes and then it glided along the cable toward the middle of the river.

Aciago had a longer swim back across the river. It wasn't any warmer, either. Gus took an axe to the cable while I dressed and we watched the boat bob out of sight.

"Happy sailing, fellers," Gus said.

"L-lets g-git out of h-here b-b'fore I f-f-freeze," I said. I could feel mud drying on my skin. Gus turned Aciago into the cavy and saddled Hoss for me while I crawled under the covers and shivered until Cookie called breakfast.

"Wash your face, Sut," Gus whispered, and I snuck around to the washbasin. The water was brown when I finished and I had to throw it out and refill the basin.

"Now, you look almost white," Gus whispered again.

"I'm damned mud brown under my clothes," I replied, and it itched, too. Cookie gave me a wink when he slapped the steak on my plate.

Jake was finished with his breakfast and he gave us instructions as we ate. He didn't usually do that, but the anticipation of the crossing and trouble to come made him anxious. Five of us knew there was no need to be anxious about trouble, and two of us knew there was reason to be anxious about a high-water crossing, but we couldn't say anything.

O and Curly had big grins at the rope corral and O slipped me two silver dollars. "What's this?" I asked.

"We *sold* them the whiskey, dollar a bottle, an' they took all eight. That's your cut." He moved off, grinning.

As usual at a river crossing, we held the cavy behind the herd. The crew was happy the cable was cut and the ferry gone. The river had actually gone down a little, but it was still muddy and heavy with trash. We watched a bloated buffalo wash by in the current. Jake had ridden ahead, his rifle across his lap, and when he saw that the ford was open, hurried back and they drove the herd into the water without stopping. It seemed the swimming was about as wide as when I first crossed the night before.

"By doggies, I think you could cut adobes off th' top o' that water," Tom said. Burly Barnes wasn't as confident as he was when he had seven or eight guns backing him, but he still demanded pay for the crossing. Jake only stared at him without saying a word as he passed, but the rest of us laughed at him. I was glad Pock was on the other side of the herd.

When the river receded, it left the ferry high and dry and too far from the water to refloat. Being unemployed, the henchmen wandered off to greener pastures when their heads ceased aching. Last we heard, some pilgrim moved in and made the boat his home while he "proved up" on the surrounding land. The spring rise floated boat and settler on down the river several miles and he homesteaded the new location, finding the time to dismantle the boat and build his house on higher ground. He had the first house made of sawn lumber in Salem County, Kansas.

There was a little village of soddies called Wichitaw on the east side of the river that had a post office. Most of us found time to visit the empty-shelved general store there, and mail a letter or two. It was here that Otha Huie, being from Arkansas, took exception to the natives calling the river, the Ar-kansas. "You spell the name of this place W-i-c-h-i-t-a," he said, indicating the letters over the mail boxes in the corner of the soddy, "and you speak it 'Wichitaw.' But then you call that river 'Arkansas' instead of its proper name pronounced 'Arkansaw.' You should be consistent in your speech and either say 'Wichitaw and Arkansaw' or 'Wichi-ta and Ar-kansas.' You do my beloved state a disservice by mispronouncing the name given to the river by the Injuns living there and proudly given to that great state. Your obstinance in this issue far exceeds your intelligence." With that, O left the store without buying a single thing, leaving the befuddled merchant to decipher his speech.

As we were leaving the store, Burly Barnes stepped behind me and shoved me hard into the mud of the street, then advanced toward me, intent on doing further damage. Only the double click of a .44 stopped his progress and he turned to look down (and I mean down) the barrel of little Gus's pistol. "Why you little . . ." he stopped when he saw Gus's finger tighten on the trigger and the gun's aim lowered to his gut. Not that Burly was afraid to die, he was afraid to die gutshot. He had witnessed that once and decided shoving me down was enough for the moment. Barnes was not about to let the matter lie. "Tell that boss of yours that he hasn't heard the last of this. I'll get my pay one way or another."

That was the moment that Pock rounded the corner of the building and stopped and listened to the speech. "That's big talk when you're talkin' to a kid, why don't you try that speech on me?"

"Why, I'll be glad to, feller. You tell that boss of . . ."

The speech was rudely interrupted by Pock's fist to Burly's mouth, rendering him speechless for some time. He spit tooth and blood out and grinned.

I heard Gus say, "O-oh no," and he was right. He moved over close to me and sniffed the air. "Sut, that ain't mud you fell in."

"What kind of hick town allows their hogs to run loose," I asked. I've seen many fights and when I stand them up against that fight, none have ever measured up to it in any way. Pock did eat Burly's lunch—eventually. But the bigger man "got a couple of sandwiches" before he was through. The third time Pock knocked him down, Burly knew he wasn't gonna win this fight without an equalizer and patted an empty holster. His gun had fallen out and I held it. When he pulled a knife from his boot, I fired a warning shot between his feet, and he cursed, "I can't beat these odds," meaning two guns and Pock's fists, "so we'll just have to settle this another day."

"Looks to me, this is settled here and now," I said. "Any other 'settlement' would be when you have an unfair advantage of us, and I am sure it would not be evenhanded."

Burly stomped around the little village bragging about what he was going ta do to Jake and his outfit. In short order, the men of the village issued an invitation to Mr. Barnes to take up his abode elsewhere. Without his gunmen, he was obliged to accept their invitation and the operation of the ferry ceased.

Pock was stoved up some, his hands swole and one eye was closed, but he insisted on carrying his load and wouldn't allow any help. Cookie made him soak his hands in cool water and stitched up a nasty split on his left cheekbone. "Must have been de devil made you do those things to that man, Pock."

"Well, Cookie, the devil told me to mash his nose an' knock his teeth out, but biting off his ear was my own idea."

We left the two children at Wichita with the parson's wife, Angel's howls ringing in our ears. Frank was so determined to go with us that we had to take him back twice. Jake had to promise him he could go with us if he were still there when we came back through on the way home. The postmaster wrote letters and found their kin back east and fortunately Frank was gone on our return.

Two days after leaving Wichita, a thunderstorm struck us while me and Gus were herdin' th' remuda. First, the air became charged and little blue lights ran back and forth on the horses' ears. Instead of running, the horses gathered around us and lowered their heads to the ground between their legs and moaned.

"Gus, we're the highest thing around, get down on the ground," I called, sliding off my horse.

"An' git trampled by these horses?" Gus called.

"They ain't goin' nowheres. Which would you choose, gettin' trampled by horses or fried by lightning?"

"Dead is dead," he retorted, but he slid off his horse and hung his gunbelt on the saddle horn.

The static crackled and the horses moved closer and I was so squeezed I sat down. I don't know how the storm could get more intense, but it did and I lay down and covered my head. One huge crash of lightning turned the rain loose on us and washed the static away. The horses relaxed some, but kept their heads down. Now, we had to stand up or drown, and we couldn't mount up because the lightning was still playing around. Most of it was in the air, but ever' once in a while a bolt would hit the ground. Sometimes a streak would split into two or three forks and hit the ground in different places at the same time.

"I don't know which is scarier, the thunder or these horses moaning," Gus called from somewhere under the horses.

"It might calm them some if we sang," I called back. I thought a moment and started singing the hymn "Never Alone." "I've seen the lightning flashing and heard the thunder roll . . ." I could feel the horses pressing me relax some. It's good they didn't know the meaning of the words.

We must have sung an hour or more until the storm blew over and moved to harass some other outfit. The horses settled down and we moved them closer to the wagon. The herd was gone.

"I don't think they ran far, boys," Cookie called. "They took off north and the storm was moving southeast." With the rain stopped, he lit the lantern and raised it up on the end of the wagon tongue. "Move the remuda after the cows so the boys can change out when they find you."

We followed the trail of the run as best we could and after a couple of miles, heard the cattle bawling. Gus rode toward them and told the first rider he met where we were.

"Good thinkin', Gus," Tom replied. "I think they only broke into two bunches. I'll tell the others. Move the horses over to the west side and near the head of this bunch and the others will find you."

We moved the horses to the west side, upwind of the cows. "Man, a herd of wet cows sure does stink," Gus said.

"And so do horses and those people who rub amongst them," I replied.

One by one, the men came in and changed horses. Curly's night horse limped in alone, his saddle askew. We saddled another of his horses and led him about a mile to where Curly was walking. "Picked up a damned badger hole and couldn't shake it off," he explained. "Does he look bad?"

"I think he's just gonna be sore a few days. You better choose another night horse for a while," I said. "It's still too dark to tell for sure, but he isn't bleeding anywhere."

He climbed on his horse and grunted a little. "Landed on my shoulder and nose," he explained and rode off.

Instead of moving up with the herd, Cookie spent his time cooking extra and hangin' wet bedding on the bushes to dry. When it got daylight, the men threw the two herds together and let them graze while they headed for the wagon. Since me an' Gus didn't have to run, we were elected to stand guard while the rest ate and looked for something dry to wear.

"This waitin' to eat all th' time is gonna stunt me," I called to Gus.

"Shoulda grabbed somethin' when we had th' chance," he replied.

Jake decided not to count heads, being satisfied we had all the cattle. After noon, we moved the herd about seven miles to fresh grass on Clear Creek. A few steers were banged up a little or sore-footed and joined the drag. That afternoon was the first time I noticed the cows watching a cloud that sprang up several miles west of us. It moved south and didn't threaten us and the cows were satisfied. We were, too, even though our bedclothes were still damp.

I wouldn't live in a country where
If you laid down you would drown
And if you stood up
Lightning would strike you.

—Settler crossing Kansas

Chapter 15
The Race

"Seems the closer we get to Abilene, the slower we go," I complained to Gus. We were a week after the big blow and only making ten miles a day.

"Now's the time to fatten the cows," Gus replied. "Enyhow, what's your hurry? We'll be th' last ones to see the elephant. Don't you dare wish for another storm. We can find something else to entertain us."

"Elephant'll be gone or dead of old age by th' time we get there," I muttered. We were sure in th' boring part of the trip. Herd horses, bring up th' drag, ride herd half th' night, sleep when you can, then get up and do it all over again. It was mighty mind-numbing. "When's th' last time you had t' think?" I called across the horses' backs.

"We wasn't hired to think, we wasn't hired t' sleep, an' you better not let Jake or Cookie be catchin' you at either one," he called back.

Cookie throwed his hat in the air and Gus took the remuda to the wagon. I moved over to take up the slack left when the first shift rode in to eat dinner.

"Watch that bobtail brindle, Sut. He's been eyein' th' far meadow all morning," O said as he rode by

"Shoulda kilt him a long time ago," I replied.

"Bullets is too rare t' waste on him. Can't afford t' lose him now, we got too much sweat an' tears invested in him," O called.

I watched him race for the wagon. *Bet Aciago can beat you in a race*. The more I thought about it, the more convinced I became. That night after supper, I said, when the time was right, "I bet Aciago can beat any horse in the remuda in a quarter-mile race."

"Nothing like stirring the pot a little," Jake grinned. "We don't bet or gamble among ourselves, Sut, house rules."

"More peaceful thata way," Tom added. "But I think you have made a brash claim there, Sut, and I hereby raises my hand in protest. Ever'one here knows my Stubbs is th' fastest quarter miler in the cavyyard."

"Ever'one 'cept Sut's Aciago an' my Sunfish," Pock said.

"Never understood why anyone would want a horse that could only run a quarter," Curly said.

"Don't need more'n a quarter if you can throw a rope," Pock replied.

The conversation waxed warm the next half hour, then waned as first one then another unspooled his bed and retired, the consensus being the question could be settled only by a race.

At breakfast, Jake announced that the race would be that evening after supper (and before any animosities or bets had time to arise in the crew). Even so, there was much discussion about the various abilities of the contestants, and possibly a bet or two were made on the sly. The subject horses were rested, and curried and warmed for the show.

"The horses are to toe the line at the far end of the run, and I want five yards between runners. Anyone violating that spacing will be disqualified. I will stand here at the finish line and drop this rag to start the race," Jake said and the contestants trotted to the line. There was some jockeying until all three gained proper spacing and toeing. Jake dropped the rag and the race was on among cheers and coaching from the infield spectators.

Aciago clearly crossed the line first and amidst enthusiastic discussion; it was agreed that the losers were in a dead heat when they crossed the line. Cookie had left the discussion early and hurried to the wagon where he did some arranging and threw his hat in the air again.

"Now, what's he up to? We gonna have another supper?" Gus asked,

"Bet he's made a pie or two," Curly said. Sure enough, two large raisin pies, one with a generous slice missing for the cook, were awaiting disposal, which promptly occurred.

Out of gratitude for Cookie's extra work, the crew unanimously volunteered me an' Gus to wash up the dishes while they unspooled and went to bed. We never realized how noisy washing metal pans and plates was until that night. Those poor boys didn't get a wink of sleep until we finished the washing.

"Bet Sunfish would beat Aciago if he had a rider as light as Sut on his back," Pock said at breakfast.

"Bet he can't," I said.

Jake had the last say when he avowed, "The race was run according to the rules of the racing commissioner and the results are final."

Final, that is, until word of our race reached the Rocking R outfit just behind us and we got a second challenge from the Circle Dot ahead of us. Thus began some spirited negotiations between the three outfits until it was determined that another race was to be held the coming Sunday afternoon.

I retired Aciago from night duty and saddled Dusky for my night horse. "Why are you resting Aciago?" Jake asked. "Don't you think he will get a little lazy before Sunday?"

"I thought I would rest him a little," I said.

"It would be better to keep him on his regular job until the race so he will be in shape and fit."

"Yes, sir," and I changed my saddle over to Aciago.

There was a lot of jobbing between the three outfits, ours

getting the most of it being in the middle, and word must have spread up and down the trail, for Saturday evening Cookie had us kill a heifer and dig a firepit. You guessed it. Me an' Gus was elected to turn the spit all night long.

"How am I going to stay up all night and still ride Aciago in the race?" I asked.

"I'll let you sleep all morning," Cookie said.

After breakfast, the wagons from the other two outfits drove in and turned to the chore of cooking for a crowd. People began riding in from up and down the trail and by noon there must have been a hundred and fifty men waiting for the race. There was some subdued betting, but the most interest was in the bet the bosses had made. The losers were to give the winner half of their pickup steers, the proceeds from the sale of these cattle to be split among the vaqueros. It would most likely exceed their earnings for making the trip. Enthusiasm ran high.

The three-boss racing commission agreed to adopt the Meeker Rules for the race, and the contestants warmed their charges up. Circle Dot entered a thoroughbred they had brought along just for the purpose of racing, and the Rocking R entered a pinto horse they had for the same purpose.

"Poor Aciago, a working horse goin' up agin racers," Gus said.

"It just may be he is in better shape," Pock said.

We stripped my saddle to the bones, even taking off the stirrups.

"How you gonna stay in the saddle without stirrups?" Gus asked.

"I'll have to grip with my knees. I have an idea about how to ride."

"Hope it's a good one, 'cause it don't look good for our side against two racers," Gus said.

The race was to begin at twelve noon, and when the time

drew near, we warmed the horses and went to the line.

"Where's your stirrups, kid?" one of the riders asked.

"I don't need them."

"You get on the end and when you fall off, be sure to fall to the outside, so you won't get trampled," the other rider said. He wasn't joking.

The Rocking R segundo was going to start the race with a gun.

Curly whispered, "Watch and go on the smoke, Sut, not the sound."

There was some trouble getting lined up because the thoroughbred was too excited. His rider finally got him to stand still long enough for the starter at the finish line to fire his gun. We all went on the smoke, so I didn't gain anything by that, but the sound of the pistol spooked the thoroughbred and the Circle Dot got a bad start.

I drew my knees up and gripped Aciago just behind his withers. With my weight almost over his shoulders, he seemed to run better. The Rocking R pinto got a good jump on us at the start, but Aciago gained on him, and by the three-quarter mark, we were even. I glimpsed back and saw the thoroughbred gaining on us, but he would never beat us to the finish line. The race was between pinto and mustang, and it was going to be close.

The finish sparked one of the greatest controversies of any happening on the Chisholm Trail that year. And the argument lasted for years, for we crossed the line exactly even. The result was instant, one spectator saying Aciago was ahead by "that much," measuring the distance between finger and thumb. Of course, someone took exception to that and the argument was on and repeated in a dozen places. One or two arguments resulted in physical contact but settled the question not a bit.

Over the years, I have met at least three hundred witnesses

who swore they were standing astraddle that finish line and their perceived results of the race were split almost 50-50 between the two horses. Without a doubt, sitting forward and with my head just behind Aciago's ears, I was closer to the finish than anyone. Aciago and I were satisfied to call it a tie. It's one of those secrets kept between man and horse. I never even told Gus.

Gus and Curly had to help me off the horse. The groin muscles and the inside of both legs were cramped to my knees and I could hardly stand. It was a miserable time for me for several days. "You're walkin' like you got a cob up your ass," Gus said. Riding a horse was sheer agony. A small dose of laudanum allowed me to sleep, but Cookie would not let me take it and do my work. "You barely got the brains to do your chores without medicine. With it, you would be dangerous." He was prob'ly right.

The tie split the payoff from Circle Dot and we only got five steers each. The profit from their sale didn't do much harm to any of us.

Now, the feed those three cooks put on was as much something to talk about as the race. We had barbeque, American chili with red or green chili on top, beef stew, and son-of-a-gun stew by the tubful. Cookie won praise for the best biscuits. His buttermilk was the difference and the extra churning we did was worth the trouble.

The wagons pulled out late evening, each with just enough feed for the unlucky ones who stayed with the herds. By sunset, everyone was gone and the old trail routine descended upon us like a plague.

★ ★ ★ ★ ★

Said the little Eohippus,
"I'm going to be a horse!
And on my middle finger-nails
To run my earthly course!
I'm going to have a flowing tail!
I'm going to have a mane!"

—Charlotte Perkins Gilman

CHAPTER 16
THE (FIRST) JAILBREAK

Now, the drive settled into a boring pattern that wasn't interrupted by anything more interesting than a thunderstorm or two until we approached the Smoky Hill River. We drove the herd into the mouth of an oxbow lake that nearly made a complete circle. We could see the cow pens across the river, and the whole sky was filled with dust from a half dozen herds holding south of the river, while a herd was loading into cattle cars.

Dos, Uno, and Chickasha left us and headed south. Abilene was white man's land and the Indian was not welcome.

Jake rode to town and the Drover's Cottage to tell the buyers we had arrived. That started a parade of buyers in buggies and horseback to look at our stock.

"From what I have seen, we've got the slickest crowd of longhorns out here," Pock said.

Cookie looked up from his cooking, "Sure hope they bring top price."

We stayed in camp until the cattle were sold. "Without a nickel in the crowd, there's nothing to do in town," O said. "Ever'thing there costs money and too much of it."

"Cain't even look at th' girls for less'n a dime," Tom said.

"Dime? You was lookin' at th' ugly ones," Pock said. "Pretty ones costs a dollar a peek—an' they still got all their clothes on."

"I don't know what you fellers are talking about, but I ain't payin' no one to look at anything, includin' wimmin'," Gus vowed.

"If they are out in the open, whether inside or outside, I'm lookin' an' not payin'," I said.

Jake was concerned about the cattle getting enough forage in the natural corral. Already, they had grazed the area down. "We will have to turn them out on the prairie to get enough graze to keep their weight up. We pay for the stock by the head in Texas, but the buyers at the tracks pay by the pound. That's why we drive slow and let the cattle graze."

"This grass ain't as good for fattenin' because of too much rain," Curly said.

"We have a buyer, but the cars won't be here until the day after tomorrow," Jake said. "We will move the herd out on the prairie tomorrow."

I groaned inside, for that meant a lot of herdin' to do. "There goes our sleep agin," Gus whispered. It was enough to make a feller grumpy.

The next morning was just like a hundred other mornings on the trail and we moved the cattle out of our corral and west a good five miles to undisturbed grass. "Them steers sure know how to 'disturb' that grass, don't they?" Gus asked.

"They do, an' we better hustle down to th' river and round up some firewood for Cookie, or he'll be skinnin' a couple of heads," I replied. We found a goodly amount of driftwood and dragged it to the wagon.

"Good," Cookie nodded his approval. "Now git down an' chop it up for the fire." Which we promptly did.

At noon a boy rode in and told Jake the cars would be ready the next morning and everything got in a hustle. We rounded up the cattle and they resumed their customary positions in the drive. "Would you look at that, Gus, they think they're still on the trail," I said.

"On th' trail to a steakhouse in th' east," he replied.

We watered them at the river and drove them on across to the pens. It seemed a little sudden and strange that we were getting rid of the herd this way. I said a silent goodbye to the good ones we had named, and good riddance to the ones who were trouble, the bobtail brindle being on the top of that list. We introduced him to an empty pen and he inspected its boundaries, and jumped and clambered over the top of that railroad tie pen. "Did you see that?" Gus asked and we turned to pursue the animal.

"Let him go, boys," Jake called. "We'll bring him back next year."

We watched that steer drink deep and ford the river and set out on a lope south.

"He'll beat us home by a month," Pock said and chuckled. "Let's finish th' job and get our pay."

While we penned the cattle, Jake settled with the buyer, taking most of the pay in notes on banks in Texas and the rest in cash for a portion of our pay. Every man who worked for Jake agreed that he would keep the balance of their pay for them until they returned to Texas. "That way you'll have money for family needs and spend it in Texas instead of Kansas. It doesn't make sense to bring a herd up here, get paid, and leave the money here also. We're just hurting ourselves and the Texas economy." We got a month's pay here and the rest at Jacksboro.

A lot was made about the fact that the ordinary cowboy spent all his hard-earned money in the saloons and dance halls of the cattle towns and left as poor as they arrived. Texas was saved and made rich by the responsible drovers and ranchers like Jake who returned to the state with the majority of the money they had made.

"Sut, Jake said we could go with the bunch and he and Tom would watch the horses," Gus yelled.

"Come on, boys," Curly called. "Me and Pock will show you how this works."

We rode down Texas Street and stopped at one of the five general merchandise stores. "Wait a minute, I thought we were going to a dance hall to look at the girls," Gus said.

Curly sniffed the air, "You go smellin' like that an' they'll kick you out th' back door with th' swine."

"So we're goin' in here to get kicked out th' back door of a general store?" I asked.

"They're used to our smell and like the smell of our silver and gold," Pock said as he trotted up the steps and across the board porch.

The two disappeared into the store an' me an' Gus peeked in the door. "Come on in, boys, don't be shy," said a man with garters around his shirtsleeves. "My, my, you *do* need new clothes." He appraised us a moment and led us to a corner of the store for boy's clothes. In no time he had us fitted out in a new suit of Levi Strauss bibless riveted overalls, a white shirt with celluloid collar, and red string tie. "Now, boys, we'll cap the ends of you with a pair of Justin boots and a Stetson sombrero."

I rounded off my stack with new underwear and socks and a California flannel long-sleeved overshirt for the fall trip back home. A linen collar was cheaper and I was only going to wear it this once in town. Boots was too expensive, but I did need a new hat.

Gus saved sixty cents by not getting fleece-lined underwear, ten cents by getting a cheaper hat, and also saved money by not buying a collar. The clerk bundled up all our clothes and we paid him. "I wanted to put my new clothes on now," Gus whispered.

The clerk wrote out my bill:

One pair of Levi Strauss bibless riveted overalls	$1.15
One white shirt	$0.83
One double breasted blue flannel shirt	$0.91
One overshirt, California flannel	$1.38
One linen collar with red string tie	$0.07
One suit fleeced wool underwear (longhandles)	$0.84
Two pair heavy Rockford socks	$0.16
One Stetson sombrero	$1.69
Total	$7.03

"You have another stop before you can put on your new clothes," the clerk said and pointed across the street to the barbershop. A sign over the door advertised a close shave, haircut, and hot bath. The other fellers were still making their purchases so we went on over to the barbershop and ordered the works. We were ushered to a back room where there was a row of tubs and a boy with buckets of hot water. We each got a tub, and the boy poured in hot water over the cold water already there until we were comfortable. Every tub had a bar of soap, a rag, and a towel. We sat and soaked and scrubbed body and hair until the water cooled and the other boys came storming in the door and demanded one of us make room, there being five of them and only six tubs.

"I was turning into a prune anyway," I said as I got out. Curly hopped into Gus's tub and as he was sitting down, I said, "Gus always pees in his tub, Curly."

"Ee-yow," he hollered. I don't think he used his arms to get out of that tub; it was like a spring under his butt went off and threw him out on the walkway. "Did you pee in that tub, Gus?" he yelled over the sound of the rest of us laughing.

"No, I never," Gus yelled back. "Dang you, Sut—"

"You never peed in the tub when you took a bath?" I asked.

"Might of once or twice when I was a kid, but not in *that* tub," he hollered.

"Sut, did you pee in your water?" Curly demanded.

"Nope. Not a drop."

Curly settled into my vacated tub and called for hot water. "Better change that tub, son, it may have been peed in." The boy grinned, but the water was not changed when the crew left for their shaves and haircuts.

We put on our new clothes and proceeded to the barbers where we got sheared but waived the unnecessary shave.

"Your white neck sure looks funny," Gus said as we walked out of the shop.

"Think yours looks any different?"

"Naw, prob'ly not. That Curly sure looked funny when you said I peed in th' tub."

"Did you see how he came outa there? He didn't touch anything, like he was shot out of a cannon."

"Yeah, it was pretty funny. I'll git even with you for that, Sut."

"I know you will, but I bet it won't be as funny."

We stowed our extra gear in our saddlebags at the livery and while we waited around for the rest to finish up at the barbershop, Gus spied a café. We found a window seat, ordered dinner, and watched for the rest of the gang. That food was so good that when the others caught up with us, we ordered again, only this time we ordered fresh peach cobbler with sweet cream at the end.

Pock pushed back his third empty plate and said, "Well, boys, it's time we got down to business and shake out some of these cobwebs. Let's go dancin'."

We followed them to the first dance hall they saw and a girl was at the door to pick up each one as they entered, except that when me an' Gus entered, no one picked us up. Gus held his hand up before his face and looked at it closely, "Nope, I ain't invisible. It must be those girls have sight problems."

"They're lookin' at th' size o' your purse an' your age," I

answered. "Truth is you are not worth the trouble in your present condition."

"Just what is my condition?" he demanded.

"You're too."

"Two, what's that mean?"

"Too short, too young, and too poor."

The two-minute song at the tinny piano by a young man with a squeaky horn ended and the boys all ushered their girls to the bar for drinks. The boys paid for two whiskeys and the girls ordered "the special" and got their drink from another bottle that contained tea. All of a sudden, the bartender came up with his sawed-off shotgun and said, "Who called that clarinet player an S.O.B.?"

Somewhere down the crowded bar someone asked, "Who called that S.O.B. a clarinet player?" The roar of laughter eased the tension and the shotgun returned to its berth beneath the bar.

"Bet the girls get a part of the amount their 'beau' spends on drinks," Gus muttered. The boys were getting pretty loose.

"Yeah, plus whatever they can get on th' side," I said, watching a couple ascend stairs to a row of rooms along the balcony.

"I gotta git outa here," Gus said and headed for the door. Outside, he breathed deep and whispered to himself, "Kilt th' last drunk I saw." His face was white and his hand shook.

"Let's see what else this town's made of," I said, and we walked down the boardwalk. "There must be a dozen saloons and dance halls." Some looked nice when we peeked in, and some were so bad we didn't have to peek.

"Only ten saloons, Sut." Gus was a counter.

"Ten saloons, five general stores, and four hotels," I said.

"Yeah, but did you notice two of those 'hotels' rented by th' hour?"

"More like th' minute," I replied.

At the end of the street, set back and away from other buildings, was the marshal's office and jail. The place looked deserted, and we were turning back to Texas Street when someone called from the barred window, "Hey, you two, seen that marshal anywhere?"

"Whut's he look like?" Gus asked.

"Squat feller, ganted legs, an' potted belly. Star onder his vest, an' tobacco spit in his beard."

"Mister, you just described near every damyankee in this town, except for th' star," I said. We walked closer so we didn't have t' yell. We could tell he was fresh off th' Chisholm Trail by his new sombrero and fresh haircut. "What are you in there for?"

"Bein' drunk an' broke, an' takin' up space layin' in th' alley b'hind that whorehouse without my new boots on, I guess. I'm shore dissatisfied with this jail. I'd git outa this town if that tin star would let me. If you see him, tell him what I said."

Gus went around to the door, but it was locked and no one was in the little office. "We'll go find that marshal for you," he called, and headed back up Texas Street. I caught up with him at th' door to the first saloon. "Gus, why do we got t' find th' law for that feller? We are here to have fun."

"Hush a minit, Sut." He walked up to the empty bar in front of the bartender and asked, "Mister, do you know where th' marshal is?"

I couldn't see his legs to judge them, but his stained beard and potbelly fit th' general description. He looked down his nose and drawled in a squeaky voice, "Shore, I know where he is, kid, what you want t' know for?"

"Well, I jist kilt a man over to th' Merchant's Hotel an' wanted t' pay my fine an' git outa this damyankee town." He mimicked the man's drawl.

"Fine for shootin' a man's thirty dollars, stabbin's worth

twenty-five, an' th' marshal's authorized me t' collect fines when he's not on dooty."

"Naw, sir, I got took by that last year an' had t' pay double when th' sheriff caught up with me. I ain't payin' no one 'cept'n th' po-leece."

"Marshal's been up all night keepin' some sort o' peace, an' he's gone home to git some sleep afore rush hour. You go wakin' him up an' he'll arrest you an' throw you in jail for disturbin' th' peace." The man spread both hands along the bar and leaned over looking down at Gus.

"Just for wakin' him up?" Gus asked.

"Charge is disturbin' th' peace—his peace—fine's five dollars."

"I'll do my disturbin' in Texas. Fine's only a dollar there, an' no jail time," I said.

"Well, if you come back by 'bout three o'clock, he'll be in here drinkin' his supper b'fore he goes on duty," the barkeep said.

We went back and told the vaquero the news and he said, "Thanks, fellers. Say, would you look to my horse? They tied him out back an' he'll need attention, 'specially waterin'."

We found the horse, a mustang, tied behind the jail, his saddle slung over the hitch rail, an' took him to the river to drink. On th' way back to the jail, Gus said to th' horse, "Say, I bet you can't pull bars from that jail window."

"Now don't you get ideas, Gus, we ain't jailbreakers," I said.

"That's a feller Texian locked up in a Yankee jail just for bein' robbed and sleepin' it off in an alley. I ain't leavin' him there."

"In broad daylight?" I asked.

"Ain't waitin' for dark."

I can't say I disagreed with his whole concept. There wasn't anything else in the town that attracted us, and we might as well be doing good for someone—and having fun doing it. The jail part of the building was made of two by fours stacked and nailed together. It wouldn't be hard to break into. We took the horse back to the hitch behind the jail and saddled him, then found a likely window where no one could see us. I tied the boy's lariat to a bar while Gus tied the other end to the saddle horn and mounted. That little mustang just walked to the end of the slack and pulled the bar and a couple of two-bys loose without hardly any effort. The barefooted feller jumped out with a whoop.

"Hush up, they'll hear you," I said.

"Whoops an' gunshots don't hardly draw attention in this town," he replied.

We headed back to town, the jailbird ducked behind one of the general stores to fish his old boots from the trash pile, and we saddled up and rode for camp out the opposite end of Texas Street.

Up at the end of town, a vaquero staggered out of the last saloon and mounted his horse after several drunken tries. "Must have started at the other end of the street and tasted every saloon he came to," I said.

Once seated as firmly as a drunk can be seated in a saddle, he started down the street and drew his gun and made the long rebel yell, shooting at every sign he met. Drunk as he was, he stopped and reloaded his revolver. "Spilled as many bullets as he loaded," Gus observed.

The cowboy was just turning and continuing his ride when a man with an express shotgun stepped out from between two buildings and ordered him, "Halt and throw down that hogleg."

"Not on your life, lawman," the rider swore and fired at the deputy. We saw the deputy stagger back, but he still was able to put two barrels of buckshot into the cowboy and several second-story windowpanes across the street behind him, sending the riderless horse trotting down the street.

The deputy staggered backwards and sat on the boardwalk, hugging an awning post. We rode back and I dismounted and trotted to the deputy. "No use worrying about that cowhand," Gus muttered.

The deputy had a hole just above his left pap that must have gone to his heart or nearby, and he was dead already, sitting and hugging that post. There were steps along the boardwalk as people came out of their hidings. They gently laid the lawman out straight and gathered around him.

Someone down the street caught the horse and brought him back. Several men lifted the vaquero across the saddle belly down and tied the body on. A slap on the rump sent the horse on his way back to his camp somewhere south of town. "Maybe when that horse gets back to camp, his buddies will come in and find out what happened," Gus said.

Such a waste of two lives. It fixed in my mind that alcohol and gunpowder are a deadly combination. Jake was in town palaverin' with a buyer and left Cookie in charge. "Can't tell th' difference from any other day," I muttered to Gus. Cookie fed us and sent us to relieve Curly and Otha. They didn't even go back to camp, just whooped it to Abilene.

Cookie looked after them. *First time any cowhands came back from the end-of-trail town sober.*

There are three degrees to drunkeness
The social degree, the lion degree,
And the hog degree.

—Jim Herron

Chapter 17
The Domino Effect

Jake sold the herd and we were waiting for the loading crew to come and take it, those that still had money "waiting" in town. The third day, all of us were laying around camp or riding herd. Me an' Gus had charge of the horses again. We were taking them back to Texas. Later drives to the tracks, the demand for horses up north in Nebraska an' th' Dakotas brought th' price of horses up so that Jake would sell them. That meant me an' Gus had a winter's worth of work breaking another bunch for th' cavyyard. It was another of those "blessing and curse" things.

I had just settled down for my after-breakfast nap when someone hailed the camp. "Come on in, cowboy," Pock called, and a young feller rode in. Cookie poured him a cup of Arbuckle's. He squatted by the wagon and sipped until it was cool enough to drink without raising blisters. After a time of polite small talk, he said, "My outfit has enough to have a baseball team, an' it looked like you did, too; how about a game this afternoon?"

Tom sat up and counted, "We only got seven counting th' cook, all right if we recruit two or three more?"

Cookie hollered, "If youse workin' up a ball game, I'm playin'."

"Shore, a couple boys over to the T bar T were interested, but they couldn't scare up a team. Bet they'd play with you."

"Me an' Gus'll go get 'em, Tom." We didn't wait for an answer, just rode to the T bar T camp. It turned out that the ball players were our friends Red and Al. They came back with us and we walked down to the field someone had laid out. Pock was the only one of us that had a glove, so we made him catcher. Tom was pitching and the rest of us found a place to play. I got third base and Gus went to right field. "Don't get many balls out there," he said and grinned. Red got first base because he was tall and needed to be to field our throws. Al was on second, and Curly got shortstop. That left Cookie in center field and O in left.

The other team, Circle Dot boys, batted first and didn't waste any time doin' it. They scored five times before we got them out. Their pitcher was pretty good and we only had three runs when O popped out to first base for the third out.

The Circle Dot took up where they had left off and we got to the middle of the second inning with the score ten to three. Al led off with a single and Gus walked because the pitcher couldn't find his little strike zone. Tom hit a double that scored Al and put Gus on third. Pock took the 0-2 pitch for a ball and Gus stole home by sliding between his legs while Tom took third. That caused a fuss, but the crowd ruled it was a fair steal, and I looked around and saw a good hundred people standing around the field watching. That was when the crowd elected an umpire for the game. He was someone from town who professed to be neutral. "Nothin' neutral 'bout a damyankee callin' a Texian ball game," Gus growled.

"Well, we're all Texians, so it might even out," I said.

Pock dribbled a roller down the first base line and Tom scored. O struck out, Cookie hit a home run to right field, and Red flied out to center. Score 7 to 10.

The game rocked on until we caught up with them in the bottom of the seventh, 15 to 15.

Tom's arm was sore and when he walked the first two men in the top of the eighth, he called a "time-out" and we all met behind the pitcher's box. "I can't get it over, my arm's too sore," Tom said. "Someone else has to pitch."

We chewed that around until the crowd got into it, and Cookie said, "I'll pitch." Before anyone could object, Tom handed him the ball and trotted out to center field. That caused another fuss, the Circle Dot boys and their fans claiming we couldn't change positions, but the umpire ruled that Tom was injured and the change was legal.

Ump gave Cookie two warm-up pitches and the game was on—and was that a revelation. Cookie's pitches smoked Pock's glove and he fanned the batter in four pitches. Pock called another time-out to the displeasure of the crowd, and stuffed a folded-up rag in his glove and the game resumed. No runner got past third base in that half inning. We didn't protest when a new pitcher warmed up, and I hit his first pitch between second and short. Curly walked and Al hit a fly ball behind second. Curly was forced out at second, putting me on third and Al on first. One out and Gus was up. He had walked every time he was up until now, but this new pitcher could hit Gus's strike zone and did. The count went to 1-2, then 2-2, and the pitcher sent one right down the middle. Gus gave a mighty swing and the ball rolled past the pitcher and died before it got to the shortstop. I shot for home and the shortstop threw to the catcher. I would have been out if he hadn't dropped the ball. Al ended up on third and Gus didn't beat the throw to second. Two out. Tom's shoulder was so sore he could barely swing and he grounded out to second. We went to the top of the ninth leading 16 to 15. I would like to say that we made a heroic stand to keep them from scoring, but we didn't. Cookie fanned them, three in a row, with only twelve pitches.

Some enterprising Yankee had brought out a couple of kegs and the crowd bought both teams mugs of cool beer. Pock took his and plunged his catching hand into it. "I think it steamed,

Pock," Red said and laughed. Pock's hand was red and beginning to swell. He favored it for a couple of days.

Our win brought a challenge from the town team and there was a lot of mouthing and betting before the game, but it was much ado about nothing, for Cookie shut them out and we won 12 to 0 in six innings. That was when the fight broke out between Texians and Kansans. Their Yankee umpire was not neutral, but couldn't do anything to change the game and we had to protect him from his fellow Kansans. We got him to the train station without getting harmed too much. He took a cattle train east and they say he never came back. We'd ask every year just to rile the Yankees. Cookie quit a couple years later and moved to Kansas City where he pitched for a Negro team and did pretty good.

While we were laying around camp, treating aching heads and busted knuckles, the man that bought our herd rode up and he and Jake had a conference. When he left, Jake called us together and said, "Lovell has a mixed herd he bought for a rancher in Nebraska, and the crew that drove them up here won't take them any farther. He wants to know if we would take the herd on through to the Ogallala Land and Cattle Company, Ogallala City, Nebraska. That's about a six-to-eight-week drive. He's willing to pay every man five dollars a month above his present salary and an extra month's pay at the end of the drive. I'm willing to go, but each of you can make up your own mind about that."

I said, "Me an' Gus'll go if you go, Jake," and got an elbow in the ribs.

"You didn't even ask me," Gus growled.

"Well, aren't you ready to go?"

"Yeah."

"An' didn't I already know that?"

"Yeah."

We put it to a vote and everyone but Pock said yes. It took some persuading and two more votes before Pock agreed to go.

"All right," Jake said, "I'll go tell Lovell and look the herd over. We'll be getting into cold weather before we are done. I'll set up an account at the Abilene General Merchandise and you all go in and buy winter gear. Don't forget heavy gloves and socks and head cover."

Those mercantile boys was just layin' for us when we walked in. They had all their winter clothes laid out and we soon had our outfits.

"Shore looks funny buying winter clothes when the temperature's a hundred, don't it?" Gus asked.

"Like that Irishman said, 'There ain't no such thing as bad weather, just poor clothes for it.' " Tom grinned as he said it.

"I thought that was a Scottish saying," O said, and started a discussion still unsettled.

We were almost done when Jake came in with Al Crow and Red Stark. "These two men need the winter clothes also," he told the clerks.

"Got a bigger herd?" Pock asked.

"Maybe a little bigger, and I bought the other outfit's hoodlum wagon and calf wagon. Those cows are still dropping calves."

I groaned and Gus looked disgusted. "Still glad we're going north?" Gus whispered, and I wasn't sure anymore. We knew who was most likely to be driving wagons, picking up bedrolls, and newborn calves—and sure enough we were right.

It took Cookie most of the day to provision the chuck wagon, and he came back mad about the prices he had to pay. Our drive to the Ogallala didn't start so smooth for some of us. We just hoped the rest of the trip would get better.

We rode over to the new herd the next morning and had a head count, Jake on one side of the gate and the old crew boss on the other. After they tallied their counts, we had 1,510 two-year-old steers, 504 three-year-old steers, 800 heifers, 1,000 cows, calf by side (calf not in count), and 500 cows, for a total of 4,314 head.

"That means five hundred calves to pick up," I said to Gus.

"You can drive th' calf wagon, I ain't drivin' nothing that carries five hundred calves," Gus replied.

"No bulls in this crowd?" Curly asked, "Gonna be some mighty dissatisfied cows."

"They are getting a bunch of Durham bulls from the east to service these ladies," Jake said. "Only a longhorn bull would survive a drive like this, and he would be mighty sore."

"Charlie Goodnight pushed his bull's nuts up high in the sack and tied th' sack off when we drove a herd to Colorado," Pock said. "Bulls made it fine after that, no more nuts bangin' around."

"You've got one more night on the' town, boys; we move this herd out at sunrise tomorrow morning," Jake said.

We didn't know how lively the town was seein' it in daylight. When the sun sat was when things got goin' good.

"Sin loves the dark," I said to Gus.

"I'm beginnin' t' cotton to it, myself," he replied.

It was quite a revelation riding into town at sunset. Riders were coming in from the east to south to west, all converging on Abilene, like arrows to a target. "And we thought we was in a crowd this afternoon," Gus said.

"All the hitching rails are full to overflowing," I said. "Let's go to the alley and hitch." It wasn't much better there.

"We could have hitched them to an awning post like those others were," Gus said.

"Something scares those horses, an' th' awnings are coming down," I replied. "I 'spect some cowboys would be in a heap of trouble if they found out who those horses belonged to."

We found two spots to tie our horses and Gus said, "Let's check out the dance hall," indicating the next building down where light and music overflowed the open back door. There was a sign over the door that announced the entrance to the Happy Hour Dance Hall. We had just passed the saloon door when it was flung open and two men threw a third man into the alley. One of the men walked over and kicked the unconscious man, gave a shrill whistle, and disappeared into the saloon. We were moving back to look at the man when a kid not more than twelve years old rushed past us and pounced on the drunk. "He's mine, didn't you hear th' whistle?"

"What's that whistle mean, kid?" I asked.

"It means that Dick Fromm says this man is mine." He rolled the man over on his back and pulled a new pair of boots off his feet. Then swiftly unbuckling his belt and unbuttoning his pants he slipped the fancy striped pants from under his rump.

"Hold on there, kid, you're not going to rob an unconscious man," I grabbed the boy and he slugged me in the gut with a sock full of coins, emptying my lungs of air. Gus jumped the boy from behind, pinning his arms while I caught my breath.

"Any day now, Sut," he grunted as the boy struggled and kicked.

I grabbed the sock and swung it at the boy's head. It made a satisfying thump and jangle and the boy went limp. Gus dropped him and we looked to the drunk. We pulled his pants back up and buttoned the top. Each of us grabbed a boot and put them on his feet. In the dark, we got them switched. We were helping him to his feet when the saloon door flew open and the kid stood there giving a shrill whistle.

"O-o-oh crap," Gus muttered.

We hustled the drunk toward the dance hall light, but we didn't make it before the bouncer Dick Fromm caught us. "Hey, what's the idea stealing this man? He's th' kid's." He grabbed the drunk by the back of his shirt and slung him to the ground. "Now, git out o' here b'fore I get mad." He kicked Gus in th' rear so hard, he left the ground. When he turned to go, I swung the sock as hard as I could and hit him in the kidney. He sort of sighed and fell to his knees. The sock burst and scattered the coins all over the place.

"Run for the light, Gus," and we ducked into the dance hall. Gus slammed the door and I slid the bar in place.

"Hey," a Happy Hour barkeep called, "Open that door, it's too warm in here."

"In a minit," I said as me an' Gus ran through the crowd for the front door. The banging on the back door had stopped before we reached the front of the dance hall.

"He's gonna be coming out th' front door!" Gus hollered.

"Not if we hurry." I rushed out the door and yelled and shot my gun into the air. It startled the horses at the hitching rail and they turned, separating the rail from its posts and sweeping the horses tied to the saloon canopy posts away with them. The canopy came down just as Fromm stepped out the door. He ducked back and was trapped inside.

The problem was that it wasn't the end of the action. As the horses ran, their excitement swept through the other horses along the street and they all stampeded, canopies falling like dominoes, stirring up clouds of dust that made it all seem unreal.

"Hell's bells, would you look at that!" I whispered to no one.

"Fellers, I think it's time to go," Pock said, and me an' Gus both took steps thataway before we realized who was behind us.

"Did you see that, Pock?" Gus asked, awestruck.

"I did, Gus, an' I seen who did it, an' if they hang around here long, they're going to be spending a lot of time in that two-by-four jail."

We heard the last of what he said while running between the buildings to the back and our horses. The alley was empty except for the naked drunk on his back, snoring. The horses in the back were agitated from hearing the stampede out front, but we had no trouble mounting ours. I was halfway down the alley before I slung my right leg over and forked my horse. *Then* he *really* ran with me whispering in his ear. Gus was fifty yards ahead and gaining when I ran clear of the last building with its fallen canopy. We ran west behind those stampeding horses for two miles and when they tired, me an' Gus turned north by the polestar and rode several miles before we turned back west and looked for camp. We would have rode right past it if it hadn't been halfway daylight. Cookie was already up. The bedrolls were all rolled up, indicating that no one had slept in them.

"Where is ever'body, Cookie?" I asked.

"Most of 'em's out lookin' fer their horses, but some are looking for a tree strong enough to hold two fellers' stretchin' hemp."

"Me an' Gus?"

"One an' th' same. How about one last breakfast?"

"Won't be no 'last breakfast' for me," Gus vowed. "I'm outa here." And he headed for the cavyyard. I hesitated long enough to grab a steak and handful of biscuits, then followed him. We caught fresh horses and lit out north along Mud Creek.

Me an' Gus hadn't gone a mile when we saw a herd of saddled horses shepherded by one man who turned out to be Pock. He threw his hat in the air, signaling for us to come on in, and we stopped a hundred yards from him. "You're ok, boys. I told the posse you lit a shuck south for No Man's Land. Help me get these horses back close to town so they can be sorted out."

"You don't think me an' Gus are gonna get within five miles of that town, do you?"

"I suppose not, Sut, but at least help me git them to th' five-mile marker." We did a little better than that, but when other riders—and walkers—showed up, we turned tail and left, which raised a lot of questions.

"I sent Dale an' JD back for a couple of strays that got away," Pock said. "Didn't see any sign of those two scoundrels. Guess they're really headin' south."

There was only one thing left for us to do, and that was to hitch up those two wagons, load the bedrolls, head up Mud Creek, and wait for the herd to catch up with us. We tied our horses behind the wagons. About ten miles up the creek, we parked under some cottonwood and elm trees and waited.

"We could just saddle up and head south," Gus said.

"Not with that posse between us and No Man's Land."

"I'm hungry."

"Me, too." I didn't mention my steak and biscuits, long gone.

Gus sat up, "Say, you reckon there's fish in this creek?"

"Wouldn't be surprised," I answered and we rummaged through our possibles until we found our fishing lines. We tied them to a couple of stout green willow sticks and stuck grasshoppers on the hooks. Half an hour later, Gus had a nice catfish he gutted and packed in mud. While he started a fire, I fished and finally caught another catfish. When the fire burned down to coals, we buried the fish in them and waited—not very patiently.

"Herd dust rising in the south," Gus said after the tenth time he had walked out on the ridge and looked.

"Ought to see Cookie's wagon before long," I said.

"I'll go look an' see," Gus said and trotted off.

He was gone long enough for the fish to finish and I took Gus's larger one and had it half eaten when he came back. "Wagon's comin'."

"Fish is done."

He scraped the mud-covered fish out of the fire and let it

cool some before handling it. "This don't look like my fish," he said.

"You had the larger one, didn't you?"

"Yeah, but . . ."

"For sure, that's th' larger fish," I said. *Well, it was after I had eaten half of his fish.*

He paused a long moment, then said, "All right." I could tell he wasn't convinced. *I'll have to keep my eyes open for some kind of retaliation.*

Half an hour later, we heard the chuck wagon and Gus ran up the bank and waved Cookie in. "Got a fire and wood all ready for you," I heard him call. He was pretty nervous about what would happen to us.

Cookie came bustling in and remade the fire to his liking and began cooking. "Tom's got a newborn 'cross his saddle he'd sure like t' get rid of."

I tightened Stripe's girth and rode out to the herd. Tom had a pretty little brindle calf across his saddle and was more than happy to turn her over to me. "Now we'll both have slobbered up saddles," I said.

"Serves you right more than me," he growled. He was sure mad about last night.

I turned the calf loose at the calf wagon, and mama took over the handling of her there. They would be in the drag in the morning, and I would pick up wobbly legs for a ride in the wagon when mama got a safe distance away.

Me an' Gus sure laid low around camp and tried to do our chores before someone mentioned the need. We sure got some mean looks, but no one said anything.

After they had eaten, Tom called for a meeting and they gathered around him. Me an' Gus stayed in the back, nothing between us and our horses.

"Is your girth tight?" Gus whispered.

"Yes, and so is yours. You're welcome."

"There was an incident in town last night that has caused much trouble for a lot of people, and it seems to be the result of actions of our two youngest members of this organization," Tom said. "Pock was witness to the incident and he will now tell us what happened."

Pock took his pipe from his mouth and began, "I was coming up the street to the Happy Hour Dance Hall when Sut and Gus ran out the door like the house was afire. Sut had his gun out and he fired through the canopy overhead and yelled at the horses tethered there, who stampeded down the street, taking all the horses with them, including the ones tied to the canopy posts on the saloon next door. The canopy fell and almost hit a man coming out the door. That stampede continued down the street taking every horse tied up there and removing every hitching bar and canopy they were tied to. It was a grand sight."

"So we heard," Curly growled. He rubbed sore feet that had to walk five dark miles in his boots. "I'm thinkin' someone ought to soak some chaps in th' creek."

"Wait a minute, boys, we haven't heard why the boys scared the horses," Jake said.

"All right," Tom said, "Sut, you and Gus have some explaining to do."

Gus stood up and said, "Well, by the time we got to town, all the parking places was taken up on the street—"

"So we went around to the back alley and found places," I continued. "When we were walking to the Happy Hour door past this saloon door, it opened and—"

"These two thugs threw a drunk into the alley," Gus said.

I held up my hand to stop him. "One of them, name of Dick Fromm, kicked the man when he was down and gave a loud whistle."

"This little kid came running up and begins stripping the

drunk," Gus said, "and we objected."

"We were carrying the drunk to the Happy Hour when the kid runs to the saloon door and whistles. This Dick Fromm comes runnin' out, throws the drunk down, and attacks Gus."

"Then Sut hits him in th' kidney and we run for the Happy Hour door and bolt it from the inside. Fromm beats on the door, then quits."

"We knew that he was headed for the front and we ran to get there ahead of him. I had to stop him some way, and short of killing him, I decided to try to get the canopy to fall on the saloon door—"

"Which he did set to a T," Gus crowed. "You should have seen it! Those canopies fell all down the street like a row of dominoes!"

Somebody chuckled and another until the whole shebang was laughing. "I was down the street in a saloon," Curly said, "and all of a sudden th' whole building shook. This old 49er hollers, 'Earthquake,' an' runs for the door. There's a general stampede for the doors an' only the ones who went through the back door survived th' quake. Unfortunately, the door, frame and all, didn't make it," Curly said. "Those that went for the front door were blocked by the canopy and there was a scramble for the back door. We figgered th' old geezer was killed in th' press of things and when we came back in, that old 49er was drinkin' up every glass left b'hind. 'Quake's over,' he said."

"I was walkin' past the gentlemen's club th' boys call the Happy Minute when the canopy fell," Al said, "only those posts propped up more than the canopy. The whole false front of th' building fell in the street. There was lots of screaming from the upstairs girls, being exposed to the world as bare as th' day they were born. It was a beautiful sight an' I saw th' mayor's white ass before they could douse th' lights."

"Me and O heard th' noise down the street, and when it went

to getting closer, the barkeep yelled 'Cyclone, duck for cover!' We all dove under the tables where there was some overcrowding. That cyclone passed by the front where the canopy cracked and groaned and fell and someone said, 'Poor horses.' Being the last building before the jail, we could get out a side window and watch a hundred horses leaving town at a gallop," said Tom.

"A few moments later, here came two riders, going hell for leather, and we thought they would come back with the horses," O said. "We waited, but they never came back."

"Which brings us to tonight's subject," Tom said. "Gus and Sut abandoned us in our time of need—"

"But we would have been hung if we had stayed around," I interrupted.

After a moment, Jake said, "That's a thing to consider. They did come back to camp and bring the hoodlum and calf wagons up here, which was their duty. If they had rounded up and brought the horses back to town, they would probably have been arrested and we would be shorthanded."

"And they did entertain us, after a fashion," Al said.

"By the way," Pock said, "we haven't heard from Red. Where were you during the action?"

"Oh, he was the other white ass on the second floor of the Happy Minute, blowing out lamps," Al said.

When the laughter died away, Curly said, "There still remains the fact that we had to walk five miles home in our boots."

"I think that portion of the event deserves some punishment," Curly said.

"How much?" Tom asked.

"Not more than three blows and *not* on bare asses," Jake said. It wasn't a suggestion, and that is where the rumor began that he was soft on us.

"Take off your chaps, Sut," Tom ordered, and Curly took them to the creek to soak. When he was satisfied, he brought them back and Pock administered the punishment. I'll admit it brought tears to my eyes, and if I had known I had to wear wet chaps the next day to keep them from getting stiff, I would have insisted Gus be whipped with his own chaps.

Wherever cattle were driven,
It took the Spanish horse to do the work.
—Frank Collinson

Chapter 18
Homecoming

There was no trail from Abilene to Ogalalla, so we struck out across the plain and made our own. Grass was hock deep and we took our time because of the slower pacing cows with calves. At the head of Mud Creek, we stayed on the divide above West Chapman Creek to its head. After that, it became a problem finding water, and we wandered from water to water clear up to the upper end of Wolf Creek. From there to Buffalo Creek, we had plentiful water.

We could see the dust of another herd behind us and it seemed they were gradually catching up with us. "Must be a steer herd to be gaining on us like that," Curly said. It seemed that one day they would get closer to us, then fall back some th' next day. "They are following us hoping we are going to th' same place they are, an' they don't know how t' get there on their own," Tom guessed.

I had seven newborn calves and seven mamas hoverin' just below boiling point following along behind. There had been several other births, but after six or eight days riding the wagon, they were strong enough to walk beside their mothers. I built up quite a bit of muscle liftin' calves in and out of that wagon. That's when my tooth got broke off by a flying hoof. Liked to of killed me until Cookie took a pair of pliers and pulled the stump. Spit blood for two days.

Gus had trouble with the bedrolls. A couple of the boys stopped rolling their beds and delegated Gus the roller-upper.

That stopped when he laid the beds out in the wagon bottom and put two wet newborn calves on them because there was no room in my wagon.

On this flat plain, the streams were the most crooked things I had ever seen. We had a big argument about which was more crooked, Wolf or Buffalo. Wolf finally won the contest, but Buffalo won the prize for the boggiest. So boggy in fact that we knew there was a good chance of losing cows crossing it.

"Looks to me it's time to build a Slaughter Bridge," Jake said our first night at the creek.

"O-o-oh no, not that," groaned Curly. None of the others looked happy. No true Texas vaquero looked kindly on manual labor.

"If you know a good alternative, I'll consider it," Jake said, but there were none proposed.

"Why can't we go around th' upper end?" I asked.

" 'Cause the upper end of Buffalo is Marsh Creek, which is boggier than Buffalo an' by th' time you get around Marsh Creek, you're ten or twelve miles from th' Republican and the best crossing of that river is just above the mouth of Buffalo, twenty-five miles south, where we lay our heads tonight," Pock answered.

"Been here b'fore, ain't you?" Curly asked.

"Yep, an' we'll be walkin' over th' bones of thirty head of two-year-old steers still bogged in Buffalo mud."

"What do you build a bridge with out here?" Tom asked.

"Lots o' brush, lots o' logs, an' lots o' sod," Pock answered.

"*A-and* lots o' blisters," Gus added.

Pock went on to explain that we would first lay a row of woven-in brush across the stream, lay six-foot-long logs crosswise on them, then cover them with tamped-down sod. "Makes a nice bridge if you don't load it too heavy."

"Where did you get this fool idea, anyway?" I asked.

"Pete Slaughter built the first bridge on Rush Creek over south of the Washita three or four years ago. I helped him an' we drove two thousand head of steers over it single file."

"Which would you boys rather do, build a bridge or pull a hundred head of cows out of the mud?" Jake asked,

"Could be doin' both," Tom said.

"Not if you build th' bridge right," Pock said.

"We'll sleep on it and start in the morning," Jake said. "Good idea to turn in early, the next couple of days will be trying." Sleep is a premium on the cattle trail and most of us took his advice. Of course, we still had our night patrol.

Progress on the trees and brush was slow, because we had only one axe and Cookie's hatchet. There was a lot of standing around jawing. Near noon, a man rode into camp. "Welcome stranger, light down and fill your cup," Cookie invited.

"Well, thank ye, boss, believe I will." He was near middle-aged, a little taller than average, lean and hard muscled. "I see you have your bridge building crew at work."

"If you can call that work, we have 'em," Cookie replied. He filled a plate and handed it to the man and while he was eating, Jake rode in and tied his horse to a wagon wheel. "Hello there, Ruben Dunn, that your outfit that's been following us?"

"Shore is, Jake, an' I thought I would ride up and find out just where we're goin'."

"Not goin' anywhere till we get across this bog they call Buffalo Creek," Jake replied. "Then I plan to follow the Republican and Platte Rivers to Ogalalla. Where are you headed?"

"Ogalalla, or to meet th' buyer along th' way, whichever comes first. We're anxious to leave for the sunny shores of Texas before we freeze to death up here."

"If you could help us get across this boggy creek, it would speed things up a lot. We got only one axe an' a bunch of grumblers."

"Well, I can add two more axes and another bunch of grumblers."

"Three axes might cut down on the mumbling and for sure make the time of construction shorter."

"Good," Rube said. "I'll get my herd set and see you first thing in the morning."

"By th' way," Jake said, "my cook is the best axe man I got. Suppose your cook could feed the bunch and free mine for th' axe work?"

"Sure, we could work that out. We'll bring up our kitchen when we come in th' morning." With that, Ruben Dunn put his utensils away and rode off to his outfit.

"Jake, I ain't lettin' no one pilfer through my kitchen," Cookie vowed. He was glad for the change of pace, even if it did mean a blister or two, but still balked at allowing a stranger access to his kitchen.

"Lay out th' common things that cook will need and hide the things you don't want him into. I'll have the boys kill a heifer for you an' we can hang it overnight to cool. Put on enough beans for both outfits. Rube has ten men he'll bring with him."

To make a long story short, we built a Slaughter Bridge over Buffalo Creek with the help of the Flying W outfit and got our herd over with only one cow falling off the bridge into the creek where she immediately got stuck.

The Flying W outfit couldn't get their herd of steers started over the bridge until I brought a calf and his mama down to lead the way. A steer will follow a cow following her bawling calf. The only thing the vaqueros had to do was to keep the steers from all trying to cross at once.

Crossing the bridge with the wagons was a little scary and very bumpy over that corduroy road, but we made it. Though it trembled and settled some, the bridge held and we left it in place for others to use.

Fording the Republican River was a snap by comparison, and we followed the river on the north side until we got to Medicine Creek. We followed that stream northeast to its headwaters and jumped over the divide to the Platte.

The new owner's range was up Birdwood Creek and his outfit met us where the Platte splits into two branches, the North and South Platte Rivers. From there, they drove straight to their range and we voted to forgo the seventy-mile ride to the city of Ogalalla and struck due south for Texas's golden shores. Already, the river margins were freezing overnight and thawing later and later the next day.

"Texas breezes are gentle zephyrs compared to this cursed north wind," Curly said through chattering teeth.

I shivered. "Sure glad we bought this winter outfit, but it don't do a lot of good north of Abilene."

"Did you ever see a land so empty?" Gus asked. "Not a house or track except th' buffalo trails."

"Lots of white bones and very few living buffalo." Jake sounded sad. "When I first came out here in '57, you could hardly see th' grass for the buffalo herd. They were thick as a trail herd bedded down for the night for as far as you could see without a break. Me an' my brother Zenas rode our horses ahead and shooed them out of th' way. When we looked behind the wagons, you couldn't see where we had been. The animals closed in behind us, sniffing our trail and fussing.

"Coyotes and wolves were abundant, always slinking through the herd looking for an easy dinner. Now, they follow the hide men and get all they can eat with no work. Such a waste, such a waste." He shook his head and rode away from us to be alone and remember.

It seemed the horses knew going south would mean warmer weather and we had little trouble keeping them together and on track. We angled a little east of due south to miss No Man's Land and picked up the Fort Dodge to Camp Supply road.

"This road's busier than an ant trail to molasses," Gus said. We couldn't squeeze in between supply wagons and had to stay to the upwind side of the train to avoid the dust. Our horse herd's dust drew the blessings of the drivers in several languages and best not be repeated here. "Hypocrites," Gus yelled back.

We stopped at a road ranch one morning to see if they had any eggs or milk. The insides stank something awful. "Smells like all they produce is bad whiskey and puke," I said.

A long-haired feller sitting reading a paper, his bare feet in the warm ashes of the stove, said, "I kin lick ever' dam Texian in th' house, an' I ain't even looked yit."

It was enough to convince us to leave . . . he wouldn't have had any eggs anyway.

The Camp Supply sutlery was run by Lee & Reynolds and we replenished our supplies there. The camp was all business; madams and card sharps deemed it too dangerous to set up business until the Indian question was settled. The Seventh Cavalry was there with the Custer brothers, George and Tom, in charge.

Everyone we talked to said going any farther south was next of kin to suicide, so we struck out due east in the Cherokee Strip for the Chisholm Trail where there would be enough traffic going south and we would be much safer.

"It would be safe anywhere in Indian Territory so long as you didn't drive right through a village. Them Injuns has hibernated for th' winter," I said

"You go ahead and take that direct route an' I'll go by the trail and beat you there," Tom said.

"How could that be, if I took th' shortcut?" I asked.

"B'cause you would be walkin' after th' second day when

those 'hibernating' Injuns took your horses, an' boots, an' coat," he replied.

"A goodly number of them would take your hair also," Pock added.

"I think I'll follow the chow wagon," Gus said, "an' maybe keep my hair in th' process."

Staying with the sure vittles and good company was fine with me. Thinking about it, I realized there was no place I particularly needed to be. Maybe if we got to the range before Christmas, me an' Gus would visit the home folks. He hadn't heard how his mother was getting along and I should see about the kids and Mom. The rest of the trip was quiet, but there was little difference in the weather. It was cold everywhere. We got to the range the last day of November and Jake put us right to work riding line and chasing off intruder cows. Our little roundup showed that there were plenty of new calves and would be a lot of branding and marking come spring.

On December 15th, 1871, me an' Gus rode south to Jack County. Homecoming was bittersweet. The Bell place was empty and Gus guessed his mom was still at our house, or had gone back to her people over east. There were four graves in our little cemetery. One was very small.

The kids mobbed us with a thousand questions until they filled their mouths with the hard candy I had bought at Jacksboro. Me an' Gus escaped to the dog trot and Mom gave both of us a big hug.

"Do you know where my mom went?" Gus asked.

Mom's voice caught and her chin quivered. "Your mom is here, Gus." She nodded toward the newer grave next to Gus's dad's. "She didn't live long after the beating. Oh, I do hope you found that man and gave him his just deserts."

Gus stared at the graves and I said, "He'll never beat another woman, Ma." That is all that was ever said about Ben Young.

I looked at Mom, "The little grave . . ."

"Would have been your youngest brother," she said and turned away.

Manley Ryman, who had stood aside and said nothing, stepped up and took my hand. "Good to have you and Gus back, Sut."

"Thank you, Manley, we are just visiting. Jake Meeker is expecting us back the first of the year." I didn't want him to think we were back to stay. It was clear to me that I would not make a dirt farmer so long as there were horses to ride and cattle on the range.

Baby Kay grabbed my hand with sticky fingers, "More candy, Sut-ter."

"No more candy for you, young lady," Mom said hastily, looking at me. "We will eat dinner in half an hour and you needn't spoil your appetite."

"But Ma—"

"Don't 'But Ma' me and go wash those hands."

Kay trotted off calling to the others, "Dinner's ready."

Mom sighed and turned toward the kitchen door, "No rest . . ."

I joined Gus at the graves. He wiped his eyes and blew his nose. "Ben Young died too easy, Sut. I wish I had him back."

"We could cut off his nose and other appendages, hang, burn, and shoot him an' he'd still get off easy," I said.

He looked at the rough crosses the children had put up and said, "Next time that travelin' stone carver comes, I'm gonna put up a nice stone for them."

"That's a good idea, Gus. I'll get one for Pa."

There were a lot of things more needful than stones for graves, but we had seen many unmarked mounds on the trail where someone had died and were hastily buried. Sometimes it would be marked by a rugged cross or maybe a name carved on a board that soon crumbled away, the grave most likely lost and forgotten as time passed. As I aged, it became more and more important to visit those graves of our forefathers and mothers just to be able to say, "This is where I came from, who I am. These were my people."

Manley had driven pegs into the inside of the log beam over the dogwalk and when the kids played outside, his old rifle was hanging there close and out of sight. Always, one of the adults—that now included Liz—found something they could do sitting on the porch—watching. Such was life in Jack County.

When we passed through Camp Supply, I bought a Model 1860 Spencer carbine. It was a breech-loading repeater that fired seven .56 caliber rimfire cartridges, loaded through the buttstock. It also came with ten tubes in a carrying case that held seven cartridges each. I also bought a box of the shells, and no, I'm not going to tell you what it cost or who I bought it from.

When I handed the rifle to Ma at the farm, she asked, "What is this, Sutter?"

"It's a Spencer repeating carbine, Ma—for you."

She hefted it and said, "It's considerable lighter than that old muzzleloader. I think I can aim it without having to rest the barrel on something."

"I'll teach you how to shoot it and reload it," I said. "You can fire it seven times without reloading."

"Really? How nice, thank you, Sutter."

I could tell she was a little taken aback, but after a time, she warmed to the idea of having her own gun and was very pleased. "Did you buy that for her protection from me?" Manley teased.

"It just might be, Manley Ryman," Ma replied. "At least it should give you pause before you raid the pie safe." It was just teasing, and I could tell she held a real affection for Manley. Next to my pa, Manley was the best thing for my mother. When she pulled her rocker out on the dogwalk to sew and watch the kids, the rifle went with her, but she was too short to hang the gun on Manley's pegs. Keeping the gun secure from kids was a problem.

"I've got a solution to that," Manley said. The next few evenings, he carved on a block of wood, shaping it to fit over the butt of the stock. When he was satisfied with the fit, he turned the block over and rounded the bottom side.

"What's he doin' with that block, Gus?" We were forking hay from the barn loft for the stock.

"I got an idea—"

"Well tell me."

"Ain't gonna," Gus declared.

"So you can say, 'I knowed it' whatever he does with it."

"No that's not what I'm thinkin' . . . tell you what; I'll write it down an' give it to Liz to keep until he shows what it is."

"You just get one guess, an' no changing it later on."

He wrote the note and gave it to Liz after supper. Ma read it and laughed, "I hardly think so, Gus."

That got me to thinking and next day, I said, "You know, Gus, this ought to be worth more than 'I told you so's.' "

"What you got in mind, Sut?"

"I don't know . . . how 'bout five or ten dollars for the winner?"

"I'm livin' in a cashless society right now, Sut, an' cash is just too precious to risk . . . I'll wager my new tooled holster an' belt agin' your new boots."

I have to admit I admired his holster and they would go real well with my new riding boots with the pointed toes and high heels. "It sounds good to me, Gus; I'll be lookin' good with that holster matchin' my boots."

"*One* of us will be lookin' good, an' t'other will be ragtag agin," he replied.

Manley was fiddling with Ma's rocking chair when we came in for supper. He had a leather strap cut out of the top of an old pair of shoes fastened to the outside of the left arm of the chair, and down on the runner he had attached his buttrest with the bottom curved to match the curve of the runner. Now, the carbine could stand fastened safely to the chair and within easy reach should Ma need it. It was a little inconvenient for her, but she was pleased with the result.

"Now, Mom, you're a regular Rocker Ranger," Liz said and laughed.

"I'm the only law in south Jacksboro," Ma declared, "and now I have the authority to enforce it." She looked very pleased with the gun and its mount.

"Mrs. Ranger, ma'am, would you read the note I gave Liz the other night?" Gus asked. He looked like he was the cat that swallowed the canary and I had a sinking feeling I would be hunting up my old brogans.

"Why, yes, Gus, it's right here in my apron." She pulled the paper out of her pocket, unfolded it, and read, "Mr. Ryman is making a buttrest to fasten to the rocking chair so the gun will be handy and safe."

I sat on the floor and pulled my new boots off for the last time. Gus just grinned. He knew better than to say anything.

The farm had done well while we were gone. Manley was a good farmer and provider for his family but there was no cash crop, so having saved most of my wages, me and Gus rode to Weatherford and bought something for each kid and Manley and Mom. We bought so much, I had to buy a packhorse to haul the stuff. We rode in after dark on Christmas Eve and found Mom, Manley, and Liz putting up a tree. Their eyes popped when they saw how much we put on and under the tree. It was a great day, with *two* roasted turkeys stuffed with dressing, yams, and giblet gravy. The airtight cans of green beans from Weatherford were an unexpected treat. "Almost like they came right from the garden," Manley declared. It was a struggle to eat with Baby Kay on my lap, but I didn't complain. She ate as much off my plate as hers and she declared green beans a finger food, but not the hot mashed yams. Each kid got an orange, but Ma confiscated the apples and made a big apple pie.

The weather turned warm and sunny, as it sometimes does around Christmas, and the kids played with their new toys outside on the sunny side of the dogwalk or in the yard. A few days later I was sitting with Ma watching the kids playing in the yard when a man emerged from the brush at the creek. He had a gun in his belt and as he approached, I stood in front of the mounted rifle. Ma put her arm on the armrest and unfastened the leather strap and held the gun in place. "It's loose, Sutter."

A man suddenly appearing like that was cause for concern, but not necessarily alarming. Guns were a common article of dress in those days. Halfway across the yard, he stopped and said, "There's a snake under that log, kids, run for the house." Amidst the general retreat, he pulled his gun and I grabbed up the Spencer and worked the lever. The man pointed his pistol at the base of the old log, but the gun continued to rise toward his intended target standing on the porch. His first shot burrowed into the floorboards at our feet. I aimed at his chest and fired, causing his second shot to go high as he fell. We buried him separated a little from the others with no name and no marker. Tuesday, Janurary 2, 1872, me an' Gus rode to the Rafter JM.

Texas was a sort of scent
And fragrance in my memory.
—Ramon Adams

Chapter 19
The Mustangs

1872

It sure was quiet around the ranch with most of the crew gone. Jake kept Cookie and Curly Treadaway and let the rest go until March first. He planned to get an earlier start on the trail drive if the cattle wintered well. There are always a lot of "ifs" in ranching and farming and to succeed at either, a man had to be flexible and always have an option in mind if his first plan didn't pan out.

We were mending fence around the small pasture when two Mexicans drove a couple dozen mustangs into the corral. One of them rode over to us and asked, "Where ees Meester Jake?"

I looked at the house just as Jake stepped out. "There he is now," I nodded toward him. "Sí." He grinned, touched the wide brim of his sombrero, prodded the horse with big roweled spurs, and rode to Jake. I heard Jake ask, "Do you ever walk, San?"

I couldn't hear his reply, but both men laughed. This man named Sanchez dismounted and they walked over to the corral to look at the horses while his partner took the horse and led him to the water trough.

"Sa-a-ay, that horse ain't gelded," Gus said.

"Mex's don't geld their horses, Gus."

"Bet that makes for int'restin' times."

"Maybe not as int'restin' as we're gonna have with those mustangs," I said.

"That looks like fun," Gus said with a grin.

"Fun, bumps, and bruises."

"S'long es they ain't no bones broke, I'll be happy," he replied.

We finished our job and went to look at the horses. They were a wooly-looking bunch, in their winter coats, and not at all used to a fence and people. We saw a lot of whites around their eyes and it wouldn't have taken much to cause a runaway. Jake and Sanchez talked low and what little we heard, they must have discussed the pros and cons of each horse in the corral. Jake wrote a figure down in his tally book for each horse and they went to the next horse.

"They're pricin' 'em one at a time like the Injuns do!" Gus whispered.

"Glad they ain't a hundred of 'em."

"Yeah, I bet Jake is, too," Gus said.

Curly had been out for a couple of days, hazing cows—ours and the neighbors'—back to their own ranges and he rode into the yard following his packhorse, who seemed more interested in finding home than Curly. We caught the horse and led him to the bunkhouse to unload Curly's gear. Gus slapped the horse's rump and he trotted over to the trough where his partner was drinking while Curly stripped the saddle off. "Looks like Jake got us some entertainment for our slack times."

"Just might slop over into our work times," I said.

"Yeah, them critters ain't been gelded yet," Gus said.

"Never heard of a gelded Mex horse," Curly replied. "They're 'bout as scarce as gelded Mexicans."

"The way they multiply, I don't see how there's *any* gelded ones," I said.

"You talkin 'bout Mexes or horses?" Curly asked.

Julio Sanchez was a *mesteñero.* He was short, rather on the smallish side, well muscled above the waist, and slightly bowed below. He had a rolling gait when he occasionally walked, his short strides almost flat-footed as if his feet hurt. His side-whiskers were long and his mustache short and there was a scar from his left eyebrow to his hairline. The little finger on his left hand was missing, probably the victim of an encounter between his lariat and saddle horn. He wore a charro jacket over his white frilled shirt and his black pantalones were tucked into his high-topped boots. His black sombrero had six woven silver galones encircling the crown. "There's a cup of beeswax inside his hat to ward off lightning," Curly said.

"Pancho," his partner, was dark with long black hair that he kept out of his eyes with a headband. Above tegua moccasins, he wore duck pants that had once been white, and his calico shirt was ragged. He seemed uncomfortable and stayed mounted, far away from us with his rifle across his lap. "Comanche doesn't trust us," Curly said.

Gus's eyes flew wide, "That's a Comanche?"

"As sure as I'm a Democrat," Curly replied. "Best horsemen on the plains."

"What's he doing with that Mexican?" I asked.

"New Mexes an' Pueblos have a peace treaty with the Comanches. That Injun is probably married to a Mexican woman, has a passel of kids, and lives in a *house*. He still kills Anglos and Mexicans who live in Texas and Mexico; they didn't make any treaty."

Sanchez worked mostly on the Llano Estacado and the country along the Pecos and Devils Rivers. Many of the wild herds had tamed horses gone wild in them, and Sanchez paid them special attention, for they were already trained and easy to return to their old habits. He sometimes returned the animal to their rightful owner; mostly, they became his to do with as he pleased. Many were glad to buy them.

"Breakin' horses just might become my specialty," I said.

"You are in for a disappointment if you think we're going t' break these horses th' customary way," Curly said. "You ain't seen horse breaking like Jake does it."

"They's only one way t' break a wild horse," Gus said.

"You notice somethin' different about Jake's horses when you rode them?" Curly asked.

I thought a moment, "You know, there *was* something different about them. Seems like they had a better attitude about their work."

"Yeah, they was willin' t' go on when they was wore out when our horses would quit," Gus added.

"Was it like they had more *spirit*?" Curly asked.

"Guess you could call it that," I said.

"Cowmen mostly break a horse by rough handling until the horse's spirit is broken," Curly said. "Injun breaking don't break his spirit, just teaches him to be used to men and do new things with his life. Funny thing; it don't take as long t' break him, an' seems like he takes to his new jobs quicker."

"Pa always liked gentle-broke horses, looked for them when he was buyin'," I said. "Said he could spend five minutes with a horse and tell how he was broke."

"Sure you can. You boys is about t' learn a lot about horse trainin'."

It didn't take long for our education to begin, for the next day we began working the horse herd. Jake studied the animals a while and pointed out the horse he wanted to Curly, who was mounted on his best cutting horse. He hazed the lineback buckskin into the adjacent corral and I slammed the gate shut.

Curly rode out of the corral and found a shady spot to tie his horse. "Get your ropes, boys, the fun is about to begin."

We all entered the corral on foot while the buckskin watched from the far side of the corral. Curly and Jake approached him from two sides and when the horse decided to change sides of the corral, two loops settled on his neck. Jake was closest to the snubbing post in the middle and wrapped his rope around it.

Curly could only dig his heels in while the horse bucked and fought the ropes. His breathing became more and more labored as the ropes tightened and soon he was standing still, his head hanging. The two men loosened their ropes and the horse began to breathe better. When it looked like he was ready to resume the struggle, the ropes tightened and forced him to calm down.

Jake looked at us and said, "Bring your rope here, Gus." He took the rope and showed Gus how to work the stubbing rope. When the loosened ropes allowed the horse to struggle some, Jake roped a front foot and gave it to me. We now had the horse pretty still, and Jake took a blanket he had hung over the gate and draped it over his arm. Slowly, very slowly, he approached the horse, grunting *hoh, hoh, hoh, hoh* with a deep voice. The horse stopped resisting the ropes and focused on this new creature making horse noises and strange motions and approaching him. Jake was close enough that the horse could have touched him and he sniffed the scent of the man. Jake breathed into his nostrils and waved the blanket before his face. Next, he rubbed the horse's nose and slipped a narrow rawhide halter on him that would pain the nerves in his nose and behind his ears when pulled. He had complete control of the animal without the aid of the ropes.

He went over every part of the horse with his fingers and hands, starting with face and neck, then striking the touched area with the blanket, always talking and making "horse" sounds. Finally, he struck the horse's back a number of times with the blanket, then laid it gently on his back. The horse bucked it off and Jake jerked the halter and replaced the blanket; after the third buck, the horse stood still and when he relaxed with the blanket on him, Jake leaned against his side. Hooking his elbows over the buckskin's back, he slowly applied his weight until the horse would not shy and resist. Eventually, he was able to mount the horse and he sat there a long time before urging the horse to move.

"He didn't buck, Gus," I whispered.

"Look how tame he is," he replied.

"That's the difference, isn't it? That horse was *tamed,* not *broke,*" I said.

I realized then and there that "broke" in the usual sense really meant the horse's spirit was broken and he would do as he was bid because he had no other choice. He still might resist—would buck—but the same rough handling that first broke him would bring him back into submission. I found that a tamed horse would do the same work as a broken horse, but with more enthusiasm and interest, abilities being the same. Too, a broken horse might with proper handling (which a good vaquero would practice) regain his spirit while retaining his taming. The argument about which method was better consumed many an evening around the campfire, the consensus being that time was a factor in determining which method was used.

Jake always chose to break horses when he had the time for blanket breaking, and it is the best method of taming a horse I know. Me and Gus learned a lot in the taming of those little mustangs and we both prefer that process.

Later on, when we were on our own, we would train horses for other people who appreciated gentle-broke horses. In fact, the bronco-busting method disappeared with the cattle drives and old-fashioned vaqueros. If they saw how we do it today, they would hoot an' holler at our "sissified" ways, then get on their "gentle-broke" horses and ride out to see how th' cows are doing. Only the really old-time cowman knew and appreciated the Indian gentle taming method.

★ ★ ★ ★ ★

A saddle seems to me
A more natural seat
Than a parlor chair.

—J. F. Dobie

CHAPTER 20
MESTEÑEROS

Jake was put out because we had only tamed two horses that day, yet our best day we only worked with three horses.

"That's partly because the days are so short," I said.

"Maybe so," Jake replied, "but we should do better. Somehow, Julio's horses take longer to tame. I don't know what he does to them."

Curly snorted and said, "He don't do enough, *that's* what he does."

"Well, I guess I prefer them like they are instead of being spoiled by the things some men do to them," Jake said. "Tomorrow, Sut and Gus will ride the horses we tamed today. Ride them morning and evening and teach them to neck rein and turn with knee pressure. Run them a little so they don't get restless in the corral. Orville will help me and Curly in the corral."

Cookie grinned. He much preferred working horses to cooking.

I grinned at Gus. There was nothing better than riding horses for fun. We had a good time that day, but the next day we had five horses t' ride and that soon turned into so many that we couldn't possibly ride them all in one day. Saturdays and Sundays they didn't tame horses and helped us ride the bunch. When a horse was well tamed, Jake would geld him and put him in the small pasture to heal up some. Me and Gus had the care of them and when they were healed enough, we began riding them again. We noticed their change in attitude.

We didn't ride the mares as much and after a time or two, turned the good ones into the big horse pasture with Jake's Morgan stud and sold the others at Jacksboro. The combination made some good cattle horses and Rafter JM horses were a popular breed with cattlemen.

"Think I've 'bout caught up on my sleep," Gus said one day at supper.

"Good, now just keep sleepin' an' store up some for th' drive next summer," Curly advised.

"Can't store up sleep," Gus said.

"Shore you can," Curly said. "How do you think we got along so well last year when you were nearly dead for not sleepin'? We was using up th' extra we had stored away in th' winter."

"Can't store up sleep," Gus insisted, but he didn't change his sleeping habits.

"We got more mares than I wanted and we need a few more horses," Jake said one night. "In a couple of days, I'll take Gus and Sut to the caprock and find a *mesteñero* with horses to sell. Curly and Orville will watch the place while we are gone."

Gus grinned like a possum picking blackberries. We spent the next day getting ready while Cookie put together food for our trip.

"Get us two mounts apiece from those new horses," Jake directed. He sent Curly with the light wagon to Jacksboro with a list of goods for trade. "Silver isn't near as valuable as flour and salt on the plains."

Curly returned with the wagon half loaded with trade goods, and me and Gus loaded the back end with our grub and bedrolls. There wasn't much light in the east when we saddled up and drove south. I lost the rock flip and drove the wagon, my horse saddled and tied to the tailgate. The Indians were holed up for the winter, but you could never count on that a hundred percent. It was good to be prepared for the worst and hope the donation of a wagonload of goods trumped chasing after horses, mules, and scalps.

We turned west on the old Fort Belknap track, then turned south at Dry Creek, not being interested in damyankee soldiers inquiring into our business. After crossing Rio Brazos, we aimed southwest until the cliffs of the caprock came into view, then we turned south and paralleled them looking for sign of horses and people. We began to see little herds of buffalo scattered about. Sometimes a solitary bull watched us go by.

The fifth day out I was driving again and as Jake rode by I called to him, "I've been watching that cloud of dust for a while and it's getting closer to us."

"Wondered when you were going t' see it," he said. "What do you make of it?"

"It's too scattered to be cavalry, so it's a herd of some kind—buffalo, horses, or cattle. I think they are being driven or chased."

"Right, Sut. I think it's time to park the wagon in the shade and see what comes by."

I turned off into a mesquite thicket and parked the wagon facing the supposed path of the runners. The mules were contented with crunching mesquite bean pods and I sat with my rifle across my knees. Gus and Jake were off to my right. It wasn't long before we saw a horse herd being chased by riders. Jake held up four fingers, indicating he saw four riders. That was a relief, we could probably handle four Comanches.

The rider nearest us was a small girl with long hair riding a grulla horse with a blanket saddle held in place by a surcingle that had loops knotted in it big enough for a toehold stirrup.

As we watched, the girl suddenly veered into a sorrel horse and, grasping its mane, slid smoothly onto its back. As she passed us, she threw a loop over his head and flipped two half hitches over the horse's nose. They veered away from the running herd and a young man, who turned out to be her brother, retrieved the grulla. They didn't look Indian.

"Where's she going?" Gus called to the boy in Spanish.

"She will return soon," he replied, but it was near three quarters of an hour before she returned on a winded and calmed horse.

The third rider proved to be the head of the family, Heliodoro Rede. "Senior Jake, ees good to see you ageen."

"Good to see you, Doro. Have you had any good luck with the horses?"

"Sí, wee have caught many good mustangs this year. You must come stay with us and see them."

"That we will, my friend. I do not need any horses, but you may have one or two I can't resist owning." Jake spoke in Spanish and that was the language of the camp while we were there. Me and Gus were getting better, but still had some trouble with the language.

Doro smiled and nodded to the youngest of the riders who turned and loped away to tell his mother they were having company

The family was from New Mexico Territory, come here to catch horses for trade. They were small people, probably endowed with a liberal helping of Indian blood. Doro had captured horses in this manner until he was too old and stove up. His wife, Paulina, had given up being a mesteñera to bear children.

The oldest son, Rubio, was fourteen. He had learned the craft, but outgrown it. He was the tallest in the family and quite heavyset, though not fat. His principal job was to tame the horses with a modified version of the blanket method that was more intense. He was not inclined to mistreat the animals and Doro would not let him. "You do have to get their attention and let them know how things are going to be," Rubio said. "But rarely is that necessary beyond the second lesson."

Zora was the twelve-year-old horse catcher. Her horse catching outfit was a tight-fitting *blusa* and loose duck pants cut off above the knees. She preferred to ride barefooted, but a pair of moccasins was tucked under her belt in case they were needed. She was pretty and petite, just beginning to fill out her feminine form, and me and Gus had a hard time keeping from staring at her. There were two younger children, Tio and Colita, both eager to learn the catcher's craft and capture horses like their big sister.

Zora rode the horse to the camp and gave him to Tio. Disappearing into the tent, she emerged with a skirt wrapped around her waist and began helping her mother with the meal.

We ate frijoles and goat stew with corn tortillas under the cool shade of the brush arbor in front of the tent. An olla of cool water, wrapped in burlap with a gourd dipper, hung from the rafters. The mealtime lasted three hours, the last two in a siesta under the arbor. I would have rested better under our wagon. I have often said that the siesta was good for your health, and I practice the custom whenever possible. The heat of the day had passed when people began to stir, and we wandered out to the corral to see the horses. They had caught the best from the herd and the foals in the bunch looked good. "We always pick the bunch with the best-looking stud," Doro said. "This one is the best we have seen this year. None are as good as my father found when I was young." He sighed. It stood to reason that without some infusion of new blood into the ranks of the wild horses that the quality of the animals would decrease.

"Those are good-looking Missouri mules you've caught," Jake observed.

"Sí, I think there are two matched pairs that have escaped from their owners," Doro replied. "They would be good for someone who only drove toward the rising sun." He chuckled.

"We travel mostly north and south, so they would do me no good," Jake replied with a smile.

I wondered if Doro would take the mules toward the *setting* sun to New Mexico Territory.

Jake said something low to Gus and he disappeared toward camp. I could see him up on our wagon and he handed a bag down to Zora, who whisked it away to her mother.

"That black colt looks good," Jake observed.

"All foals come with their mare," Doro replied, and I groaned, another darned mare. Jake commented on several other animals, but didn't make any offers. Gus didn't return to us and I found him sitting under the arbor with Zora. Gus had given her a ten-pound bag of flour and all the family was excited about having flour tortillas for supper.

The whole family went to bed at sunset except Zora, who took her father's old shotgun and headed for the corral. Some time in the night, Tio would replace her, then Doro would take the last third of the night watch. It might be that there were no horse thieves around, but it also might be that there were—red, white, or brown.

It was Jake's habit to move his bed from where he unrolled it into the brush after dark, and we slept under the wagon away from the arbor where someone was a big snorer. Gus usually has to get up in the night to relieve pressure on his bladder, and I didn't think anything of it when he left except that it was earlier than usual. The stars told me he had been gone a long time when he kicked me out of my warm spot. "You sick?" I muttered.

"Nah. Go to sleep," he whispered.

Just then, Zora walked by on her way to bed. "You been out there with—"

"Shut up an' go back to sleep," he hissed, and it wasn't a suggestion.

Thus began the period of our lives I call "The Courtship of Gus." It seems his attentions had awakened that latent drive in Zora and Gus encouraged her—until it scared him. By then it was too late to rein in her emotions and Gus became the object of her affections. The only thing that held her back was the need to keep their "relationship" secret from Rubio and her parents.

The horse trading was proceeding at a slow pace and the third night, Gus didn't get up and go after Zora.

"What'sa matter, ain't you gonna go see your sweetheart?" I asked.

"Shut up," Gus growled.

"Taught her to kiss, didn't you?"

"Shut—*up*!" he spat. He was quiet a few moments, then he whispered, "She wants to do things that would get me kilt." It was almost a plea for aid, and I very nearly lost it. I had a coughing fit to cover up my laughing. Gus punched my ribs so hard I lost my breath.

"What . . . you . . . want . . . me . . . t' do?" I grunted.

"Pay her some attention."

"O-o-o-oh no, I'm not gonna do that." Then after a moment, "You want *me* to git killed instead of you?"

"Ain't that what friends are for? Bible says, 'Greater love hath no man—' "

"I know what it says, but I ain't wastin' my life when all you got t' do is run away."

"Right into 'Pache arrers."

"Least you'd have a fightin' chance." I drifted off to sleep and only woke up when Zora coming off her watch kicked me hard in the ribs, thinking I was Gus—I hope. Gus woke up and stumbled off on his nightly trip. There was some kind of disturbance and in a few moments, he returned and crawled into bed.

"Try t' take my pants off, will you . . ." He muttered to himself.

Now being a year older than Gus, I might have *helped* some good-looking girl take my clothes off, but that's the difference between boys and mature men. Zora made life interesting the next few days. Doro suspended catching horses to deal with Jake and we broke the horses he had already bought.

The four kids came out and watched us. The three oldest helped us ride the tamed horses and we got on good until Gus got thrown and hurt his arm.

"It isn't broken," Jake said after feeling around on it, "but it probably is cracked. You'll have to keep it quiet for a while to let it heal."

And that's how sweetheart Zora became nurse Zora.

"Can't tell much difference b'tween th' two," Gus complained. But the sling on his arm limited any physical contact and he used that to good advantage. Paulina's attention kept stolen kisses to a minimum, and Zora had an unusual number of errands to run.

Jake paid Rubio to help us with the horses and we stayed there eight days, trading and taming the horses so we could drive them home. We had fifteen horses plus four good-looking colts with their mamas. The ninth morning we tied the horses in two rows, nose to tail, put the two youngest colts in the mostly empty wagon, and Gus drove the wagon ahead of the parade. Tio and Colita escorted us a little way while Doro, Rubio, and Zora prepared to go catch horses. Our trade goods allowed the mesteñeros to stay longer and gather an extra bunch of horses. It was a very good year for them.

★ ★ ★ ★ ★

Let him kiss me with the kisses of his mouth:
For thy love is better than wine.
—Song of Solomon 1:2

Chapter 21
The Goodnight-Loving Trail

If you don't count hard work and little sleep, the trip back to the Rafter JM was uneventful. Uneventful, that is until just before we got there and found a riderless horse with blood on his saddle.

"Now what is this all about?" Jake asked. "Do either of you recognize that brand?"

It was plain on the horse's hip, a long vertical line with a crook on the upper end like a walking stick.

"We never saw it before today," I said.

"Speak for yourself," Gus said and popped my shoulder with his fist.

"You know that brand, Gus?" Jake asked.

"No, but I can speak for myself," he replied, glaring at me.

"Well, it's for sure someone is in trouble somewhere," Jake said. "You two take these horses on into the ranch and water and corral them. Tell Curly and Orville where I am."

"It would be better if we could tell them where you're gonna be," I said.

"It would be even better if *I* knew where I was gonna be," Jake retorted. "Now get goin' and tell Curly I'm backtrackin' this horse's tracks, an' he'll find me at the end of them."

"Yes, sir," came twin replies, and we turned to our business while Jake took up the stray's reins and followed his meandering trail.

"Saw the whites o' your eyes, Sut," Gus said low across the

horses' backs.

"Say that to my face an' we'll see how red your nose blood is. Push 'em hard, Jake's gonna need some help an' soon." There was a lot of danger being alone out here, especially with your eyes on the ground most of the time tracking. I was torn between racing for Curly or turning around and catching up with Jake. To be prepared, I changed to a fresh horse. "Gus, there won't be enough daylight left for Curly to find Jake if we wait to tell him."

"He wouldn't know where to start, either," Gus said.

"I'm gonna go back and follow Jake."

"I think you should, Sut. I can handle these horses so long as they're tied to the wagon. We'll get to the ranch midafternoon."

"Well, I'm gone," I said, turning back to the place we found the horse. Gus made no reply, slapped the reins, and they trotted on. My horse loped away, glad to be free. An hour later, I was following Jake through the brush—and this is where a mystery began. I noticed almost immediately that my horse was following the trail of the other horses without my guidance. That constant Texas wind had to have blown any airborne scents away, so he must have taken his clues from the bushes we brushed through, and he followed without hesitation. I figured it must have been his former herd mate that he was following. The stray was a stranger to him.

Jake had a two-hour head start on me and I kept one eye on the trail and the other on the setting sun. I had to find him before dark. I kept urging hoss on and he seemed to understand. The sun had set and the light fading when a horse nickered somewhere in the brush, and my horse nickered a reply. He would have walked on and I had to rein him in. "It isn't polite to enter another camp without knocking," I whispered. "Hello the camp."

Jake replied, "Come on in, Sutter."

"Uh-oh, hoss, we're in trouble," I whispered. Jake's fire, tucked under a cedar bush, didn't look much larger than a candle. I could have passed it by twenty feet away and never seen or smelt it. The only thing it could offer Jake was light and a little warmth.

"You forgot your canteen." I handed it to him and untied my greasy sack lunch and pulled out the Bull Durham bag of ground coffee. We brewed it in our tin cups and chewed tough beef jerky. Jake didn't say anything about my coming after him, but I think he was glad. We picketed the horses and rolled up in blankets and slept.

At sunrise, he said, "I haven't found the rider, and the trail ends where the horse comes out of the creek."

I realized with a start that this was Cameron Creek, which flowed by the ranch house. "This might not be good, Jake."

"You're telling me? I would have ridden on in last night except for the fact that I might miss the rider of that horse or might ride into an ambush at the ranch. I could tell enough that the horse came upstream, probably looking for water."

Cameron was mostly dry, with a few water holes here and there. "What do you want to do now?" I asked.

"Since you're here, why don't you ride down the creek looking for that rider and I'll climb up on top, cut across Squaw Mountain, and come into the ranch from behind in case something funny is going on there. You won't have to track, only keep an eye out for where he might have come into the creek bottom."

"I can do that. I'll take the lost horse in case I need him or he tells me where to look," I said.

"Stay out of the trees as much as you can and keep your eyes moving."

"Yes, sir."

Without another word, he mounted up and climbed the north

bank of the creek, leaving me to saddle both horses. The banks of the creek were heavily timbered and in a lot of places the trees arched over so that we were going through a tunnel. The riderless horse took the lead, pulling us along and occasionally stopping to sniff the air or the ground, then moving on. I rode with my rifle ready, watching the sides of the creek. There were places where both banks were over my head sitting on hoss's back and we were all spooked. No one lingered there.

The hunting horse stopped at the west end of one of those long tunnels and lowered his head to a black spot on the rocks. He made soft sounds in his throat I had never heard a horse make. I got down for a closer look and realized that it was blood—lots of blood—between the rocks where it had coagulated. It looked like someone had stuck a hog there. "If that's human blood, ol' hoss, he didn't make it."

He stood there, head down, while I looked around for signs. There were none and there was no body. I searched for an hour and didn't find so much as a bent grass blade or disturbed gravel. Nothing. It was as though the body lifted up and floated away. *"If that's what happened, Lord, take me the same way when my time comes."*

I went back to the blood and studied it for the third time. The horse had quit making that sound and when I stooped to look closer, he licked my ear. "All right, ol' hoss we'll go," and he moved around the blood as I mounted and that horse walked beside us all the way to the ranch.

All was quiet at the ranch. Jake had ridden in to find the three working with the horses and peace elsewhere. They had not seen another soul for several days and then it was when Orville drove to Jacksboro for groceries. Cookie watched the place while I took the other three back to the blood. I rode the stranger's horse and he visited the blood again while we searched the grounds and wished two Ute vaqueros were here.

We gave up in time to get to the ranch by suppertime. Afterward, we sat around the veranda smoking and waiting for bedtime.

"Do you think it was Injuns, Sut?" I hate it when Gus starts a conversation in the middle like that.

"Injuns doin' what?"

"Killing that man that was riding the cane horse."

"Walking stick brand? You mean the *walking stick* branded horse?"

"Yeah."

"I don't know . . . they wouldn't haul a dead white body around, just taken his scalp and left him layin' there."

"Woulda mutilated his body so's he could go to hell," Curly said.

Gus stirred his coffee with his finger, then sucked it. "Seems like he just flew away, like the angels taken him."

"Swing low, sweet chariot," Cookie sang.

"It may be that he wasn't dead," Jake smoked that in his pipe for a couple of puffs, "but he couldn't have lived long enough to get him to the squaws."

"And th' squaws would have tortured him to death," Gus said.

Curly grunted. "Hah, they would have been mad at the warriors for bringing in a captive so near dead. They want healthy prisoners to torture. They last longer."

Jake relit his pipe. "Injun women are meaner than the men. I would much rather be killed and mutilated by warriors than have those women turned loose on me."

"They mutilate *before* you're dead, do they?"

"You know they do, Sut, and I'm gonna make damn sure I don't feel my mutilation, if it comes to that."

Me, too.

"But if that cane horse—"

"Walking stick."

"—could have smelled the way he came, why couldn't he sniff where his master went?" Gus asked.

"Good question, Gus. I suppose it is because he knew by the blood that the man was dead," Jake said.

"Horses are a lot smarter than we know, aren't they?"

Curly nodded, "And they ain't tellin' us all they know, either, Sut."

As long as we were in that country, we never found what happened to the rider of that horse. We watched, but never found hide, hair, or bone. Cookie had the most plausible answer with his sweet chariot theory.

In the year 1872 the tracks got to Dodge City, Kansas, and Joseph McCoy sent word that the cattle would be shipped from there. This meant blazing a new trail to Dodge. Cattle prices looked to be fair, but by some method, Jake found that the prices were better in New Mexico Territory where fewer cattle were available. The trick would be to get there with your herd. Somewhere—anywhere—along the Goodnight-Loving Trail, the herd would likely be taken over by Comanches. With luck, you could keep your scalp, but you would have to walk home.

Given all these advantages, Jake Meeker could not ignore the opportunity. Thus, early in January he put out the word to his customary crew that the drive would begin early. He immediately began to buy up cattle and we busied ourselves driving them to the ranch and applying a road brand. We would no sooner get the branding done on one bunch than someone would drive in another fifty or one hundred head for the brand. We were almost finished by the middle of March.

"We won't have as much to do today," I said at breakfast. "I branded that last fifty in my sleep last night."

Gus growled, "I know. You kept callin' for a hot iron all night, even though I always had one ready. You sure are impatient."

"Business is business."

"From now on, get someone else to heat your dreamin' irons an' don't be botherin' me."

The crew wandered in the next week or so, one or two at a time. Thomas Stepp and Pock came in one day with a hundred head. We woke one morning to find Otha Huie in his bunk.

Gus grinned and kicked his bunk, "Thought I was dreamin' when I heard your snore."

"You couldn't have heard my snore over the sawmills already going," O retorted. "It got so dark coming in that I would have passed the ranch if I hadn't heard the ungodly noise from this bunkhouse. 'That's ol' Tom Stepp or I'm not Jed Huie's son,' I told my hoss. 'And danged if it ain't that Curly joinin' in on th' chorus! Hoss, we're home.' Shore 'nough that snorin' led me right to the door."

Two days later, we were resting on the porch when Red Stark, Al Crow, and a man named Ep Ross drove two hundred head of T bar T three year olds into the yard. The T bar wasn't making a drive this year and sold part of their herd to Jake. Al, Red, and Ep were to go with us and Uno and Dos would stay and watch the ranch. Jake didn't want to expose them to the hostility of the Comanche warriors.

We hadn't met Ep Ross before. He had not made last year's T bar T drive north. I guessed by looking at him that he was around twenty years old. His hair was sandy, long, and stringy. He was taller than Pock but shorter than Al and skinnier than both. His shirtsleeves ending above his wrist bone made his hands look extra large. He had a firm grip, and his friendly grin showed that he had donated a tooth to a calf's hoof. If there was one thing that was worth remarking about him, it was his special care of his outfit. His saddle was in top shape and he cleaned his guns every night after his daily target practice. He had a thirty-foot hair rope and showed his skill with it when we rode into the big pasture and picked out three strings of horses for the three new men.

He wouldn't tell us his whole name, only said his grandpa as head of the tribe had given him a Bible name. Red said the only name his Biblical research could come up with was Ephesians. Ep was a good hand and fit right into the outfit.

Gus looked at the T bar T steers and groaned, "Here we go again. When is that Jake gonna say 'enough'?"

"That puts us to twenty-four hundred twos and threes," Curly said.

"You're not counting those mossy horned sea lions as cattle, are you?" Pock asked.

Tom looked up from his whittling, "Where did those things come from? I thought Shanghai Pierce had a monopoly on them."

"They were on loan to someone south of Fort Worth an' he got tired of their shenanigans an' sold them to Jake when he heard Jake was going west this year," Curly said. That was just a tale. We all knew Jake would not buy cattle without a clear bill of sale. Still, how those steers got from the coast to the heart of Texas was curious.

When we started the first of April, 1873, we had 2,350 twos and threes, and fifty of those sea lions four to six years old. They naturally assumed command of the herd.

We camped on Briar Creek after that customary first day's hard drive. O and Ep rode out to spell me and Gus while we ate, and it was then that five men rode out of the brush and into the cavyyard, shooting and scaring them into a run.

"I saw Otha fall!" Cookie yelled, and we all scrambled for our horses.

"Ep's staying with 'em," Gus yelled and whipped his horse into a gallop. Ep was laying low on his horse and flying for the lead horses to turn them and the thieves were shooting at him from across the herd. In a sudden move, Ep sat straight up, and fired three quick shots at the lead thief who slumped forward, then fell from his horse.

Jake, with Pock and Tom, divided the outlaws' attentions and there was a running fight for a few moments. Two more outlaws fell and a fourth man was unseated when his horse fell. The fight was over and all left to do was to stop the run.

Me and Gus got them turned and after a short mill, they spread and rested, catching their breath. Curly rode close and started to dismount, "Blood on my saddle . . ." He slumped to the ground and we rushed to him.

"Where are you hit, Curly?" I asked, but he didn't hear.

"Is he gone?" Gus whispered.

I laid him out and that is when we saw that the inside of his left pants leg was soaked with blood from above his knee. It ran out of his boot top. A bullet had nicked the artery when it passed through his thigh and imbedded in the tough stirrup skirt. He didn't know he was bleeding to death as he rode.

Jake and the others rode up, Otha pale and with his shirttail wrapped around his arm. It's a picture I will always carry with me, nine men standing around their fallen companion, bare heads bowed and more than one with tears stinging his eyes.

"Tom, would you go get the hoodlum wagon?" Jake quietly asked.

Tom nodded and rode for the wagon, wiping his face with his bandanna.

I suddenly realized I had an urgent need to relieve myself and barely made it to the brush.

Presently, Tom drove up with the emptied wagon and we unrolled Curly's bedroll for the last time. Someone handed Jake the possibles bag and we gently laid Curly on his bed. Six of us laid him out in the wagon, and Tom drove slowly back to camp with Curly's horse tied to the tailgate and the prisoner walking behind.

Me an' Gus stayed with the cavyyard. "Did you see what that feller looked like?" I asked Gus.

"Looked like a damned horse thief and murderer to me. Needs hangin'."

"I'm pretty sure I saw him in Jacksboro a while back."

Gus didn't hear what I said. "Real nice t' know all horse thiefs ain't red, ain't it?"

"Gus, you're not listenin' to me."

"What you want, Sut, I'm still bein' mad."

"That prisoner an' a couple other of them guys was from Jacksboro."

"Shoulda shot them th' day they showed up."

Even as close as Jacksboro was, it would take too long to carry Curly back there, so the boys dug a grave on the top of a little hill not far from the camp. They were waiting for us when we drove the cavy in for the night. All of us gathered there with Curly laid beside the grave. We all passed by and said our "good-byes" and Jake read some scripture about the resurrection. Each of us took turns with the shovel after we had lowered the body into the grave. It was a strange and hard thing for me to do. I'm not ashamed to say I cried.

The crew caught their night horses and me an' Gus moved the cavy away after we ate.

"Sa-ay," Gus said, "I didn't see that prisoner anywhere."

It was the first time I had thought about him. "Me neither, they might have put him to stretchin' hemp early and leavin' us out of it like they did at Johnny Jump's grave."

"When do you ever think we're gonna become men?" Gus asked.

"If bein' a man means I can hang someone, I don't want to be one. Don' know, but it's probably best this way."

"Prob'bly so, but I would have gotten some satisfaction from seein' him dance."

"Me, too," I said. "We can look around and find him if you want to. Might be just about as satisfying." We found him hanging from a cottonwood and I had to stop Gus from shooting him. We threw rocks at the body and that was almost as satisfying.

(Sutter failed to mention the other three thieves killed in the incident. Ed.)

We counted the horses and found that the lone thief who got away had taken twenty-one horses with him. With such a head start, going after him was useless.

Our path took us southwest. After we crossed the Colorado, the tanks were numerous and held adequate water, but they got more scarce as we approached Big Spring. We stopped near the spring creek and let the cattle rest a couple of days and get as much as they could out of the grazing. We were resting after supper with Al and Tom on first watch at the herd and Ep with the horses.

"Grass just has a hint of green, not much for a cow to eat," Gus said.

"But he has plenty of water," Pock added.

"Those winter-starved Injun ponies won't be ready to raid for another month," Jake said. "We shouldn't have trouble with them on this trip. Herds that follow the Goodnight-Loving in June will be lucky to get through without Comanche-Kioway visitations."

"One 'visitation' I could live without," I said.

Jake nodded, "For sure you could die with it, Sut. We still need to be very alert out here. Indians could be about and we know all horse and cattle thieves are not red." When the herd had two full days of rest, he called us together after supper.

"We're going to water the herd tomorrow morning, then get them strung out for Horsehead Crossing on the Pecos. If we were on the Goodnight-Loving, we would have a couple of watering places in the next eighty miles. But we are north of the trail and I'm not depending on finding water before Castle Mountain, some seventy-five miles from here. Sut, you and Gus be sure Cookie's barrels are full of water and all of us will leave the spring with full canteens.

"We'll drive the herd late and stop when the moon sets. I expect the cattle will begin to suffer the second day if we don't find water, and we will drive them all night and most of the next day without stopping. We'll aim for the middle of Castle Mountain where there is a gap and a spring at the west end of it. If we let the herd string out before the gap, it will be easier to handle them at the water. Take care of your horses. It's going to be a rough trip."

We had a couple of dry drives last year on the way to Ogalalla, and I didn't like them at all. This posed to be the driest, and I hardly slept a wink thinking about all the things that could go wrong and all the things we needed to get ready. Gus didn't do much better.

Watering the cavyyard was early and we threw them out on Cookie's wagon tracks. The sun was on the downhill side of noon when we caught up with Cookie. He was parked on the opposite bank of a draw that had several pools in it. Later on, someone told us it was called Mustang Draw.

"Danged if he ain't found water, Gus," I called, "how 'bout that?" We watered the horses and drove them across the draw downwind of the wagon. Gus turned and rode for the wagon and a plate. When he returned, I asked, "Ever think about your partner? He might of needed food more'n you."

"Brung you a biscuit to give you strength to stagger in on." He tossed me a biscuit, staying well out of the range of my quirt and rode on.

"Smart aleck. Did you check the barrels?"

"Did this morning," faded with the wind and distance.

Jake still anticipated a dry run and we drove on until sunset and made a dry camp.

The next day we crossed two dry draws and would have made another dry camp if Cookie's mules hadn't smelled water and detoured a couple miles south to a draw with a couple of pools.

Cookie saw me peeking into one of the water barrels and said, "Don't add any water to those barrels, it's gyppy."

Later, Pock gave his opinion of the water, "Might be a little gyppy, but not enough to oil your casters." Some time in the night, he changed his mind.

This was the second time we had found water where we didn't expect any but Jake figgered we still had forty or fifty miles to Castle Gap. There were still some hard miles to go.

Some secrets of equine senses
Have not been found out by man.
I think that wild horses
Have more secrets than gentle ones.
—J. F. Dobie

CHAPTER 22
AN APACHE VISIT

We paralleled Johnson Draw on the south side, one or the other of us checking to see if there was any water in it, but there wasn't. Where the draw turned west, we turned a little more south and trudged on in the alkie dust. Toward evening, we came to some small tanks, mostly drying and alkali. Cookie picked the best-looking one to camp by, but we couldn't drink it.

We were finishing supper when this feller hales th' camp from th' brush. He's speakin' Spanish an' Jake calls him in. Well, sir, in rides this feller on a mustang mare. You can bet that causes a stir on th' picket line. Even geldings' got feelin's. Cookie's layin' out a cup an' slappin' steak an' beans on a plate.

It took us a while to see it, but this feller's a youngster, maybe fourteen or fifteen. He's wearin' a rough suit of buckskin, turned black with wear. A strung bow an' arrow lays across his lap. His red hair hangs ragged to his shoulder blades, tied back with a dirty red sash. At his sight, two o' th' boys fades into th' brush an' me an' Gus stands up, plates in one hand an' empty hand near our gun hip.

Jake stands up an' says, "Light down, friend, an' have a cup with us."

"Gracias," he says an' gits down *on th' mare's right side.* He drops th' rein an' that little mare stands right there th' whole time. Jake don't offer t' picket th' horse, knows th' commotion that'd cause. "Our horses aren't used to a mare in camp," he says right easy an' sits down.

Cookie sidles up an' hands th' man his plate an' a cup of coffee. This feller cross-legs on th' ground, bow an' plate in his lap.

"I'm Jake Meeker an' this is Cookie, Gus, an' Sut." He waves his hand at us an' frowns us t' sit.

"My name is Rojo Pelo," he says through a bite of steak. He eats slow an' thoughtful-like, seemin' t' like coffee th' most. Cookie refills his cup, sumthin' he don't do fer us. Gus grunts an' glares at him.

This Rojo Pelo finishes eatin' an' says polite as a gen'leman in th' parlor, "Thank you." "Knows American, too." Gus cocked his head sideways, "Seems t' have a German accent, don't he?" he whispered.

"German accent? He ain't said ten words an' yo're hearin' accents?" I whispered back.

"Yuh know anythin' 'bout th' trail t' Horsehead?" Jake was always about business.

"Tanks are drying up but you should have enough water to get you to the river. Rio Pecos was swimming, but passable three—maybe four days ago," he says in Spanish. "Big Comanche party crossed going southwest, to Mexico, likely."

He spoke slow, choosing the words like he hadn't used the language in a while.

Gus punched my ribs, "He *is* German," he hissed.

"Water's fairly plentiful goin' northeast," Jake offered. It ain't perlite to ask personal questions like "Where you goin'?"

"Your horses are ganted," this Rojo Pelo said.

"We lost half our remuda to thieves and can't afford to let these left graze at night or we would be hoofing it to New Mexico Territory," Jake answered. He didn't mention that we had a runnin' fight with th' thieves an' that they was mostly whites; that we had buried Curly Treadaway an' left one o' th' thieves swingin' from a cottonwood limb.

This feller scratches in the dirt with a stick a minute and says, "I have some horses that could help you if we could make a trade or two."

"I'd be interested, for sure," Jake replied.

Act too interested an' it'll cost yuh more.

"I need a gun and a pistol with ammunition and a bowie knife," Rojo Pelo says.

Jake Meeker gives that some thought, rubbing his stubbly chin an' knowin' all th' time we've got poor Curly's outfit right down to his saddle an' extra shirts. "We can scratch around an' maybe come up with something," he allows.

"I will bring my horses to your camp when you stop after the morning march," this feller says, and he leans forward and lifts himself up just with his crossed legs.

"Yuh see that, Gus, can *you* do that?"

The feller takes his plate to the wreck pan. Danged if Cookie don't hand him another steak rolled up in a newspaper. You'd think they growed on trees, and us with only a half dozen heifers in th' lot t' git us to summer.

Pelo speaks to his horse and the little mare perks up.

"Bet he can mount that horse from either side," Gus Bell allowed.

"How's come?"

"He's talkin' German to him."

Shore 'nuf that feller mounts from th' left and rides slow upwind of th' picket line. I thought for a minute those geldin's was gonna uproot th' mesquites they was tied to. "Done that a-purpose," Gus growled. The other hands eased back into the firelight.

"Now ain't that spookier'n a horse on loco weed?" one of them asked.

"Think I'll bed down up by th' picket line," I said.

"You could have solid men sleepin' head t' toe around that

remuda an' he'll still git away with them horses," Jake said, "an' leave you sleepin' like a baby."

Even so, he put an extra man on th' night herd crews and kept his night horse tied to a chuck wagon wheel. You can bet there was some sleepy discontent amongst th' crew. No one complained about breakin' th' monotony of a long hot cattle drive, though.

Twice th' next morning I nearly fell off my horse when he took after a stray while I was dozing. Sometimes I think he does it a-purpose. "One of us has t' stay awake, ol boy, an' you have t' see where you's goin'. You kin sleep on th' picket line while I'm ridin' herd." He shook his head an' made his ears flop like a mule's. "I *knowed* there was some jackass in yore lineage sommers." Even rubbin' tobacco juice in my eyes didn't help.

Our shadows had tucked up underfoot when we saw th' smoke of Cookie's fire an' before we got there, we run on to this Pelo feller. He had seven horses b'sides his mare tied to bushes. We noted that only two of them had th' same brand.

"That grulla come from th' Lazy C outfit up on Salt Fork," Pock said.

"Huh," Tom said, "I rode that dun for th' Half Moon Xes."

Jake looked at Pelo, expectin' an answer.

"I took these from the Apaches because they were stolen and still had their shoes. They will be useful to you and you can return them to their owners when your drive is over."

"What's t' keep us from just takin' them an' not payin' a thing?" Gus muttered.

"Tell you what, Gus, you take th' first one an' we'll git th' rest," Tom answered.

Cookie throwed his hat up an' first crew rode in to eat. Jake an' th' Injun scooched up under a bush an' palavered.

Pelo insisted on dealing one horse at a time an' by th' time they were through, he had 'most all of poor ol' Curly's outfit, including his extra shirts. We rode in to eat and that feller rode with us. First thing he did was strip off his buckskin outfit. The shirt kept th' same shape as it did when he wore it. "Coulda been bulletproof." Gus chuckled.

There he stood, knee-high moccasins an' breechclout. He pulled one of those white shirts on and wrapped the gun belt around his waist—cinched to th' last notch—and stuck th' bowie sheath under the belt.

" 'Cept fer his hair, here stands a 'Pache Warrior," Jake observed.

"My father was Elkhorn, the Mescalero chief, and my mother was Little Bird," Pelo said.

"Who were your white folks?" Jake asked.

"I do not remember them, they are dead." The Injun in him said it without a sign of emotion.

"Injuns don't talk about dead folk," I whispered to Gus.

He elbowed me in th' ribs. "I knowed that."

"You knowed that like you knowed Adam."

The Injun inspected his firearms and noted Curly's name carved into the rifle stock. "White men would hang me if they found me with this gun. I would trade anyone for one without a name." He spoke Spanish, seemed more comfortable with it.

"I knew Curly and his family well," Tom said. He went to his horse and pulled his rifle out of its boot. "I will trade you my no-name rifle for it." The guns were just alike and both traders seemed satisfied. When we got back home, Tom gave that gun to Curly's middle boy. He made points with one of Curly's girls and squired her for some time—until he run out of jingle. Preached many a sermon about fickle greedy women after that.

"I knowed 'bout fire 'thout gettin' burned ever' time I built one." I mentioned it to him only once. Seems th' thought was painful for his heart and for my shoulder an' ribs.

Rojo Pelo ate with us an' that Cookie wrapped up another

steak for his greasy sack.

"Hope I done read those papers," Gus said loud enough for Cookie t' hear.

"Yer 'readin' only extends to pictures in ads for women's union suits an' corsets an' I wrapped that grub in th' front pages that's only got words an' which you never look at," Cookie retorted, waving his iron poker in a threatening manner.

"I'm gonna throw that poker in th' next river we cross," Gus muttered.

"Won't do no good, th' nex' river's Rio Pecos an' th' rod'd float just like Moses's rod in th' Nile."

"Didn' throw his rod in th' Nile. That's heresy."

"Well, he coulda," I retorted. Who made *him* a Moses expert, anyway.

We found Rojo Pelo's camp and discovered he kept two horses, one we didn't ever see.

"Probably his best horse, and probably a racer," O said.

"Where's he goin' and why he's out here so far from 'Pacheland," Gus wondered.

"Stole horses from the Mescaleros, traveling by hisself and heading north toward the Llano—bet he's fixin' to become a Comanche or Kioway," Pock said.

"Bet his folks lived among those Germans living around San Antonio an' Fredericksburg," Ep said. "Make good beer down thataway."

I asked, "What do you know about that country, Ep?"

"Well, I was born in a covered wagon in Austin, New Braunfels, and San Antone. We was movin' at th' time. Ma spoke Louisiana Cajun an' Pa spoke German. They couldn't talk to each other for a long time, but Ma said their feelin's for each other was plain. Pa started for Texas an' two days later, Ma caught up with him in a buggy with her dowry trunk tied on behind. Her brothers was followin' her, set on 'defending her honor' an' neuterin' Pa. 'Course, Pa objected an' convinced th' boys t' leave his *testiculos* alone. Uncle Ollie decided to stay with us, and Uncle Brisco returned to Acadia. We settled at Uvalde where Uncle Ollie bought a saloon and Pa owned a ranch. I grew up poppin' brush and speaking Cajun, German, Mexican, and American with just a little Lipan Apache thrown in."

Tom snorted. "Thought I seen sign of brush poppin' on you."

"More fun than a room full of rattlers, you should try it some time," Ep said.

"We git all th' poppin' right here without goin' huntin' for it," I said.

"Me, too, Sut," Ep agreed.

The next day we made one of the driest drives I have ever made. We drove those steers and horses thirty hours straight with empty water barrels and canteens. We joined the Goodnight Trail just before we got to Castle Gap, and Jake signaled us to take the horses ahead. They smelled water as soon as we entered the canyon. Cookie had set up near an old rock Butterfield station and helped us keep the horses from foundering at the log water trough.

The last horses were still drinking when the first steers pushed in and began to drink. They were so strung out that we didn't have much trouble keeping the process moving. The spring couldn't quite keep up with the demand and some of the cows licked the bottom of the trough until enough had flowed in. The drags were the most pitiful example of a cow you could imagine. They revived with the water, but we found one dead the next morning. We left eight dead scattered along our trail. The next day was a rest day, and that water trough never did overflow the whole time we were there.

Jake and me and Gus rode the fifteen miles to Horsehead Crossing to check out the river. The road was lined with the bones and scraps of dried hide of cattle and horses that didn't make it. There are no trees lining the river and we rode right up on its sheer banks almost before we knew it. The crossing was a little ways downstream and it was the only place in a long ways they could safely get to the water.

"Look at that row of horse heads," Gus exclaimed. "There must be a hundred."

"Someone spent some time gatherin' them up," Jake observed. "Don't let your horse drink too much at a time. I imagine that most of these bones were from animals who didn't get here or drank too much when they did."

I tasted the water and it was so slick I almost swallowed it before I could spit it out. "Yuck, that's awful."

Jake and Gus were grinning at me. "You should chew it a little before swallowing," Gus said.

Jake chuckled. "Makes you want to be sure the barrels are full of that spring water before we leave the gap, don't it?"

"There's no trail north on the west side of the river, so if the trail goes up the east side, why are we coming to the crossing?" I asked.

"They tell me this is the only place the cattle can get to the water for a long ways either way," Jake said.

There were no signs of Indians or others crossing or watering here, which was a relief. We turned to go and caught sight of a grave. "Huh," Gus said, "there's another one beside it . . . and another and another . . . there's eleven graves here!"

"Mr. Goodnight told me only one of them died from natural causes or water starvation; the rest died in gunfights," Jake said. "Don't make sense, does it?

"The advantages of traveling on the east side of the Pecos is that there are no tributaries coming from the east, the grass is more plentiful, and the Apaches are on the west side. The river is the boundary line between Apache and Comanche, though either will cross the river if the enticement is good enough. Comanches don't come this far west, as a rule."

Some of those crossings were good, like the Salt Crossing north of Horsehead, and some were so narrow and steep we had to water the cows two at a time. They had to back out of them after getting a drink.

"Look at that cow backing up out of that cut," I said to Gus.

Gus grinned. "Didn't know they could do that, did you?"

"When did you ever see them goin' up a hill back'ards?"

"By going back'ards, his toes dig in and he has better traction," O said. "They only learns it when they has to, but then they never forgets. I've seen 'em back into a rock hollow or thicket an' like a 'coon in a log stand or lie there watchin' us lookin' for them."

We stayed on the west side of the river until Pope's Crossing just south of the state line, where there was a freshwater spring on the east side. We traveled north on the west side to get fresher water from the rivers flowing out of the Guadalupe Mountains, then crossed back to the east side near where Eddy is now to put the river between us and the Mescalero Apaches.

"These Fort Sumner folks need to get the entertainment committee Abilene has to set things up here for them," Gus griped.

"Don't get near the traffic here that Abilene gets," Ep observed.

Al looked up, "Does more traffic get more entertainment or does more entertainment get more traffic?"

Red lifted his sombrero off his nose, "You done stopped cowboyin' and started 'whatif'n' agin, Al. I keep tellin' you if the boss gets wind of that, you're a goner."

"Feller can wear two hats if he wants to," Al said.

"Just so's you keep the cowboyin' hat on top," O said.

"You jist cain't mix 'em when you're forkin' a horse. Let the horse do th' philosifyin' an' you keep yore mind on th' job," Tom advised.

"Can't do that if the horse is smarter than th' rider," Al said, looking at the recumbent Red.

Red raised his hat and cocked one eye at Al. "Was you talkin' at me, or was that just a crow fussin'?"

It took Jake a couple of days to get the cattle sale finished, then he had us pick out three horses to keep from our string and sold the rest of the cavyyard. "No use trying to take the whole herd back and lose them to some bunch of Indians—red or white.

"We don't have any choice but to go back the way we came, but we can take our time. I hear that the entertainment isn't too good around here, so we will stop at a couple of places going home that might have better prospects."

"Well, there ain't a couple of places, there's only that mud town they call Roswell with its barrel and plank bar in th' back o' th' mercantile," said Gus.

"Could be nothing," I said. "Could be they ran out of beer an' they're saving the whiskey for sick folks."

"Who wants to have a drink with old women starin' an' shakin' their fingers an' talkin' 'bout us bein' too young t' drink?"

"You *are* too young to be drinking, Gus, and I'm here to see that you don't do much of it," Tom said. "One or two beers is plenty for you half-pints, and there won't be any of the hard stuff for you."

"We work just as hard as you do and we deserve th' same privileges," Gus declared.

That conversation continued for the next twenty miles with both sides standing firm on their convictions and the rest of us trying to stay out of the sound of battle.

After the nooning, when the same conversation started up as soon as we were in the saddle, Pock drew his gun and said, "If I hear one more word about babes having or not having the right to drink, I'll shoot the one that starts it." It was quiet for a long time and conversations wandered off to other subjects.

Two days later, we camped on the Rio Hondo a mile above Roswell Town. "We'll stay a couple of days and rest up the horses," Jake said after supper.

Red stood and stretched, "Well, that's settled, I think I'll wander in an' see if the mercantile is still open."

"I mind I'll go with you, and see if I can keep you out of trouble," Al said.

"And who's gonna keep *you* outa trouble?" O asked. "I notice a new mud house goin' up down there an' I can't tell if it's a jail or saloon. Either one would be trouble for you two. Guess I'll have to tag along an' watch out for you."

There followed a general exodus that soon left the camp empty save for me and Gus and Cookie.

"Damned if I'm gonna let some half-cocked cowboy keep me from having my share of the fun," Gus declared.

"Who's gonna watch th' horses?" I asked.

"You can, I'm gone." He mounted and loped off to town.

I watched him go for a moment, then mounted up and turned to check the horses. We had them hobbled and picketed around the camp. They all were secure and contented to graze on the abundant grass. Back at the wagon, I started to dismount and Cookie said, "Whoa there, Sut, get yourself on down there and check Gus's hobbles. He's been there just long enough to get hisself into something he can't back out of. I'll watch the horses for a bottle—or two—of beer, now git."

And I got. The Rafter JM horses were all tied up at the front of the new building. A sign above the door read FIRST CHANCE SALOON and down below in smaller letters, & JAIL. Inside, the crew was all lined up at a regular bar along the right wall. In the back of the room was an iron bar cell with one occupant who was obviously very drunk.

Right in the middle of the bar stood Gus on a chair.

"Hey, look who's here," Pock hollered. "Pull up a chair—"

"Ain't gonna stand—" before I could finish Pock and Red lifted me up and Jake slid a chair under my feet.

Gus looked at me with foam on his upper lip and said, "Hey Sut, we're th' tallest fellers at the bar."

"How many beers have you had?"

"Jus' this one, an' I ain't gettin' drunk. How you like the picture?" He nodded toward a large picture hanging behind the bar. It depicted a garden with two very naked people in the foreground. "Adam and Eve, Sut, ain't it great?"

I looked at the picture and shook my head. Barkeep handed me a mug of beer.

"What's th' matter, Sut, you don't like the picture?"

"I like the picture, but it ain't Adam and Eve."

"Sure it is, says so on th' bottom." He indicated a brass plate on the bottom of the frame that declared "Adam and Eve in the Garden."

"Don't care what it says, that ain't Adam or Eve."

"Sure it is," Tom said at my elbow.

"What makes you think it isn't?" Pock asked from Gus's side

"They got navels."

"Wha-a-at? Ever'one got navels!" Gus declared.

"Adam an' Eve didn't."

"Why do you say that?" Tom asked.

" 'cause God made them."

"My ma said we got navels b'cause when God finished makin' us, he punched each one of us in th' stomach with his finger an' said, 'You're done an' you're done, an you're done.' "

"She said that b'cause she didn't want to tell you that the navel was where she fed the baby when it was in her stomach."

"Why don't Adam an' Eve have navels?"

"They were not ever inside a mother's stomach and didn't need a navel."

"He may have something there," O said from down the bar. "Wasn't any need for them to have a navel."

"Adam's got nipples an' he doesn't need them, does he?" Al asked.

"Useless as the tits . . ." Red drank from his mug, ". . . on a boar hog."

"We'd look funny without 'em," Jake said.

"Yeah, and just as queer without a navel," Gus declared. I noticed his glass wasn't going down much and that was good. If he just sipped, he wouldn't get drunk. I took a sip and didn't like the taste. It was also too warm.

"They was only two people in th' world without navels an' it was Adam and Eve. It was the mark that God gave to show that he made them," I said.

O looked at the picture, "Kind of like they was mavericks, ain't it?"

Pock set his mug down with a bang, "They was God's mavericks. Barkeep, we has met and determined that your picture is a fake. Therefore, if you please, put the word 'NOT' before that brass plate."

"Gentlemen," he said, "I perceive your knowledge is on a firm theo-logical foundation, and as soon as it is convenient, I will comply with your request."

(It might be noted here that the picture and its brass plate was unchanged some years later when we happened by. It sparked another heated discussion, which resulted in me and Gus retiring to another saloon down the street that had a less controversial nude behind the bar.)

Conversation drifted away from the navels to other subjects, less interesting and controversial. During a lull while me and Gus pretended to sip our beers, I said, "You know, there's something else wrong about Adam and Eve looking thataway."

"Now, what's wrong with it?" Tom asked amid groans up and down both sides of the bar.

"They're white."

"WHAT?" Gus yelled, "You telling me they *wasn't* white?"

"Not at all, likely," I replied calmly.

Now it was Gus's time to bang his mug down, "If that ain't the stupidest . . ." Words failed him.

"You know what, Gus? He's probably right," Jake said. "Where was the Garden of Eden? Somewhere in the east, probably around the Tigris and Euphrates Rivers. Folks in that country are dark. Some Ethiopians are plumb black. It is very likely Adam and Eve were dark skinned with black kinky hair."

There was a shuffling up and down the bar as the imbibers changed feet on the rail and refilled before the start of the debate.

"If they was so dark, how did we get so white?" Gus demanded.

It was quiet for a moment, then Ep, who had not participated in the first debate, said, "Selective breeding."

O rubbed his stubbled chin. "By George . . . you could be right, Ep. When th' crowd split up at the Tower of Babble, some of those folks moved north, an th' farther north they traveled, th' colder it got and th' more they covered up—"

"And th' weaker the sun shone," Jake added.

"We get darker in th' sun an' lighter in th' winter when we are out of it more. I can see that," Pock said. I looked his way just in time to see his bottle retreating from Gus's mug. So that's it, Gus ain't sipping and Pock is refilling on the sly. I opened my mouth to say something and Pock shook his head no. His look said he was up to something and I didn't interfere so long as it didn't do Gus damage.

"And our hair gets lighter," Al said, looking at Red's hair.

"I don't know about that . . ." Gus the Doubter said.

"You know there's more people of color in th' world than white folk, don't you?" Jake asked. "There's black folks and brown and red and olive folks—"

"An' them yeller Chinks," Ep added.

"I know," Gus said, "but all them old painters painted white Adams—"

"B'cause they was white an' just natural thought Adam and Eve and God was white," Ep said.

"Now you go makin' God dark too?" Gus nearly yelled. He was getting mad. "You fellers go find someone else to job, I'm tired of this tomfoolery." He took a long drink of his beer, wiped his foamy lips on his sleeve, and grinned at me.

He ain't sipping an' he is getting drunk. Now's not th' time to mention that God might not be male.

Everybody is ignorant,
Only on different subjects.

—Will Rogers

Chapter 23
A Battle Plan Busted

"Pock, what are you doing to Gus?" I whispered behind Gus's back.

"Teachin' him how not to drink."

"By getting him drunk?" I asked.

"By showin' him how *not* to drink," Pock repeated. "You can learn from him."

"I've already learned: Don't drink."

Just then, Gus stood up straight and staggered back against the chair back. "What you two whisperin' 'bout 'hind my back?" He would have flipped over the back if Pock and I hadn't caught him.

"Seems you're tall enough t' stand on the floor, now," Pock said as he whisked the chair away lest Gus re-ascend. I removed my chair and we bellied—no, more like chested and chinned up to the bar, Gus standing on the rail with both feet.

"I'll sure be glad to grow a lot taller," I said. Those prospects were not too promising, both Pa and my mother were short people. Gus's prospects at a decent height were better, considering his stock. B.R., his pa, was near six feet.

"Gus, I'm hungry, let's have a sandwich." Pock handed the boy a rolled tortilla filled with spicy meat and chili. "Shouldn't drink on an empty stomach."

"Yeshsiree," Gus said and ate the tortilla and another. It took a few moments for the anticipated to take effect, but Gus's sudden rush for the back door signaled success.

"There," Pock said. "Now the learnin' begins."

In a few moments, Gus returned, pale and clammy and a little unsteady on his feet.

"There you are, Gus, where you been?"

Gus opened his mouth to speak, thought better of it, and returned to the alley. After a few minutes he returned and slumped weakly into his former platform, considerably sobered.

"You see, Sut, Gus just showed us the way *not* to drink with his buddies. Beer is a social drink a fellow takes with his friends; whiskey is for getting drunk. When we come to the bar with our friends, it's a time of fellowship and getting mellow, not for getting drunk. Therefore, we take our beer slowly and savor both the drink and the conversation."

For once, Gus was quiet. I think he was afraid to open his mouth.

We had hoped to cross the river to the safer side, but the river was on the rise and we were too impatient to wait for her to behave.

"If we're lucky, they are having a revival at the reservation and won't be out looking for mischief," I said.

"Don't plan on it, Sut, I been havin' this chill a'tween my shoulder blades for the last two days," O said. "It started the moment we left Roswell."

"He's right, Sut."

"Those hills have eyes that never close," Jake said, indicating the Guadalupe Mountains and their foothills.

"How are we gonna avoid losing our horses?" I asked.

"Vigilance and strength, but mostly luck," Ep sang out.

"Luck is a mighty fickle lady t' be countin' on," Tom said. "I'll take vigilance an' a .44-40 any day against those creatures."

"We could travel at night and hole up in th' day," Gus said.

"And chance riding up on one of these arroyos in the dark?"

Ep asked as they looked for a way to get across a steep-sided wash.

"We could if th' bottom was lined with goose feathers instead of those boulders," said Pock.

"Normally they are until a rain washes them away," Al said, then to himself, "So many feathers an' so many washes from here on down, the Pecos oughta be called Feather River."

"Not many choices left to us," Jake said. "We'll just have to be careful from now on. If it isn't Mescalero, it'll be Comanche or Kioway or Cheyenne from here to the ranch."

That very night, the second night after we left Roswell, in spite of hobbles and pickets, the Indians stole every spare horse we had. "Damn 'em, Damn 'em to hell," Tom declared. "Damn any people who think stealing an' murder is a virtue. I'm goin' after them."

He turned to follow the tracks and Jake called, "Hold on there, Tom, let's think about this a minute." One of the good things about Tom Stepp is that he had a flash point, but got over it pretty quick. He turned back and came back to where we were gathered. Jake got down and squatted in the shade of his horse and we joined him in a circle, reins over our shoulders.

"We can't all go. Some of us will have to stay here with Cookie and the wagon. If we push them hard, they'll run our horses to death."

"But if they get to the reservation, they'll have their friends to help them and the agent won't give us permission to get our horses back," Red said.

"I'm not askin' some do-goody Quaker if I can go get my property from the thief that stole it," Jake said, barely holding his temper.

"What's your plan, Jake?" Ep asked.

"Three of us should be able to protect the wagon with Cookie helping. We'll find a place to hide it and wait for the rest of us to return." He thought a moment, "The rest of us will go after the horses. I will send a note to the agent . . . no I won't. All the rest of us will go get our horses back without asking anyone's permission."

"They have a good head start, so there is no use wearing our horses out running after them," Al said. "If we take our time, they might think we aren't going to follow."

"A-a-nd they'll think they are safe when they get to the reservation where white men can't go," Ep added.

"We just have to be quick enough that they haven't scattered our horses all over the reservation," O said.

"Probably they will turn the animals in with the herd on the community pasture. They would be easy to get there," Pock said.

Jake held a fistful of grass stems, "Let's hope so. Here is a fistful of grass. The shortest ones get to go get the horses. There are three long ones for the ones who get to stay."

Pock, O, and Red got the long straws. That left Jake, Al, Ep, Tom, and me and Gus to chase the horses.

"Those boys should stay with the wagon," Pock said in the hopes he would get to go.

"They carry their load the same as the rest of us, so they can go," Jake said.

"Them's th' short stick rules," Ep added.

Pock grinned. "You're right, we just might leave this wagon out in th' open an' see what varmints gets drawed to it. Might be more fun than herdin' horses."

Jake grinned. "You can do that if Cookie agrees and you're willing to chance going back to Jacksboro without any food."

"Not much of a chance of that happening, is there?" Pock said.

"There ain't *no* chance that gone be happenin'," Cookie said. He had walked out and joined the conference.

We had camped just north of Eagle Creek and it wasn't hard to find a place to hide the wagon in the arroyo and above what looked like the flood line of the creek. Getting the wagon there was another thing. Cow horses don't harness up at all and we could only pull the wagon with our ropes. My punishment was steering the tongue while the others pulled. It was late afternoon and after much pulling and yelling at the driver, the wagon was where Cookie wanted it.

We left late in the night after the horses were rested and the cooling air came down out of the mountains. Before the eastern sky got very bright, we found an arroyo off Eagle Creek with decent grass and picketed our horses well out of sight. After the sun set behind the far Sacramentos, we took up our march up Eagle Creek. Jake and Ep had tracked the horses and were pretty certain they had stayed with the creek up to near the reservation.

We found a place to hide early and Jake and Ep scouted for the horses' trail. They returned well after dark and we gathered to hear the plan. "The horses turned southwest to the trail on the divide between Eagle and Rio Peñasco. They are resting a couple of miles inside the reservation. We will turn northwest to the divide between Eagle and Rio Felix and come at them from the north and west. They won't be expecting that and we will be lined up to drive the horses off the reservation quickly and in the direction we need to go. After that, I don't know what we'll do. If we don't get the Indian horses, they'll just follow us and get our horses again."

"Might anyway," Ep said, "those 'Paches can run as good as the horses, only not quite as fast."

"Any plan we got has to have a big dose of luck to work," Tom said.

"As Granny Ruth used to say, 'Time's a-wasting,' let's go," Jake said, and we "got."

We found a well-used trail on the divide above Rio Felix and followed it into the reservation. "These Injuns sure travel a lot outside their homeland, don't they?" Gus observed.

"Got it made," Al said. "Gover'ment feeds them up so they can go out and steal and rape and sometimes kill, and if they can get back to the reservation, they can holler 'home free,' an' no one can touch them."

That was a situation white men had to deal with from all of the reservations around us, Comanche/Kiowa from Indian Territory, Apache from Fort Sill, and Mescalero and beyond, even from the Navajo out west. The fighting went on into the early 1900s.

The horse thieves had followed Rio Peñasco into Elk Canyon and turned them loose in the canyon and camped near the reservation line to stop anyone following them. We saw their campfires and heard their drum from the bluff above and rode upstream until we were beyond the horses and able to find a gully that ran into the canyon.

The going was slow in the dark and we waited at the mouth of the gully for moonrise. Then we moved out into the canyon and spread out, gently hazing the horses down the river, the wind in our faces. I looked at the herd. "Know what, Gus? I'm gonna trade in my tired horse for one of these an' let mine rest."

"Say, that's a good idea, Sut, an' I'm gonna do th' same." Soon we all had new mounts, not quite rested, but fresher than the ones we turned loose. There were twice as many Indian ponies as our mustangs in the herd and we kept them all together. They had wandered several miles up the canyon and we drove them to within a mile of the camp. It was three quarters of an hour after the drum had stopped that Jake signaled to start the herd moving. Faster and faster we went until the herd was galloping right through the Indian camp. Two tipis fell and people scattered everywhere. I saw one Indian mount a pony on the fly, but a blow from someone's rifle butt unseated him. A young girl was standing by the ruins of a tipi about to be run over by the horses. I grabbed her up as I ran by and sat her behind me. She hung on tightly until we were clear of the run, then she began to hit and claw and scratch me until I twisted around and knocked her off. I left her sitting in the dust yelling Apache curses at my back. Such gratitude.

Another half mile and the horses began to slow and we kept them at a fast walk. "Now, it's our turn to keep the Indians away," Jake called. "Sut and Gus, you're in charge of the cavy. The rest of us will be rear guard. Keep them moving, but don't wear them out. We can still outpace the Indians afoot, but if they get mounted, we're going to have a big fight."

"Always got the rockin' chair," Gus muttered.

"They'll be after the horses, Gus, not interested in fighting a bunch of mad whites. Put your rifle up and keep your pistol in your hand."

"Yes, sir, Gener'l Catfish." He saluted and I backhanded him in the face with my sombrero.

"Oww! That hurt," he yelled.

"Coulda shot you."

Gus squinted at me closer in the gathering light and asked, "You run under a limb somewheres?"

"Not that I remember."

"Well you must have, that's not sweat running down your neck an' soakin' your bandanna, it's blood."

"Blood! That dang girl I picked up clawed me something awful before I knocked her off." I untied my bandanna and took it off. It was soaked where the scratches were. I wrapped the cloth around my neck and tied it.

"You gotta get better at pickin' your wimmen."

"You're out of range of my hat, but you can't outrun these bullets."

"Anywhere over twenty feet an' I'm safe, but you might hit my horse an' he's innocent."

"Hey! You two quit jawin' an' keep those horses together and moving," someone from behind us yelled.

"O-o-ops," Gus muttered and rode off to bring a stray back. Elk Canyon had petered out and there was more room to wander. We drove the herd nearly forty miles southeast and rested them in Fourmile Draw where there was a little water.

"These horses go any farther without rest and they are gonna start dying," Jake said.

"Damned Injuns," Tom cursed. "We're in a no-win situation. They're following us on foot and we can't go far enough to get out of their range. They steal our horses and we get them back and they steal them again."

"They're pushing us to stand and fight or give them the horses," Al said.

"I'll stand and fight before I give up," Tom vowed.

"Standin' will put us in a defensive position," Jake said. "We have to take the fight to them if we get out of this whole."

"Well, they're forcin' th' issue on us by following," Ep said. "It's time to hit it hard and make good medicine."

"The last I saw them, there were six, but one was lagging well behind and has probably dropped out of the race. That leaves five men camping out there somewhere. We gained on them some at the last, but it is certain they will be coming on, either in the dark or at dawn. I think the best thing to do is draw the moths to the fire and ambush them."

He thought a moment and making up his mind, he said, "Sut, you and Gus move the herd on down the wash as far as you can go before dark. Gus, you hide and stay with the horses. Sut, you take the mules and light out for the wagon. Go down the wash to where it runs into a river. That is the Peñasco. The next stream north of it is Eagle Creek. All you have to do is go down the creek to the wagon. Tell Cookie to drive to the Peñasco and set up out of sight there. You and O stay with him and send Pock and Red our way with food and ammunition—wait, don't go until you hear the rest of the plan."

Looking around at the wash banks, he said, "This looks as good a place as any to make camp. We'll build a fire in the bottom and set up like we usually do, then set an ambush around the herd from both sides."

Ep shuffled uneasily, "They'll have the same idea, Jake."

"Sure they will. We will be a few yards back from the edges of the banks and before they attack, we will get them from behind. Stay low to keep from shooting each other across the wash. As soon as we are set up, Ep, you and Tom take the south side. Al and I will take the north side. Stay back far enough to let any warrior get in between you and the bank. Wait for them to make the first move, then give them no mercy. That's the only way we get out of this somewhat whole. Gus, any man showing is an enemy. Aim carefully if you can. *Now* you can go."

We mounted fresher horses and eased the cavy down the wash. All of us were tired, and there wasn't any worry about that bunch of horses wandering far. The wash, when it ran, had a nice pool in it, but it had dried along with the rest of the stream; the extra moisture there had been good for the grass and the herd naturally stopped to graze. "Think you can handle them here, Gus."

"Probably the best place until they get thirsty," he replied.

"Then it'll be a different story, for sure," I said. "Where you want t' hide?"

"Looks like that cutbank would be th' best place." He indicated the north bank of the wash where the sod still clung together and overhung the bank. He could back up under it and not be seen from above. A little rock fort building and he would be pretty snug and safe.

"All right," I said. "Guess I'll load up those mules and ride. You be careful."

"Same to yuh."

I could tell he was nervous about being left by himself, and so was I—for both of us. The mules were stubborn about leaving green grass unmowed and I had to tie them in a string, nose to tail. The first mile was a struggle, but after that, they settled some and we moved faster. I was surprised the Peñasco was so close. We crossed and climbed the low divide between that and Eagle Creek. The mules smelled water and needed no encouragement. I can't say there was enough water to fill them, but they all got a good drink before I pulled them on down the stream. If it had been full dark, I would have missed the wagon, and I guess it was doubly fortunate it wasn't very dark, or Red might have shot us. "That you, Gus?" he called.

"No, it ain't Gus an' you know it," I growled back.

"I swear, I can't tell you two apart unless you're together," he lied.

O took the animals and Cookie handed me a plate of beans and steak while I gave them Jake's instructions. The coffee was hot and strong and I dug in. I woke up from a troubled sleep bouncing along on top of the bedrolls in the hoodlum wagon.

O glanced back as I sat up and said, "Hello, Rip Van Winkle, how was your nap?"

I lay back down and groaned. "Too short."

"Cookie's savin' your breakfast you never finished. We tried to wake you up, and couldn't, but since you were still breathin', we throwed you up on top and brought you along."

"Thanks," said I, and lay back and dozed.

The stillness scared me and I awoke with a start and lay very still until I remembered where I was. I had sunk down into the bedrolls and couldn't look around without moving, so I listened for a moment. I could hear the soft voices of Cookie and O and smell Cookie's fire going. By that I figured everything was good and struggled out of my bed. It was a long drop to the ground.

"See, I told you we should keep him as long as he breathed," O said to the cook.

"Huh, he didn't even finish his steak and spilled his coffee," Cookie growled.

"Growing boys have to have their rest," O said.

"Where are we?" I asked.

"We're above the wetlands on Rio Peñasco. I calculate about five miles below Fourmile Draw," said O.

"I've got to go help Gus with the cavyyard." I began looking around for my gear.

"Your rifle's still in the boot on your saddle, and your saddle and bridle are on th' hoodlum," O said. "What did Jake say for you to do?"

"He said for me to stay with you and send Pock and Red to him with food and shells."

"Those two are riding up Fourmile right now, don't you think they can take care of Gus?"

"Yeah, but—"

"You gonna leave Cookie and a shot-up me to take care of this while you go on a jog up the creek? We're all in this together and you need to do your duty and be where you were told to be. You can trust those boys to take care of Gus just as well as you would, Sut."

Of course, he was right, but that didn't make me feel much better. I should be there with him facing whatever Gus faced.

As told by Gus

I backed up under that bank and watched Sut struggle with those mules. They could be a handful, but I was in no mood to help. There was a fort to build. There was a boulder the size and shape of ma's sow laying against the cutbank a few feet to my right. It was just the right size and place to make one side of my fort. On the far side was a hollow in the dirt big enough to hold the rock. I could sit in the hole and watch the horses over the boulder. It took a few minutes to stack rocks for the wall on my backside.

I settled into my nest. Even sitting there alone guarding horses Injuns was set on stealing wasn't enough to keep me from nodding off. Something disturbed me and I awoke with a start. The moon was up, and I could make out the horses, all standing and staring at the north bank a few yards downstream from me. To crawl out where I could see over the bank would also expose me, so I set my rifle over the boulder and waited.

A hoof clipped a rock upstream and two riders were coming down the wash. They had on sombreros and I prayed they were not Injuns with hat trophies. As they got closer, I recognized Pock by the way he rode and could breathe again. Red was with him. As they approached, I whistled our secret signal and they stopped not ten feet from my nest.

"Who's there?" Pock whispered. Neither man turned his head, just stared at the horses.

"Gus—under the bank. Trouble's down there on top of th' bank."

Red began untying a bag from his horn, "Here's some chow—" The flat pop of a rifle interrupted his speech and he fell from his horse. At the same instant, the herd turned and raced up the wash right at us.

"Run with them, Pock, I got Red," I shouted and ran for the man just sitting up. I grabbed him under his arms and dragged him into the fort, jumping behind my stacked rock wall.

With Pock leading the way, the herd rumbled by, not yet to full speed. Pock might be able to slow or stop them within the confines of the wash before they trampled our bedrolls to pieces.

There were shots fired on both sides of the wash as the others joined the fight. If one Indian escaped, he would be sure to bring down th' whole tribe on us.

A figure arose from the brush on the far bank and both of us fired at him. When the smoke cleared, he was gone. "Did we get him?" Red asked.

"Don't know, prob'ly not."

Someone stomped the overhang above us and showered us with dirt and gravels. I fired into the overhang and the shower stopped. "Are you bleeding, Red?"

He grunted, "Yeah, my hair's been parted on th' wrong side."

I peeked over the wall and saw he was sitting up folding his bandanna into a bandage to tie around his head. "Git yer head down, Gus, I got this," he ordered, but nothing more was heard or seen of the Indians. They were following the horses. At least, Jake and the others were after them. They might have a chance to keep the Injuns out of the horses.

"There's food in that bag, Gus, if you want to try for it."

Before he was finished, I raced out and grabbed the bag and his flattened sombrero and raced back unopposed. The bag dripped tomato juice from a couple of mashed cans. I opened one a little more and gave it to Red. The tomatoes were good, but the juice would have been much better. The sound of firing echoed off the banks down to us.

"We better move on up there and see if we can give a hand," Red said.

"You feel like walkin'?"

"Yeah, it's just a scratch. Bleedin's stopped. I'm sure the 'Paches that were down here are chasin' the herd, but you better sneak down and climb up on top and make sure no one is waitin' on us to show. I'll cover the far side."

Well, you know he wasn't a hundred percent or he would

have gone himself. I guess it takes a bullet to someone's head to allow me and Sut to do a man's work. I didn't say anything, just skittered down under the bank to find a place to climb out, then eased through the brush to where I thought the fort was. There was no one around, and it was easy to find with the top stomped down. The grass felt wet and sticky. I had drawn blood. I felt a scrap of leather and folded it into my pocket.

"Red? There isn't anyone up here but me. You want me to come down and help you?"

"Nah, I can make it, just a little light-headed an' achy like a beer buzz."

"I'll walk up here until there's a way to get down. Ready when you are. Walk out a ways where I can see you and keep up."

He scratched gravel and grunted out of the hole and walked out so I could watch him, his battered hat tight on his head. Keeping up meant I had to slow way down and we took a Sunday stroll up the wash. I found a stout stick and tossed it to him for a cane. He didn't go any faster, but he was steadier. Presently, a rider hove into view, leading two saddled horses that must be Red's and mine.

"Nice night for a stroll, is it?" Al asked. "Got a spare horse or two if you want t' ride a ways."

"Think I will, how 'bout you, Gus?"

"Soon's I get down from here," I said.

It took Red three tries to mount up. Al didn't offer to help.

"He's had his hair parted, Al."

"I see that, but I discern it wasn't deep enough to allow a little of his stubborn out."

"When I need it, I'll let you help me," Red growled. He held on to his staff.

"Not even a drop," Al muttered.

Fortunately, they had stopped the horses before they had

made shambles of the camp and I had to walk past the camp to get off the bank.

Everyone was admiring Red's wound. It didn't go to the bone, but that doesn't mean it didn't bleed a lot. His bandanna was soaked as was his shirt.

"You know, Red, I don't think it needs a stitch," Doctor Cookie said. "Pullin' it together an' holdin' it there would work."

"That would be good if I had three hands, Cookie, I need these two to work." Red was getting grumpy.

"I'll get my needle and catgut," said our doctor. Let me note here that you don't want to rile Cookie before he sews you up.

"You're lucky, Red, quarter inch over an' that bullet would have ricocheted off that rock-hard skull and hurt someone," Ep said. "They or their widow would have to sue you and the marshal would arrest you for assault with a deadly weapon."

"Go pee up a rope, Ep."

"Here, Red, sip on this." Al handed him a steaming cup of coffee that looked mighty weak and smelled funny.

"Thanks, Al, at least I have one friend."

Jake rode up on a lathered horse, "You boys quit admirin' Red's head and get these horses settled. Ep, take Gus and scout that north bank. See if you can find any sign of those Apaches. Pock, come watch while I scout the south side. The rest of you watch that herd."

I mounted and Ep handed me his reins. "I'll walk and look for sign, Gus. You look for trouble and don't let it get near."

We didn't find any sign for a long ways, which meant no one had followed the herd when they took their little run. Ep found a few drops of blood near the spot over my fort and that reminded me of the piece of leather I had found in the dark. I fished it out of my pocket and unfolded it. It was a bloody piece of moccasin and something fell out of it and Ep caught it before it hit the grass.

"Dang, Gus, what you carrying this around for?" He opened his hand and a toenail with some skin and meat attached lay in his palm.

"I picked it up in the dark and couldn't see what it was. One of them Injuns was stomping on the bank there over our heads and I shot up through it. Guess I got some part of him."

"At least one toe." Ep grinned. "You see any other parts layin' around, a nose or ear or somethin'?"

"Nope, just a little blood." We moved on down a hundred yards or so and found a dead Indian. He had been shot in the chest.

"Got him from across the wash," Ep said. "I wouldn't shoot a man in the back and I bet whoever was behind this man on this side hesitated also. The good thing is that someone got him."

The fact that he was still laying there told us that none of his companions had found him. His Winchester was laying by him and he had a nice bowie in his belt. Ep picked up the rifle and turned it over. "Lookee here," he exclaimed. Someone's initials were carved on the stock.

"Stole it," I said.

"Most likely jerked it from his dead hands," Ep growled. "You know, Gus, I don't mind fighting a man on level ground, even if he ambushes me, but it sure sticks in my craw that these Mescaleros have a safe haven they can run from and steal and kill, then run back to when the going gets rough. They think it's smart, but I think it's cowardly."

"Do you think if we were in that place we would think differently?"

"I *have* thought about it and I don't think I would feel any different—for myself at least."

We didn't find any more sign and decided that the man we found must have been the one that stampeded the herd.

"Let's go back and see if we can find where ol' Fourtoes got off to," Ep said.

We picked up his trail until he stopped and wrapped his foot with something, then after a few steps his trail just disappeared. "One got away," Ep said. "By th' time he limps to the reservation, we'll be long gone."

"Fightin' Comanches, most likely."

Ep nodded, "Most likely."

There was only one dented can of peaches left when we got back to the camp. The others had an airtight of one flavor or the other and since I had a can of tomatoes, they saved the peaches for Ep. He offered me half, but I declined. I gave Red the half can of peach syrup Ep gave me. Red was awful peaked and Jake made him drive the hoodlum wagon. That meant I got to ride a horse with the rest of the crew.

Since there was no longer a need to hide, we spent the rest of the day joining up with Cookie, O, and Sut, and moving down Rio Pecos

He dreamed of Injuns
Feelin' for his hair.

—Pete Whetstone

Chapter 24
The Dry Scrape

About the hundredth time Gus started bragging that he had stopped the rustlers by shooting off a toe, I left him and rode over by Red who was driving the hoodlum. "Red, aren't you feeling good enough to ride?"

"What's th' matter, Sut, your ass getting tired, or is it your ears?" He grinned a lopsided grin that made him look funny with his bandage and semi-destroyed hat with two bullet holes in it.

"It dang sure ain't my rear end," I vowed.

"Sut, I got th' dangest headache I ever had. I can feel ever' time these mules roll us over a mesquite bean. I shore wish I could lay down."

"Hold up and let me tie this horse to the tailgate and you can crawl on the bedrolls and rest." All I needed to say was "Hold up." He was sprawled on the beds before I could finish tying the horse to the tailgate. Red isn't soft or lazy, but that blow to his head did more damage inside than outside. In an ideal situation, he would have been put to bed to stay there until he was well—probably longer than he wanted to be. In this wilderness Indian country, he understood why that couldn't be.

About sundown, we found a jinglebob cow with a yearling calf that hadn't been jinglebobed or branded. The calf died, and we found a quiet out-of-the-way place and beefed him. Mama was upset, but what else could we do?

Cookie wrapped the carcass that was left and threw it in the hoodlum wagon. The bedrolls piled on top of it would keep it some cooler and discourage flies.

We crossed the Pecos at the Salt Crossing, hoping we could get to some of those tanks thirty miles away before they dried up. It isn't hard for horses to make a thirty-mile trip in a day's time, but they need water at the end, and we didn't find any. All the tanks were dry.

"Plumb across th' ponds an' nothin' but mud—and most of it cracked and baked," Gus said.

Jake rode by and said, "We'll give them a rest and move on after it cools. Our next hope is Johnson Draw."

"Twenty-five miles to the head and another twenty miles to the hope for water," Cookie called as he rattled past. "I ain't got much hope." He didn't fix much for supper and none of us felt like eating much without coffee or water.

Filling ten canteens emptied one water barrel, and there had been some used out of the other barrel. "This is not near so worrisome as not havin' water for th' horses," Pock said. "They are the ones that will get us out of this scrape, an' they don't have a drop to drink."

O nodded, "You're better off keeping your horse watered than drinking it yourself, Sut."

"I ain't got a five-gallon canteen," I replied.

"No, but you can wash his mouth out some and keep his nostrils clear."

"And trust him," Tom added. "Just like them cattle, he can smell water a long ways before you can see it, and he'll take you to it."

The drinking gourd was halfway around the polestar when Jake kicked us up and we loaded up, hitched up, and moved the cavy out. "Sut, you and Gus take the left side and keep the horses close. Tom doesn't have a night horse and he'll drive the hoodlum wagon and Red."

The wagons with those half camel mules drove on ahead and were soon beyond hearing.

We rode to the north side of the bunch and Gus said, "Wake me when th' sun comes up, I didn't get my nap out."

"I'll wake you with the business end of this quirt if you so much as blink—and if you should get far enough to snore, I'll shoot you an' tell the boys an Injun done it. Stop wastin' your spit talkin'."

The moon was setting behind us and it seemed like it got darker and darker. We rode close to the horses and followed them by sound. I grabbed the fork when we suddenly dropped into a ditch and scrambled up the other side.

"What was that?" Gus asked.

"A ditch, I guess." We rode on probably two or more hours with the cavy until we began to see enough to count the horses. There were eight horses in front of us. Off to the right where the rest of the cavy should have been was emptiness.

"Dang, Sut, where is everybody?"

I stopped and stood in the stirrups and looked all around, "I don't know."

"These damned horses took us astray." Gus looked at the horses and growled at them. They had stopped when we did and just stood, heads hanging down, not interested in any grazing. "What now?"

"Gus, I bet that ditch we crossed was Johnson Draw."

"We ain't crossed anything else like a draw . . . so if we bear south, we'll run into the draw and hopefully th' rest of them."

"I don't even see any dust, do you?"

"No. Let's change horses and turn this bunch southeastward." I washed out my horse's mouth and the new mount's mouth with the last of my water and we turned the horses southeast, watching for signs of activity. That was the emptiest country I ever passed through. It was as if we were the only living things in the world. Not a jackrabbit or even a lizard disturbed the stillness. The horses plodded on, heads down, one or the other stumbling occasionally. I got off and walked a ways, as far as I could. We came to the draw hidden under a hill and the horses perked up.

"Water, mayhap?" Gus hoped, but the only thing we found was a little mud where the creek had dried.

"They've passed by here, Gus," I said, pointing to the tracks.

He hardly noticed, looking at that mudhole. "Reckon we could dig a well, Sut?"

"With our hands?"

"I have my little shovel. There could be water under this mud."

"It's either that or ride for the wagons. We prob'ly can't do both."

"I'm diggin' or dyin'." He picked a spot and dug his shovel in. When he tired, I dug and we took turns that way.

"I think it's getting wetter," I said.

Gus peered into the hole, "Think you're right, Sut. Mayhap a little deeper, we'll hit something." By the time he had dug out another ten inches or so, water was seeping into the well.

"Give me the shovel an' I'll start another hole," I said. We dug with more enthusiasm, occasionally checking the first well and noting the rise of the water. It wasn't clear, and didn't taste good, but it was wet. When the water was high enough, Gus filled his sombrero and began watering the horses. I struck water and moved to make another well several feet away.

The horses had visibly improved by the second round of hat drinks and we decided to spend the night right there. Every time I woke up, a horse was drinking at one of those wells. There wasn't any need of washing up for breakfast—there was nothing to eat. We saddled up and rode down the draw.

Midmorning we met Jake and Pock riding to meet us. "Where

have you been?" Pock asked. "We were coming back to cut your trail and bring your bodies in for your ma's t' weep over."

"Even more important, where did you find water?" Jake asked.

"In the bottom of three wells we dug," I answered.

"It was a little gyppy, but wet an' the horses liked it," Gus added. We were both eyeing the lunch bags hanging from their forks and Pock threw his to me. Cold biscuits and jerky never tasted so good.

"Get your head out of that feed bag," Gus said as he grabbed the sack. It was his turn. Two hours later, we rode into camp beside a pool of green water. "I'm not dumpin' my canteen for that," Gus muttered. And we didn't, although Cookie did beg me out of my water for coffee. Everyone was thankful for that. We rounded up the horses and moved on down the draw looking for better water.

"This hole is th' same shade of green as th' first one," Tom said. "I give a grade of ten."

The next water was a pale green and Tom said, "I'd call that about a five." Another five and we rode up on a hole where the green growth was in islands. "This is what a three looks like, gentlemen," Tom solemnly pronounced.

I grinned. "You can dump your well water, Gus."

"Think I'll wait just a little longer," he said, but he did drink from the pool and pronounced it "good."

After Johnson Draw joined Mustang Draw, the stream trickled from hole to hole and we didn't worry about water anymore. Big Spring was extra welcome and we spent a couple of days there along the outflow creek someone named Beals Creek. "Bet th' Injuns got a name for the creek older than Methuselah," Ep said.

"They did, but old man Beal couldn't pronounce it and gave it a good Methodist Democrat name instead," O said.

"Must have been trying th' 'Pache name," Jake said. "Child

of the Big Spring is easy in Comanche."

It was a nice stream by any name and we made full use of it, washing clothes and bodies. Me and Gus set about catchin' up on th' meals we had missed, Cookie huffing and puffing to keep ahead of us. Al and Tom rode out and killed three antelope, which proved fortunate for us later.

On the plains,
The rivers run at night.

—Andy Adams

Chapter 25
The Cavalry Rescue

"This is where that redheaded A-pache was coming," Gus said, "wonder where he is now."

"He's been seen riding with Quanah Parker," Jake said.

"Redheaded?" Al asked.

"Red enough to be Red's older brother," I said.

"There's been talk of folks seein' him with Comanche and Cheyenne raiders up on the Smoky Hill and Platte Rivers," Ep said.

"Better he be a redheaded Injun than a damyankee Republican," Pock said.

"That's a story we'll never hear from him," I whispered to Gus.

"That's all the politics we're gonna talk about today," Jake declared. He generally steered conversation away from politics and religion in his camps. It avoided hard feelings and harsh words.

"Sorry, boss," Pock said.

"I'll tell you now while I'm talkin'. We're gonna move after dark tonight. I've been watching the skies and saw a smoke signal coming from the mesa above the spring. I think it's a good possibility we'll have visitors tonight or tomorrow night. Make sure the barrels and canteens are filled and be ready to move."

There's not much you can do for a sneak move before night, so me and Gus went for a last swim and dressed and brought the herd in for the change to night horses.

"Take the horses south, but not far enough that the Indians could get between the herd and camp," Jake said.

"Now don't go acting like somethin's up," Ep warned, "keep your rifles in their boot, but don't let your hand get more'n six inches from your pistol."

"Keep your eyes under your hat, but don't miss anything bigger than a sand flea," O said.

We rode off with the herd and when they were set where we wanted them, Gus said, "I gotta go back, them yokels forgot to tell me how to breathe."

"We must be awful shy o' somethin' t' git all that *un*necessary coachin'."

"Yuh think they would shut up if we could grow a beard?"

I nodded, "Prob'ly help. That dang grulla of Tom's is sneakin' out agin. You get him back and I'll circle around this other way. Be careful."

"There *you* go giving unnecessary advice," Gus said over his shoulder. "It must be catchin'," he said to his horse. "You git it an' I'm shootin' you."

We heard the wagons coming and rounded the cavy closer and drove them south. The other men spread around the herd without a word and we drove southeast toward the North Concho River all night and found water a mile down the river from where we hit it at dawn.

Cookie got us busy gathering wood while he worked on a meal.

"Never ate breakfast this late in th' morning," Pock said, "think I'll call it lunch an' worry 'bout namin' the other meals as they come."

"You might not have t' worry about namin' another meal today if them Injuns catches up to us," Cookie called.

"You just keep cookin'there, Orville; I've told them redbirds we ain't fightin' 'til after we eat," Ep said.

"You think it bothers Jake when we talk about Injuns, bein' he's three quarters?" I asked.

"Nah, it don't bother him none, he knows we're talkin' 'bout wild Injuns, not the civilized half of the Cherokee Nation."

"So you mean there's Injuns an' there's civilized Indians?" I asked.

"Yeah—"

"Just like they's civilized negroes an' they's no good Republican niggers," Cookie interjected. "Some day those niggers is liable t' get a bunch of us negroes kilt."

"Dust comin' up the river," Ep called from the cavy.

We all watched as the dust approached. Down under the dust rode a dozen men, and when they were closer, we discerned that they were soldiers, and when they got close enough, we discerned they were black—all except the white officer who rode at the front. Beside him was a flag bearer with a little blue flag with a white "A" on it. We watched as they rode up and Jake invited them to "light and rest a spell, Cookie has the coffee hot."

"Thank you, sir, this is a detachment of A Company, Ninth Cavalry out of Fort Concho and I am Lieutenant Patrick Cusack." The soldiers dismounted, rummaged through their possibles bags for their cups, and lined up for a taste of Cookie's coffee. It was good to get reacquainted with several of them. We knew Bull Boone, Silent Sam, Bandy Huein, Oke, Sad Sack, Ike Casey, and Fears Nothing from our past encounters with the cavalry. They entertained us with their lively banter as they drank and visited with us. Jake and Lieutenant Cusack sat aside and talked. Jake told him about the Indians following us and they had their heads together planning something.

Cookie understood the meaning of that and began cooking up a meal and passing out orders to anyone who happened to be near. Soon we were all busy under his command and a kettle of water was heating over an enlarged fire, a bag of rice waiting for it to boil while the cook mixed up a big batch of biscuits. Tom dug out the last antelope carcass and began carving it up according to the grub boss's instructions.

Presently, Cusack stood and addressed his men. "Men, this outfit has been running before a large party of Indians set on stealing their horses and taking a few scalps. I have proposed that we band together and set a trap for these savages and Mr. Meeker has agreed. He has invited us to eat with them while we make plans."

First priority for the soldiers was to care for their mounts and as soon as that was done a couple of them volunteered to help Cookie. When the rice was almost ready, he stirred in a whole box of raisins to make spotted puppy.

When all was ready, Cookie called "Come an' git it," and the soldiers gathered for their meal. Cookie sent O to the lieutenant with a plate of food and coffee. The soldiers ate with gusto and emptied all the containers of food.

"Would you still call this second table lunch or give it another name?" Red asked Pock

Pock pondered the question, "In light of the time and proximity to the lunch, I will call it Second Table."

"You can also call it 'gone,' " I said.

"Those fellers must be hollow." Gus marveled at the amount of food that had disappeared.

"We was, most near," Bull Boone said.

"Forty miles a day on beans and hay ain't all that nutritious," his pal Bandy said.

"And we has t' feed th' hay to th' horses," Ike added. The unfaded portion above his three stripes indicated he had fallen from a higher rank to his present position.

Gus elbowed me, "They's several fellers been demoted there."

"Ain't many black soljers at Fort Concho kept th' stripes they come there with," Bandy said. "Folks there just natural figger a darkie in any uniform is an enemy. They don't think he should stand up to a bar and drink like them. Sometimes we has to fight for that right."

"Them cowboys an' gamblers get beat up by a darkie soljer, they goes crying to th' sheriff an' he comes out to the base demandin' justice."

"Which they usually means lead poisonin' or hemp stretchin' from a telegraph pole," Bull added. "We prefers army justice which might mean a few nights in th' jail an' sheddin' a stripe or two."

"Some o' those boys has been up an' down th' stripe ladder so many times, they's done wore out their blouse sleeves," Oke said, grinning. His sleeves recorded the rise and fall of his fortunes.

Jake and the lieutenant could not come up with a good plan to catch the Indians, so they decided that the best thing they could do on that flat plain was for us to stay here for the night while the soldiers stayed out of sight in the riverbed. Toward dark, we brought the horses in and hobbled them, and two of us rode herd as we usually do. When it was fully dark, the cavalry rode out and scattered around the cavy.

It was all for nothing. No Indians appeared and disappointment, relief, and a certain amount of grumpiness were breakfast companions. We had just finished removing the hobbles when a dozen Indians rose from the cutbank of the river, yelling and waving blankets. Me and Gus were caught on the ground in the middle of a stampeding herd of horses. I grabbed a handful of mane and vaulted onto the back of a passing horse and was relieved to see Gus mounted ahead of me. Without bridle or hackamore, it was impossible to control the horses and we found ourselves trapped in the herd. There were shots behind us and we laid low on the horses—and that is when I remembered the hobbles stuffed in my hip pockets. It's pretty hard making a headstall laying on a bareback running horse, and getting it over his nose was another proposition. Gus was still napping, the forgotten loose ends of his hobbles slapping a regular rhythm on his horse's back.

My second headstall was a little easier and I guided my horse over to Gus and put it on his mount. "There, Gus, let's get out of here." I looked back and the Indians were a quarter to a half mile behind us. Farther back came the cavalry. "Turn 'em, Gus, let's go back to camp."

We managed to turn them and when they began to slow, I fired my gun and reignited their desire to run. Half of those Indians were afoot and, already having run nearly a mile, were a little tired. The vision of the herd turning on them was enough to change their intentions and they found a companion to ride behind.

The herd ran right through them and one rider's horse that was slow to turn was knocked down and caused a minor jam. The pursuing cavalry split and went around the running horses, intent on the Indians. We heard shooting behind us before we got the horses stopped at the camp.

"Jake didn't say anything about running those horses, just to take their hobbles off," Cookie said as we walked our horses to camp.

"Is ever'body chasin' Injuns?" Gus asked.

"No. I ain't," Cookie said, "and I ain't gonna, nuther."

Gus looked at me, "Reckon they need a little help?"

"The best way you can help is stir this kettle of beans."

Gus looked at the kettle, "You got too many in th' pot, Cookie, they'll never cook through like that."

"They will with you on this paddle, keeping them stirred." He handed Gus the paddle and directed him to the kettle.

"Well, don't just stand there gawking, Sut. Get on your wheels and snake up some more firewood. We're gonna need it. Those darkies is gonna come back here starvin' an' I hardly have anything t' feed them."

He was right, and it was a long ways to a store. It looked like we would be hungry before we got there.

"Want I should kill a horse for you, Cookie?" I asked as I rode away.

"Smart-assed kids is more tender," he called.

"Ain't enough of us t' feed this gang."

I had to go a ways to find some driftwood and by the time I got back to camp, the cavalry was back, lingering around the kitchen. "I ain't gettin' anything done with you hangin' 'round underfoot, so get out of th' way," Cookie ordered, "go on, now, shoo! Shoo!"

The soldiers reluctantly moved away, gathering in a bunch, eyeing Cookie and the food.

"Last time he ran *us* out, he had a butcher knife in his hand," Gus said.

"Sho do get jealous 'bout his space," Bandy said. He was a short, stout feller without a drop of fat on him. His legs were horse-belly bowed and he looked like a cub bear with crane legs.

"Guess that's why they call him Bandy," Gus had whispered the first time we saw him afoot.

I grinned. "Name fits, don't it?"

The Apaches had gotten away with five horses, two of them Jake's spares. They carried off one man who was obviously dead and several others left blood behind. Two soldiers were wounded, one looked pretty serious.

Pock came back with his bloody bandanna tied around his upper arm. "I'm gonna need some sewing up, Cookie."

"Well, you can take an old cold biscuit and wait until I finish this feast," he replied.

Pock turned to me, "Sut can you—"

"Not on your li—well might be on your life, but not on a scratch like that."

"How you gonna know to sew him up 'on his life' if you don't practice on little things?" Gus asked.

"You keep out of this, Gus Bell, it ain't any of your business."

" 'Tis if I need stitches an' you're the only one around," he yelled. "I'll sew you up, Pock, an' even try to do it neat. I think more of my buddies than t' not know how to doctor them."

"Atta boy, Gus," Cookie called, "kit's on th' top shelf of th' pantry. Be sure to stick the needle in the fire first."

Gus did a pretty good job on Pock's arm, and he let me put in the last three stitches for practice.

De only t'ing dis country good for
Is t' git somewheres else.

—Isaac Casey

Chapter 26

Sangaree and the Saint Angela Fire

Jake had not planned to go to Fort Concho, but the Buffalo Soldier drain on our food bank forced us to go, seeking food for the last leg of our trip. We expected to restock from the fort sutlery, but a collection of brothels and saloons called Saint Angela also had a good general store and we stopped there.

"I suppose you all want a little time here, so we will stay over one night," Jake said. "If you get into trouble, don't get caught, for I intend to leave tomorrow, with or without you." Jake didn't like any loud demonstrations, so we all whispered "whoopee" and hastened through our chores. Cookie wasn't cooking (there being practically nothing to cook) so me and Gus headed for town and some good grub.

"Only one fly-blown excuse for a restaurant in th' whole town," I grumbled.

"Looks like they specialize in liquid diets," Gus said. "If you're interested in good food, I see a Mexican cantina down the street. They will most likely have good food."

"I'm all for that," said I, and we "sallied forth," as the lieutenant said.

Orville the Cook came stomping out of a saloon called the Fallen Angel and looked up and down the street, pale and shaking, obviously mad, a condition we were used to and could spot a hundred yards away.

"Hey, Cookie, what's goin' on?" Gus asked, ignoring the obvious.

"Nothing you'd understand, not bein' black."

"Don't serve blacks," I said. It was an affront to us as well as Orville. We worked beside him day in and day out, ate his cooking, slept on the same ground. He more than carried his own weight. "We're going to the cantina, they'll serve all of us."

"Thanks, Sut, believe I will.

The cantina was busy, quiet, and clean, so we knew the food would be good. We waited for seats at a table and when there was room, we availed ourselves of mounds of tamales, chili con carne, and refried beans, which Cookie never served.

"No sense in cooking a bean twice when once would do," he said, but he asked for a second helping. There was no tea and too hot for coffee, so the waitress brought us a fruit drink called sañgaree.

As was our custom at that time, we ordered another meal when the first was finished. Orville called it quits and left to go to the general store. The waiter brought a big pitcher of their sañgaree with lemon and orange slices in it.

"Are those slices for real?" Gus asked. "How did they get out here?"

"They bring them up on the freight wagons from San Antonio," a vaquero at the next table said.

The fiery food demanded a lot of quenching and we drained the pitcher and ate the orange and even the lemon slices. I stood up to get my money out of my pocket and had to grab the chair to keep from falling

Gus looked at me and giggled like a girl, "Sut, that drink had wine in it."

"O-o-oh, too late you are telling me," I said. I paid our tab and wove my way out for some fresh air. Gus had made it as far as the ramada and sat on a bench, elbows on knees and chin cradled in his hands.

"That was good, but that sañgaree is sneaky."

"I'll say. We should walk it off a little bit."

"Hafta stay in th' road, the sidewalk is to-o-o narrow."

So we wove our way down the dusty street until a buggy near run over us. The man yelled, "Git outa th' street, you drunks," as he passed us so close the wheel hub struck behind my knee and knocked me down.

"D' he run over you, Sut?"

"Jus' hit my leg. Wha's your hurry, mis'er?" I yelled. "Can't you go 'round?"

He replied with a vulgar gesture.

"Tha' man needs some manners," said Gus.

We were still contemplating the appropriate lesson for our rude driver when shots in the saloon two doors ahead of us interrupted our somewhat labored chain of thought.

"Uh-oh, trouble in the Fallen Angel, Gus."

"Better see if it's any of our buddies," Gus said.

We were nearly to the door of the saloon when the batwings swung open and Bull Boone pushed his way out, half carrying Ike Casey, who had blood soaking his lower right leg. Bandy Huein followed, backing out, gun in hand.

Gus stopped, "Wha' happen, Bull?"

"We broke two house rules," Bull gritted, "Don't serve blacks. Don't serve soldiers."

"But they do shoot blacks," Ike growled. He pulled his pant leg up to reveal a hole through the meat of his calf. It was bleeding profusely.

We sat him down on the edge of the boardwalk and bandaged his wound with his pant leg while Bull brought up their horses. "We'll be back and have another vote on those rules," he vowed as they departed for the fort.

We found our horses and rode out of town, our conversation two horses wide and three miles long. "Bet th' rules get changed," I said.

"But not before more lead flies and more of our friends get

shot," Gus said.

"We'll help them," I said, knowing not one of our Rafter JD friends would lend a black soldier a helping hand in a fight.

"Jus' you an' me?" Gus asked. "What good would we do b'sides gettin' ourselves shot up?"

"Well—"

"Let's work on preventing a fight."

"How's that, Gus? How's that?"

"Them solders gonna hafta wait 'til after taps an' ever'one's asleep to come in there and have a vote on those rules . . ."

"What if th' rules is already changed?" I asked.

"Only way we can change those rules is with lead."

I thought a moment, "What if those solders marched in there an' th' place was gone?"

"What you gonna do . . . burn th' place!"

"Why not?" I asked.

"Might burn th' whole town."

"It could, but every saloon has th' same rules, an' only th' dark girls are allowed to entertain the black men."

Gus snapped his fingers and flinched at the sound. "There goes another rule."

"If we do it, we'll have to do it before taps." I stopped and thought

"How? What'd you stop for?"

"No use going to camp, we'd just have to turn right around," said I. "You got any ideas?"

"No-o-o. Gonna need something to start it with . . . with that dry wood, once it's started, there's no stoppin' it." Our two-horse-wide conversation continued back to town. By the time we reached the back alley, all we had settled on was the fact we needed coal oil and didn't need anyone to know we had it.

I fumbled around in my saddlebag and brought out a package of firecrackers. "Was gonna save them for July 4th, but they might come in handy now."

Gus peeked in the back room of the Fallen Angel where the owner/operator lived, motioned for me, and stepped inside. By the time I got there, he had a Coleman lantern burning brightly, removed the reservoir cap, and poured its contents on the cot and its cotton bedclothes. I found the coal oil jug and splashed it around on the walls and floor.

"What say we light it and run," Gus said.

"If anyone sees us run, they'll know who set the fire."

"We could yell 'Fire!' "

I shook my head, "No, too soon and they could put out the fire."

"Well, what then, smarty?"

"Give me one of them Maud Mullers you bought."

"I ain't opened them yet."

"Open them and give me one," I demanded.

Gus fished out the pack of store-bought cigarettes and handed me one. "You owe me."

I lit the cigarette and carefully worked the fuse of one of those firecrackers into the other end of it.

"A-a-aah," Gus grinned and fished out another cigarette. In all, we scattered four of our bombs around the room where they would fire and catch the coal oil on fire. We would be far away by then. With that done, we took a leisurely ride to camp. We had gone a good mile when we heard three bangs in town and a moment later, a fourth.

"There'll be a hot time in Saint Angela tonight," Gus sang as he turned back toward camp.

By the time we had gone another mile and looked back, there was a column of smoke drifting north with the wind. The fire spread to the brothel next door and people were running everywhere.

"House rules are retracted," Gus said with a grin.

"Let's get scarce." And we proceeded to do just that.

Cookie wanted to know why we were back so early and all Gus would say was, "Sañgaree an' coal oil."

The rest of the crew straggled in near morning, sooty and smelling of smoke. Tom kicked my feet as he shuffled by and asked, "Where were you when half th' town burned?"

I sat up and acted surprised, "Town burned down?"

"Yeah, an' we spent all our time fightin' it," Pock growled as he shucked his blackened overalls. "Where were you two?" This last said with suspicion.

"Sleepin off a sañgaree headache," Gus growled back. "An' it ain't quite gone, so hush yer bellyachin'."

"Huh," Pock said and lay down.

Gus suddenly sat up and then grabbed his head. When the world stopped spinning, he said, "Say, Pock, move them pants; they're stinkin' th' place up an' we're downwind."

"Move 'em yerself, but not too far away," he replied.

Gus groaned and lay down a moment, then growled and jumped up. Stooping to get the pants proved too much for his head and stomach and he threw up on the overalls.

"Now, look what you done!" Pock yelled. "Lay back down and smell that for a while—an' yuh ruined my pants!"

"Hold it down over there, we're trying to stay alive, here," Ep called.

The smell turned my stomach and I had to swallow the vomit in my mouth. I dragged our bed away and eased back into it very carefully.

"Why are you on my side?" Gus asked.

"So you'll be downwind."

"Shurrup," Tom demanded.

Under the circumstances, Jake, who had also been fighting the fire, delayed our leaving half a day.

Some feller calling himself a marshal came out asking for me and Gus. "You two were seen leaving the Fallen Angel the back way before the fire broke out. Do you know anything about the fire?"

"It wasn't on fire when we went through," I said.

"We went out that way 'cause our horses were tied out there, and Sut needed to pee," Gus said. "Someone was sleepin' it off on th' cot an' there was a lantern on th' table."

"What did this feller look like?" he asked.

"Drunk," I said. "We smelled him more than we saw him."

"Did you see anything or anybody suspicious when you left?"

"All that bunch looks suspicious," Gus said.

"We were a mile this way when we heard four gunshots from town. Next time we looked, the place was on fire," I said. I could tell he had suspicions about us, but we put on our most sincere and innocent looks and after talking to the others, he went back to what was left of town.

"Those two don't fool me one bit," Cookie muttered under his breath.

"You didn't tell th' marshal if that lantern was lighted or not," I said.

Gus grinned. "He didn't ask."

It was a tired and hungover crowd that "Pointed Them North" that afternoon.

It's better to travel than to arrive.

—Outback saying

CHAPTER 27
THE SEARCHER

"Where did you say that Saint Angela fire started?" Cookie asked for the third time.

"I didn't say 'cause we was two miles away when it started," I said, and Cookie grinned.

"Started in th' Fallen Angel, Fallen Angel, Fallen Angel," Cookie sang.

"At least he's in a good mood," Gus muttered out th' side of his mouth.

"You ain't bellyachin' my chow, is you, Gus?"

"Weather's changed," I said.

"No, sir, Cookie, I was just commentin' on your good mood," Gus said.

"That so, Sut?" He waved his meat cleaver threateningly.

"You're too far away to threaten with that thing," I said. "Yes, he said you were in a good mood."

"I don't have to be closer with this cleaver, I can throw it straight and true." He made a chopping motion like he was going to throw it.

"My bullet's faster," I said.

A stranger hailing the camp interrupted our conversation and we called him in. He was an older man with a salt and pepper grizzly beard, a slouch sombrero hid his eyes, and his unkempt hair hung to his shoulders. His bib overalls were patched at the knees and the cuffs were ragged from dragging the ground. He wore a well-kept gun and holster and I noted the long leather tie-down thongs hanging from the muzzle end of the holster.

His horse was well bred and formed, but a little ganted and I stared at his brand. It was the walking stick.

"Thought you would never notice," Gus whispered.

"Step down and look at your saddle," Jake invited. "Cookie's got a plate and cup for you."

The man got down, stiff from a long ride, and turned to survey the camp. He hesitated, then decided not to tie his holster down. "Thank you, boss. Name's Clois. Folks call me Clo."

"I'm Jake Meeker, and this is my cross to bear," he said, waving his hand at me and Gus.

"Looks like a big load," the man said and grinned. He took the plate and cup Cookie offered him and ate his meal in silence. After putting his tools in the wreck pan, he squatted by the fire and rolled a cigarette. "I came by the Rafter JM ranch and talked to your man there about the walking stick horse you found, and he told me you should be somewhere on your way back from the Pecos country. He told me about finding the horse and showed me the saddle. It belongs to my brother Toby. Can you show me where you found it? I might be able to pick up his trail from there."

"That horse could show you the place better than me," Jake said. "But I'll be glad to show you and help you find him if possible."

"I'd be much obliged to you."

That was all that was said between the two men about the subject. The man was going to search for his brother and Jake was going to help. In their minds, the deed was as good as done. This was back when a man's word was his bond. We've seen men make fifty thousand dollar deals on a handshake. The deal would go as agreed or either man would die trying, and his folks would take on the obligation and see that the word was kept.

We struck Cameron Creek just below the headwaters—only there was no water—and followed it down to the spot where we found the blood on the rocks.

"This is the last sign of your brother that we found. By the amount of blood, we knew we were looking for a body," Jake said to Clo. "But try as we might, and there were four of us, all pretty good trackers, we never found the least sign of where that body went from here."

"It's as if he just lifted up and flew," I said.

"It may be I could find something," Clois said. "I don't want to cast doubt on you-all's tracking abilities, but I have to satisfy myself."

"We understand," Jake said, "we would be the same way about our kin."

"It's been too long, there won't be any sign left there," Gus whispered.

"Th' man has to satisfy himself. And as far as he knows, we could be his brother's killers," I whispered back.

The old man began circling the blood in ever-larger spirals, seeming to look at every blade of grass. He disappeared into the brush and was gone quite a while. When he reappeared, he was behind us and the first thing I noticed was that he had tied down his holster.

"You were the last ones to see my brother—"

"No, we never saw him," Jake said very firmly. "The only thing we saw was that horse coming to us with fresh blood on the saddle. He led us to this spot and we found enough blood here to believe someone had died. All of us have looked for signs of activity here from time to time and never found a thing. We are completely stumped."

"What did your brother look like?" Tom asked.

The old man dug out a tintype from his shirt pocket and we passed it around. It showed a young man with light hair and smooth face. He was a big man, as evidenced by the six-shooter he held. It looked like a toy in his hand.

None of us recognized him until back at the ranch when Pock handed the picture to Cookie, who exclaimed, "I seen him in Jacksboro!"

"When, Orville?" Jake asked.

"When I went in and provisioned up before you went mustangin'. He was sittin' on Martin's dock watchin' us load the wagon and joshin' Martin about . . . about losing in a card game the night before. He asked me if we needed any more hands an' I looked at that big man an' realized I would have to buy another wagonload of food to keep him fed. So I said, 'No, suh, da boss done got his full crew.' " Cookie shook his head, "Never saw a man so big."

"*When* was that?" Clo asked.

"He went to Jacksboro the first week of October last year," Jake said. "We found your horse the second week of November. The blood on the saddle was dried some, but still held its color."

This Clois Lynch looked from one of us to the other, his right thumb hooked behind his belt near his gun. "Toby was carrying the proceeds of our trail herd we sold in Kansas, about thirty thousand in silver. There's a lot of folks on th' Nueces needin' that money."

"You might get a couple of us, feller, but you'll die never knowing what happened to your brother. And all for nothing, we never saw him," Jake repeated.

In those days, a man developed a pretty good sense of knowing when a man was telling the truth and when he lied. I guess Clo finally saw that we were not lying to him and he relaxed. "Just had to know you were telling me the truth."

"Funny way of saying he's sorry," I muttered.

" 'Cause he *ain't sorry,* Sut," Gus muttered.

"I'll bet if you got on his trail at Jacksboro, you would get a pretty good idea of what happened to him," Jake said. "Come with us and rest your horses at the ranch, then hit Toby's back trail."

"Tough people around there, and some of them stray from th' law quite often," Pock said. "I'll be glad to go with you, if you want."

"Do better not worrying about those around me," Clo said.

"You're too damned independent, Clo, you make a hog on ice look steady as a rock," Ep said and we laughed.

That broke the tension and Clois allowed he would take Jake up on his offer and rest a few days before taking on his brother's back trail and Jacksboro.

The next morning, Jake sent Tom Stepp to Jacksboro on an errand of some kind and the rest of us began the regular old ranch chores. Me and Gus rode to the south, hazing strays, showing visiting cows the door, and sending wayward JM cows back home.

"Be th' same thing tomorrow—and prob'ly th' same cows," I said.

"Let's send our bunch—"

"To hell," I said and turned my tired horse to catch a backsliding steer. Roping him was easy, but when I tried to bust him like Pock does, something in my method was wrong, and I ended up with a broke girth raising dust and riding cactus behind a stampeding steer. Gus threw his loop at the steer's hind legs and got one. It was enough to stop him, but he stood there three-legged, cussing us while I dismounted a prickly pear clump.

"Took your danged time," I growled "and did half th' job."

"Stopped him, didn't I?"

"Now what?" I said as we watched my horse hitting the high

spots for the ranch.

"Well, looks like you got a long walk."

"I ain't walkin' nowhere. Git rid of that steer an' head for th' house b'fore that rescue squad finds us sitting here."

"If I shake this loop off his hoof, he's gonna come for you or that saddle an' since that saddle don't move, he'll take care of th' mover first—how fast are you, Sut?"

"Just where d'yuh think I'd run? They ain't a tree closer than Jacksboro an' th' run'll kill me if that steer don't."

"Well, why don't you just walk up there and ask Mr. Steer to give you back your rope? Tell him I'll turn loose his leg if he does."

"Gus, ease around toward his free leg an' when I say, jerk hard and he might go down." I eased over to the saddle over the steer's protests and got my piggin' strings. "Now, I'm ready."

Gus turned away and jerked hard enough to knock the steer off his hind legs and a short drag brought him to his side just as I reached his horns and twisted his neck so he had to stay. Gus grabbed the piggin's and had the steer tied in no time.

I retrieved my rope and coiled it. "Ride up here close and I'll take off the strings and hop on." When he was ready, I jerked the ties off and climbed on behind Gus. We were sixty yards away and fading when the steer was on his all fours, looking for someone to blame for his troubles. The last enemy left on the field of battle was a battered saddle, and he tore into it with a gusto seldom seen in a bovine. We could only watch helplessly as he shook and tore parts off.

"Don't ever doubt a cow don't know how to use those horns," I said as the steer stabbed the remains and impaled the saddle on his horn. Unable to shake it off, he trotted away, head high, proudly displaying his trophy for all to see.

"Wanna pick up th' pieces?" Gus asked.

"Well, there's my rifle and blanket roll. That stirrup may still be good."

We were gathering the remains when two riders topped the hill leading my horse.

Gus squinted, "Looks like Ep and O."

"—and my horse."

"Where's your saddle, Sut?" O asked as they rode up.

"Donated it to that steer," I said, indicating the saddle bouncing away.

"Why he don't even know how to wear it!" Ep exclaimed.

"Looks like you'll be barebackin'it for a while, Sut," O observed.

"Say, there's that ol' hull in th' barn you could use until you get to town to get another one. I saw it yesterday hanging from a rafter," Ep said.

"Go get it, Sut, and we'll help Gus guard th' border 'til you get back. You can spend the night in the line shack with us."

Ep nodded, "While you're at it, borry a bag of flour and a dab of Cookie's sourdough starter. Ours died when it got accidentally cooked—"

" 'Bout as accidental as sunrise," O growled "You're th' most confused cook I ever saw."

Ep grinned, "What you get for havin' me cook."

"Bet you'd really be upset if you was forever banned from th' kitchen, wouldn't you?" Gus said. Ep just smiled.

I got to the ranch house with a whole list of things to get for the shack and found everything but women, cookstove, and running water. That old saddle looked like it should have been burned about twenty years ago, and when I stepped into the stirrup, it ripped off the saddle. I wound up standing on the ground with my boot still in the stirrup, watching that horse do the two-step on the bag of provisions. I had to start over.

Jake had been gone a couple of days, making arrangements

with neighboring ranchers to gather a herd for Dodge City next spring. He rode in while I was sorting out the remains of that feed bag and chatted with me a few minutes. "I have to write a note for you to deliver, Sut, so don't leave until you see me." He went to the bunkhouse for pencil and paper.

He was still writing when I finished. Folding the paper and sealing it in an envelope, he handed it to me and said, "Take my saddle and a couple of horses and you and Gus take this note to Tom in Jacksboro. You can get a new saddle on my account at Ifeld's and pay me back as you can. If Tom needs you, help him out or scamper back here. At any rate, don't be gone more than five days."

I said, "Yes, sir," and beat it for the bunkhouse for some more clothes for us before I rode out in the pasture and gathered me two savvy-looking horses to ride.

Five minutes after I found him, me and Gus were riding for Jacksboro. We found Tom at the hotel sleeping off an all-night card game. "What you two doing in town? Playing hooky?"

"Nope, Jake sent you a message—"

"And Sut needs a new saddle," Gus put in.

"What happened to your old saddle?" Whereupon Gus had to tell the whole expanded story, exaggerations included.

Tom grinned. "Gus, you're gettin' to be a right accomplished liar, keep it up and they'll be callin' you a cowboy. Tell Jake I'm makin' progress. I know the two tinhorns who cheated Toby out of his money, and I'm close to naming his killers."

"He wants you to write him a letter about what all you have found. Clo is restless and we can't convince him to stay much longer," I said.

"Don't look so constipated, Tom, we'll spell the big words for you," Gus added.

"Go get your saddle and I'll have a note ready when you get back. I don't want you lingering around here after dark. The wrong people are getting suspicious of my antics and might do you harm to find out what my game is."

We went over to Ifeld's and I tried out three saddles before I found one suitable. It cost fifty dollars, but it was the only one that worked for me.

"If a man is gonna be sitting in his office all day, he wants a chair he can be comfortable in," the clerk said.

"Yeah, but it's a shame the 'chair' costs more than the 'office,' " I replied. We bought some other things needful, including a couple boxes of shells, and headed back to Tom's room. The clerk stopped us at the desk and handed us the envelope we had given Tom. "Mr. Stepp had to run an errand and left this for you."

Gus took the envelope and we left. "This envelope is damp, Sut; Tom must have sweated over that note."

"Or a desk clerk tampered with it. Did you see how nervous he acted? Didn't look us in th' face once."

"Well, stow this in your new saddlebag and let's pretend dumb and get out of here."

A mile from town, Tom rode out of the brush into our path. "Here's the real note for Jake. I wanted to see if that clerk was honest. Show me the note he gave you."

I pulled it out of the bag and gave it to him. "Uh-huh, it's been tampered with."

"Desk clerk seemed awful nervous," Gus said.

"He'll be hallucinating when I get through with him," Tom vowed.

"Anything we can do for you?" I asked.

"Yeah, git that note to Jake as soon as you can."

"Good as done," Gus said, and Tom faded into the brush.

"You know, Gus, Tom's got his neck stuck 'way out there by hisself. He needs someone to have his back."

"Bet you know just th' one t' do that, don't you?"

"One of us would do, but I—"

"Shut up and give me the letter."

"—was thinking you would be best since I drew a lot of attention buying that saddle. Not as many people would recognize you."

"Wha-a . . . you're jobbin' me, ain't you?"

"No, Gus, I ain't. Get to town and see if you can tail Tom without anyone knowing it." I turned and left him sitting there, slack-jawed. "It's time you took on more responsibility, now git."

I rode hard to get to the ranch as quick as I could. When my horse began to tire, I rode the other one. We loped into the yard an hour after dark. It seemed like Jake was expecting me, he was sitting in the bunkhouse drinking coffee with Clo and Cookie. After he read the note, he said, "Clo, Tom has found out who the two tinhorns are who cheated your brother out of his money. He thinks he will have the names of the killers within a day or two. He wants you to go to an abandoned house a mile north of town and wait for him there."

"Why doesn't he go to the sheriff?" I asked.

"Because he suspects one of the killers is a deputy and he doesn't trust the sheriff."

"And why am I not surprised," I said.

"Shady characters get elected sheriff or judge as much as honest men, Sut. A lot of well-meaning voters find that out after the election. In time the mistake is corrected," said Jake. "A lot of men, sheriffs and deputies, walk on both sides of the law."

"Reckon I'll be going t' town in th' morning," Clo said.

"I'll send Sut to show you the old Adams place. You know where it is, don't you, Sut?"

"Yes, sir, I do."

"Where's Gus?" Jake asked.

"He's tailing Tom in case he needs him," I said. I didn't mention that it was our idea and not Tom's.

"As soon as he's not needed, you two hightail it back to the south range and redo what those ornery cows have undone while you were gone."

Cookie chuckled. "Knows his cows pretty well, don't he?"

"Some day this range will be all fenced up and tame an' we'll know our cows by name," Jake predicted. Sadly, he was right.

Am I my brother's keeper?

—Cain, Genesis 4:9 King James Version

Chapter 28
A Town Cleansing

The ridgepole of the Adams cabin had broken in the middle and the ends were laying on top of the log walls. After a little work, we could get the horses under one end of the roof and we had the other end for our camp. Clois went to some trouble wiping out our tracks all the way back to the trail past the house while I made supper.

"After supper, we'll walk into town and have a look around," he said as we waited for the coffee to boil.

"You don't think we will need the horses? It's a good two miles into town."

"Horses make a lot of noise and without them we can hide in the brush and not have to run or leave our horses in town."

It was a good idea, but I couldn't wear my soft-soled moccasins in the dark. I was sore-footed when we got to town. We found Tom at the Dixie Queen Saloon in a card game with three other men, two of which were obvious tinhorn gamblers. Clois went right in and ordered a drink. I stayed in the shadows, for the fourth was the hotel clerk. When I saw a back window where I could hear the table conversation, I slipped down the alley, kicking bottles and a cat out of my way. A familiar figure was already at the window and I tossed a pebble at him. "That you, Gus?"

"You know it is, be quiet." He had his gun in his hand.

"Whatcha doin?"

"Shut up."

I listened a moment to the desultory conversation and pulled a reluctant Gus away so we could talk. "Tell me what's going on, Gus."

"That clerk is the deputy that shot Toby Lynch and he's got his gun in his lap. I got to get back." We both hurried to the window, guns in hand.

Clois walked over, drink in his left hand, and observed the game a while. "Mind if I join?"

The elder gambler looked up with a gotched eye and said, "Sorry, four's th' limit at this table."

"Well, we could move over to that table and play five, or I could buy out one of you fellers. How about you, feller, are you playing with yourself or is that your gun you're holding in your lap?"

The desk clerk deputy flushed and started to rise, raising his gun until the barrel caught on the edge of the table. Clois kicked the table into his midsection and he fell back into his chair. Tom reached over and slapped the clerk's face forehand and backhand, pulling the gun out of his hand.

An ugly-looking little derringer had suddenly appeared in the gotch-eyed tinhorn's hand and he fired at Clois. The other gambler pulled a knife from his boot top and lunged for Clo's back. Two shots from the window stopped him and he fell heavily.

Clois grabbed the man by the throat with his left hand and lifted him to his tiptoes, squeezing until the man's face began to turn from red to purple. He flailed Clois with the empty pistol to no avail and slowly collapsed. Clois dropped him and stared at the window through the powder smoke. "Who do you think you are interfering with another man's fight—and there's *two* of you? I'll thank you to tend to your doin's from now on and don't go meddling in another man's business." Blood had soaked his shirtsleeve and was dripping off his fingertips from an ugly wound in his shoulder.

I couldn't believe my ears and Gus just stood there slack-jawed. "You had that man with a knife at your back and you think we *interfered*?"

"We'll damned well interfere when we see someone backstabbing someone, an' especially a friend of ours," I yelled. We both scrambled through the window as the man on the floor slowly sat up and fumbled with his sleeve gun. I grabbed it and ripped it off his arm, taking a little hair and flesh with it.

Tom helped the man up and Gus shoved a chair into his legs so he sat down. Tom got in his face and said, "We have a new religion, feller, they call us the Temple Cleansers, and you have just become our chief missionary and evangelist. Here's a list of your friends we wish to reach with a message of love and wonder. Our prophets have had a vision of an apocalypse and the only way you and your friends can avoid it is to be out of town by sunrise, as the Lord said, *'Let them which be in Judea flee into the mountains: Let him which is on the house top not come down to take any thing out of his house: Neither let him which is in the field return back to take his clothes.'* And again, He said, *'For then shall be great tribulation, such as was not since the beginning of the world to this time, no, nor ever shall be.'* "

The man grabbed the slip of paper with a smirk on his face that faded as he read the list. "You don't think you can make these men leave without a fight, do you?"

"Oh, of course not. In fact, we are having a drill of our soldiers tonight. Let's step to the front door and I'll give you the privilege of reviewing the troops before you start on your mission."

We all went to the door and stepped out on the porch, Tom pushing the deputy/desk clerk before him. There, filling the street must have been a hundred men, all armed and waiting. At its head stood the sheriff. "Aren't you inspired, seeing all these men backing you up on your journey? The sheriff and his deputy dog have volunteered to lead you from the desolation to come to the safety of far lands. And now, great missionary, go forth and conquer."

He shoved the gambler off the porch and the army began their march. "Look down the street, Gus," I said.

There were groups of men standing at the door of every saloon and house of entertainment along the street, and as the van of the army approached, men and women were pushed into the front of the march. Except for some woman screaming hysterically, the march was silent. They were met at the edge of the town by a troop of cavalry from Fort Richardson who took charge of the new converts and escorted them to the fort; there they were sifted and sorted into those whose presence was requested in other jurisdictions and those whose sins had not found them out and thus reluctantly turned out to hopefully go and sin no more.

Me and Gus and Tom, not wasting time waiting around, headed back to the ranch where Tom resumed his duties and me and Gus went about ours, sorting strays at the south border.

Clois Lynch hung around Fort Richardson visiting with old troopers and scouts he had campaigned and scouted with and keeping an eye on certain of the prisoners.

Whether it was by design or accidental, the army released Hotel Clerk Deputy Dog and the sheriff the same day and they rode out of the fort together. Clois followed them to the campsite for passing travelers where they ran off a family of travelers and lay around until evening. Unable to wait longer, Deputy Dog scraped the fire aside and began digging within the fire circle before dark. Soon, he pulled two canvas bags out of the hole and set them with a clank outside the circle. Then he carefully restored the ground and fire.

This must have been the moment that Clois Lynch entered

the picture, for nearby residents heard gunfire. Supposing it to be target shooting, they went about their business of gathering eggs and milking. The ex-sheriff and his deputy were never seen in that area again and no one missed them.

Me and Gus rode in to the line shack one evening to find Clois Lynch sitting by the fire talking to Otha and Ep. "How are you doing, boys?" He stood and shook our hands.

"We're doing fine, Mr. Lynch, how are you?" Gus replied.

"I'm fine as a fiddle. Found Toby's body and gave him a proper burial at Fort Richardson. Since he was a scout for the army, they allowed him to be buried there. I've got all his earthly belongings and I'm heading for my ranch and the family."

He didn't say anything about how that all came about and we didn't ask. Some of those bags jingled like silver when he loaded them on his packhorses and rode south the next morning.

In the uncertainty of punishment following crime,
Lies the weakness of our halting justice.
—Isaac Parker

CHAPTER 29
A GALLING MATTER

Fall 1873

He rode into the yard on a fine thoroughbred, followed by a pair of wagons pulled by six mules and driven by an older fellow not much taller than my five foot six. The rider wore strange clothes, some sort of britches baggy at the top and narrow below the knee, so as to fit into his high-top brown boots. His coat had long tails that flared over the horse's sides. We called his hat a two-way cap, for it had a bill front and back and did nothing at all to protect his sunburned face and neck.

He rode up to where we were working and looking at us down his long nose said, "I say, where is your mauster?"

You could see the red climbing from his collar to his ears, and Ep replied, "The S.O.B. ain't been born yet."

Pock stood up and said, "I'm boss of this outfit, what do you want?"

"I am Sir Percival Hampton-Halley and I have come to search this area for the bones of prehistoric creatures that once roamed here."

"Bones here are mostly buffalo and cow," I said. "You can have all you want."

He glanced my way and dismissed me with a backhanded wave like brushing away flies. "I will camp nearby and beg the loan of one of your servants," nodding our direction, "to guide and assist me in finding what I seek."

Jake had emerged from the ranch house and quietly joined us

as the man spoke.

"These men are not servants; they are hired to assist in running this ranch and they are free to come and go as they please. You may offer employment to them if you wish."

Sir Percival glared at Pock, realizing he had been jobbed, and turned to Jake. Before he could speak, Jake said, "I'm Jake Meeker, welcome to the Rafter JM. Step down and have a cup of coffee with us."

Sir Percival smiled, but it didn't look like a friendly smile, "Thank you, Mr. Meeker. Bob, take care of Thunder, and the mules," he commanded and followed Jake to the bunkhouse kitchen where Cookie served them cups of steaming coffee. They sat at the table and talked.

Bob "Grey with an 'e,' " as he said it, led the horse to the trough while we aided him by unharnessing the mules and leading them to the water.

Bob, without his high-heeled boots, would be shorter than me and a little taller than Gus, but he must have been at least in his mid-thirties. He was wiry with rough strong hands. He removed Thunder's funny-looking little saddle and brushed him good before he released him into the corral. He obviously held more esteem for the mules than the horse and was pleased we treated them well. "Oi thanks ye f' bein' so koind to me pals," he said. "They can be buggers, but they're good workers. Oi've convinced Sir Percy to take them back t' Hengland wi' us, th'likes 'as niver been seen there."

It took all of us to translate that into American and Ep said, "These are Missouri mules, the best bred in the world."

"Jake used to raise them back in Arkansas. Says he sold a passel of 'em to th' army," Pock said.

Cookie rang the bell and we all trooped to the kitchen for dinner. Sir Percy ate his steak an' 'tater hurriedly and left the table early.

" 'E don't often eat wi' th' sarvants," Bob explained.

" 'E ain't et wi' but one 'ere," Pock mocked Bob's talk and grinned at him.

"Ye don't have to be called a sarvant in the USA lessin' ye wants to," Gus said.

"It hain't a bad word in Hengland," Bob said. "Me line goes back foive generations wi' th' Halleys. Me great-grandfaither Robert was head trainer o' th' Halley stables."

"So you were named for your great-grandfather?" I asked.

"An' me grandfaither an' me faither."

"How do ye keep straight which Robert you're talkin 'bout?" Gus asked.

"We all have middle names we go by when mauster ain't around. Th' custom is that the firstborn son be named Robert and work to take his faither's place."

Pock nodded, "I see, it's so 'mauster' doesn't have to learn a new name ever' time someone dies an' another takes his place."

The current Bob smiled. Sir Percival insisted on dealing with Jake for our services, and Jake insisted that he deal directly with us. That prospect was so distasteful and beneath his station that he commanded Bob to do the job. Of course, Bob got nowhere, even when he doubled the pay we were getting. He was in a real fix. Failure would not be acceptable, and he was reduced to begging me and Gus to go with them.

"I don't mind goin'," Gus said, "but I ain't takin' orders from that stuffed shirt."

"Yeah, Bob, if we can work for you, we'll go, but we won't take orders from 'Sir Percy,' " I said.

That seemed to be good with the two foreigners, Sir Percy seldom condescended to speak to the "sarvants," except for Bob, and he would relay orders to us.

We rode to the "Henglish" camp at sunup and helped Bob feed and water the mules. Sir Percy had not made an appearance from his tent and Bob cooked his breakfast and took it in to him. He returned and ate his breakfast by the fire. " 'E allows me to eat when 'e does out 'ere to save time. At 'ome, the sarvants wait until the mauster has eaten, then they eat."

When he finished his meal Sir Percy called Bob, who hurried in and carried out the breakfast tray with its dishes and jars of jelly and other condiments. He washed the dishes and carefully stored them with the condiments in a large chest.

Sir Percy presently emerged from the tent in his dressing robe and pajamas and addressed Bob, "We will leave the hind wagon here, but you may take all your mules. The *boys* are to strike and set the tent each day and curry Thunder every evening. When breakfast is over, I expect to find Thunder at my tent, saddled and ready to go. You are to have the mules hitched and we will move on immediately. As you know, we are looking for limestone formations and you are to instruct the *boys* to direct us to the nearest outcropping and we will dig to find the fossils we seek."

"Bet I know the 'we' who'll be doing the diggin'," Gus muttered from the side of his mouth.

I dug my elbow in his side, "Sh-h-h."

He listed several other dictums about deportment and camp duties, and how to address His Highness, which in essence was not to be done, then returned to his tent "to prepare for the day's ride."

"I'm beginnin' t' hate the sight of him, and we haven't even started," I whispered to Gus.

"I can't stand even his name," he replied. It was then that we agreed to call him SP.

Bob turned to us and began, "You are in charge of the tent—"

"Never mind, Bob, we got it straight from the ass's mouth," I said.

"Does 'strike the tent' mean take it down?" Gus asked.

"Yes, Gus."

"How we gonna do that with him in it?"

"We'll wait until he is out, then do the striking," I said.

We hurried and helped Bob hitch the mules, then he showed us how SP liked his horse saddled and stationed at the tent flap. Thunder was no sooner in place than SP emerged in his fancy riding suit. We immediately began taking down the tent when SP sharply admonished, "Bob tell your *boys* to empty the tent first."

Gus looked inside, "Dammit."

There were bedclothes and a cot to be folded and three trunks to be loaded. "The blankets go in that trunk," Bob instructed.

Then we folded the tent while SP sat his horse, giving Bob instructions on how to properly fold and stow the equipment—as if he hadn't done it a hundred times before. Last of all the rug Bob called the Persian was rolled up and carefully stowed in a long box made for the purpose.

"Well, Bob, where shall we go?" SP demanded.

Me and Gus had decided the nearest and easiest to get to limestone was along Salt Creek down to the Brazos River, all over west of us. "I will show you the way," I said and turned to lead the procession and got a sharp tap with a quirt.

"*I* will lead, you tell me the way." SP brushed past, Thunder shouldering my horse aside.

"We're going west," I called and he struck out on a trackless march. The routine, Bob told us, was to travel until just after noon, stop for a while, then move on until "tea time," whatever that is, and stop for the evening and pitch camp and let the animals rest. Me and Gus were familiar with the land and knew where the wagon could and could not go. Several times during the day, SP found himself leading no one while the wagon made its way over smoother ground or around some arroyo. He had to hustle to regain his leadership position. We ignored him, while an uncomfortable Bob followed our instructions.

There were three hours of daylight left when SP called a halt. "This is tea time?" I asked.

"Yes," Bob said and hurried to take Thunder from his waiting master.

"We ain't come fifteen miles," Gus said. "We're never going to get there."

"Or back," I added.

SP had called a halt in a little clearing on the banks of Brushy Creek. "Put the tent there." He indicated a spot on the bank of the creek.

"This creek is liable to sudden rises and you are likely to get your tent flooded if you set it up there," I said.

He looked at me down that nose and said, "It hasn't rained. *Put the tent there*," and he walked over to criticize Gus's currying job on Thunder.

I began the process of laying out the tent while Bob and Gus tended the animals. When they were nearly through, Gus came to help me raise the tent and fill it with the furniture. SP inspected the work and admonished Bob because we had not unfolded the cot and laid out the blankets. It passed inspection with a sniff and expectation that we would be more efficient "from now on."

"Where we gonna go after we kill him?" Gus whispered.

"Back to the ranch and be heroes," I said.

Me and Gus took note of the flashes of lightning to the north of us and to Bob and the animals, camped on higher ground. When SP swung his feet to the rug next morning, he stepped into ankle-deep water. We anticipated his call and "hurried" to his rescue. "Why didn't you warn me?" he demanded.

"I only warn once," I said.

Fortunately, the trunks were waterproof, but the boots floated enough to topple and fill with muddy water. Rings on the low cot legs showed that the rise lacked an inch reaching His Highness's hindquarter. How unfortunate.

The Persian was soaked and so muddy we couldn't make out the pattern. We spent a good hour in the creek washing it and it rode spread over the canvas top of the wagon.

At least the ass paid more attention to routes the wagon could take, but still occasionally made the wrong turn and found himself leader of nothing. We struck Little Salt Creek and followed it down to where it joined Salt Creek. SP was excited at the exposed limestone and chose a spot above the creek for his camp this time.

While we set up camp—above the high-water mark—SP took a little shorthandled pick and went along the limestone shelf pecking on the rock, marking places he wanted to come back to. "He keeps up that peck-peck-pecking he'll wear out his pecker," Gus observed.

"And thereby saving Britain and the rest of the world the burden of his progeny," I said.

"I guess you know what you said, *I* say he couldn't reproduce little SPs to harass th' rest o' th' world."

"Good point, Gus."

The next morning, we learned what our job was going to be in this operation. Bob rummaged through the wagon and came out with three more of those little picks and little whisk brooms. SP led us to the rock shelf and at his first marked spot he demonstrated the correct method of digging out fossils from the limestone. He pointed out a smooth piece of rock and said, "That is a petrified bone. I want one of you—you," pointing to me "—to dig this bone out without breaking or chipping it."

He moved farther down the shelf and put Gus to work digging out what he called a tooth. We set about pecking away at our projects. "Look at this, Sut. Ain't nothin' in th' world big enough t' have a mouth full of this."

Gus had dug most of the tooth out and it looked like one of those chewing teeth behind the biting teeth in your mouth, only it was as big as a baseball.

"That's one big tooth, Gus."

"Yeah, wouldn't want t' meet up with him when he was hungry."

"If this is a bone, it's from something bigger than an elephant," I said, "and it's liable to reach plumb to where you are. I think it's some kind of tree trunk."

Bob walked by on his way to make tea, "Found the jawbone that tooth would fit into," he said in passing.

We both went down to Bob's "dig" and saw a huge jawbone half dug out of the surrounding rock. "Jehoshaphat, what a jaw," I said.

"No wonder Samson slew all those Philistines with a jawbone," Gus said

"Why are you two loafing around down here?" SP stood behind us, slapping his leg with his quirt, "Get back to your work. I'll tell you when it's time to lollygag around, now move."

We turned without a word and returned to our projects. "I'm gonna feed him that quirt before this is over," Gus vowed, and I didn't doubt him.

"You'll have to beat me to it," I replied. Both of us determined within ourselves that he would get only one blow on either of us before judgment descended upon him. SP must have suspected that, for he never raised it to either of us, and after a few days, he laid it aside. But that didn't change his overbearing attitude and all three of us got tired of it. Bob got a tongue-lashing because the jawbone was only half there. I got chewed on because I was too slow digging out that tree trunk, and Gus got chewed on just for being there.

We were there two weeks, and all I did was dig out that tree trunk. It was a tree until I got to one end and found the joint bones. SP declared it a leg bone and when I lay down beside it, it was longer than I am.

"What kind of creature was this?" Gus asked. He held up the tooth he had extracted from the limestone.

"I don't know, you'll have to ask SP."

"I wouldn't ask him th' time of day."

I got two thirds of the diameter of that rock bone exposed, but to free it from the limestone was going to take a lot of digging, and SP was impatient to find a whole monster, so he decided we would move on down toward the river. With tooth and jawbone carefully packed away in the wagon we drove on down the Salt Creek a couple of miles where the king called a halt.

"You will set my tent up . . . there," he pointed to a little level place above on the hillside and we got busy while he looked for limestone treasure.

We lugged the tent up the hill to his chosen spot.

"Don't think he's gonna want to sleep here," Gus said as we watched a skunk duck into a burrow. We peered into a ring of tiny noses and eyes peering up at these curious creatures invading their space.

"Oh, he doesn't allow little things like that to stop him from living where he wants to live." I leveled the ground, kicked off the rocks, and unrolled the Persian, fixing it so the back edge was just over the burrow so the skunks could come and go as they pleased.

We pitched the tent over the rug and made it secure at the bottom as directed, to keep out invading creatures.

A slight skunk scent in the air prompted His Highness to make sure the tent flap was extra secure when he retired for the night. *Those poor men out there where a skunk could get to them . . . Oh well, time for bed.*

Five little mouths taxed mom's ability to nurse them and the urge to hunt sustenance was insistent. The extinguishing of the light was to her the sunset and signaled the time to forage, so out she came, pushing her way from under the Persian.

Sir Percy, having retired, heard the slight sounds of the creature, but the concentration of the odor was the signal for action. He sprang from the bed giving loud voice to his fears and in so springing, kicked mother skunk, who reacted as the emergency dictated. Fortunately or unfortunately in accordance to the individual's perspective, mother's aim was off and her weapon of defense was directed to the Persian.

Disoriented and without light, our lord fumbled to find the door. The odor was intense to the point of tasting and he threw up on the poor mistreated rug. As if finding the door was hard enough, he now had to untie all the ties that secured the tent flap—only down to knee height and not below for fear of another furry encounter. He squeezed through the opened slit, ripping either tent or flap as he loudly exited the tent to confront three "anxious servants" who were thankful their facial features could not be seen.

"Are you hurt, m'lord?" Robert asked anxiously.

"Yes, yes, you dolt, can't you smell? I've been poisoned." He began tearing off his clothes, leaving them strewn along his path to the creek. We heard him splash into the water. "Bring me soap and a cloth," his shout demanded.

It took the three of us some moments to light a lantern and cautiously peer into the tent. All was quiet, mother having retreated to her lair to protect her babies. The overwhelming odor prevented even the most venturesome of us from entering.

"We better air out the tent first," I said, and me and Gus began raising the sides while Bob found soap, towel, and rag.

"Whe-e-ew that skunk did a job on this place," I said. "We

need to roll up that poor rug and take it to the creek."

"I ain't touchin' that with my bare hands, and for sure not with a good pair of gloves," Gus declared.

"Grab that corner and we'll drag it," I said, and we dragged it to the creek, leaving it on the bank until later.

With the rug gone, mother found room to lead her kits away to a quieter neighborhood. When they were all gone, we sat one of the big trunks over the hole to prevent reoccupation, but most importantly to hide the hole. Exclamations, orders, and curses from the creek indicated that the bath was not over. We declared the tent uninhabitable and moved SP's cot to a level spot downwind from our bedrolls. He appeared wrapped in a blanket, bedraggled and silent. I almost felt sorry for him until Gus giggled, then I had to have a coughing fit.

Bob showed the man his bed and tucked him in and semi-quiet settled on the camp.

"Crimey, that man stinks," Bob whispered. "Used up a whole bar of soap, 'e did, and it never did a bit o' good."

"Did he get sprayed?" Gus asked.

"No, th' stench just seemed to settle on 'im and won't go away. How did that skunk get in the tent?"

"Musta dug under the edge," Gus said, "a skunk will dig like a gopher."

Bob sat up and looked around, "Where is it now?"

"Headed for a quieter neighborhood, I imagine," said I. "That reminds me, we should sleep with the cover over our heads in case sh—it comes back. Tomorrow we need to get these beds up off the ground."

"They can't climb trees, can they?" Bob was working on a plan.

"Not that I ever knowed," Gus replied.

"Go to sleep, you two," I demanded.

The Persian was ruined. No amount of washing, airing, or

sunning diminished the smell. We stretched it over the bushes and just left it there when we returned to the ranch. It was two years later that I ran across it hunting cows. The print had faded in the sun and it was showing signs of wear. Some animal—probably a cow—had chewed off a corner. As I passed on, the breeze brought me the definite odor of skunk perfume.

Although he was quieter, the skunk episode didn't dampen SP's ardor for a dinosaur.

Gus struck the chisel a hard blow, sending chips flying. "How can a man claim he found a dinosaur when he never turns his hand to the work?"

"Because we be merely dumb 'sarvents,' " I replied.

"Well, I'll be glad when that tent is properly aired out an' he sleeps in again. His snoring would wake th' dead."

"Kept me awake last night," I said. "Tonight, we'll have to give him the cure."

"Hey, that's right, we know how t' cure him," Gus exclaimed.

Bob had walked up to hear that last exchange. "You can cure his snoring?"

"Sometimes, but it usually takes several treatments for it to work," I said.

"We must try it," Bob said.

"Do you have any bitters in your plunder?" I asked.

"As a matter of fact . . . yes, we do. I'll get it for you."

"Not now," I hastened to say. "You can get it for me tonight after he has gone to sleep. I'll also need the salt."

Now that the plan was set, we were eager to put it into play and the afternoon dragged by. SP was pleased with another tooth Gus had retrieved from the rock, and I was nearly done excavating the largest egg I had ever seen. It lay in a nest of petrified twigs that we were going to try to save.

Gus peered over my shoulder, "Take a big skillet t' fry that egg, wouldn't it?"

"Take an army t' eat it," Bob said in passing to start supper.

"It has sure taken a lot of blisters to free it," I said. "Sneak me the bitters when you can," I whispered.

"Righto."

"Righto? Is that a word?" Gus asked.

"Only on the other side of the ocean." I lay my tools aside, "Let's eat."

As was his custom, SP went to bed with the sunset and we sat around the fire until he began to sing his nightly song. I poured out about a teaspoon of salt into a large spoon. Then I stirred in a few drops of the bitters—and it *was* bitter. The two started to follow me when I crept over to the royal bed and I waved them back. SP lay on his back, his face so much like a slack-jawed cadaver that I shuddered. The vision troubled my dreams for days. Very carefully, I scraped the concoction into his mouth and retreated.

"You would think a feller who slept with his mouth that wide would attract bugs," Gus whispered.

"Sometimes he does," Bob said. "It sure causes a fuss."

It took a few minutes for the sleeper to recognize the taste in his mouth. He inhaled sharply and smacked his lips several times; finally coughing and turning to his side, he slept quietly. Half an hour later, he was loudly proclaiming he had returned to his back. I administered another dose with the same result. We had all gone to bed when he snored again. I dosed him and was under my covers when SP awoke coughing and choking.

"Robert, Robert," he called until Bob was awake enough to reply.

"Yes, me-lord."

"Bring me water, a lot of it, and the medicine case. My gall has busted."

★ ★ ★ ★ ★

He sedom listened to good advice.

—Robert J. Casey

Chapter 30
How Sir Percival Lost the Dinosaur

Robert encouraged Sir Percival to return home to seek medical attention, but the man would not, believing he must complete his mission before his condition worsened. In the end, the treatment backfired on us somewhat, for he was far more insistent

His condition repeated itself a couple of nights, and we "sarvants" worked hard to complete the airing and cleaning of the tent. The galling episodes ended when he returned to sleep in the tent, and Sir Percival blamed sleeping in the dews and damps for his discomfort. Our snore-free sleep was unaffected by said dews and damps.

It was beginning to look like our quest would have no end until we found "the whole elephant," so to speak, and the longer we suffered SP, the more likely the violent death of an English knight in Texas would cause an international incident. So me and Gus made a plan.

We put it in motion one night during supper: "New moon tonight," Gus said, looking at me as if that were a fact of some significance.

"This is the last one?" I asked.

"Last what?" the impatient SP demanded.

"Last new moon before the Comanche Moon," I replied.

"Pray tell me what this 'Comanche Moon' is."

"It's the time the Comanche and Kioway Indians come down from the Llano Estacado and raid the settlements," I said.

SP made his backhanded swipe to wipe the thought away,

"That means nothing to me."

"They raid anyone they find on the prairie, lookin' for scalps," Gus said. "Does that mean anything to you, Sir Percival? It does to me, an' I don't expect to be out here chippin' rock under the Comanche Moon."

"You'll do as I say—"

"Your 'say' ends where my scalp begins, Sir Percival, and me and Gus will be at the ranch under Squaw Mountain or at Jacksboro when that full moon comes up in about twenty-eight days."

"You can stay if you want to, the Injuns like English hair," Gus said.

Bob was taking all this in, his discomfort growing. "I do not wish to donate my scalp to some heathen Indian, my lord."

For a moment I thought the man would strike his servant, and I'm sure he would have if his quirt had been in his hand. "I will not have you speak—"

"Sir Percival, the eighth day from today I will be riding back to the ranch, with or without you." I stood and looked down on him to emphasize my intent.

Even then he did not accept our intention, believing he was still in control of the situation and disbelieving a mere servant would stand up to him. "We shall see."

When we arose the next morning, me and Gus strapped on our guns and that is how we worked the next six days. The seventh day in the afternoon we packed our things and prepared to ride out without the wagon. Bob did an extraordinary thing: he struck the tent, folded it, and stowed it in the wagon.

When SP returned from his searching, his cot was set up near the fire. Not a word was said, and when morning came, Sir Percival mounted Thunder and led us east to the ranch. We arrived the evening before the full moon.

"Hey, Gus, look, there's Uno and Dos," I called. The two

Utes were sitting on the bunkhouse porch weaving horsehair hackamores.

It was gratifying that Jake's first greeting was, "Come in ahead of th' Comanche Moon, did you?"

SP looked surprised, "It was a matter of necessity. We were low on supplies."

"Th' idiot still won't admit we were right," Gus said through a set jaw.

Nevertheless, Sir Percival requested that Thunder be shut up in the barn. Two nights later, Indians stole him and SP was livid. Ever the impatient one, Sir Percival and Bob left for Fort Worth the next day, and we gladly said goodbye to SP for the last time, we hoped.

"Thunder being all they took," Tom said after breakfast, "means they are still headin' east an' intend to stop back by for the rest on the way home."

"That gives us a chance to cook up a welcoming party and might get Thunder back," I said.

"Not likely there'll be much left of that horse by then," Jake said. "Let's see if we can get our horses out of harm's way, then you can set up a party for the Injuns."

"They ain't a place in Texas those horses are safe from that bunch of thieves. Our best bet is to ring th' herd with 'bout a thousand rifles," Gus said.

"You're right, Gus, but there may be a safe place to keep the horses and protect them with less rifles," Tom said. "Jake, do you think we could keep them safe in that box canyon south of where Lodge Creek runs into th' Trinity?"

"Probably our best bet without leaving Texas," he said, grinning at Gus. "We can't fight them off enough to save the horses, but we could fool them."

"How?" I asked.

"Don't know just yet, Sut, but it will come to us if we work at it . . . First of all, we have to keep the scouts from finding the herd."

Tom squatted and drew a map of the area. "If we took the horses west a ways . . . and say, cross the river at the ford, only not cross, but drive them down the river to Lodge Creek and up the canyon . . ."

"We ain't got enough men t' keep those cayuses in th' water an' not wander everwhere," I said.

"We could just take a few at a time," Gus suggested.

"A few at a time, and we would not have to wade the river so much," Jake said.

"Jake, how far ahead of th' pack do those scouts run?" I asked.

Jake considered, "Half a day, might be a day out sometimes."

"What if we let them find the horses here, then moved them after the scout leaves and set up our ambush here without the horses being around?"

There was a long silence while they considered my idea.

"Could work if we knew when we were scouted," Tom said.

"We can depend on Uno and Dos to determine that," Gus said.

"You gone draw dem Injuns here an' fight 'em off?" Cookie's interjection startled us.

"Where'd *you* come from?" Gus demanded.

"Where d'ya think?"

"We'll have to know when they scout us," Jake continued. "Then move fast. We'll need more men."

"Jacksboro men would help—and pay *us* for the priviledge," I said.

"We wouldn't have to hide tracks, since they would attack us at night," Gus added.

"Still, it wouldn't hurt to hide th' tracks around the place," Tom said.

"You gone do it, ain't you?" Cookie demanded.

"You can help us, Orville," Tom said.

"I'll help by buryin' my pots an' pans an' kettles an fightin' t' keep my nappy hair," he snapped.

"Knew we could depend on him," Gus muttered.

"We'll bury the kitchenware for you, Orville; I have something else for you to do," Jake said. "Take these two chowhounds and go over and close up the mouth to that canyon. Tom, go to Jacksboro tomorrow and gather some help, if possible. I have an errand to run, may be gone a couple of days."

That's how the plan started. We modified it as we progressed with the end result that the country was full of spies who would warn us when the Comanche approached, and we had twenty-seven men join us from town. Every one of them had lost something to the raiders, from stock to family members and burnt houses and barns. We all had a singular purpose.

The posse was not going to arrive until the Indians were reported in the area. With family safely forted up in town, they rode in with the waning half moon. "They're about a day out," one of them said, "scouts half a day ahead."

"Good, all we have to do now is know when those scouts get here. Don't you two interfere with them in any way," Jake shook his finger at two grinning Utes.

"Hurry up and wait," I said. "I wish those Injuns would get here."

"So you can get shot by an arrow or bullet you never saw?" Gus was always looking on the dark side of things.

"No. So I can get my sights on some no-good thievin' Injun that just might have killed my pa or your dad. I'd knock off a little of him at a time until there wasn't enough left t' bury, then I'd turn th' hogs on him." My anger surprised me as much as it surprised Gus. I didn't know I felt so intense about the

Comanche-Kiowa-Arapaho raiders; it just came out, and there it was.

"I'll have to remember not to make you that mad at me," Gus said.

"Just don't kill my people," I said, then hastily added, "I know you wouldn't, Gus, I'm just mad, that's all."

We were sitting on the bunkhouse porch watching Uno and Dos weave. Of a sudden, Dos looked at Uno and nodded. They quickly tied off their weavings, left them hanging on the post nails, and disappeared around the house. We didn't see them again for three days after glimpsing two naked and painted Indians leaving the horse corral.

"Now what tipped them off?" Gus asked.

"Some sixth sense told them trouble was near," I answered.

"Now there you go again. What is a sixth sense?"

"They are much closer to nature than we are. They responded to something they smelled, saw, felt, heard. Something we are not attuned to."

"Like the time you shot the skunk?"

"Yeah."

One night at the line shack, a rabid skunk came through the open door. His aroma woke me and I reached for my gun and waited. I tracked him across the floor by the sound of his sniffing, though I couldn't see him.

Gus stirred in his bunk, "Where is he?"

Otha and Ep bunked across the room and I heard them stirring. "As soon as he's out of your line of fire, I'm gonna shoot him," I said.

"You're talking about that skunk and not Ep, aren't you?" O asked.

It seemed that every skunk we saw was rabid. We naturally shot them if we found one moving around in daylight. Several people sleeping on the ground have been bitten by the skunks and died from rabies.

"Where is he?" Gus asked again.

"Hush and listen," I answered. I followed the sounds of the animal and when he was well out of the line with O and Ep, I fired twice and the skunk fired once, causing a hasty exit of four men from the shack.

"You either got him or scared the stink out of him," Ep said.

"I'm pretty sure I got him at least once," I said, sniffing my blanket. The odor was so strong we could smell it in our clothes.

"That's the worst-smelling skunk I ever smelled," O said.

Ep snorted to clear his nose, "You could cut that smell with a knife, an' with two slices of bread, have a sandwich."

We slept outside in just the blankets we were lucky enough to grab and the horse blankets still damp from the day's riding.

"Think I'll be sleeping outside for a while," said Gus, and we all agreed. We found the dead skunk and hauled our odor-saturated clothes and beds out and had a washday.

"Sut?" Gus called and I opened my eyes. We were laying in our bedrolls, relaxing before sleep, when he called me from the start of a pleasant dream.

"What?"

"You didn't see that skunk when you shot him, did you?"

"No, I followed him by sound."

"So it was just a lucky sound shot."

"N-n-no-o, I was sure of his location." I hadn't thought much about it, but now that Gus was asking, I tried to remember what I was thinking when I shot. I remember I had no doubt about where the skunk was and I was aiming for his head and disgusted when I hit him behind the shoulder. I later determined that my head shot had missed and my second shot killed him.

"How could you know where *she* was and not see her?"

I thought about that a moment and said, "I saw *her* in my

mind moving across a place I knew, beyond where I knew O and Ep were. It was just like I could see those things because I was so familiar with them."

"So you remembered where everything was?"

"Not *every*thing, but the things I needed to remember at that moment."

"I don't understand."

"Well, I didn't have to remember you since you were in your bunk and not in a possible line of sight. I guess my mind knew where I was without me having to think about it. I only needed to know where the skunk was and what was beyond him that could be harmed by my shot."

"I still don't understand," Gus said to the stars.

"You're not conscious of the things your body knows that you don't have to think about."

"What do you mean?"

"Say if you wanted a bridle you left hanging on a nail in the barn. Your feet know how many steps there are to the nail, and your hand will reach and pick up the bridle without fumbling around in the dark. When it's daylight, we don't think about it; we think our eyes see how far it is to the saddle and they direct our hands to pick up the bridle. We give our eyes too much credit. At night, if we don't rely on the memories of our limbs, we fumble around trying to make our eyes do all the work." I sat up, "For instance, I bet you could go to your saddle and pick up the piggin' strings on the horn without fumbling around."

"Bull."

"You can if you don't think about how you are going to do that without light and just get up and do it. Go ahead, try it."

"I can't, I just thought about it."

We lay there a few minutes, drifting off to sleep, and I said, "Gus, go get me those piggin' strings on your saddle." I heard him get up and shuffle off and presently he came to me with the strings.

"See, you can do it."

"Did it in my sleep."

"That may be, or it may be that you were so sleepy you didn't think about it and your feet and hands took over. They got you to the saddle and piggin' string, then they got you to my bunk, all without using your eyes. Well, go to bed, we'll talk about it in the morning," I said. He shuffled off.

"Find it all right?"

"Yeah," he grunted and I smiled. *Didn't think about it, did you?* I don't know when I became aware of it, but I know I can lay something down in daylight or dark and go back to that item in the dark and unfailingly find it without fumbling around all over the place. Apparently, we all have the talent to some extent, for Gus just demonstrated it by finding the strings, finding me and then his bed.

"I guess you can close your eyes and find the Wagon Box Spring," Gus said as we rode the next day.

"No, I use my eyes and the information directs my compass to know where the spring is," I said.

"Even out here where there are no landmarks?" He waved at the featureless Llano.

"Yes. My mind sees details too minute for me to note, but it can process it and deduct where we are and where we need to go." On that featureless plain, you develop a keener sense of location and direction. The biggest thing you have to learn is to trust yourself.

No one slept in that shack until winter forced us to dig up the floor and haul in new dirt.

★ ★ ★ ★ ★

MEANWHILE, BACK AT THE RANCH

That night, we rounded up the horses and drove them to the box canyon south of the mouth of Lodge Creek. Jake left Tom and three of the town men there to guard the horses. About midmorning the next day on the porch, Gus stood up and stretched. "Think I'll see what Cookie has for a sack lunch. You go saddle our horses."

"Givin' orders now, are you?"

"You want t' go talk to Cookie?" Gus got along with the cook better than I did. It's like Cookie takes up for Gus because he's th' youngest and smallest in th' outfit.

"I'll put your saddle on backwards so you can keep an eye on what's behind us without strainin' your neck."

I can't print his reply. He came into the barn with a greasy sack and we sat back in the gloom and watched the yard and beyond. We sat there until Cookie beat the pan for dinner, then went to eat. Men had been coming in a few at a time for the last three days. We found ourselves back on the front porch after dinner, listening to the talk.

A feller from down on Keechi Creek rode in and said, "I saw a big dust down south last evening an' knew it had to be th' Injuns, so I hitched up and left the wife and kids forted up in Jacksboro and rode on out."

"They hit Weatherford pretty hard, stripped 'er clean of horses an' milk cows. Feller said them give out cows was spread from there to East Keechi," another man said.

They all had been admiring the hackamores and one of the men said to me, "I'd pay a dollar for one of those when they're finished."

"They get two and a half for them," I lied.

"Too rich for me," he said and sat on the edge of the porch puffing his pipe.

Cameron Creek flows north to the Trinity through the narrow canyon Jake had chosen for his headquarters. This was also the only trail to the ranch from the south and the Indians would have to pass through it to get to the horses in the big corral. The house sat back in a little arm of the valley away from the trail that ran on north to the river. The logical thing for the Indians to do was for some of them to run the horses north and turn west at the river to rejoin their comrades holding the main herd.

Jake had made little forts high on the hillsides along the valley and as the men arrived assigned them two-by-two to the forts. He even put some men on the hillsides north of the ranch house. The men were surprised to find a stick of Little Giant dynamite and a punk in each fort.

"You can use the dynamite to push the Indians on through the canyon. Don't stop them but don't let them lollygag along, either. It wouldn't be bad for none of them to reach the ranch. Our next job will be to capture the stolen animals."

It was clear he didn't expect the whole Indian party to drive through the canyon, but that they would send a few men to get our horses and meet the main bunch west of the ranch. That wasn't to be, for the thieves were so confident they drove their entire herd through the valley, probably thinking they could take over the ranch with little or no resistance.

Jake had put me and Gus to guard the buildings with Cookie, his shotgun, and the leftover dynamite. He had gone on down toward the Trinity to help those few men stationed there. When the stolen animals crowded into the open area around the ranch buildings, they spread out, and the Indians still alive after running the first gauntlet could not round them up. Instead, they continued on through the canyon driving a small part of the herd that had continued running.

Cookie had fired one shot at an Indian that rode by the

kitchen door. That's the only shot we got from the buildings and Gus was disgusted. "I'm shore tired of being at the back of the crowd," he complained.

"Next time we'll do something about that," I said, and we did later on.

Everyone stayed in his place for the night, just so they wouldn't become someone's target. They found only one dead Indian and three dead Indian ponies in the upper valley, but there was a lot of blood. Several of those ponies running north may have had wounded warriors laying on their backs that we could not see in the dark.

"Most likely the wounded ones will die for the lack of good doctoring," someone said, and that was all right with me.

When they rode in, Dos had three fresh scalps and an arrow through his leg. Uno sported a black eye and a hen-egg knot on his forehead. He had one new scalp on his lance.

Sir Percival and Robert had taken in all this with big eyes, staying in the background and saying little. We found Thunder in the crowd that had remained in the valley. He was in sad shape, wind-broke and sore-footed. SP was greatly upset and I think he actually mourned for the horse. "Got more feelin's for that dang horse than he has for people," Gus growled.

Jake traded a nice horse for Thunder with the idea that he might be good at stud, which he was, and our horse herd was materially improved. A few days later, the Englishmen rode out on their long trip back to "Hengland," without so much as a thank-you or fare-thee-well.

"All that work and he didn't pay us a penny," I hollered so he could hear. He didn't even flinch, just rode on.

"Good riddance," Cookie declared, and there were a lot of nodding heads and grins.

"He'd still be here if he had found his monster," Gus said.

"Too bad," I couldn't help grinning.

"You know somethin', don't you?" Tom charged.

"Yup," I said and couldn't help chuckling.

"What did you do?" Gus demanded.

"I found a whole dinasaur head with the neck bone still attatched to it."

"And you didn't tell Sir Percival?" Jake asked.

"No, he was such an ass he didn't deserve it, and we would still be digging that thing out of the hillside if he had known about it."

"Well, we at least got a chance at a good stud out of his visit," Jake said, shaking his head and laughing. "What are you going to do with your dinasaur?"

"We'll keep him hidden until a good rock man comes along that has his own men to dig for him."

Two years later, a Baylor University man visited us. "Calls himself an arch-e-olo-gist," Cookie said.

"Those four syllable words come about six to the pound," Tom observed.

I looked at Gus, "He's looking for fossils."

"What kind of feller is he?"

"Seem like da only t'ing you can hold agin him is he's a Baptist," Methodist Episcopal Cookie said.

"Yeah, but he brought diggers along with him," Gus said.

After determining his attitude, me and Gus showed him the fossil head, and he and his men dug up a whole dinasaur. It's on display at the Baylor museum.

Scripture tells us God made the Universe.
Science tries to tell us how He did it.

—Unknown

Chapter 31
The Return of Robert Grey

There were four hundred and forty-seven horses in the herd we took from the Indians. Some of the brands were from ranches nearly to San Antonio. There was a lot of discussion about how to handle the horses, and no one could come up with a satisfactory plan. No one wanted to keep the herd on their range, eating up grass their own stock needed. The problem was solved when a squad of Rangers showed up. They had gotten on the Indians' trail late and had no chance of catching up to them. We convinced them the Indians had been taken care of and that they should take the horses back south and distribute them back to their rightful owners.

"How did they do that?" Gus asked as we sat around the table after breakfast and watched it rain.

"Do what?"

"Convince those Rangers to take that herd."

"By liberal application of Jacksboro tonsil varnish and the prospect of good eating at ranches grateful to see their horses returned. With luck and a little planning, they won't have to cook a single camp meal between here and San Antone," Jake said.

Gus grinned. "Sounds like a good plan to me. Did you ever eat some of that German food around Fredericksburg, Sut?"

"We came in from the north. I haven't been south of Fort Worth," I said.

"Pretty good eatin'," Tom agreed.

Gus grinned at me, "We'll have to go some day."

"It'll be after we break that new string of horses—"

"—And after we road-brand about ten thousand steers, two and three year old," Tom interjected.

"—And put them on the trail to Dodge," Gus added.

"You gone hafta es-cort dem steers all da way t' Dodge," Cookie declared from the kitchen door.

I grinned. "Shore glad it ain't Abilene."

Tom snapped his finger. "That reminds me—I saw a wanted poster at the marshal's office in Jacksboro describing two fellers wanted for vandalism and rustling horses in Abilene, Kansas. Descriptions shore fit you two, an' th' marshal's mighty suspicious."

"You never!" Gus exclaimed. "Th' only one who knew what happened was Pock an' he wouldn't tell."

"Yeah, they're just guessing we had something to do with that night," I said.

"Here, fellers, have some bear sign." Cookie plopped a pan of steaming donuts on the table.

Gus grabbed one and dropped it on his plate. "Not 'til they've cooled some. Those things are hot enough t' melt your teeth."

"Just right," Jake said, licking his fingers.

"Take a bite and cool it with this coffee, Gus. It's only boiling," I said.

"Listen!" Jake held up his hand. Very faintly we could hear the rattle of a wagon coming down the creek. We all grabbed a hot bear sign and stood on the porch watching as the wagon pulled by six mules appeared. The driver looked familiar and we all recognized him about the same time.

"Oh no," Jake said.

"Dammit," Gus cursed.

"Well, I'll be . . ." Tom was grinning.

"I'm gittin' me shootgun," Cookie declared from the door.

"A good day to ye, gen'lemen," Robert Grey saluted from the wagon seat. "I come bearing good news: Sir Percival Hampton-Halley has left this earthly orb."

Cookie's "shootgun" stock thumped on the floor. "Glory be," he whispered.

Jake laughed. "I think you just saved a shooting, Bob. Park your wagon and we'll help you with your mules."

Cookie disappeared into the house and Bob drove on to the wagon park. We followed and helped unhitch the mules and rub them down with hands full of hay.

"Cookie's got beans and steak ready for you. Come on in and eat and we'll hear all about your doin's, Bob," Jake said.

We sat on the porch out of the drip while Bob ate and carried on a conversation with Cookie. Eventually he emerged in dry clothes, bringing a cane-bottom chair with him.

"Well, gen'lemen, 'ow 'ave ye been since Oi left? Where did all those 'orses go? Are ye goin' to trail a 'erd this spring?"

"We're doin' fine. Sent the horses home. Gonna take a herd to perdition an' hope th' Devil will let us come back," Tom answered.

"Devil can't think of a worser hell than herdin' a bunch of longhorns. He'll congratulate us and send us back for more," Jake said with a laugh. Even though we complained, we were all drawn to the trail with a herd of cattle.

"With your permission, Oi would like to assist you in your next excursion on the trail." Bob was always courteous. By contrast, it made SP's deportment all the more galling.

"You ain't goin' nowhere 'til you tell us what happened after you left here," I said.

Bob grinned and tilted his chair against the wall, found himself under a drip, and scooted over to a drier spot. "We left 'ere and went to San Antonio via Fort Worth and Sir Percival retrieved the money 'e 'ad deposited in the bank there. Oi 'ad to ask 'im for me stipend an' 'e only gave me 'alf of me wage, saying that's all Oi was entitled to. We 'ad words, but 'e refused my due, even though Oi knew 'e 'ad abundant resources."

(*I know how tiresome the missing and displaced "h"s and the "Oi" personal pronouns can become to you, dear reader, so I have taken the liberty to translate Bob's "Henglish" into Vaquero English for the remainder of this story. Ed.*)

"You can't imagine how upsetting it is that a man would treat his brother in such a fashion, and I contemplated retribution—"

"Wait a minute," Tom interrupted. "You said brother?"

"Yes—well half brother anyway. The Lord Oswald caught me mother raking hay one evening and I resulted. I was educated with my half brothers and sisters and spent much of my life in the manor, me mom bein' upstairs maid and all.

"When it was determined that Percival would seek his fortune in the west, Lord Oswald sent me to be his companion. Percy determined that I should be his valet when he promoted himself to his lordship."

"You mean Percival isn't a lord?" Gus asked.

"Wasn't. Oh no, and never will be. All the inheritance goes to the eldest son. It's customary for the lord to set up his other children with a remittance for their inheritance. Lord Oswald gave Percy a remittance and included money for my wages, but Percy kept most of it.

"Well, you can see that I was quite upset by this and plotted to get what was rightfully mine. Percy checked himself into the Menger Hotel in San Antonio and left me to my own devices. I was soon reduced to cleaning out livery stables so I could sleep in the loft and catch a meal here and there. I had to stay close, for he was the only means for me to get back home. Percy would summon me when he needed something or I needed to write his letters for him."

"He couldn't write?" I asked.

"Yes, he could, but he early determined that I should write letters to the family in his name so he wouldn't have to. Sometimes he would dictate what I wrote and he had to read every letter.

"I noticed he had become very familiar with his chambermaid at the Menger, and one day I caught him in a romp with her—"

"Never heard it called that before," Gus said.

"She was a pretty señorita newly married to a young vaquero of proud heritage. Somehow, he heard of the tryst [Bob winked) and one day the management found Lord Percy naked in his bed, carved to a fare-thee-well and the chambermaid gone. The newlyweds had left town on a honeymoon.

"I was summoned to the hotel by the management and found 'poor Percy' laid out on a board covered by a sheet. What to do? I couldn't write home telling of his death in the same hand I had used to communicate with them before. I would not have another write the letter. After giving it some thought, I wrote the family that our beloved brother Robert Grey had been murdered and was buried in San Antonio, mourned by all who knew him. I vowed to follow the murderers until I caught them and justice was done for poor Robert.

"I also included in the letter that his dying wish was that his mother would come and say an Ave over his grave. The return letter from my half sister said that the Lord Oswald had granted poor Robert's request and booked passage for his mother to come to San Antonio. That can be read between the lines that his Lordship was glad to rid himself of my mother, for she had grown older with him, and that he had his lecherous eye on a young maiden to warm his bed and soon be an upstairs maid. I debated returning to England and giving his Lordship some of what his son had gotten, but the remittance will be more of a justice for my mother." Robert stood and concluded, "So there, gen'lemen is 'ow Oi became Percy 'ampton-'alley with a remittance so long as Oi live and breathe, but ye can still call me Bob."

" 'Ow very satisfying, me man," I mocked.

"Thankye kindly," Bob said with a little bow.

"Is your mother here now?" Jake asked.

"Yes, sir, she is. When she got over the shock of seeing her son alive and well, we left San Antonio and bought a small tavern in Fredericksburg where she is 'appily engaged in serving Henglish 'ospitality to the public."

It was a quite satisfying story, not so much the murder, but the restoration of balance and justice in the universe. For days, it was the topic of our conversation. Bob stayed with us and made a decent hand, especially with the horses. On our occasional trips to San Antonio, he would visit the cemetery and lay flowers on his brother's grave.

He got great satisfaction in seeing the Baylor excavation of the dinosaur.

He was a good hand, but never could overcome
Being English.

—Jake Meeker

Chapter 32
The Devil and the Mountain Man

Jake Meeker had traded his way into the cattle business not intentionally, but by way of taking in cows in trade for his horses. It was his intention when he moved to the open range to concentrate on breeding good horses and keeping the cattle until time to sell them. Gradually, his herd grew and imposed on him so that his time was primarily spent on them instead of his horse herd.

Many cattlemen got their start in Texas in an entirely different manner. The country was full of unbranded cattle after the war and their only worth was making tallow and selling their hides. Both markets were so flooded they gave no prospect of prosperity. Until, that is, a man named McCoy saw the profit of shipping Texas cattle east to meat-hungry Yankees. Thus began the era of the great trail herds.

Thus also began the era of the rustler. A rustler was a man who ventured into the prairies and brush to catch and brand the maverick cattle that were there for the taking. At first, it was thought of as an honorable profession by men with ambition, and many a big cattleman got his start this way. Men like Charles Goodnight disliked mavericking, likening it to theft, especially when it was done on another man's range. As the maverick population decreased, the sight of a calf having a different last name than his mama became more common, and the name "rustler" was sullied. This form of rustling became a hanging offense and a few men found swinging from a cottonwood limb served to discourage others of the profession.

The stealing of whole herds of cattle was called just that—stealing.

Men who participated in this activity were called cattle thieves, not rustlers. Practically the whole of the Comanche-Kiowa-Arapaho tribes were cattle thieves, trading their stolen herds to New Mexican comancheros for their goods. We are concerned here with the Anglo and Mexican-American breeds of thief and not the Indian.

At first, we thought the cow we found on the "back forty" had just died, but the neat hole in her forehead and full udder said otherwise. "Damned thief cost us two cows," Gus cursed. "Let's see if we can follow him," I said, and we tracked the horse with a broken near forefoot shoe for several miles up the Trinity until we caught sight of smoke rising from the dugout stack. "Let's watch a while and see what happens," I said, so we hid the horses up a wash and watched.

Presently the cowhide over the door parted and a grizzled man with hair all over his face and down below his shoulders stepped out. He wore a wide-brimmed floppy hat, and a stained buckskin shirt over striped pants tucked into knee-high moccasins. The belt around his shirt at the waist held a long Green River knife and he carried a Sharps rifle.

"Bet he's a squaw man beaver hunter," Gus murmered.

"Wouldn't take that bet myself," I answered. I had no more than finished than a toddler waddled through the doorway and a dark-skinned woman stepped out to stop the escape attempt.

"Right again," Gus said with a grin.

We watched the activity around the dugout until dark, then I sneaked up to a hide hanging on a limb and dragged it off like an animal would do, hoping the drag would hide my tracks. We rode away and Gus said, "You ain't gonna fool him, he knows a coyote don't ride horses."

"Maybe he'll be more cautious about stealing calves and killing cows."

At the line shack we examined the skin and found the brand

had been partiallly cut out with only the rafter remaining. "Wonder where in the JM the rest of it went," Gus mused.

I threw down the hide and said, "We better tell Jake about this."

"We can handle it, or we're not full growed hands," Gus declared.

"Don't get the idea I'm gonna go in there and run that wildcat out of his den."

"Bet we could smoke him out," said Gus.

"Yeah, an' then what would we do with him?"

"Don' know, haven't got to that yet."

I grinned. "Well, you better get th' rest of your plan together before you start th' first of it. Somehow you got to persuade that mountain man this climate ain't healthy for him or his family."

Gus thought a while, "You think that man is superstitious?"

"If he ain't, his woman will be."

Gus's eyes lit, "Shore she is."

"That attitude is catching, if she gets wound up, it might affect him," I said. "Now what kind of spirit are you gonna make?"

"Think I'll sleep on that," he said and retired to his bunk. I was not too far behind him. There was no inspiration in Gus's dreams, but I awoke with an idea. I spent the next few days looking at different animal hooves and finally settled on hog hooves for my project.

A feral hog had been tearing up the horse pasture and we let his squeal out one night. He got baconed, chopped, hammed, ribbed, and rendered, and we threw hide and hooves in a ravine a long ways from the ranch house. I could hold my nose long enough to retrieve the hooves, and was sitting on the outside bench working on them when Gus came in from riding the range line. He sat on the steps and took off his boots, looking at the soles before setting them aside. "Did you step in something bad or die?" he asked.

"Nothing on my boots . . . might be these pig feet for dinner."

"You can eat rotten feet if you want to, but you ain't cookin' them in the house or in any of the pots."

"Thought I'd cook 'em in th' brandin' fire, if you don't mind," I said.

"That's fine if you get the wind from th' right direction."

"Shore pa'ticular, ain't you?"

Gus sniffed. "Got th' stink in your clothes, too."

"You didn't think I would do this when it was my turn t' do th' laundry, did you?"

"You're gonna wait a lo-o-ng time if you expect me to touch those clothes."

"You shore are a sissy, Gus."

The hind feet looked like they would fit my plans best and I cleaned and worked on them all afternoon, spreading the cleft and reshaping the hoof. I bored holes in them to lace them to my boots and when I tried them out, they worked fine. "How do these tracks look, Gus?"

He studied the tracks some and said, "Don't look like any track I've ever seen. Might be scary knowing this creature only has two feet."

"Might be that half-goat half-man that toots his horn?"

"Or the devil. You need horns and a tail."

"We'll find a buffalo skull with horns we can borrow, and Cookie was butchering when we left the ranch house, so I can have what's left of that tail."

We spent the next day huntin' horns and retrieving the small end of that tail and the cow's ears. I have to admit the outfit looked pretty spooky on Gus. It would be just right for that mountain man.

"What else you got in mind?" Gus asked.

"We need some powder and a bucket for water and I think we'll be set," I answered.

"Tonight, we'll make a visit."

The dugout faced a little east of due south, so I planned to make my appearance to the west of the door, silhouetted against the late sunset sky. We watched until the light went out in the dugout at sundown and waited until they should be asleep. The sky was just right when I walked up to the door, then tracked on west. When I came into sight, Gus dropped a handful of gunpowder down the cast-iron pipe chimney, and when it flared, followed it with the quart of water, making a ghostly mixture of black smoke and steam.

It was amazing how fast that mountain man appeared at the door, Sharps .50 in hand. Behind him, his wife screamed and pointed at me. The rifle was coming to bear when I dropped over the bank and disappeared.

The man would have followed if he hadn't been constrained by a hysterical woman. They disappeared behind the cowskin door and a loud conversation followed. After a time, sanity returned to the woman and the man's temper cooled. Silence descended on the household.

We retired to the line shack and checked on the squatters a couple of times the next couple of weeks. They seemed to be settled in for the winter and not interested in moving on. One day we saw the man in the pasture chousing a cow and calf toward the brush. When we rode toward him, he abandoned his herd and left.

We drove the cow and calf back to the river bottoms, watched, no doubt, by an angry mountain man with an itchy "trigger finger," as Gus would say.

"My hair's still standing up on my neck," Gus said as we dropped from sight in a draw.

I have to admit I had a tickling between my shoulder blades until we were more than a mile from the edge of the brush where he watched us. "Time for another visit from the devil," I said.

Our visit came that very night while the memory of the cow stealing attempt was still fresh on Mountain Man's mind. This time there was more powder poured, producing a satisfying "whoosh" with the smoke and steam. The reaction was much the same except the victim fired and missed, and the devil danced and laughed until the rifle came up a second time and he made a hasty disappearance.

"You hear that woman screaming?" Gus asked.

"Couldn't have helped it if I'd been deaf," I said.

"That oughta get their movin'-on itch goin'."

"Depends on how thick that beaver killer's skin is. He just might get his dander up and want to collect the devil's ears," I said.

Cattle kept disappearing and a couple of weeks later when we figgered the man had tired of night watching, we visited the dugout one night just to check on the activity there. We crept up to the smokestack and found the man had covered it with a huge slab of stone set on four rocks that left a gap between pipe and slab so the smoke could escape. There was no moving that rock.

"Now, what?" Gus whispered

I frowned. "Let's go home and think about this," and we did.

"Where in the world did someone get that cast-iron pipe?" I asked.

"Yeah an' why did they haul it 'way out here? What are we gonna do now?"

"You know, Gus, I didn't see sign of that woman anywhere."

"Me neither, an' they wasn't but two horses in that corral. You suppose she's left him?"

"We need to find out." Three days of spying confirmed that the woman and child were no longer with the man.

"That makes it easier," Gus declared. "We can catch him gone and tear the dugout down."

"I hate to lose a good dugout that way, but it looks like the only way," I said. "We need to get a couple of sticks of that Little Giant at the ranch."

"I'll bet Tom will bring us some when we meet riding the north line." We rode the line north every other day until we met Tom riding the line south from the ranch house. He would bring us supplies as we needed them and it would be no problem for him to bring us a couple of sticks of dynamite. "I'll tell him we need to blast out a spring that's stopped up," Gus said.

"Better tell him we need some more beans and flour, too," I said. Gus would meet Tom the next day while I rode the line south. It would be two days after that before we got the goods. Meanwhile, I could spy on the thief on my south patrol and see when he is away from the place.

I found him in a corral full of calves branding a new one. Somewhere on our range there was a dead cow. The waste and disregard for another man's property made me angry. I couldn't wait to get that dynamite—and I didn't care much if that piece of work was home or not when I lit it.

Gus brought the supplies in the third night and we made plans. Sunrise found us watching the dugout, and just before the sun popped up, the old mountain man came out and caught his horse. We watched him ride away and gave him time before we advanced on the dugout.

"Can we get a stick into that pipe, Gus?"

"I think so . . . we can try and see if it will go."

"I'll crawl under there and try it," I said, "and we'll have a spare stick to finish the job if we need to." It was a tight squeeze getting under that rock, but there was plenty room for the dynamite to go into the pipe. I lit the two-minute fuse and dropped it into the pipe. Scrambling to back out of the hole, I got stuck. "I'm stuck, Gus, pull me out!"

"What?" His voice came from a distance.

"Pull me out, pull me out!" A dark smoke from the burning fuse wafted in my nose. "Pull me out!" I almost screamed and I felt him grab my ankles. A boot came off and he grunted, grabbed again, and gave a mighty pull. I came out, my head banging across the rock above, and my chin digging a channel. I rolled over and hollered, "Run!" and we did, me hobbling on a bare foot. We barely had time to reach a safe distance and turn around before the stick blew with a roar. The big slab of rock lifted about a foot, broke in half, and fell back to the ground. If I had still been there, I would have been crushed. My hat that I had laid aside scooted across the ground, lifted on its brim, and rolled away with the blast wind. The ridgepole was dislodged and settled to the floor, taking the roof with it, and what was once a dugout became a sinkhole in the prairie.

"Da-a-a-mm," Gus whispered.

"That was close," I said, spitting dirt and wiping muddy blood from my chin. "He's close enough to have heard that, and he'll be back in a minute or two. I'll stay up here," (because my legs were too shaky to run) "and you get down there behind the creek bank so you will be behind him when he rides in."

We could see him racing toward us and Gus barely got hidden under the bank before he splashed across and ran into the yard. I stood above the ruined dugout with my rifle ready. His horse skidded to a stop thirty yards away and the man's rifle came to his shoulder. I called, but he didn't stop and I knew he was going to fire. Three shots sounded almost as one, and the impact of the .50 caliber slug spun me around and I fell.

I came to with Gus anxiously washing my face and talking,

"Don't die, Sut, don't die on me now."

I inhaled to speak, and the pain was so sharp all I could do was let the air out as slowly as I could. My ribs on the left side were on fire.

"You been gutshot, Sutter . . . you can't die . . . don't die on me." Tears were rolling down his cheeks.

I reached across my body and felt my side. There was a long hole like a rip in my skin, and my hand was sticky and gritty with blood and little bits of bone. "Ain't gutshot," I gasped; that was all I could say.

Every breath was excruciating, but desperately necessary. "Bleeding much?" I asked.

Gus examined the wound closer. "No, it's not too bad, but your ribs are showing and one is broken."

"Wrap me up."

"Sure, Sut, I have to go find something." He hurried away and I lay back and dreamed. Ma came to me and said, "It will be all right, Sutter, come to me to heal."

I heard me say, "I will, Ma," and Gus said "What, Sut?" He was ripping up a sheet he had found somewhere. He helped me sit up so he could take my shirt off. Then he cleaned the wound and pushed the skin together as much as he could. He wrapped a strip around my chest to hold the padded dressing in place.

"Sut, can you stand so I can wrap your ribs?" He had retrieved my boot and was putting it on my foot.

"Uh-huh, if you can help me." He got me up, but I couldn't stand alone. I had to sit back down on that big slab rock while Gus led one of the horses to me. I could stand holding on to the saddle while Gus wrapped my ribs tight. My knees kept wanting to buckle and Gus had to practically lift me into the saddle. He was gone a few minutes, chasing the calves out of the corral and catching up Mountain Man's horse. We left the man where he lay and started toward home, Gus pushing the calves along.

It was hard to tell which was slower, me or those calves. Either way, we didn't hurry. All I remember about that trip is that it was very long and I don't remember it ending. I remember Doc Pritchert coming into the bunkhouse and I remember the smell of ether. When I woke up, Ma and Liz were there, listening to the doctor giving instructions. Liz sat on the edge of the bunk holding my hand. I squeezed it and grinned at her.

"He should lie still a couple of days before trying to move. The skin is pulled pretty tight and needs time to knit together before he is very active. I've treated the wound with sulfa, but keep a close watch for infection. There may be bone fragments come to the surface of the skin from time to time. We can remove them later when he is well. When you take him home, stop by Jacksboro and let me look at him." That's the last I heard and when I woke again, he was gone and Ma was rocking in Jake's chair by my bed.

I waved my hand at her and she grabbed it and said, "Sutter Lowery, what ever am I going to do with you?" I could only grin and drift back to sleep. That darn ether.

It was three days before I could stand to sit up some, and on the fourth day I abandoned that bunk most of the day. It made me awful tired.

The boys had turned the bunkhouse over to me and the women and slept in the house. They had rebranded seventeen calves and kept them in the horse pasture for the time being.

They had buried Mountain Man in the dugout and brought what little they could salvage back to the ranch. That .50 Sharps stood in a corner of the bunkhouse and the boys said I could have it, but I didn't want it. Ma took it home with her and it stayed around the house until one of the boys took it when he left home.

The seventh day we went through Jacksboro and saw Doc Pritchert. He was satisfied with my progress and told Ma she could take out every other stitch the tenth day and the rest when she felt it was time.

I could get around pretty good by the second week. The stitches still pulled and everyone kept hollerin' at me to "stand up straight," especially Baby Kay. I was afraid to let Ma take the stitches out the tenth day, and she talked me out of them the fourteenth day after Doc had installed them. Two weeks later, I thought the rest could be taken out without me bustin' out again.

A month after I got shot, Gus rode down to see me and when he left after a couple days, I went back to the ranch with him.

The need for murder
Is all in the eye of the beholder.

—Doc Pierce

Chapter 33
Scouting for Mackenzie

Fall 1874

We trailed a herd of steers, two's and three's, to Dodge in the early spring of '74. There were the usual adventures and mishaps, the bulk of which I have fortunately forgotten. In August we trailed a small herd of steers to Fort Griffin for the army. We had taken a couple of days' rest, camping just outside of the the Flat, the settlement below the fort. Lieutenant William A. Thompson rode into camp and had a long conversation with Jake, the upshot of which was that Jake agreed to be a scout for the lieutenant and his commander, Colonel Ranald Mackenzie. Their forces were part of a coordinated campaign against the rebel Comanche, Cheyenne, and Kiowa-Arapaho Indians who had never come into the reservations.

Me and Gus immediately volunteered and the lieutenant accepted our offer, much to Jake's misgivings. "We're as good scouts as any of those scouts at Fort Richardson," I said with just a little truth stretching.

"I'm not going to coddle you," Jake said, "You'll be on your own."

"Good enough," Gus said. "We can take care of ourselves." The truth of that was yet to be seen, but we were optimistic. After all, three trail drives had toughened us and taught us a lot. We had grown some in the last three years. In fact, Gus was now taller than I am and still growing. By the time he was twenty, he had topped out just under six feet. I only made five foot nine—and that in my bootheels.

The next few days were really busy. We had to catch up horses that had been let out for the winter and choose the ones we would take with us. Jake had us select four horses each, including a night horse. We had to stock up on ammunition, since the army had Springfields and we carried Winchester .44-40's.

"Better take all the winter clothes we can manage," I said. "Nothin' between us an' th' north pole up there on that caprock."

Gus made a face. "My new Union suit will stop that."

"Not if it's soaking wet," Jake said. "Make sure your yellow slicker don't leak, 'specially around the collar—and be sure to take plenty wool socks. You'll be needing to change them two or three times a day, not once a month like you do now."

"I change my socks ever' day," Gus growled. He was sensitive about foot odors. Setting his boots on the porch improved the air quality in the bunkhouse considerably.

"We ain't got enough blankets, an' this old tarp leaks," I said. Me and Gus would share a bedroll to keep our load lighter. Two more blankets and a new tarp from the Flat completed our hotel. Our saddlebags were stuffed with heavy winter clothes, gloves and scarves and wool socks. The army would feed us.

The second day after signing up, we rode with Lieutenant Thompson and his sergeant, John Charlton, to Fort Concho where Colonel Mackenzie was gathering his troops for the campaign.

Thompson's scouts consisted of thirty-five men, three Lipans, thirteen Negro Seminoles, one of them being a Mexican half-breed comanchero, Jose Piedad Tafoya. Job, Johnson (a half-blood), and Henry were among the twelve Tonkawas. Me and Gus, Jake, Henry Strong, and Irish McCabe were five of the six whites. I don't remember who the sixth man was.

Me and Gus were assigned to Sergeant Charlton's scouts

with Major Anderson's supply train, and Jake stayed with Lieutenant Thompson and Colonel Mackenzie. We left Fort Concho August 23, aiming for the old supply camp the army had used in past campaigns.

Our job was to range out around the column watching for Indians and Indian trails. The last days of August were hot, but the nights were cool and a change in the seasons was evident. Adequate forage was a problem.

"I signed on to find Injuns, not look for grass," Gus griped.

"You can look for Injuns while you look for grass," I said. "If we don't feed our horses, we'll be walking, an' th' Injuns'll be findin' us."

We followed the Colorado River until it turned west, then drove up the drying Deep Creek and found water on the Double Mountain Fork of the Brazos. North Fork had water, but we didn't get wet feet crossing that Salt Fork farther north.

The trip with those slow wagons took us eleven days and we arrived at the campsite late in the afternoon of the third of September.

"Where is this place, anyway?" I asked.

"Major Anderson says it's on the White River, but Johnson says it's on Running Water Creek," Gus said through a mouthful of buffalo hump steak.

"No, no, we are on the Freshwater Fork of the Brazos," Irish McCabe said. His grin betrayed some sort of joke. "They also call it Catfish Creek."

"So this . . . stream, here, is called Freshwater *and* Catfish?" I asked.

"And Running Water and White River," Irish said, grinning.

"Four names for the same river?" Gus exclaimed. "And I still don't know where we are."

"We are on the White Running Freshwater Catfish River Creek Fork of the Brazos River," I said, and ducked a flying short rib. It didn't even have any meat on it.

The next morning was a mass of activity as the drivers and soldiers set up camp. Major Anderson was everywhere directing the work. "You scouts mount up and reconnoiter the area. Look for Indian sign and get familiar with the area. Get to it, I expect Colonel Mackenzie is not far behind us and things will start popping when he arrives."

When we returned that evening, we were met with a wall of supplies surrounding a large open space where the animals, including a small herd of cattle for beefing, were to be kept at night.

"Welcome to Anderson's Fort, gentlemen," Sergeant Charlton said as we rode into what became known as Anderson's parade ground.

We rode out every day, patrolling the perimeter of the camp, even riding several miles out looking for Indian sign. It was turning out to be a wet September with lots of rain and wind that as often as not turned into a cold norther. It was miserable scouting with everything wet.

"Br-r-r-r, it's too cold to ride circles around this blasted camp. Tell Charlton I'm takin' today off to keep my blankets warm for tonight," I said to Gus.

"Tell him yourself, I'm so wound up in blankets it'll be noon afore I'm free."

"If ye both donna get up and dressed for r-r-roll call, ye'll be *walkin'* those circles 'round this camp, r-r-rain and shine," Irish McCabe warned as he rolled his bed. "Charlton's got somethin' cookin' and you might want a bite or two."

After breakfast we generally had a sort of roll call, and Charlton gave out our assignments for the day. He told off everyone except me and Gus and Henry, the Tonkawa scout. To us, he said, "Gather your things and saddle up and bring a packhorse for a two-day scout. I've drawn rations and corn for the horses, but we don't need to load that packhorse too much; we need to travel light and far."

"Which of these horses is most likely t' travel a straight line?" Gus asked. "They've gone in circles so long, I don't know if they are able to do anything else."

"Pick any one of them and when he asks, tell him it's gonna be a great big circle an' you'll tell him when to turn."

The sun arose September 18th to look down on dark and somber clouds scudding north across the sky. The air was hazy, limiting visibility. We scouts traveled quickly over familiar grounds, then slowed and spread out to search new ground. It was late in the evening that we found a faint trail crossing our pathway.

"How many do you think passed this way, Henry?" Charlton asked.

"Not know, rain wash tracks away."

"It rained yesterday, so the trail is older than a day or two," I said.

Henry pointed east, "They go there, may go to Pease River, yes."

Sergeant Charlton looked at the sky and thought a moment, "Let's go on north a ways and see if we find anything more." In less than a mile, we found a similar trail and half a mile further was a third. All seemed to be about the same age and all were pointing toward the Pease.

We rode two more miles north without finding anything and Charlton said, "This is far enough, men. We'll rest the horses here and eat a little, then ride for camp—all night if we have to."

"And that's just what we did," Gus said as we rode through Anderson's Fort gate late on the afternoon of the 19th. We took care of the horses while Charlton and Henry reported their findings.

"Lookee there, Gus, the late Colonel Mackenzie and Jake have arrived," I said.

"Things'll start poppin' now, I'm gonna eat supper and get scarce." And that's just what he did, only to be called out and ordered across the river with the rest of us scouts, riding a fresh horse and towing another behind. Twenty of us rode north behind Sergeant Charlton. We rode all night and were still south of the first cross trail at sunrise.

"We'll rest here, men, and eat a cold breakfast after you have changed your saddles to your fresh horse."

No one delayed changing horses. The last thing a man wanted was to ride a tired horse in a time of need for action when his companions had fresh ones. We sat on the ground eating with our saddled horses' reins draped over our shoulders while the newly retired horses grazed around us.

I looked up and was startled, "Gus, look at the Tonks," I whispered.

"Uh-oh, somethin's up."

We both pulled our rifles across our knees and watched. I slowly cranked a shell into the chamber, watching the Indian scouts. "They are looking toward that arroyo behind us."

"Not all of them, some are looking at that gully north of us," Gus replied.

I stood up and as casually as I could tightened my saddle girth, all the time watching the trail and arroyo south of us. "Watch to the north, Gus."

The instant a meadowlark called from the prairie, screaming Indians rose simultaneously from both arroyos. The loose horses raced out of our midst, a couple of saddled horses with them and the rest jerking on their reins in panic. For a few moments, we all had our hands full trying to keep our mounts, but most of us were soon mounted and chasing our horses. The Indians lined up opposing us as young warriors-to-be gathered the horses and drove them away.

It was obvious the objective of the enemy was stealing the horses, but they were more than willing to do battle with us. We parted, trying to ride around both flanks of their lines, but the Indians also split riding between the retreating herd and us.

Firing became heavy and a horse behind me screamed and fell, dumping his rider. Gus fired three quick shots and hollered "Yeah," when an Indian fell. His companions picked him up and the whole line turned and retreated with the stolen horses. It became a running battle. We didn't run a mile before Sergeant Charlton gathered us and said, "No use wearing our horses out going after horses we'll never catch. We'll turn back and report to Colonel Mackenzie, and I'm sure he can do more damage to those Injuns than we can."

We met three scouts left afoot, the two Anglos who lost their mounts and the Seminole who had his horse shot from under him limping along.

With that, we headed for the fort, the injured Seminole riding behind a companion and the other two walking. After an hour, the sergeant picked a Tonkawa who had a good horse and sent him ahead with a message to Mackenzie. When we arrived, the camp was alive with activity, preparing to move.

We rode north the next days through cold rain and winds that turned into howling northers. The rain washed out any sign of the Indians. Some of the horses began to drop out and Mackenzie had them shot to keep them out of the enemy's hands. It was a hard time.

We stopped at Quitaque Creek and camped in a driving rain, the creek roaring its defiance. Lieutenant Lawton's supply wagons had bogged in the mud, but he rode in with twelve mule loads of supplies.

Smoky fires of wet buffalo chips did little to cook the steaks, and it was in just such conditions that me and Gus learned to eat rare meat.

Gus had his socks off drying his feet, "Rub between your toes, Sut, or they'll web up."

The weather was so bad, the colonel decided to stay in camp for the day and we welcomed the rest.

"What gets you wetter, running in the rain or walking?" I asked.

"If you run, you collide with more drops than if you walk," Jake said. We were all huddled up under our new tarp, which still shed most of the rain.

"But if you walk, you're in the rain longer," Gus added.

"You might be able to dodge between the drops walkin'," I said.

"Ain't no spaces between these drops," Gus declared. "In fact, they ain't no drops, just streams of water coming down. I hafta breathe in my hat to get air." A hailstone thumped on the tarp. "Good," Gus said, "they's air between hailstones."

After the hail came that cold north wind and we wrapped in the damp blankets. "You'll stay warmer if you don't wiggle," I said.

"Does that include your jawbone?" Jake asked. Even he got grumpy in this weather.

"The only thing good about this weather is the damn Injuns are not pokin' around in it," Irish McCabe said as he pushed under the tarp.

"No boots on the blankets, Irish," I called over the thumping ice. We heard the curious snap, crackle, and boom when lightning strikes too close, and all ducked.

All was quiet a moment and Gus asked, "Where did it hit?"

"Donno," I said, "but I smell smoke."

" 'Tis fire and brimstone," Irish said.

"They'll be warm, won't they?" I asked.

"Just like hell, me friend."

"Hell ain't all fire and brimstone, parts of it are wind and rain and cold," Gus said.

> There is something about the Irish temperament
> That is not ideal for exploration;
> It is too quick, too mercurial, too imaginative,
> Too headstrong, and paradoxically too brave.
>
> —Alan Moorehead

Chapter 34
The Palo Duro Fight

If anything, Quitaque Creek was higher the next morning and we broke camp and slogged up the creek, climbing out on the Llano about midafternoon, as best we could tell. By some miracle, Lawton got his train up on top of the caprock, and after about four miles on the plain, we stopped and hunkered down under another norther.

For the next days, scouts with small detachments of soldiers searched the prairie never finding Indians, just their tracks and trails.

Lieutenant Thompson looked down to let the rain drain from his hat brim before looking up as we rode in. "Find anything, men?"

"Just tracks, sir," I said, "just tracks."

"Lots of tracks. Tracks goin' here, tracks goin' there, an' no Injuns t' go with 'em," Gus said.

"Mackenzie has split us into two battalions. You two will go with your detachment in his battalion in the morning. I'm going with the other battalion and we'll meet in three days north of here at the head of Tule Canyon."

We moved south and west over the plain, finding fewer trails and most of them older than the ones up north.

"I feel like a salamander goin' from one wet place to another," Gus said as he crawled into the damp bedroll.

"Just think of those Injuns sittin' in their cozy tipis by a warm fire, all toasty and warm an' laughin' at us out here dragging through mud and rain lookin' for them," I said.

"Ain't nothin' like it, is there? I don't have any notion of living like a king, I want t' live like an Injun with two or three wives t' do all th' work an' me to lay around an' be taken care of," he said.

I fell asleep to the sound of his voice and woke to it the next morning. "I hope you slept some time during the night."

After a couple of days scouting, we moved north toward the rendezvous at Tule Canyon. "These Injun trails are getting more and more frequent," I observed

"Any fresher, and we be seein' th' makers," Irish McCabe said. "The clouds are a-settin' right on our heads."

"Look how fresh these tracks are," I said. "They haven't even filled with water." The three of us turned and followed the tracks.

"I see shadows," Gus exclaimed in a low voice.

"Don't see 'em, Gus where?"

"Straight ahead . . . now they are gone."

We picked up our pace a little and soon I could see shadowy figures moving along ahead of us. "Here's where we stop," Irish said, pointing to where six new travelers joined the twelve or fourteen tracks we had been following.

"You got no argument from me on that," I said, and we turned and groped our way back to the scout camp and reported to Lieutenant Thompson, who requested that the scouts follow the trail.

September 25, 1874

We were out as soon as there was light enough to see and the sun rose above a speckled sky.

"What is that thing?" Gus asked, shading his eyes.

I squinted at the sun. "Don't know, but it looks like it's mildewed around the edges."

"*I'm* mildewed all over."

"I know, I can smell you."

We stopped at noon and ate some hardtack and salt back. Sergeant Charlton stood and looked north under the shade of his hat. "I see a bunch of buffalo coming our way, Lieutenant."

Thompson rose and dug his binoculars out of his saddlebag. "They are Indians, Sergeant, and they are going to attack us. Get your men ready for action."

Charlton gave six men charge of the horses and formed us in a line around the horses.

The lieutenant watched the approaching Indians and called to us, "Form a skirmish line, men, they outnumber us four to one."

"Thirty-one of us, so there's a hundred twenty . . . four of them," I said.

Gus handed me a bag of shells from my saddlebag, "Don't need all that ciphering, Sut, an' don't quit when you've shot your four."

"Hold steady, men, and reserve your fire until they are in easy reach," Lieutenant Thompson called. He was quite calm in the face of what seemed to some of us certain death by a horde of savages. One determined charge through our position would be the end.

The Indians charged at full gallop and when they were within about sixty yards veered right and began circling our formation.

"Why did they do that?" Gus asked as he took aim and fired.

"Don't look gift horses in the mouth or try to figure an Indian's mind," I said.

Irish McCabe was reloading his gun, "Saints be thanked, they turned instead of running straight over us."

"Must have seen your ugly mug an' scared th' horses," the man next to him said.

We fired, then fell back, step by step. "Is anyone sure we're retreating toward the command?" someone asked.

"You let the lieutenant do th' navigating an' you do th' shootin'," Gus demanded over the noise of the fight.

"You're very good at shooting, Gus, just not too good at hitting," the man replied.

"What's that idiot on the white horse doing?" someone asked.

"He challenge one of us come out and fight him, yes," Job said.

"I'll fight him from right here," I said and took careful aim—as apparently did three or four others. The warrior fell and his horse trotted away and joined his circling companions. It wasn't long until he had another rider who had been unhorsed.

We fought and retreated all afternoon and near sundown reached the trail of our battalion. When the Indians saw that, they retreated southward, thinking the larger army was near.

"Disappeared as if by magic," a grimy-faced Sergeant Charlton said.

Henry fired at the last retreating Comanche and killed his horse. The Indian was thrown on his head and arose dazed. Henry, who had ridden out to him, tried to draw his pistol bound up in his blanket and couldn't find it. The Comanche, recovering his senses, dragged Henry off his horse and for want of a weapon began beating him with his bow.

Henry was getting the worst of it and dancing around calling to us, "Why you no shoot? Why you no sho-o-o-ot?"

We were laughing so hard no one could hold sight on the warrior, and every time someone was ready, some antic in the battle caused him to lose composure. Finally, one of us got the shot and ended the dance. A disheveled Henry took his scalp and was angry with us for several days.

We found the reunited command with the supply wagons at the head of Tule Canyon after dark and Lieutenant Thompson wrote his report of the fight. He commended us for our bravery under fire and estimated we had killed fifteen warriors who were carried away by their friends, leaving only dead horses scattered along the route of our retreat.

Several detachments had reported increased signs of large numbers of Indians. Expectations ran high that a fight was soon to happen. Mackenzie called for the 26th and 27th to be rest days while the scouts did their reconnaissance.

The rest of us washed in a buffalo wallow, ate supper, and rolled up in our beds. I didn't know anything until Sergeant Charlton shook me awake in the early morning darkness, "Get up you two and get ready to ride."

"Sut, Sut, I just had a dream Charlton told us to ride," Gus mumbled.

"You had a nightmare and it's true," I said. "Get us something to eat and I'll get our horses." At least we were ready before Charlton. "Couldn't find these Injuns," he muttered as he passed, two shadowy figures riding behind. They turned out to be Job and Johnson, the Tonkawas.

We rode north across a sea of waving grass until we suddenly came upon a huge gash in the earth. A hundred yards away, there was no indication it was there, and I shuddered at what could happen if one came upon it in the dark.

Me and Gus held their horses while Johnson and Charlton crawled up to the brink and looked. I heard Johnson say, "Heap Injun, yes," and saw Charlton nod agreement. They looked and talked for a few minutes while we danced from foot to foot. Finally, they crawled back several feet and rose to allow us to take a look.

It was our turn to crawl the last five yards to the brink of a sheer cliff. Job pointed to two side gullies that ran into the main gulch and said, "Cita Blanka." Gus whispered reverently, "It must be a thousand feet deep if it's an inch." Sheer cliffs rose a half mile—or was it a mile—across the canyon, striped with a dozen shades of red and orange and white earth. A tiny stream ran in the bottom and hundreds of horses looking like sheep grazed its banks. Hundreds of tipis strung along the bottoms made a village three miles long. We looked and looked until Charlton called us back, and we crawdaded back from the rim.

I've seen and experienced it time after time, this crawl by visitors to that enormous canyon's rim. It's as if one is overcome by the awesome sight and approaches the rim cautiously, almost reverently, speaking in hushed tones in the presence of some mighty wonder of God's creation. The stark contrast from the flat featureless Llano Estacado is very striking—and somewhat disconcerting.

Disregarding the possibility of encountering hostiles, we rode the twenty-five miles to the Tule camp as fast as our jaded horses could go and arrived about ten o'clock that night. Charlton rode straight to the lieutenant and made his report. The two then went to Mackenzie and they had a long talk.

When he returned, I asked Charlton hopefully, "Tomorrow?"

"No, Sut. He wants to rest the horses one more day before starting something."

That was fine with me, and when I went to bed, Gus was already snoring. It started raining.

September 26

There was no reveille and we woke up just as the sun popped free of the horizon—and thirty Indians attacked the camp from the south. There was no stealing our hobbled and sidelined horses so they concentrated on harassing the camp, staying just out of range of our carbines. Every once in a while, one of the scouts let loose with his Sharps .50, and usually, a man or beast fell.

At officer's call that evening, Mackenzie said, "See that your men are fed before dark. I want the horses hobbled, picketed, and sidelined. Place the men in a circle around the herd; they can sleep in uniform and armed. We'll have a surprise for those Indians when they come to steal our horses."

There was a full moon, "Bright enough to read by," Gus avowed. Anticipation was high and we napped some.

"Watch there," Job pointed to a bush on the plain about a hundred fifty yards away, and we watched and watched.

"Wake me when that bush starts to move," Gus said and laid his head on his arm. It seemed like an hour later that I did see some movement at the base of the bush and as if by magic, dozens of Indians appeared, screaming and charging for the horses. Company A held their fire until they were within thirty yards, then cut them down and broke the attack. Meanwhile, a company of infantry escorting ten wagons loaded with ammunition and forage drove noisily into camp, led by wagon master James O'Neal.

The attack failed and the Indians retreated and harassed the camp the rest of the night, but did not attempt another charge. The only damage they did was to wound a few horses and interrupt our sleep.

September 27

Almost every scout that went out reported encounters with Indians. It seemed that there was a very large encampment somewhere south of our position. Me and Gus were left in camp to rest up and be available if Colonel Mackenzie needed us.

The harassment went on all morning and toward noon, I saw a flurry of activity in Lieutenant Boehm's detachment. "Get your horse ready, Gus, somethin's gonna happen."

"As ready as I'll ever be, Sut." There he sat on his horse. We rode over to the back of the mounted detachment and made ourselves as inconspicuous as we could while Boehm rode to where Mackenzie was watching the Indians.

Without even dismounting, he asked the colonel, "Sir, permission to pursue."

"Yes, Boehm, take two companies, but remember Fetterman and don't get trapped. Go no further than two miles."

Boehm, already turning to leave, replied, "Yes, sir."

The companies were moving before he reached us and he assumed his position in front with his scout, Irish McCabe. Me and Gus moved out on the flanks of the formation, watching.

The Indians led us south, staying just out of range on their fresher ponies. They slowed as we approached our two-mile limit and I heard Irish call, "I don't like this, Lieutenant, they're lurin' us into somethin'."

Boehm threw up his arm and said, "No, they aren't. Blow our friends a kiss, men, this is as far as we go today." The veteran soldiers nodded their approval, while the new recruits expressed disappointment. They were not familiar with Fetterman and the trap he had led his men into.

The Indians moved even closer, yelling insults and vulgarities at us as the formation turned. Boehm put the companies through several maneuvers, showing our disdain of the Indians.

"Very good, Boehm," was all the colonel said when the lieutenant reported.

The Indians continued their harassment and about midafternoon, Mackenzie moved the entire command south in pursuit. We stopped early for supper before sunset and made camp for the night. Orders were for us to keep our horses ready. It was overcast and very dark near nine o'clock when the order came to mount up, and we rode north as fast as it was possible.

★ ★ ★ ★ ★

September 28

Just as day was breaking, we came to the Palo Duro again, south of the big bend where the canyon turns west. All the scouts joined Lieutenant Thompson at the head of the column and Colonel Mackenzie rode over and said, "Mr. Thompson, take your men down and open the fight."

"Very well, sir," and we began our descent to the bottom of the canyon on a steep buffalo trail. It was too steep to ride and we had to lead our horses single file. As he stepped over the brink, Irish McCabe murmured, "And not even a cup of coffee for me stommick."

Two thirds of the way down, an Indian leaped out from behind a rock. His yell and the following shot that ended his life aroused the whole camp. The warriors had an opportunity to stop the attack at the trail, but instead chose to protect the women and children as they escaped the conflict. Their decision virtually decided the outcome of the battle before it was good and started.

The first to attack us were Kiowa, Arapaho, and Comanche warriors in front of us and from behind rocks and bushes on the canyon sides. It was a hot battle for a few minutes. As soon as we were down, Thompson mounted us, and our charge broke up the Indian attack in the floor of the canyon and gave Colonel Beaumont's Second Battalion room to form up. We quickly took care of the Indians before us on the valley floor, but the snipers behind rocks and trees were another story. We couldn't locate several Indians on a ledge behind treetops above us. They gave us fits and brought us nearly to a standstill. Sergeant Charlton's best friend, a man named Comfort, came running by with a hatful of cartridges and yelled at Charlton, "Come on." He ran ahead a hundred yards or so, Charlton following in spite of Mackenzie's call to come back. They sat down in the middle of the valley, bullets flying thick as bees, and began firing at the now exposed Indians on the ledge. They had run them out by the time the troops had advanced to their position. Later on, Mackenzie put Charlton under arrest a few hours for disobeying an order. It was this kind of discipline that made the Fourth Cavalry one of the best in the army.

A trooper named McGowan had his horse shot and instead of running for cover, began rummaging through his belongings while bullets whizzed around him. Colonel Mackenzie yelled at him to seek shelter, the second time pretty sharply, and McGowan replied, "Damned if I do before I get my ammunition and tobacco." Mackenzie gave up and turned back to directing the battle. He sent two companies to join us in a sweep through the camps while the other two companies guarded the flanks.

We rode pell-mell through the camps, scattering people everywhere and doing battle with the warriors who resisted. At the end of the villages, we saw the horse herd and Beaumont determined to capture it.

Mackenzie became concerned that Beaumont would be cut off by the Indians and sent word for him to turn back. The commander delayed obeying the order long enough for us to round up the Indian horse herd and drive them back through the villages.

Already, the Second Battalion was burning the tipis, piling the tent poles on to big fires. There was a lot of anger in the men, for much of the winter's supplies they found had been issued to the Indians at their reservations. It was the same old story we had seen before: Stock up on supplies from the agency and go out and kill civilians and soldiers.

Thompson led us back to Colonel Mackenzie for further orders and while he was waiting on him, I spied a group of

Indians moving toward the trail we had entered the canyon on. "Sergeant Charlton, they are going to block our exit," I called, pointing.

The colonel heard me and said, "Captain Gunther, secure the trail."

Sebastion Gunther and H Company beat the Indians to the trailhead and secured it. The fighting was for all purposes over and we were ordered to help with the horse herd, about 2,000 head, we guessed.

The Indians had made their escape from the canyon to the caprock without food, shelter, or horses and Mackenzie called back all pursuit.

It was Colonel Mackenzie's ironclad rule that only the bodies found on the field would be counted as casualties. Lieutenant Boehm was given responsibility for the count, and he found only three dead Indians in the whole field. The practice of carrying away their dead kept the count low.

"I killed seven of the ten Indians known to have been killed in this fight," Henry Strong said later. Another soldier recalled years later that "we passed over dead Indians everywhere," and another veteran of the fight said an Indian told him that fifty or sixty warriors had died. This may include men who later died from their wounds.

We herded the horses out of the Palo Duro and formed a box around them and herded them toward our Tule camp, arriving after midnight.

September 29

"Does anyone remember th' last time we slept?" Gus asked.

"It was just after Christmas, wasn't it," Jake replied.

One of the soldiers said, "We haven't slept in forty-eight hours."

"Well by that, I figger you got about forty-eight more before you catch up with us," I said.

"Looks like we need another trail drive to catch up on our sleep, Gus," Jake said with a grin. "I should never hear you complain about lost sleep on a drive."

"But you know you will," I said and laughed.

The colonel called out the rested companies that had been left with the camp to guard duty and the rest of us slept.

We had a late breakfast and Mackenzie gave permission for the scouts to pick some ponies from the herd. Johnson was allowed forty horses for finding the canyon. I knew the horse I wanted above all others and searched until I found him, a horse obviously kept by the Indians for racing. He came along quietly, making me think he was used to white men. The four other ponies I chose didn't like my smell and resisted.

"That Quanah's horse, King, yes it is so," Job said when he saw the horse. He seemed disappointed I had him. "The Apache Rojo Pelo gave it to him when he became a Comanche."

Rojo Pelo is the name the Indians gave a captive redheaded German who became a fierce warrior with the Comanche Indians. He is said to be Quanah's adopted son. I wondered how Job knew so much about the horse but didn't ask.

The command was turned out to separate the animals capable of serving army needs from the rest, and there were a little over a thousand ponies, horses, and mules left. It was then that Mackenzie gave the order to kill all of them. It was like one of those pictures of Hades. I saw more than one trooper with tears running down his face as he carried out the grisly task.

September 30

Midmorning, Gus rolled over on his back and lay there a moment mumbling and grunting. He flung the covers back and sat up, "How can a feller sleep with all that howling and growling going on?"

"I could, except for all that mumbling and growling from you," I said. "Be still and quiet or go away."

"I'm going and I'm gonna kill me a few coyotes and wolves for disturbin' my sleep." He grunted on his boots, stood up, and stomped them on.

"Make as much noise as you can. Cover the bed before it gets wet, and go away," I ordered.

"A-a-aw, get up and help me find something to eat before my stomach grows to my backbone. I haven't eaten in a week."

It was no use trying, I wasn't going to get any peace until I got up and hunted something to fill his stomach. "Gus, you're th' beatin'est rascal I know." I threw the covers back, sat up, and put my sombrero on.

"Cover the bed, it's getting wet," Gus mocked.

I swung my boot and caught him on the shin.

"Ouch!"

I stomped my boots on and we spooled the bed and went looking for food. The mess tent was busy and we ate a meal—not knowing which mealtime it was—with Sergeant Charlton and Jake.

"That noise in the canyon wake you up?" Jake asked.

"It did me," Gus said.

"Th' dang noise and fuss in my bedroll woke me up," I growled.

Chandler laughed. "Sounds to me it's time to split the blankets."

"Way past that," I said.

Gus ignored the conversation and went back for another plate of beans.

We finished our meal and walked out to see a sky filling with buzzards coming from all directions.

"How can they know with th' rain an' coming from upwind of th' place?" Gus asked.

"Buzzards can smell a cow a mile away and know when she's gonna calf," Jake said. "I've seen them start circling before the cow lays down. If she don't fight them off, the black vulture will be on the calf before it stands up, pecking its eyes out. They can kill a calf in no time."

"Won't have to do any killing here," I said. We rested all day and October the first moved camp away from that terrible place.

Mackenzie sent us back to the battle site to find where the Indians had gone while the command followed. All of October was spent finding trails and campsites, but no Indians. The only action we saw was the capture of two groups of Mexicans that Jose Tafoya said were comancheros. We burned their carts and goods and being out of beef, killed their oxen and ate them. Two or three of the Mexicans agreed to serve as guides, but we suspected they were not trying to find their wild customers.

"These Mixicans are no good scouts," Henry Strong said. "They have only led us on wild goose chases."

"And on purpose," Jake said. "They're worse than nothing."

"Mexicans no good scouts," Henry the Tonkawa agreed, and Lieutenant Thompson dismissed the Mexicans without pay. That night all the comancheros left camp. We tracked them the next day until they joined the tracks of their Indian comrades.

"Let's keep after them, Sergeant," I called. "We'll catch them all and unburdon the world of their souls."

We never caught up with them, but the very same ones were captured when they came all the way to the Comanche reservation to trade in 1875. Sadly, the women had no hides to work into robes and decorate for trade, and it was the last time we knew of that the comancheros sought the Indians for trade.

★ ★ ★ ★ ★

If one were to choose the great factors
In the development of the west . . .
The great freight wagons would be represented.
—Clarence Mulford

Chapter 35
The Caprock Range

1875

All of October and on into the first week of November, we chased Indians over the Llano in some of the coldest and wettest weather ever experienced by white men in this country. The Indians called it "the time of the wrinkled hands."

The soldiers were not prepared for this kind of weather and suffered greatly. Jake's foresight saved us from a lot of discomfort, but we still suffered. When Mackenzie took the command back to Anderson's Fort, the three of us resigned. It was striking, the difference in the weather between the caprock and the lower lands.

"No wonder the Indians chose the Palo Duro for their winter camps," Gus said as we rode to the ranch.

"That caprock is not a place for cattle in the winter, but it sure has good grass for summer grazing," Jake said. He had been pretty quiet since we left the army and we suspected something big was brewing in his mind.

"I know what you are thinking, Jake Meeker," I said. "You are thinking about moving the ranch."

"A-a-aw, you wouldn't do that, would you?" Gus whined.

"That country is going to be open for settlement after the Indians are corralled, and I haven't seen better grazing land in a long time," Jake replied. "It's sure a tempting possibility. I'm thinking we won't make a drive this year." He paused a few minutes, then said, "We just might buy up a bunch of two year olds and fatten them on the Llano if we can find water for them."

"I noticed a lot of ponds and wallows full of water up there," I said. "They would have water in them almost 'til July. After that you would need to find a spring or something."

"If nothing else, we could drive them down and graze them under the caprock and drive them to the ranch for the winter." Jake was really thinking about doing the move, but I noticed he would keep the ranch where it is.

"Grazing on the Llano, then driving them to the ranch for the winter is a good idea," I said.

"It all depends on when the Indian question is settled, but when it is, we'll have to move fast to stake our claim."

"You think we could do that before the Injuns are run out?" Gus asked.

"Risky, but possible," Jake replied. "We've got a pretty salty crew and as long as we are careful and friendly to the Indians, we might get away with settling there early."

"They're gonna be hungry come spring. Better take some beef you could afford to lose if we go early."

"You have a point there, Sut. I'll think some more on it before we do anything."

It made me and Gus feel good to be included in Jake's planning. I tried riding King some, but he proved to be no good working stock. Every time we went after a straying horse, he took it to be a race and couldn't be convinced it wasn't. He always won, most of the time leaving us a quarter mile away from the herd. He behaved very well in the horse herd, assuming the lead as was proper for a racehorse of his standing. Jake was pleased we had him and planned to use him for stud duty. It was many years before he could be beaten in a race, and he never tired of the sport.

Back at the ranch, Jake sent word to the crew to meet about

the same time in March, then he left on a buying expedition. Gathering neglected and strayed cattle from neighboring ranges and clearing our range of visitors took up all our time.

"Wish Jake had told those boys to come on now," Gus said as we cooked our supper.

"Yeah, whoever reps for us this spring is gonna have his hands full," I said.

"I wouldn't envy him."

That night, Tom rode in and spent the night with us. "Jake sent a couple hundred steers to us yesterday and I need you to go back with me and help with the branding."

Gus groaned, "Here we go again. Ain't it awful early to be starting that?"

"Doesn't look like it will be as bad as it sounds," Tom said.

I noticed his grin. Something was up.

Gus popped Tom's rear with a towel. "I saw that look, Tom Stepp, an' you're holdin' out somethin' on us."

"Just a couple hundred head needin' a brand," he replied, but the grin remained.

"Well, that just about gives it away, Gus. Bet none of them is over two years," I said.

"That's what I'm thinkin' an' I'm gonna nominate Tom to be th' top man."

Now, it was Tom's turn to be puzzled. By his own admission, he had never been farther west and had not seen the caprock country. "What's a top man, Gus?"

"He's th' man who stays on th' caprock ranch after we drive those steers back here for the winter."

"Think of it, a whole winter with nothin' t' do but keep our range cleared of buffalo and other folks' cattle."

"That's mighty generous of you, Gus, but I've been sniffin' somethin' strange in your offer. Think I'll pass 'til I sees th' whole hog." Tom's suspicions were well founded.

We heard the bawling before we saw anything of the calves and when we did, Gus learned to cuss. "Those are weaners, an' we gotta brand 'em? They ain't old enough t' show their manhood . . . so we brand them now and th' brand grows with them so that when their manhood finally comes down we cut them and brand them again."

I spit and said, "Don't get th' brand too hot, Gus, you'll burn right through those skinny hips."

"Hold on, Sut, I think I'm hearin' th' Lord callin' me to preach, an' preachers don't mangle little calves with hot irons."

"Don't preach usin' th' language you just been usin'." Tom laughed out loud and slapped his gloves on his leg, which caused his mount to do the sidestep dance.

Gus sat and looked at the calves, "How many did he get an' how much did they pay him t' take 'em?"

"I coulda swore a couple of them were still wet from birthin' when they came in here," Tom said. "Feller over toward Weatherford has a dairy and a surplus of calves. 'Most half of them are heifers."

"Not much longhorn in 'em," I observed.

"Not any," Tom said, "they're some mix of Durham and Jersey milk cow."

"How many are they?" Gus asked.

"He's only got about fifty head. Th' rest are two-year-old longhorns. Said he got such a good deal, he's gonna check out a couple of other dairies."

My groan was drowned out by Gus's fall from grace. "I ain't gonna do it, I ain't."

"How did they get here, Tom? In wagons?" I asked.

"No, a goatherd brought 'em."

"They ain't much bigger than a goat, are they?" I said.

"These Mexican kids come ramblin' in here one evening with their goat herd mixed all in these calves. We penned th' whole bunch in the horse pasture and next morning all the goats had filtered through that fence and were grazing on the mesquite bushes, leaving the calves bawlin' in the pen. I swear they're bawlin' because their goat friends have left."

If the weaners looked little, those longhorns looked big. "Must be a new giant breed of cow to have two year olds that big," I said.

"Two and a half year old, I figger," Tom said. "We better start with them, then tackle the babies."

"Yeah, and give the babies time to grow a little," I said. Gus had ridden on to the barn and I heard him arguing with Cookie in the kitchen.

We tackled those two and a halfs next morning and by the time we finished with all fifty of them, Jake and Otha Huie drove fifty more into the corrals. We branded them before we took on the weaners. After handling those big steers, the little ones were easy. It didn't help my disposition any that one of those babies kicked me in the mouth and loosened a couple of my teeth.

The middle of April, we lined five hundred head of two year olds and fifty weaners west for the Llano Estacado. It was necessarily slow going, primarily because of Gus's Weaners, as we called them, but also because we didn't know exactly where we were going. Jake would take one of us with him and ride ahead to scout a route and also explore the land. Once we found a fresh Indian trail, leading north toward Indian Territory. There were a lot of footprints, mostly small and bare, and only one horse in the bunch, the sign of their poor condition. Jake sent me back to bring up a steer from the drag, and we followed the Indians until we caught up with the stragglers, where Jake called to them and shot the steer. We rode away as the Indians gathered around the carcass and began butchering it.

"Hungry women and children is a poor sight, Sut, no matter

if they are friend or foe. And maybe this will keep them from helping themselves to our cattle." We went back to the herd and hurried them on their way. That was the only group of Indians we saw that summer, being well south of the Palo Duro. We turned northwest and followed the Pease River to near its headwaters and waited at Quitaque Creek while Jake and Pock scouted for a place to establish a range.

Gus stood looking at the red cliffs of the caprock. "That sure is pretty in th' morning sun, but I never saw such tore up land gettin' from here to there. These steers need to be half or two thirds goat to cross that."

"I sure don't see any way of getting up on top without wings, once we get to the bluff," I said.

"All you have t' do is find an Injun trail an' foller it," O said. "They go up an' down that bluff like it wasn't there."

"Goin' up one of those trails might expose you to some Comanche comin' down, an' they ain't in no mood t' be friendly."

"When was they ever in a friendly mood?" Tom asked. "Problem is, you'll probably never see th' Comanch' that kills you."

"Wasn't much fight in those we saw th' other day," I said.

Cookie waved a long-handled spoon and said, "Feed them a little an' the fight comes back. How will we ever get this wagon up there, even if they find a way for the critturs?"

"I don't know, Cookie, but it's for sure I'm not strayin' too far from that feed wagon," Tom said.

We waited two days for the two scouts to come back. "They'll be in today," Cookie announced at breakfast the third morning.

"How do you know that?" Gus asked.

" 'Cause they ran out of food yesterday," Cookie replied, "an' nuther one of 'em eats grass."

"Whether they show up or not, we're goin' to be movin' this

herd to new pasture," I said.

Tom stood up and dusted off his pants, "You are sure right there, Sut. Go catch up the mules and help Cookie hook up. We'll move them over to another flat up the river where there's a good pool for their drinkin' pleasure."

We only moved the herd a couple of miles. They were pleased to find new grass and scattered over the pasture. Cookie grumbled the wagon over and parked it behind a rock outcrop that would give him some afternoon shade and hide his fire from prying eyes.

Gus helped unhitch the mules and led them to the water. "Is it a requirement that cooks be grumpy, or do they get thata way with th' job?" he asked around the fire that evening.

"That's been debated around a lot of fires," Tom said.

"I was on a drive with about the gripin'est cook I ever knew," O said. "He was so bad that a man named Sims shot him dead when he threatened him with a cleaver. We buried him up by the Red River and some of the boys tamping down the grave did a little jig on it."

"What did you do with the killer?" I asked.

"Why, we made him cook, of course. Wasn't two days until he started gettin' grumpy. We formed a committee and warned him of the dangers of grumpiness. It improved his attitude quite a bit. He got t' likin' th' job and made a good trail cook. When he got too old for trailin', he opened a little place at Weatherford called the Chuck Wagon."

"I've eaten there," Tom said. "He had an old chuck wagon right there in the room and cooked off it. Served us on tin plates."

"You know some of those old fellers too old or too fat to go up th' trail used t' come in there an' sit on th' floor agin th' wall an' eat out of their laps," O said.

"Trailin' gets in your blood, I guess," Tom said.

Just then, Jake "helloed" the camp and rode in with Pock and two jaded horses. Me an' Gus took the horses and Cookie threw a couple of steaks in the pan. The two scouts were eating when we returned to the fire. When they finished, Jake packed his pipe, and when it was lit, sat back and said, "Up by the headwaters of the river is a wash with a trail wide enough for the wagon, but it'll take all of us pulling to get it up the slope. We'll drive the herd there, then turn them north to a good range with a lot of tanks and some pretty good-sized sinks that should hold water well into June. We'll need to get an early start in the morning." With that, he tapped out his pipe and unspooled his bedroll, but not before Pock had bedded down.

Imagine yourself standing in a plain
To which your eye can see no bounds.
Its sublimity arises from its unbounded extent,
Its still, unmoved, calm, stern, almost self-confident
grandeur . . .

—Albert Pike

Chapter 36
Ghost Comes to Camp

Tom had first watch and climbed up on the rock where we had made a watcher's nest. We could see the camp on one side and the pasture on the other. The horses were picketed between camp and the riverbed. I had third watch and Gus and O had the last watch.

Gus kicked me up a little early, as usual, and I climbed to our perch. That drinking gourd crept around the polestar slower than usual, and I think it stopped a time or two. I didn't dare wake O early for fear of revenge and it made for a long watch for me. That dang Gus. I could see by the setting half moon that the scattered cattle were bedded down and quiet, but when I turned back to check the camp, every horse's head was up, ears pricked. I strained to see what they were looking at, but could detect no object or movement. The fact that they continued to be restless worried me.

I tried to scan the area like Jake had taught us, "Keep your eyes moving, don't look straight at something you want to see in the dark, look a little above it or to the side and you can see it better. Don't look at the fire or any other light, even the moon. Move your eyes and if you have to move your head, do it very slow."

Moving would reveal my position and most likely make me a target if someone was out there watching. A well-placed arrow would make no sound and possibly eliminate my giving a warning. The horse at the south end stomped and backed to the end of his picket. I could see nothing. Time passed and still nothing showed, then I heard a soft whine like from a wolf or coyote—maybe even a dog.

There was movement among the sleepers and I saw O sit up. Glancing at the polestar, I saw that it was well past time for his watch. I heard him lever a cartridge into his rifle as he crept toward me, keeping low. He disappeared under the rim of the rock and I whispered, "O, can you hear me?"

"Yeah, Sut, what is it?"

"There's something over by the horses. Look at the one on the right end."

"Can you see anything?"

"No, but I heard a whine like an animal."

"Not a whine like a person?"

"Don't think so. Come on up here and I'll slip off the back side and try to get behind whatever it is," I said.

"All right, go ahead, but be careful. Anything happens, fire your gun."

I crawled out of the nest and rolled over the ridge, trying to be as quiet as possible. There was no cover for a ways and I crawdaded across the open space to a cedar bush. From there it was easier to creep in a big circle to get behind the place I thought the creature would be. I dropped down over the cutbank at the river to possibly see movement against the skyline. The eastern horizon behind me was a black line against a lighter sky, foretelling sunrise.

That end horse stayed at the end of his picket and occasionally stomped a hoof. The other horses showed less and less interest as their distance from the center of concern increased. Two or three on the far end resumed their grazing with only an occasional look our way. And still there was nothing to see, so I started at the end picket stake and covered every inch from there out in front of me. The only thing that seemed out of place was what looked like an arrow sticking up out of the taller grass. I finished my scan and looked back at the arrow, and it stood at a different angle.

Cookie began banging around his "kitchen" and with that, I jumped up on the bank and walked toward that arrow. I could tell as I approached that it was embedded in an animal of some kind and I made a noise. I couldn't tell if I was looking at a wolf or dog when it raised its head to look at me. Something on his chest flashed in the firelight and I knew he had a collar on. I approached the animal, talking to him and hoping O was watching out for me while I concentrated on the creature. He lay very still and watched me approach. It was obvious he was hurt and my only fear was that he might bite. Was he mad?

He laid his head on his paws and sniffed the back of my hand. A tail somewhere at the other end of his long body thumped twice. He didn't object when I petted his head. The arrow was sticking out of the ribs close to his right front leg. He had bled a lot and I was concerned about how deep the arrow had gone. With my right hand under his jaw, thumb hooked in his collar, I slowly rubbed his back and side until I could reach the arrow. It couldn't have gone in too deep unless it was unusually long.

"What you got there, Sut?" The dog—if that was what he was—and I both jumped. We hadn't noticed Pock approaching.

"A wounded animal," I said, not yet sure what he was.

"Why, that's a Russian wolfhound, Sut. Probably came out here with some army man and got himself lost and shot by a hungry Comanche."

"Dogeaters?"

Pock grinned. "Some of the best. Think he'll let me look at that arrow?"

"He seems pretty tame and for sure he's pretty weak," I said.

"You talk to him and let me look." Pock petted the dog's

back and moved his hand to the arrow. Feeling around the wound, he grunted. "The arrowhead hit his ribs perpendicular to the way they run and is stuck between two of them. He's probably just weak from losing blood, but I could tell his ribs were sore." He tried to pull the arrow out and the shaft came loose, but the iron arrowhead was stuck tight. Pock looked toward the wagon and called, "Yo, Gus, bring me those tongs out of the toolbox."

The tongs arrived and Pock said, "Take a boot off, Gus."

"What?"

"Give me a boot, Gus. Your ears awake yet?"

Gus pulled a boot off and stood balanced on one foot. Pock set the boot on the dog's side against the wound and gripped the arrowhead with the tongs, prying it across the toe of the boot until the missile came loose. "There you go, boy, you're free," he said.

Gus grunted the boot on. "You mashed the toe of my boot, Pock."

"All for a good cause, Gus, thank you."

I showed the dog the arrow shaft and he growled and snapped it in two with one bite. "That's what you think of it, huh?" Gus asked.

Tom showed up with a bit of half-cooked steak. "Cookie sent this to you, feller, how about a bite?" The dog took the meat eagerly and sat up on his forelegs. He couldn't get his hind legs under him until I lifted him by his backsides; then he took faltering steps toward the fire.

"Sure is gaunt, ain't he?" O observed.

"Cookie will cure that if he stays around here long," Jake said with a grin. "Last dog we had got so fat we had to roll him around in a wheelbarrow and keep him away from the kitchen."

"That's the longest legged dog I've ever seen," Gus said, and he was right. Standing, his back was at my waist at his shoulders.

He was shaggy and rough coated. We realized later that someone had kept his hair trimmed from his eyes. He looked around the camp a moment and tottered over to Tom's bedroll and lay down with a sigh. "Don't you bleed on my tarp, dog."

Pock laughed. "Think I'll go spool up my bedroll."

I got a pan of water and took it to the dog and he lapped up every drop.

Cookie called, "Biscuits done," and sent over a little larger piece of meat that quickly disappeared.

"Where did you ever see wolfhounds, Pock?" Gus asked as he returned from the wreck pan.

Pock swallowed biscuit, drank some coffee, and said, "When I finish my meal, I'll tell you, now be quiet."

Chastised for his breach of camp etiquette, Gus sat by the sleeping dog and waited until all had finished and were packing pipes. He looked at Pock expectantly and didn't say anything.

Pock lit his pipe, took three puffs, and eyed Gus. " 'Dog' Kelly up at Dodge had a kennel of those hounds and ran coyotes with them. Only dog I know that could run down a coyote. He took them out one day and let them run in the heat. They never caught a coyote, but they sure did die, every one of them. Rowdy Joe Lowe never let him forget it, either."

The dog's wound was small and "Doc" Cookie only put two stitches in it. When the dog went to the river, I waded into the water with him and washed the blood off as best I could. He smelled much better after that.

The brass tag on the dog's heavy collar said his name was Ghost. There had been more on the back of the tag that probably named the dog's owner, but it had been worn off against his chest. Pock drilled a small hole in the shank of the arrow and added it to his collar. Ghost gained strength quickly and was soon traveling with us as we herded the cattle. He always knew when mealtime was and when he disappeared toward the wagon, we knew to follow. He was a good watchdog and we had no need of a night watchman around camp or ranch house.

He hated Indians except for Uno and Dos, but those two seldom came this far east anymore, having a herd of their own on the Ute reservation in Colorado. Cookie kept Ghost well fed, but he was so active he never got fat. One year at the ranch he kept disappearing for a day or so at a time until one day he came into the yard with two romping puppies that were obviously half wolf.

Try as he might, Ghost couldn't train the dogs to be good ranch hands, even with our help. One day they attacked and killed a newborn calf and before I could draw a bead, Ghost tore into them and killed one while the other ran, but my bullet ran faster. That was the last time Ghost tried to augment our watchdog corps, though we continued to notice very long-legged rough-coated wolves from time to time.

No one could guess how old he was, but he stayed with the ranch five years, even making a couple drives to Dodge City. When he got tired or foot-sore, he rode on the wagon seat with Cookie, who was his best friend. He slept at the foot of Cookie's bed at the ranch and one morning Cookie discovered he had died in the night.

Cookie was heartbroken and the rest of us were not much better off. We had a funeral and buried him on a mound above the yard overlooking the creek. Later on, there were a couple of men buried with him, but Ghost was the first in that cemetery.

The pioneer dog deserves a dignified story,
For he was a part of the serious business
Of his pioneer owner.

—John E. Baur

Chapter 37
On the Llano Estacado

We rounded up the herd and set them toward the arroyo that led to the top. Cookie struggled with the wagon over that rough ground and me and Gus were delegated to help him.

"You go on ahead and find an easy drive and I'll stay with the wagon," Gus instructed.

I glared at him, "Who made you boss?"

"Just like cream rises to the top."

"Keep it up and I'll be churnin' butter outa ya."

Cookie called from the wagon, "Sut, get up there and pick me out an easy way to go before I get *really* mad."

"It's true, Sut, 'really mad' is a lot worse than his usual mad." Gus grinned at me and dodged my quirt.

The truth was that there wasn't any "easy way," and we were awful glad that wagon had iron axles and we had a spare wheel. After the cattle were on top, Jake, Pock, and Tom came back, rolling big rocks out of the way as they came down the draw.

"Be careful rolling rocks, if you roll too many yu'll open up the earth and fall through," I called.

"Nothin' but rocks twixt here and hell," Gus called.

"Thought we were in it an' climbin' out," Tom replied.

"You gonna see hell's-a-poppin' if you don't tie onto this wagon an' help these mules climb outa here," Cookie yelled.

We tied on and wore out four mules and four horses pulling that blessed wagon to the caprock.

"It's flatter'n a table up here," Cookie exclaimed as the

winded animals rested.

"Just miles and miles of miles and miles," Pock said.

It was like driving into another world. Below in the breaks it was warm and sheltered. Up here, six or eight hundred feet above, it was definitely cooler, drier, windier, and there was no windbreak in sight. Jake led us north to a small lake in a sinkhole that could have been hollowed out by buffalo wallowing. This is where we set up camp. Cookie moved the wagon several times to get as much shelter from the south wind as he could. We ended up sleeping in a little gulley that drained into the lake to get out of that blessed wind.

While Jake and O ran the north line of our range, Tom and Pock rode well south of our "road" off the plain and set monuments of piled rocks for the south line. Me and Gus were set to work finding a good site for a dugout.

"Don't face it north or west," Cookie called. "Don't set it where it will flood or be too high in this wind."

"There's a darn good place for one about twelve miles north of Jacksboro," Gus yelled back.

Cookie approved the third location we found in the sink above the high-water line on the northwest side where the entrance would be to the southeast and the bank would give a little afternoon shade on the front "porch." He drew off the shape of the dugout with his boot toe and said, "Good, fellers, now all you have to do is dig it. Throw the dirt in a mound around the edge of the hole. If you do it right you won't have to go so deep. Shovels are in the wagon."

"Those handles don't fit my hand," I said.

"A few applications of the business end of that shovel to your ass-end might fix that," Cookie said.

"You got something for blisters?" Gus asked.

"Wear your gloves, Gus, and yes, I got somethin'."

"Not a dab of sympathy," I muttered.

"A big dab for you, Sut, might be a thimbleful."

The digging began after many protests, mostly not heard and all ignored, the wagon being on the other side of the lake. We ate when the others came back and then had a lot of help with the dugout. It was pretty important to get it built soon, for the cyclone season was upon us. Tom went back to the ranch and got a light buggy with a boxed bed full of firewood and two barrels fixed to it for water that we would have to bring up from the river below.

We had a cedar roof, from ridgepole to rafters to cedar thatch, all under six inches of packed dirt and sod. After a season or two the place just looked like a little mound on the edge of the sink—so much so that we had to fence it off to keep cattle from climbing up to see the countryside.

There was room inside for a two-story bunk on both sides and a little cast-iron stove at the back. It could hold six men or more, but I want to tell you about the time it held only two men and two horses.

Me and Gus spent a lot of time on that blessed caprock riding the range lines and keeping our cattle at home and sending visitors home as the range became occupied by other outfits. Midsummer, there was a lot of dragging cows out of boggy ponds.

"They're perverse, a servant of th' devil," I said one day as we escaped from a mad cow we had just pulled from a boggy tank.

"That's th' second time for that ol' girl. Third time, she gets lead poisoning," Gus called as he and his horse outran the "ol' girl."

"Better let her calve first or Jake will have you by the short hairs."

"If her calf is as dumb as she is, it would just double our troubles," Gus replied

"What time do you think it is?" I asked squinting at the darkening sky. The hot wind was very strong out of the south, but the clouds were boiling in from the west.

Gus grunted and squeezed his dollar watch out of his fifth pocket. "Dang. It says it's three o'clock."

"Missed dinner again," I said. Which wasn't strictly true, we ate whenever we felt like it, or got by the dugout during the day.

"I ain't stayin' around to watch it rain, see you at the dugout." He turned and we raced the mile to shelter. Huge drops of icy cold rain hit us, cold as the ice it had been a few hundred feet above. The horses increased their pace without prompting. A roaring noise grew behind us. "Here comes the hail," Gus called.

The wind picked up clouds of dust. Sheet lightning lit up the clouds and we bent low over our horses. Just as we reached headquarters, the whole roof of the loafing shed lifted and lay over upside down. "Take 'em to the dugout, Gus." It was probably unnecessary to say and just as probable that he didn't hear. I pulled up and let him get ahead. He landed against the door of the dugout and shouldered it open. His horse pushed him into the dark hole and had hardly gotten his rump past the threshold when my horse followed before I could dismount. I kicked out of the stirrups. The door, sides and top, scraped me off and I slid down off his rump. I had to push him to one side to close the door. *Oh my Lord,* I thought, and it wasn't a byword, either.

"Get us a light, Sut," Gus called over the roar of the storm. We could hear the hail hitting the ground. An occasional one rattled the door. "Bi-i-ig ones," Gus yelled.

"You've got the candle back there, Gus."

There was a pause, then, "Got a match?"

"Damn," and *that* was a byword. I made my way past the two trembling horses by the searing white light invading the cracks in and around the door.

"Where is the candle?" I asked, striking a match. Gus offered the candle and just as it lit, air rushed out of the room extinguishing match and candle, breaking the door in two. The roof lifted a little. then settled with a sigh, showering us with dried cedar needles, dirt, and a scorpion or two. It seemed to suck the very air out of our lungs. Both horses groaned and fell to their knees. Had I not known better, I would have sworn a train passed by our door, then retreated to leave all quiet except for the patter of a gentle rain.

We inched past the horses and through the remains of the door. The cloud was low enough to touch, rolling northeast. The sun peeked under the straight line of its western edge. The horses emerged from the dugout to the sound of a breaking bunk. When they calmed down, we mounted to see the damage.

We found the path of the cyclone by the flattened grass. "My gosh, Sut, it was a mile wide!"

"More like a half mile," I said, "but wide enough." The first time these storms were called tornadoes was when one wiped out Mobeetie in the panhandle. By any name, they are no good. This one had sucked all the water out of the tanks it crossed. Whether by luck or design, there were no cattle or horse victims in the path of the storm. We rode east to the edge of the rock.

"Look, Sut, the storm skipped a ways below, then hit th' ground again."

"Yeah, and look what it dropped off the bluff." I pointed to three dead cows scattered below.

"That thing could pick up three cows?"

"And probably a whole lot of other stuff with them," I said, and turned west along the storm path. The only other damage we found was a steer with a broken leg that we butchered and ate, proving Jake had lied to us about Rafter JM beef being bitter to eat.

We found the place where the twister first set down and

stopped and looked southwest for any other signs of damage. The sun broke full from under the rim of the cloud and millions of droplets sparkled on the waving grass across the plain as far as our eyes could see. Gus shaded his eyes aganst the sun's glare and I heard him whisper, "Miles and miles of miles and miles."

We turned for camp and saw twin rainbows arcing high in the sky.

I do set my bow in the cloud,
And it shall be for a token of a covenant
Between me and the earth.

—Genesis 9:13

LIST OF HISTORICAL FIGURES

In the Approximate Order of Their Appearance

Bass Reeves: U.S. Deputy Marshal.
J. Clay McSparren: Shanghai Pierce's trail boss.
Lee & Reynolds: Camp Supply sutlers.
Custers, George and Tom: American Cavalry officers.
Charles Goodnight: Texas cattleman and co-founder of Goodnight-Loving Trail.
Shanghai Pierce: Pioneer Texas cattleman.
Quanah Parker: Comanche son of white captive, Cynthia Ann Parker.
Lieutenant Patrick Cusack: Company A, Ninth Cavalry.
Lieutenant William A. Thompson: Mackenzie's Chief of Scouts.
Sergeant John B. Charlton: Sergeant of Scouts.
Colonel Ranald Slidell Mackenzie: Commander, Fort Concho.
Henry, Job, and Johnson: Tonkawa Scouts.
Irish McCabe: Scout.
Jose Piedad Tafoya: Seminole Mexican Scout.
Lieutenant Boehm: Cavalry Company Commander.
Comfort: Charlton's bunkmate.
McGowan: Cavalry trooper.
Colonel Eugene Beaumont: Commander, A Troop.

Captain Sebastian Gunther: H Company Commander.

Henry Strong: Scout.

James O'Neal: Wagon master.

Rojo Pelo: Redheaded Comanche (captive German boy who became a warrior).

"Dog" Kelly: Dodge saloon owner.

Rowdy Joe Lowe: Dodge gambler and saloon operator.

ABOUT THE AUTHOR

James D. Crownover grew up in the fields and woods of central Arkansas. After graduating from the University of Arkansas with a Civil Engineering degree, he was commissioned Second Lieutenant in the U.S. Air Force, receiving his pilot training at Webb Air Force Base, Texas. His first tour of duty was Vietnam where he flew more than 150 combat missions.

Returning to civilian life, he spent the next thirty years as a structural design engineer. He has always had an interest in frontier history and has an extensive collection of nonfiction accounts of life on the frontier A few years after retiring, he began writing historical frontier novels based on the knowledge he has acquired.

The employees of Five Star Publishing hope you have enjoyed this book.

Our Five Star novels explore little-known chapters from America's history, stories told from unique perspectives that will entertain a broad range of readers.

Other Five Star books are available at your local library, bookstore, all major book distributors, and directly from Five Star/Gale.

Connect with Five Star Publishing

Website:
gale.com/five-star

Facebook:
facebook.com/FiveStarCengage

Twitter:
twitter.com/FiveStarCengage

Email:
FiveStar@cengage.com

For information about titles and placing orders:
(800) 223-1244
gale.orders@cengage.com

To share your comments, write to us:
Five Star Publishing
Attn: Publisher
10 Water St., Suite 310
Waterville, ME 04901